17/3 12/2

CW01604675

Liz
Langley Street

Carol Rivers, whose family comes from the Isle of Dogs, East London, now lives in Dorset. *Lizzie of Langley Street* is her first novel.

Carol Rivers

Lizzie of Langley Street

POCKET BOOKS
LONDON • SYDNEY • NEW YORK • TORONTO

First published in Great Britain by Simon & Schuster UK Ltd, 2004
A CBS COMPANY
This edition first published by Pocket Books, 2004
An imprint of Simon & Schuster UK

Copyright © Carol Rivers, 2004

This book is copyright under the Berne Convention.
No reproduction without permission.
® and © 1997 Simon & Schuster Inc. All rights reserved.
Pocket Books & Design is a registered trademark of Simon & Schuster

The right of Carol Rivers to be identified as author of this work
has been asserted by her in accordance with sections 77 and 78
of the Copyright, Designs and Patents Act, 1988.

5 7 9 10 8 6 4

Simon & Schuster UK Ltd
1st Floor
222 Gray's Inn Road
London WC1X 8HB

www.simonandschuster.co.uk

Simon & Schuster Australia
Sydney

A CIP catalogue record for this book is available from
the British Library

ISBN 978-1-84739-794-2

This book is a work of fiction. Names, characters, places and incidents are either a product of the author's imagination or are used fictitiously. Any resemblance to actual people living or dead, events or locales is entirely coincidental.

Typeset by SX Composing DTP, Rayleigh, Essex
Printed and bound in Great Britain by
Cox & Wyman Ltd, Reading, Berkshire

This book is dedicated to May and Bill Skeels

Book One

Chapter One

November 1920
Isle of Dogs
East London

Lizzie sat up in bed, her heart pounding.

The crash had brought her awake with a start. Taking care not to disturb her sisters, she slipped from their large double bed, glancing back at the two small forms snuggled together under the worn blankets. Nothing ever woke Babs or Flo. They managed to sleep their way through every disruption in the house, of which there were many. Lizzie pushed her tangled hair from her face and shivered in her thin nightdress. The temptation to climb back in beside them was enormous. Resisting it, she opened the bedroom door. Once her eyes adjusted to the dark she saw the shapes of her two brothers on the half-landing. Bert's huge bulk was unmistakable as he bent over Vinnie, who, on all fours, appeared to be trying to crawl up the stairs.

When light from the gas-mantle flickered on in the passage downstairs, Lizzie's heart sank. She waited for the inevitable, a full-scale row in the middle of the night. As she had feared, Kate Allen came belting up the stairs just as Bert and Vinnie staggered on to the landing.

Vinnie was promptly sick.

'You filthy sod!' Kate gasped breathlessly as she arrived beside her younger son. The stench was overpowering. But Vinnie didn't hear. He had fallen flat on his face in his own vomit.

'What have you two buggers been up to?' Kate demanded of Bert, who was still on his feet. 'This is the second night running you've come in late!'

At only thirty-nine years of age, Kate Allen looked a haggard old woman. A darned woollen shawl was pulled around her nightdress, covering the straggly grey plait that hung down her back; her face was the colour of parchment and prematurely aged by deep lines of worry.

Lizzie watched Bert's jaw fall open. His eyes were red and unfocused. She was well aware that Bert, at eighteen, was known throughout the Isle of Dogs as the gentle giant. His great shoulders, tree trunks of legs and barrel chest set him apart from other people. But despite his abnormal physique, he was not to be feared. Bert possessed a heart of gold, but unfortunately lacked any brains to go with it.

Lizzie had watched Vinnie capitalize on this. Though small and wiry in stature and a year younger than Bert, he was quick-witted with a sly, mean spirit. What she disliked most was the way he used Bert for his own ends, whilst Bert's loyalty to Vinnie was unquestionable.

'Well?' demanded Kate, her face puffed and blotchy

with anger. 'What have you got to say for yerself, you dopey great lump?'

As usual when flummoxed, Bert fiddled with his cap, turning it round and round in his big, gnarled hands. 'We just come from the pub, Ma,' he mumbled, unable to meet Kate's blazing eyes. 'Got a bit 'eld up on the way 'cos Vinnie took ill, like. Something upset him, he said – them eels, he thinks it was.'

Lizzie knew Bert was carrying the can for Vinnie, who would have primed Bert earlier in the evening with the story of the eels, no doubt having a laugh at Bert's expense.

'I'll give you eels. He ain't poisoned, he's pissed!' Kate bellowed as she glared at the prostrate body on the landing. Vinnie's mouth gaped open, a gurgle coming from the back of his throat. 'Look at his face! It ain't turned that colour from eating eels. He's had another bashing by the looks of it.'

'Yeah, he looks a bit peaky, don't he?' Bert agreed vaguely.

'Peaky? *Peaky*!' spluttered Kate. 'He's bleedin' unconscious!'

'You go back to bed,' Lizzie told her mother gently, trying to avert disaster. 'Me and Bert'll clean up the landing and put Vin to bed.' At fifteen and the eldest girl of the family, Lizzie was accused by Babs of being a bossy cow. Babs, at fourteen, was strong willed and already a beauty, with waist-length auburn hair and innocent brown eyes that attracted the boys. She refused to be dominated by anyone, whilst Lizzie took her role of Kate's helper seriously, even if Babs hated her for it.

Kate shook her head miserably. 'God in heaven, help me. What have I brought into this world?'

'Aw, don't take it to 'eart, Ma,' Bert said, adding fuel to the fire. 'You know what our Vin's like. A bit 'igh spirited when he's had a few, that's all.'

'High spirits? Is that what you call it—' Kate stopped, slapping her hand on her heart. What colour there was in her cheeks drained away. She reached out to grip the banister.

'What's the matter, Ma?' Lizzie stepped over Vinnie and took her mother's arm.

'It was running up those stairs like that,' Kate croaked. 'I'll be all right when I get back to bed.'

Bert helped to take his mother's weight, and slowly the three of them descended the stairs, turning into the gloomy passage below.

'What's going on out there?' roared a voice from the front room. Lizzie's heart sank to her boots. Their father was awake.

Bert pushed open the door of the parlour, which had been converted to a bedroom. Tom Allen lay on a large iron bedstead, his bristly grey hair standing on end, his small eyes narrowed under gauzy cataracts, the result of mustard gas poisoning during the war. Lizzie had never quite got used to the sight of her father as a cripple. She remembered him as tall and handsome, with two strong legs. Now he had only stumps where his legs had been. Blown up in the trenches of Flanders, Tom Allen was one of the few men to return alive.

'It's only us, Pa,' Lizzie answered, fully aware she would now receive the force of his temper. The real culprit was lying unconscious upstairs on the landing, and, what was worse, Lizzie wouldn't put it past Vinnie to remember nothing of the trouble he caused in the morning.

'I know it ain't Father sodding Christmas,' Tom Allen yelled, clad in a pair of long johns, the loose ends drawn up and pinned to his waist. He supported the weight of his torso by his muscular forearms, lifting the two small stumps in front of him in an agitated jerk. 'Well? I asked yer a question, gel!'

'Ma had one of her faintin' spells,' Lizzie answered swiftly, giving Bert the eye to keep quiet. 'We're just helping her back to bed.'

'And in the morning I'll 'elp you lot to me belt,' Tom Allen growled, an empty threat, as everyone knew, in his condition. Despite his anger, Lizzie felt a pang of compassion for him. She knew he had become more aggressive to compensate for his legs. But he was still her father and she loved him.

'Leave the kids be for now, Tom. They mean no harm,' Kate pleaded wearily, sinking down on the bed. She looked deathly white, and Lizzie anxiously pulled the bedclothes round her.

Tom Allen shuffled himself clumsily across the bed in order to make room for his wife. Lizzie averted her eyes from the covered stumps that never failed to fill her with a deep, pitying sadness. She was terrified it would show. Her father hated sympathy and was swift to discern it.

'I know where I'd like to leave the bloody lot of 'em. Now if I hear another sound I'm taking me belt to all five of you, legs or no legs. And don't forget, Lizzie gel, we're up first thing for the market.'

Lizzie wanted to ask her mother if there was anything more she could do, but catching Bert's arm she led him away. Given half the chance he would open his big mouth, and cause another row.

The rift in the family had started in earnest when her father had returned from the war, unable to exert discipline over his household. In his youth, Tom Allen had worked as a stevedore on the big cargo boats that docked in the Port of London. His wage hadn't made them rich, but it was regular work and they were no poorer than anyone else in Langley Street. Many of the dockers and their families lived in the smoke-blackened two-up, two-down terraced houses that led down to the wharves. Dirty and overcrowded, their backyards brimmed with junk and washing lines. No one grew flowers or vegetables and weeds thrived.

On Friday and Saturday nights the men spent their wage in the pub. The women waited to duck the drunken punches on their return and pray a few pennies remained. Lizzie knew that unlike many households, where the men would beat their wives, her father never raised a hand to their mother. Despite all their troubles, he worshipped the ground she walked on.

Before the war, he'd ruled the family with an iron fist. Being strong and healthy, his rules were obeyed. That was the way things were; not a wonderful life by any means but they felt secure and knew their boundaries. After the war it was a different story. Many men didn't return; in the Allens' case, it wasn't death, but disability that ended the family's happiness.

As half a man, Tom Allen lost respect in himself, and without legs he would never regain it. A cold lack of regard had grown between Vinnie and his father. Lizzie knew there was nothing Tom could do about it, especially since they only survived with the money Vinnie brought in. Where it came from was a bone of contention. Vinnie worked for a villain, a hard man of the East End, and it had broken his parents' hearts.

As for Babs, she was almost sick at the sight of the stumps. She only tolerated the gruesome spectacle by ignoring her father. Flo, however, at ten, was too young to remember him clearly before he enlisted. She accepted him as he was and did her best, but Tom would have none of it. Lizzie knew he was frightened of seeing the same look of revulsion in Flo's eyes as he had seen in Babs'.

Once back out in the passage, Lizzie glared up at her brother. 'You're daft, you are, Bert Allen. Ain't you got no sense at all in that whopping great 'ead of yours? I ask you, going on about eels, what good was that?'

Bert stared down at his muddy boots. 'Vin told me to fink of a good story,' he admitted sheepishly.

'Well, he must've forgot that thinking ain't exactly a natural state for you,' Lizzie answered sharply, pushing her brother up the stairs. Then, immediately regretting her words, she added gently, 'Still, I ain't having a go at you, Bert. When all is said and done, you probably saved him a worse hiding.'

Bert brightened at the unexpected flattery. 'I 'ope so, gel. 'Cos our Vin was on one 'ell of a bender ternight and nuffin' I could say would stop 'im. One minute 'e was drinkin' wiv 'is mates, the next 'e was in a fight out the back, all 'is mates vanished.'

'Fine friends our Vin has if they all do a bunk,' Lizzie sniffed.

'It ain't Vin's fault,' Bert replied loyally. 'He's got 'imself in deep with Mik Ferreter but 'e says he's gonna sort 'imself out soon.'

'What, as a bookie's runner! Betting's illegal and you know it, Bert Allen.'

Bert hung his head.

Again she regretted her tone, but she was worried for Bert, terrified he might get blamed on Vinnie's account. She sighed as she stared down at Vinnie. The swelling was right up now, covering his close-set eyes and distorting his thin mouth. It was strange how he resembled no one else in the family, Lizzie thought, not for the first time. She herself had long curling black hair and deep green eyes, like their mother. Vinnie's dark brown hair was dead straight and his eyes were jet black beads, always moving in their small sockets. Babs' big brown eyes were flecked with gold and Flo's were a lovely soft brown, like a doe's. Where Vinnie got his hard look from she didn't know.

Perhaps Vinnie was a throwback, she thought now, as

she studied the unpleasant sight. Both maternal and paternal grandparents were born and bred on the Isle of Dogs but they had died long ago. Three of her uncles, Tom's brothers, had been killed during the war. On her mother's side there were two sisters, who had married and left the island, their own families scattered far and wide. So if Vinnie resembled any relative, they were destined never to know.

'We'd better get 'im to bed,' Lizzie said as Vinnie stirred, 'then I'll clean up.'

'I'll sort out 'is mess, gel,' Bert said cheerfully. 'Don't you worry, leave it to me. You get yer 'ead down.'

Lizzie watched Bert haul Vinnie over his shoulder as though he was lifting a sack of feathers. Brute strength and ignorance, she thought, smiling to herself. Vinnie's dangling arms disappeared along the landing and she heaved a sigh of relief. Selfish and greedy, that was Vinnie. He gave money to Kate only to boast of his role as breadwinner. It gave him power to sneer at others, including Tom. Not that Kate had been able to refuse the money; with business at Cox Street market being so slack, it was all that had kept a roof over their heads and food on the table.

Lizzie tiptoed downstairs to the scullery, squeezing past the Bath chair and its detachable tray on which were displayed the ribbons and souvenirs that were her father's livelihood; the Seaman's Rest Home at Greenwich provided sources of goods for disabled veterans. Lizzie had left school at thirteen, when Tom came home from the war and her mother needed help, and for the past year she had pushed him in the Bath chair from Cubitt Town to Cox Street market, Poplar, on Mondays, Wednesdays and Saturdays, then all the way home again.

Lizzie lifted the galvanized iron pail that stood behind the back door. She filled it with cold water from the tap over the china sink. Next to the sink was the boiler and beside this, during the day, a kettle boiled perpetually on the hob.

The bucket half full, Lizzie hauled it over the sink, careful not to spill any on the large oak table. Her mother scrubbed the table religiously and fed her family well on it. The few extra pennies she earned taking in sewing all went on food. Lizzie glanced fondly at the big rocking chair squeezed in one corner. Her mother sat there at night, head bent over a needle that flashed incessantly through every cloth known to mankind.

A shiny black roach fell on to the back of the chair. Lizzie watched it skid down a rung, keeping its balance with agility. The porous distempered walls were infested with bugs, skittish black insects that acrobatically stuck to any surface and were the devil to kill.

She ignored it, going quietly upstairs. The house was silent. It was music to her ears, no fights or rows taking place. Langley Street was where they had grown up, where her maternal grandparents had lived. All their history was in this house. A roof to call their own was more than a lot of families had. At school, one of her friends had been taken to an orphanage along with her six brothers and sisters, her parents unable to pay the rent and evicted from their home. Destitution hadn't befallen the

Allens; and whilst she had breath in her body, Lizzie vowed it never would.

Upstairs she lowered the bucket to the boards. Bert had done the proverbial vanishing act. She went and looked in their bedroom. Bert lay beside his brother on the big double bed, fully dressed, boots sticking up like tombstones. Despite his injuries, Vinnie snored loudly, and Bert was no longer in the land of the living.

Lizzie returned to the landing and began to clean up the vomit. It was more trouble than it was worth to rouse either of her brothers. As usual, it was quicker to repair the damage herself.

At four o'clock in the morning, a sepia light filled the scullery. Always the first to rise on market days, Lizzie turned on the lamp. Her clothes were folded on a chair, and she struggled into them, pulling one jersey on top of another.

She cut a slight little figure. Most of her clothes were second-hand from Cox Street market. Every stitch was someone else's, darned, patched and lengthened. Several shades of blue ran round the hem of her skirt, a clue to the number of its previous owners. The jerseys were darned and had squares of cloth from her mother's work-box sewn over the elbows. Her boots had been outgrown by their neighbour's daughter, Blakies hammered into their soles.

She reached behind her, scooped up her long dark hair and plaited it. Then she poured water into the kettle and warmed her hands beside it. Next, she sliced the big crusty loaf that was purchased from the baker's roundsman, also referred to as the Midnight Baker because he delivered at night. Kate bought bread and milk from him twice a week. On Fridays, when she had money, and on Tuesdays, when she had none. Her debt was recorded on the slate. Lizzie knew it was robbing Peter to pay Paul but that was how people survived on the island.

When she had finished her chores, she went outside to the lavatory. The path to the wooden shed in the backyard was covered in frost. Sitting on the cold seat, she left the door wide open and shivered as she gazed up at the stars still lighting the sky. With luck, it would be a fine, dry day and business would be brisk at market.

Lizzie's heart raced at the thought of seeing Danny Flowers, the tall, blond-haired barrow boy whom she secretly worshipped. She thought of the silk ribbons lying on the tray, imagining them tied in her own curling black hair. Ribbons were all the rage, favoured by the young women who travelled down from the West End. Gentry were always dressed impeccably. Lizzie was fascinated with their clothes and loved to study the fashions. It was the only opportunity she had to do so and she made the most of it.

Thoughts of Danny and beautiful clothes vanished as she returned to the house, stifling a yawn. It was time to wake her father and she'd only had three hours' sleep. All because of Vinnie. His drinking was becoming worse and so were his black moods.

The stink of disinfectant flowed out as she opened the bedroom door. It was the only antidote the islanders had to bugs and mice. Distributed free at the local park each week, Kate used it in the bedroom, which, because of Tom's injuries and the risk of infection, was the priority.

Once acclimatized, Lizzie pushed the Bath chair up to the bed. Her father groaned as she parted the heavy curtains.

Kate woke and sat up on the edge of the bed. 'Wait, Lizzie. I'll help you get 'im into the chair. You'll do yer back in if you try it on yer own.'

'I'll manage, Ma, you couldn't have got much sleep last night.'

'Oh, I'm all right now, love.' Still sitting, Kate wound her long grey plait into a bun. 'Let's get your father dressed, then,' she sighed, rising slowly.

As usual, Tom complained throughout the performance. It was not until he was washed and fully clothed that Lizzie had time to notice how ill her mother looked.

'You sure you feel all right, Ma?' Lizzie asked at the breakfast table.

'I'll be right as rain when I get me second breath.' Kate poured tea into three enamel mugs. 'Spread the drippin', gel, will you?'

Lizzie's mouth watered as she spread the thick, juicy paste scooped off the top of the stock. Kate rarely cooked a joint of beef now. They wouldn't eat another one for at least a month. Lizzie remembered how every Sunday before the war they ate thick slices of succulent roast beef, the leftovers fried as bubble and squeak the next day. The rich brown juice was made into broth, eked out over the week. They had taken the beef for granted then. Now, even the dripping was a delicacy.

'Eat up, you two,' Kate told them briskly. 'You won't get much more before the day's out.'

Lizzie bolted her food. She noticed Kate hadn't eaten a crumb. 'Why don't you go back to bed, Ma? Babs could take Flo to school today.'

'Aw, stop fussing,' Kate scolded. 'Anyone would think I'm on me last legs.'

'It's them lazy buggers upstairs that's the cause of the trouble,' muttered Tom angrily, pushing himself away from the table, his breakfast uneaten. 'They treat this house like a bloody lodgings. I tell you, I've had enough of it. If they can't abide by the rules they can clear out. Idle good for nothing layabouts—'

'I'll get yer coat and scarf, Pa,' Lizzie said quickly, catching her mother's look of dismay.

'And wrap up warm,' Kate called after her. 'I don't want you both coming down with pneumonia. And who knows, if the weather holds, you might have a good day and we can settle the rent with old Symons.'

A remark that didn't make Tom Allen any the happier as, swathed in coats, scarves and mittens, they left the house and Lizzie began the long push from Cubitt Town to Poplar. It was a sombre beginning to the day, but Lizzie knew their spirits would lift when they saw their friends. For her, one in particular: Danny Flowers.

The Isle of Dogs was still asleep as she pushed her father through the empty streets of Cubitt Town. Only Island Gardens, the park where she brought her sisters to play, was alive with birdsong. Soon they had reached the Mudchute, years ago a mountainous health hazard of rotting silt. Now the islanders grew vegetables there. It was barricaded with wooden fences so the kids wouldn't get in.

Lizzie was proud of the island's ancient roots. She had learned at school that the Isle of Dogs had first been recorded on the maps in the sixteenth century. Over time, the rough horseshoe of land, surrounded on three sides by water, had become the centre of the capital's trade and industry.

Glancing seaward she spotted a tall ship's mast over the roofs of the tatty cottages. Hooters echoed, oil and tar blew in on the wind, another day of sea trading had begun. Her grandfather and great-grandfather had sailed on the big, ocean going vessels, the *Triton* and the *Oceanides*.

It had been nothing, once, to see the bowsprit of a ship leaning over a backyard. Children had swung from the long poles, pretending to be pirates, and up above them the main masts had seemed to pierce the sky. Lizzie could remember her brothers playing along the wharves. She could see them now, scavenging under the furnaces of the factories, black with ash. Bert had a deep voice even as a boy. He'd often sung sea shanties with the sailors and Vinnie had dug in the silt, convinced he'd find treasure.

The war had seemed a long way away then.

Her father huddled down under his scarves. His jaw jutted out against the wind, and she pushed on, her efforts keeping her warm as the November day dawned, bright and clear. Horses and carts trotted by, women whitened their doorsteps.

'A Good Pull-Up at Carmen', announced a notice over one door. Lizzie waved at the owner, standing outside his café fastening his apron. The Carmen was no more than a shack, with a corrugated roof and a flap that came down over the front, but the smell of cheesecake was tantalizing. She'd never tasted the pastries covered in thick coconut, but they were always lined up on trays inside. The aroma of hot dough and coconut made her mouth water.

On they went, her load heavier now. Some of the girls from the pickle factory said hello. They all looked and smelled the same. Their hair was hidden under white caps and they walked noisily on their clogs. Their white coats were stained with yellow from the onions and they stank of vinegar.

Lizzie had always feared having to work at the pickle factory. Then one day her mother had remarked, 'It's better than the sacking factory. The dust fills up your lungs and chokes you to death. Listen to the women coughing and you know they work with sack.' After that, the pickle factory seemed like heaven.

As they skirted the docks a small band of men huddled on the stones. 'There must be a skin boat in. Poor sods,' her father sighed. These were older men, casual labour, waiting for work. No man in his right mind would work with animal skins from abroad, her father had once commented. The skins were riddled with disease. And there were rats. Vermin as big as dogs. But these men were starving and they'd resort to anything to feed their families.

Lizzie shivered. There were always anthrax deaths on the island. The stories were gruesome. At least Bert and Vinnie had never had to unload skins, she thought more cheerfully. Perhaps being a bookie's runner wasn't so bad after all.

The market stalls were suddenly in sight and Lizzie quickened her step. Would Danny be there with his barrow? Eagerly she looked for his fair head and broad shoulders, her heart beating fast as her eyes scanned the crowd. Colour, laughter and early morning jokes abounded. The traders were busy erecting stalls and insulting one another. Fruit and vegetables, fish, meat, materials, china. It was all there, like Aladdin's cave, spread out over the tables.

It seemed as though she hadn't lived till this minute.

The beautiful features of the young woman were enhanced by a soft smile as she drew the delicate pink silk through her fingers. 'How much are these ribbons?' she asked in a refined accent.

'A penny's worth there, miss.' Lizzie gazed up, fascinated by the aura of wealth and respectability. 'The blue would look lovely on you.'

'Do you think so?'

'Why don't you try one on, miss?' Lizzie held up one of the blue ribbons. It matched the girl's powder blue coat and velvet hat with an upturned brim.

'Have you a mirror?'

'No, but Freda has. Over there on the fruit and veg stall. Freda'll hold your hat whilst you try them on.' Lizzie knew that Fat Freda, who was always putting on her red lipstick and smacking her lips in a big, cracked mirror, would gladly offer her help. She watched the girl walk gracefully to Fat Freda's stall.

The next moment Freda was holding her mirror up and giving Lizzie a wink on the sly. Lizzie knew once those ribbons were in the girl's hair she'd be hooked. The girl didn't give Freda her hat, just held the ribbons against her peaches and cream cheek and Lizzie knew it was enough. She would be opening her purse any moment.

Freda raised her pencilled eyebrows behind the mirror.

Lizzie giggled.

'Off you go, gel.' Tom Allen gave his daughter a nudge. 'Stop staring at the customers and go and find Dickie for me. Tell him to come up for a chat if he's done all his business.'

'But Pa—!' The girl was walking back, a satisfied look on her face.

Tom Allen pulled down his scarf with an irritable jerk. 'Ain't you awake yet, gel? Did you hear what I said?'

'Yes, Pa.' Lizzie glanced at their customer one last time before walking away. She liked selling, but it wasn't often Tom let her. He preferred her to push the chair or run errands, like now, irritably dispatching her to find Dickie Potts, one of his friends.

'How'd it go?' Fat Freda asked as Lizzie passed her stall.

'She'll buy 'em I think. Thanks for the loan of the mirror.'

'Yer old man oughta let you flog stuff more often,' Freda exclaimed. 'You're a natural, gel. You'd sell sand to an Arab.'

Lizzie liked Fat Freda, so named because of her immense girth and chins. She was not from the island, but hailed from Poplar. Freda was a widow with a large family and numerous grandchildren. She attended the market each week and was known for her loud singing voice and hammering out tunes on the pub piano. Tickling the ivories, as she called it.

'You seen Danny yet?' Freda asked, winking.

Lizzie blushed and tried to pretend she hadn't heard.

'He's along there with his barra,' Freda said loudly enough for the whole market to hear. 'Down the end of the row.'

Lizzie went scarlet. She kept her head down as she left Freda's stall. She had to take the long route in order to pass Danny and she hoped no one would notice. Her heart was pounding as she walked through the crowd. Would Danny speak when he saw her? Or would he be too busy selling chestnuts and not notice her pass by? Lizzie couldn't see anything but bodies squashed together, and a sense of panic filled her. What if she couldn't find him? What if he hadn't come?

'Enough brass monkeys for you?' a voice called and she spun round. Danny's barrow, slightly set back from the stalls, was brimming with hot roasting chestnuts. He was standing there, tall and handsome in his cloth cap and waistcoat, warming his hands over the brazier. 'Come and have a warm up,' he called, his blue eyes inviting.

Lizzie flushed with pleasure. 'Can't yet, Danny. I'll be over later.'

'You make sure you are.' Danny winked as he tilted his cap. 'Me day don't start till you come over and have a chat.'

'Get on with you, you saucy bugger,' called the stallholder next to the barrow. 'Leave the poor girl alone. She ain't got time to spend with the likes of you, silly sod.'

Lizzie smiled and caught Danny's eye again.

By the time she found Dickie Potts he was counting his change and totting up the morning's sales. 'How's yer dad, Lizzie?' Dickie grinned, displaying big, brown, horse-like teeth.

'Said he'd like to have a chat, Dickie.' Lizzie tried to dodge the spray of spittle.

'Yeah, all right, gel. I'm almost done.' Dickie had survived Flanders like her father. He suffered from a hacking cough, the effects of gas poisoning. He had sold newspapers before the war and was still selling them now. Newspapers were his passion.

'Have a butchers at this.' Dickie lowered a newspaper and Lizzie was able to read the headlines. 'Marshall Foch Salutes Unknown Warrior!'

'Bloody liars and hypocrites!' exclaimed Dickie. Like her father, Dickie didn't believe the printed word, but he wanted to read the lies all the same. By the time the afternoon came, the newspaper seller and her father would have analysed every article in the paper from cover to cover.

Lizzie knew that the war had changed their beliefs, as it had millions of others who had lived to tell the tale. The government's words, her father said, were at variance with its deeds. He'd heard all their promises and been the victim of the broken ones. No one came to relieve him or Dickie in the trenches. From the minute he woke in hospital and saw his two stumps, he knew the government's promises of an acre of land and a pig for every soldier after the war was a myth.

Dickie himself was a hive of knowledge. He and her father were always debating politics. Both held allegiance to no one after the atrocities they'd witnessed. War disgusted them along with the warmongers on both sides that had sent millions of men to their deaths.

'Why is he called "Unknown", Dickie?' Lizzie asked as Dickie licked the spittle from his lips.

''Cos 'e represents the unknown dead,' Dickie replied gravely. 'The French are takin' six unidentified dead bodies to a hut at Saint Pol, near Arras. Then they're gonna get an officer to close 'is eyes, rest 'is hand on one of them there coffins, and that'll be the poor bastard who'll travel to England in a box.' Dickie sucked his teeth grimly. Suddenly he looked very far away. 'The coffin's going from Boulogne to Dover on the British destroyer, *Verdun*. Another destroyer, the *Vendetta*, is gonna accompany her across the Channel, very regal like. As a special tribute, they're gonna fly the

White Ensign at 'alf mast and dock to a nineteen gun salute.'

Lizzie was silent for a moment, the gravity and importance of what Dickie had just told her bringing a lump to her throat. 'What's gonna happen then?' she asked quietly.

Dickie coughed loudly and wiped his nose with a grubby sleeve. 'The coffin goes by train to London, gel. They'll put a bloody great wreath on top of the gun carriage and take it from the Cenotaph to Westminster Abbey. King George'll be there and Queen Mary.' Dickie's face darkened. 'All I say is, why couldn't they bloody shake the poor devil's hand when 'e was alive, before 'e 'ad to spill 'is guts for King and Country? A bloodbath that's what it was – for the working classes and kids! We was expendable.' Dickie shook his head slowly. 'Nah. It's too late to honour 'em now. And I wouldn't mind bettin' 'alf the country thinks so too.'

Lizzie had heard the rumours of unrest at market. She knew her father was of the same opinion as Dickie. Ex-servicemen, the unemployed, every one of them was disillusioned with their meagre lot.

'Would you believe Foch is sending over one 'undred sandbags of French earth?' Dickie went on in a low voice. 'They're gonna line 'is grave with it. French earth or British, what does it matter? All earth's got worms, don't matter where it comes from. The maggots'll get a bellyful just the same. It ain't going to matter to the corpse, is it?'

Lizzie shuddered. She felt sorry for Dickie, but sometimes he frightened her. She knew that, like her father, he would never recover mentally from the terrifying experiences of war.

'Saw 'undreds o' worms, I did, saw 'em crawlin' over torsos and limbs, burrowin' their way inside flesh and bone. Worms has filthy 'abits. Worms ain't fussed wevver it's the Boche or the Allies.' Dickie cackled lewdly. 'All rot tastes the same.'

A shiver went down Lizzie's spine. 'Is there anything else in the papers?' she asked, changing the subject quickly, hoping he would hurry up and get his things together. She wanted to see to Danny again.

Dickie looked at her and blinked. Then he stabbed a filthy finger at the paper. 'Yeah, a big burglary up West. They coshed a night watchman and got away with two 'undred quid's worth of stuff from a jewellers. One of 'em was seen by a passer-by. They think they can trace him with a bit of luck. Two 'undred smackers in one night, more 'n' I make in a lifetime. Big, 'e was, a bloody big bloke.' Dickie licked his lips thoughtfully. 'Says 'ere over six foot. Gotta big 'ead and long arms. Like a bleedin' great gorilla.'

Lizzie instantly thought of Bert. He had a big head and long arms. 'When was it?' she asked, telling herself not to be silly.

'Thursday,' Dickie read, 'in the wee small hours.'

Bert and Vinnie had been out on Thursday night. She recalled her mother's words as she had run up the stairs. *The second night running . . .*

Dickie folded away his paper and stuffed it in his pocket. He lifted his floppy sack bag over his shoulder. 'Come on then, gel. Lead the way.'

Lizzie walked through the market in a daze as Dickie's voice went in one ear and out the other.

Chapter Two

''Ello Dickie.' Lizzie saw that her father was looking pleased with himself when they arrived back. The tray in front of him had large gaps in it and his money bag was open as he counted the pennies.

'You done some business then.' Dickie dumped his sack by the Bath chair.

'Yeah, business is brisk. And it's only the middle of the morning.'

'What d'you put that down to?' Dickie asked.

'Everyone's talkin' about next week,' Tom replied. 'They seem to be doing a fair bit of spending at the same time.'

'You mean Armistice Day,' Dickie said with a nod. 'Well, we ought to 'ave a bleeding big funeral every week if it 'elps business. One of them there politicians would do for starters. I can think of a few of 'em I'd be pleased to see six feet under.'

'I'll go along with you there all right.'

Dickie made himself comfortable on an orange box and began to read the newspaper aloud.

Lizzie's thoughts, though, were still on the robbery. She didn't know why she was so worried. There must be lots of big men involved in robberies all over London, so why suspect Bert? He was not the right sort of material for a thief. He was slow moving and clumsy, but what worried her was that Vinnie might use his influence to involve Bert.

She could still hear Vi Catcher telling her about Vinnie the other day. Vi lived opposite at number seventy-nine. She was the street's gossip and made it her business to know everyone else's. She was always dressed in her apron and turban, but never seemed to do much work. She stood at her front door, watching the world go by, her plump arms folded over her pinny. Kate said Vi was harmless enough, but Lizzie tried to avoid her if she could.

'Off out then, gel?' Vi had asked as she walked down Langley Street one morning.

'Just doing some errands for Ma, Vi.' Lizzie knew it was a mistake to pause, but she didn't want to appear rude.

'Heard the Old Bill collared your Vinnie in the pub last night,' Vi said with a gleam in her eye. 'That Mik Ferreter slipped the copper a few quid, apparently, to get him off the hook.'

'You know more than I do, then, Vi,' Lizzie retorted sharply. Vinnie hadn't mentioned any of this at home and Vi knew it.

'I hope I ain't put me foot in it, gel. But I know how much your mum worries about you kids and I thought, well, *someone* ought to know. Just in case, like.'

Lizzie had got away quickly, then. She didn't want to hear any more. A lot of it was gossip, but what Vi had said worried her. Mik Ferreter's reputation preceded him in the East End. Not only was he a bookie who tolerated no debt, but he was said to have some of the police in his pay. His criminal exploits in the underworld were legendary, and if Vi's information was correct there was no doubt of the hold he had over Vinnie.

Someone tapped her on the shoulder and Lizzie jumped.

'Blimey, gel, your nerves are in a bad way.' Danny Flowers grinned down at her. His blue eyes twinkled under his mop of blond hair.

'Oh, it's you, Danny.'

'Who did you think it was,' he answered with a straight face. 'The Old Bill?'

Lizzie went white. 'Course not!'

'Crikey, I only came up to say hello. I might as well not have bothered.' Danny stuck his thumbs in his waistcoat and rocked on his heels.

Lizzie smiled faintly. 'Sorry, Danny. I got a lot on me mind.'

'Like what for instance?'

'Nothing important, not really.'

'In which case, you're doing a lot of frowning and jumping for something that ain't important,' Danny remarked astutely. 'Why don't you walk down to the barra with me and 'ave some chestnuts. Yer dad'll let you come if you ask 'im nicely.'

'I ain't saying nothing about what's on me mind, Danny Flowers,' she warned him, knowing that it would be a surprise to both of them if she kept her mouth shut. 'It's me own business and I don't want no one poking their nose in.'

'Me? Poke me nose in? The name's Danny Flowers not Pinocchio.' Danny looked affronted.

Danny always made her laugh. 'Just for a few minutes then. I'll just tell Pa.'

Lizzie walked over to the Bath chair and asked her father if she could go with Danny. 'As long as he don't come the old nonsense,' Tom said suspiciously. 'I don't trust any of them costermongers further than I could throw them.'

Costermongers were regarded by shopkeepers and stall-holders as disreputable moving from street to street, often selling goods at dirt-cheap prices. The Flowers family, however, had reformed years ago and now ran a greengrocery business on Ebondale Street.

'Danny ain't a costermonger, Pa,' Lizzie reminded him once more, hoping Danny couldn't hear. 'He just brings the barra up to the market on Saturday for his dad.'

'A leopard don't change his spots. Just you remember that, my girl.'

Lizzie escaped whilst she could, though her inclination to argue the point was strong. Bill Flowers' shop was a bit scruffy and you had to watch some of the stuff he sold but he had gained a reputation for fairness. She couldn't see the difference, anyway, between selling from a Bath chair and a barrow. Danny had been in the war, too. He was just sixteen when he had enlisted the year before armistice. He had done his bit for king and country.

Danny was liked on the island, but Danny's older bother, Frank, was not well regarded. Frank helped in the shop, but had once worked on the docks as a guard. He had been exempt from conscription because of this. Tom Allen had once remarked that Frank Flowers must have a trunk full of white feathers by now.

'How's yer dad and Gertie?' Lizzie asked as they walked together down Cox Street.

Bill Flowers had been a widower since Danny was born nineteen years ago. His wife, Daisy, had died in childbirth. Danny and Frank were the reason Bill had given up his roving way of life. With a new born baby and a little boy of three to look after, a shop was the only way he could earn a living.

The barrow was all that remained of the old way of life. Gertie Spooner was Bill's right-hand man. Bill had hired her to help look after the baby after Daisy's death and Gertie had been at his side ever since. As well as looking after the two boys, she knew the business back to front.

'Dad don't change,' Danny grinned. 'All work and no play, that's me dad. Gertie still manages to get him down the Quarry on Saturdays though. Between you and me, I reckon she wears the trousers. They should have got spliced those two. Might as well have, for all the time they spend together.'

Lizzie liked Gertie, who always had time to stop and say a few words in the shop, even when she was busy.

Kate had been a regular customer in the old days but not so much lately. Market prices were all she could afford.

When they reached the barrow the chestnuts were sizzling on the brazier. Their succulent aroma filled the air and Lizzie held her hands over the heat. The warmth penetrated her old green coat and seeped into her cold bones.

'Sit down, gel. I'll do you some.' Danny rubbed a tin plate clean on his elbow before tipping out some chestnuts.

Lizzie hadn't eaten since breakfast. She sat down on an upturned box. Her mouth was watering as Danny passed her the plate. She stripped them hurriedly, tossing the hot brown nuts quickly between each hand.

'You're a sight for sore eyes, Lizzie Allen,' he chuckled. 'Blimey, if all my customers had your appetite – and a full purse – I'd be a millionaire.'

She licked her lips. 'I could eat these all day long. They're lovely.'

'Like someone else I could name.' Danny folded his arms and leaned against the barrow, tilting his cap over his forehead. 'So when are you gonna say yes and marry me, then, Lizzie Allen?' Danny was always teasing her like this. She wondered what he would say if she answered, 'Whenever you like.' But she never quite had the nerve to spring that one on him.

'When you've made enough money to keep me like a lady,' she said instead. 'I've expensive tastes, you know.'

'Blimey, hark at it. All right then. If you won't marry me, when are you gonna let me take you out on the town?'

'Oh, I've heard that one before, Danny Flowers.'

Lizzie thought he probably said the same to all the girls. She wouldn't mind betting all those girls had lovely clothes, too. He was so handsome, her Danny, his white shirtsleeves rolled up to his elbows, his shirt open at the neck. There wasn't anyone she'd ever met who made her feel this way, all sort of shivery inside. She'd rather die than let him know, of course. He probably thought she was still a kid. He'd known her ever since she was small, seen her trailing round the market with her sisters in tow. But the way she felt about him wasn't the way a child felt.

'How do you fancy a night up the Queens?' he said, with a serious expression on his face.

Lizzie stared at him. 'The Queens? Up Poplar?'

'Where else?'

She almost died of shock. 'You mean . . . just you and me?'

Danny laughed. 'Blimey, gel, I ain't speaking French, am I?' He looked at her with amusement, then, leaning towards her, raised one eyebrow. 'Saturday is Amateur Night. We'd have a bit of fun sitting up there in the gods.'

The gods! Had she heard him right? She couldn't believe it.

Suddenly Danny was staring at her, and his eyes were telling her that he didn't think of her as a kid any longer. Oh no, she'd been wrong there.

'Course if you didn't fancy the Queens, we could go to the Lyric,' he shrugged. 'It's over Hammersmith, but Dad would let us borrow the 'orse and cart.'

'The Lyric,' Lizzie breathed in wonder. 'At Hammersmith.'

'Beggar's Opera, it's called. The most popular show in town.'

Lizzie knew exactly what the Beggar's Opera was. Dickie had read aloud all about it from an article in the newspaper; the show was packed with popular music, songs, dancing and puns. Lizzie swallowed. Not only had Danny Flowers actually asked her to go out with him, but he'd asked her to go to the theatre.

She'd never even been in one. The nearest she'd ever got was looking at the posters outside the Queens. Life-sized colour posters of actors and actresses, singers and dancers, comedians and acrobats.

This was a dream come true. Her and Danny at the Beggar's Opera.

Then reality came back with a crash. Besides not having any clothes – or money – her father would refuse to let her go. She couldn't tell Danny that Tom didn't approve of him. Danny would be angry then, and he might never talk to her again, let alone ask her out.

Thinking quickly, she made a joke of it. 'I'll think about it,' she told him. 'If I've got time, I might. I've got a schedule to keep you know.'

She held her breath. Maybe she had got away with it.

'Don't keep me waiting too long,' he warned her. 'I've got a schedule to keep an' all.' His blue eyes were twinkling.

Lizzie stood up, intending to leave whilst the going was good.

'Yer not off already?'

'I'd better. Pa said not to be away too long.'

Danny came to stand beside her. He was so tall and handsome. She felt weak at the knees. 'Incidentally,' he said as he looked down at her, 'how's that brother of yours – Vinnie?'

Her heart banged against her ribs. 'Why?' she blurted, immediately on the defensive.

Danny shrugged. 'Nothin' really. It's just that I was down the Quarry the other night. Someone said he was in a spot of bother.'

'Not that I know of.' Lizzie turned and walked away, her heart still pounding.

But Danny caught up with her and took her arm. His eyes were kind as he said gently, 'You can trust me, Lizzie, you know that. A trouble shared is a trouble halved.'

She really wanted to tell him, but she couldn't. She still had her pride and didn't want Danny to think less of her for something Vinnie had done. 'Vinnie is old enough to look after himself,' she said, tossing back her thick black curls. 'He don't tell me his business and I don't ask.'

Danny raised his eyebrows and let her go. 'Pardon me for breathing.'

Lizzie felt a moment's regret as she looked into his eyes.

'When am I gonna see you again?'

She smiled a halting little smile. 'Next Saturday. I'll be here with Pa as usual.'

He grinned. 'Looks like I'm gonna have to wait another week for me answer, then.'

She knew what the answer was already, but she wasn't going to tell him. She'd have to think up a good excuse over the next seven days. She had as much chance of seeing the inside of the Lyric as going to Buckingham Palace for tea.

When she got back, her father and Dickie were still engrossed in the newspaper. 'Me old mate's right,' Tom hailed her as if she'd been sitting there listening for the last half-hour. 'Our strife will all be forgot. In time to come no one will remember we fought a war.'

'The kids these days don't know what life is about,' agreed Dickie, folding the newspaper carefully and sliding it back in the sack. Politics, religion and the unions had been ripped apart and put to rights again. Now it was time to get on with what remained of the day.

'Push me by Elfie Goldblum's stall,' Tom instructed her. 'No doubt he'll be catchin' a few latecomers.' Though the traders had to have licences for their pitches, disabled veterans were given the freedom of the streets, and Lizzie pushed the Bath chair beside Elfie Goldblum's stall for their last stop of the day.

'How you doing, my son?' Elfie called, emerging from the back.

'Had a good day, Elfie. And you?'

'Could be better, could be better.' Elfie Goldblum regularly denied making a fortune. He dealt in second-hand jewellery and curios. He was tiny and wizened with a small brown face like a gnome. He had kept a stall at the market for years and was a very astute businessman. Tom liked to be near him in the afternoons because interest waned in the food as the day wore on but people were always keen to look at Elfie's fascinating stock. Rings, necklaces, bracelets, small pieces of china, teapots, brass and second-hand clocks. Elfie craftily replaced the gaps as he sold and his stall always looked inviting.

Lizzie was still thinking about Danny, the Lyric and Hammersmith when a cultured voice broke in on her thoughts. 'How much are the mints?' A well-dressed man pointed to the small bundle of sweets remaining on Tom's tray.

'Four ounces for a ha'penny, all done up in nice packets,' replied Tom, before Lizzie could speak. 'Lizzie, pass the gent a packet.'

Lizzie passed the mints, and after some examination their customer nodded. 'I'll take those three, one for each of my children.'

Lizzie stared at the gentleman, dressed in quality clothing, a brown trilby, leather gloves and a silk tie. What was it like to have money to spend and nice clothes to wear and be able to lead a life that wasn't always overshadowed by poverty, she wondered as the man nodded to her father and went on his way.

'You all right, gel?' Dickie asked, nudging her arm.

Lizzie nodded. 'Yes, Dickie, I'm fine.'

'Just as long as that flash 'arry with the barra ain't upset yer.'

'No, he hasn't, and he's not flash, Dickie.' Lizzie knew there wasn't much point in arguing. Dickie and her father were set in their ways and ideas. She could argue till she was blue in the face on Danny's behalf. It would make no difference. To some people on the island the Flowers would always be known as costermongers.

It was growing foggy again and the crowd was thinning out. Dickie rubbed his mittened hands together as another customer passed over a penny. 'Blimey, it's like Christmas arrived early,' Dickie chuckled as he gazed down at Tom's depleted tray. All that was left was a small pile of written commemorations for Armistice Day.

Tom nodded in satisfaction. 'I'll be able to knock a bit off the rent. Kate'll be pleased about that.'

Dickie scratched his chin, his dirty nails raking against the grey stubble. 'Talking of next week, are you going up to the city?'

Tom shook his head. 'That ain't likely now.'

Lizzie had been eagerly awaiting their trip to the Cenotaph even if she did have to push the chair all the way. 'Why can't we go, Pa? We could still sell them commemorations and buy some more stock besides.'

'You know the score as well as I do,' Tom answered her gruffly. 'You heard yer mother this morning. The rent's got to be paid. What money is left won't buy us enough to make a trip to the city worthwhile. And don't make those cow's eyes at me, gel, 'cos I can't bloody well work miracles, now, can I?'

Lizzie turned away. She loved going up West. It would be the only chance she had to see the city before Christmas. But the tone of her father's voice told her that his decision was final.

She glanced down the street. Danny would be one of the last traders to leave, the contents of his barrow a welcome warmth for the remaining few empty stomachs.

'I'm off now,' Dickie said, hoisting his sack over his shoulder. 'Me pins are killing me. And the fog's comin' down quick off the river.'

'Yeah, it's gonna be a pea-souper.' Lizzie saw her father shiver under his blanket. It was time to go home. She wouldn't see Danny again for a whole week. And when she did, she'd have to have a good excuse up her sleeve for not going out with him.

'Take me home,' Tom said.

Lizzie waved to Dickie, then started the long push home.

On the Sunday before Armistice Day 1920 the news was broadcast to the nation that King George V would unveil the new Cenotaph in Whitehall. As Lizzie and her family gathered round the table in the kitchen, eating boiled potatoes and mutton stew, the talk was of the city in mourning.

Lizzie had helped Kate peel the potatoes and prepare the table. There were more vegetables than meat in the stew but Lizzie knew it would fill a gap in each of the seven hungry stomachs. Her father was silent and withdrawn, but Kate was smiling. Lizzie had watched her tuck the rent money safely in the Ovaltine tin. 'The old Cenotaph was an eyesore anyway,' Kate remarked as she surveyed her family. 'No one liked it.'

'What's an eyesore?' This from ten-year-old Flo.

'A blooming great monstrosity, that's what.' Kate frowned at her youngest daughter. 'In other words, a fake. It was erected in Whitehall, temporary like, for the peace celebrations in 1919. But a bloke called Sir Edward Lutyens 'as designed the new one. And there ain't a word on it about religion, mind.'

'Why's that?' asked Flo.

'Because the blokes commemorated on it were of all creeds and none.'

'What's—' began Flo again, only to be swiftly silenced by Tom, who scowled at her across the table.

Vinnie and Babs looked bored. Bert was almost asleep, his hands clasped over his stomach.

'Can I 'ave Babs' carrots?' asked Flo, willing the food off her sister's plate.

'You've already had three helpings,' Kate scolded.

Flo pushed her fringe from her eyes. 'I could eat an 'orse, I could.'

'She can have them,' Babs shrugged. 'I'm sick of veg.'

'Well, I certainly ain't gonnna have those carrots wasted,' sighed Kate, passing the leftovers to Flo. 'There's souls out there who'd give their right arm for food like this.'

Flo picked up her spoon. 'Slowly, gel,' Kate reproved her. 'Anyone'd think you were starving. Just you watch yer digestion.'

'What's di . . . dig—?'

'Innards,' clarified Kate as Vinnie and Bert yawned loudly, twiddling their braces. They were eager to leave the table and have forty winks. Lizzie was relieved that neither of the boys had returned to the Quarry since Friday. Despite his injuries, Vinnie had joined the family for Sunday dinner. His face was still yellow and blue but the swelling had gone down.

'As I was saying about the Cenotaph . . .' Kate picked up the thread of her conversation but was stopped by Babs.

'I don't see what all the fuss is about.' Babs spoke truculently, with a swift glance from under her eyelashes at Lizzie. 'The war's over and done with. Besides, who'd want to go up West on a day when all the shops are shut, anyway?'

Lizzie knew the remark was aimed at her. Leaving school that summer had given Babs a precocious air and she thought she knew it all. She had been taken under the wing of the women who came from the affluent parts of the city, and she helped give out hot soup and tea at Hailing House, the old family home now used for the destitute. Lizzie knew Babs had envied her the visit to the city even though Babs wouldn't be seen dead pushing a Bath chair.

Kate intervened. 'I don't want to hear no talk like that, young lady. The war's over, but like yer father tells you, at a cost to nearly every family on this island. Thank Gawd yer brothers were too young to enlist or they might not be here today, just like poor Lil's two sons, who didn't even survive the first year.'

Lil Sharpe and her husband Doug lived next door at number eighty-four. Kate had helped Lil over the terrible period following the two boys' deaths in 1915. Kate and Lil were close friends as well as neighbours, and it was Ethel, their daughter, whose clothes and boots were handed down to Lizzie. Ethel was now married and had moved to Blackheath. She had two small children of her own.

'Miss Hailing says that all the other kings in Europe is gone,' Babs continued airily, 'and only our one's left. She says that God was on our side. That's why we won.'

Tom began to shake his head, his fingers tightening into fists on the arms of the Bath chair. 'God was on no man's side, gel. The whole world lost.'

'That ain't what Miss Hailing says. She says—'

'Listen here, young lady . . .' Tom leaned forward, his face flushed with anger. 'You tell this to your Miss Hailing from me. We've got strikes, we've got unemployment, we've got civil war with the Irish and the king don't give a toss. All he gives us is a load of blarney and expects us to swallow it. But we don't want talk, we want jobs, food on the table, our kids' bellies full. We want what they promised us when we laid down our lives for their future. But what we want we ain't never going to get. They told us lies in the trenches and they're still telling us them. What in God's name have we got to live for?'

Babs had long since stopped listening and was staring disinterestedly into space. Tom looked hard at his family, his pale eyes going over them one by one. No one answered. Vinnie got up, belched loudly and left the room.

Tom turned to Lizzie, his thin lips quivering. 'Fetch me cap, Lizzie, and me coat and push me out into the yard.'

'Oh, Tom, you shouldn't upset yerself,' Kate wailed, her hand going up to her mouth. 'You haven't eaten yer pudding. It's yer favourite, Spotted Dick.'

'I don't want it,' Tom growled.

Lizzie rose from the table and did as her father told her. If she didn't there would be another full scale row. 'You carry on with dinner,' she said to her mother as she helped her father on with his clothes. 'I'll do the washing-up.'

Kate's head was averted. Lizzie knew she was wiping away a tear. Tom's aggression was getting worse and Babs and Vinnie did nothing to ease it.

Lizzie wheeled the Bath chair from the kitchen and into the yard. Here, in the freezing November afternoon, she turned her father towards the broken fence that divided the two backyards. Beyond the fence Doug Sharpe attempted to thrust a spade into the earth.

'There's Mr Sharpe, Pa. Why don't you have a chat?' Doug and Tom were old friends. Lil and Doug had lived next to the Allens for twenty years. If anyone was able to understand her father, Doug was. But her father shook his head and said quietly, 'Leave me alone, Lizzie.'

'But Pa—'

'Go in, girl. Eat yer dinner.'

Lizzie stood for a moment. Sadness overwhelmed her at the sight of his slumped shoulders. She had seen desperation in his eyes and heard a new bitterness in his voice. Vinnie and Babs could be relied upon to upset the apple-cart, but what satisfaction they derived from it, Lizzie was at a loss to know.

Chapter Three

It was Monday and wash day in Langley Street.

'I tell you, Lil, one morning I ain't going to see the light of day,' Kate Allen complained to her neighbour as they stood gossiping over the garden fence. 'I'll be laying there in me bed, me heart stopped dead, the kids screaming their heads off, and what'll happen to the lot of 'em then, I ask you?'

'Well, one thing's for sure, if you're dead you won't know a bugger about it,' Lil Sharpe responded dryly.

Laughing, the women continued to peg out their washing. Minutes later, two neat rows of clothes were blowing gently on each line. Steam rose in the frosty air, the smell of carbolic and Sunlight mingling.

'Your Tom ready for Wednesday?' Lil called out as she draped a pair of long johns over the line.

'He's only going as far as Poplar now. He had a good day on Saturday, so he ain't got that much left to sell.'

'Probably a good thing,' Lil remarked. 'They're bringing the coffin from Dover, arriving at Victoria, so I hear. The city'll be chock-a-block.' Lil took a spare wooden peg from between her teeth and clamped it on the line. 'Your Lizzie still pushing Tom, then?'

'Better at pushing the chair than her brothers.' Kate lowered her voice, returning to the fence. Lil joined her there. 'Bert's so big and ugly he frightens off the women. Vinnie makes himself scarce at the mention of the chair.'

'You think he'd be proud to push his father on Armistice Day,' Lil commented, folding her thin arms across her chest. 'There ain't many blokes round 'ere lost two legs to the Kaiser. One maybe. Or an arm. But not two legs. You can't do much these days without yer old pins to walk on.'

Kate sighed. 'Yeah . . . and don't I know it.'

Lil raised her pencilled eyebrows. 'Least you ain't up the spout again. 'S'pose that's a comfort for you, gel.'

Reluctantly, Kate agreed. 'Nor likely to be, either, with what that shell did.'

'Don't make a man feel like a man, I 'spect.'

The subject of sex always dismayed Kate, for Tom was disabled in all respects and her only release was to pretend that she had gone off it too. Not that it was the sex that mattered so much, rather the tenderness and affection that her husband had once lavished on her. She longed to be taken into his arms and hugged; she didn't care that he was crippled. She loved him for what he was, her man. In fact, his disability had made her love him all the more. But she knew he felt he was repulsive to her. He recoiled when she slid her arms around him at night, and often she wept into the pillow, sleep evading her. But tears did no good. Her husband's heart had hardened.

Kate glanced at her neighbour and changed the subject. 'We had another ruckus Friday night. Gawd knows what I'm going to do about our Vinnie. Pissed to the eyeballs, he was, his face as black as a bruised plum. I tell you, me heart is having real problems catching up with me breath these days.'

'At least you got your Lizzie. She's a good girl, your Lizzie is.'

Kate nodded. 'Yeah. At least I got her, poor little cow.'

'And your Flo's coming on nicely. She's bright as a button for ten.'

This brought a smile to Kate's face. 'Ain't she just. Always askin' questions, that girl. Gawd help her teachers if there are more like her at school.'

'She's a real card, too. You can have a good laugh with your Flo,' Lil agreed with a chuckle. 'And Babs, well, she knows her own mind, that one. And with all that red hair, she turns heads all right. She's gonna be a stunner when she gets older.'

'Don't I know it,' Kate nodded. 'Up with all them posh ladies at the House.' Kate was secretly proud of the fact that the ladies of Hailing House had asked Babs if she'd like to help in the soup kitchens. It didn't matter that it was charity work. Babs would get on if she behaved herself.

'As for your Bert,' Lil continued, but in softer tones this time, 'he hasn't got a bad bone in his body, and me and Doug love him for it.'

Kate was aware that Bert reminded Lil of her two sons. They were only young when they had been killed in action in France. They'd been fine, strapping lads. Greg was sixteen and Neil seventeen. Though Greg had been a little older than Bert, they had been good mates. It had been five years since their deaths. Kate knew her friend had never really recovered.

'And I've got a bit of rent for old Symons on Friday,' Kate said cheerfully, avoiding the subject of the boys.

'That's a relief, ain't it?' Lil pulled her turban round her ears to keep out the cold. 'Maybe Christmas will see us all right, after all.'

And maybe she'd be crowned queen of England, Kate thought as the racing beat in her heart started once more. She took a breath and nodded at her neighbour's hopeful words. She didn't want to depress Lil, who had her own troubles. And to complain she'd had this funny feeling inside her for some months now would only cause her friend to worry. It was probably just a bit of indigestion. She'd take a double dose of salts and that was sure to ease it.

'What we need is a bloody good party,' Lil said suddenly. 'Like what we had at the end of the war.'

Kate sighed. Life was full of wars. When one ended another started. Tom had come home from the German war to the war of survival, not in the trenches, but in family life with all its pains and very few pleasures.

'Yeah, I s'pose so,' she agreed distractedly.

'Come on, gel, keep yer pecker up!' Lil laughed. 'It ain't the end of the world yet.'

'Course not.' Kate galvanized herself into action, shaking out a wet sheet. 'You're right. We should all get together at Christmas and have a knees-up.'

Lil nodded enthusiastically. ''Ere, I'll get Doug on 'is spoons, Lizzie can sing and we'll get our Eth on the Joanna. Some of the keys is missing, but never mind, no one will notice.'

'That'll be nice.' A sharp pain went across Kate's chest and she dropped the sheet back into the tub. Keeping her face averted from Lil, she breathed slowly, the way she'd been trying to do lately. It sometimes helped to make the pain go away. Lil was trying to cheer her up, bless her. She was a cheery spark, for all that had happened. It made Kate feel that she was lucky to have all her family alive. She'd miscarried the twins, but they had just been scraps, no life in their minute bodies and only a brief agony. Lil carried her dead sons in her heart – bravely and without complaint.

'You sure you're all right, gel? You look a bit pale.'

Kate nodded. 'Right as rain, Lil. But I'd better get meself back indoors. Gotta think of somethin' to give 'em for dinner.'

'You do that.' Lil Sharpe winked. 'And don't forget about Christmas.'

Kate picked up the sheet gingerly. She was relieved to find the movement caused her no discomfort. At last the pain was receding. Bloody indigestion. She began to mull over what she was going to put on the table. Should she borrow from the rent or make do? There was nothing except spuds in the pantry. Well, she could boil the bones from yesterday that she'd saved from the mutton. Yes, she'd do that just as soon as she sat down for a bit.

*

That evening Lizzie and Flo were in their bedroom. They were pretending to be nuns, with coats over their heads. Lizzie had a strong, husky voice and could reach any note she attempted, high or low. Flo stayed in tune as long as she concentrated.

Babs had gone next door with Kate and Lizzie was trying to amuse Flo. Normally she would have died rather than let anyone see she was acting out a part in her old coat, pretending she was a famous actress. But her mind kept going back to Danny and the one and only chance she'd probably ever have of going to the theatre.

'I ain't seen Mary Pickford being a nun,' said Flo doubtfully. 'A singin' nun, anyway.'

'We're just imaginin', Flo. Nuns have lovely voices, like what we heard on His Master's Voice.' Lizzie pulled her green coat firmly round her head, doing the button up under her chin. She'd always taken the part of Mary Pickford when she was younger. But now it was Flo who had been given the honour. Charlie Chaplin was usually left to Flo, who was the comic of the family.

Flo pushed back her straight brown hair and hugged her knees. 'Is that real nuns singing the Nuns' Chorus, Lizzie?'

'Course it is. Or else it wouldn't be called a Nuns' Chorus, would it?'

'How do you know?'

'It's written on the label of one of them shiny records that Pa got from the Seamen's Rest, over Greenwich. If it's on the label then it must be true.'

'I wish we could listen to it now,' Flo said wistfully. 'Then we could join in with them.'

'Pa ain't gonna let us bring his gramophone up here, is he?' It was from a battered black box that the strains of such music as Cavalleria Rusticana could sometimes be heard in their parents' bedroom.

'Don't see why not,' Flo complained. 'We wouldn't 'urt it.'

'Well, you ask him then,' said Lizzie challengingly, knowing that would stop Flo's questions. They had often lain awake in bed at nights listening to the gramophone downstairs. Lizzie had an ear for music and it was not long before she had memorized each tune.

'What do nuns do all day?' Flo asked, ignoring Lizzie's last remark.

'They pray for people's sins. To save the world.'

'We ain't been saved though,' Flo spluttered. 'Pa says that if God loved the world he would have stopped the wars and all them soldiers what's been killed would be alive today. And it's God that them nuns pray to, ain't it?'

'Flo, d'you wanna be Mary Pickford or not?' Lizzie was getting exasperated. She wanted to think about Danny, not answer all these questions.

Flo yawned. 'I'm tired,' she mumbled.

'Then undress and get into bed,' Lizzie told her. 'I'll tell you a story.'

'What sort of story?'

'Flo!' Lizzie yelled. She'd had enough. Flo pulled a face, but she did as she was told. Lizzie removed the coat from her head and tidied away the tattered old clothes they had used to dress up in.

By the time Lizzie had finished the story of a poor girl

marrying a prince and having a ball gown to wear every day of her life, Flo was fast asleep. Lizzie went quietly out on to the landing, closing the door behind her. She expected to hear Bert and Vinnie in their bedroom, but was surprised to hear voices downstairs.

She leaned over the banister as Bert came up the stairs. 'We're off out,' he said, squeezing his cap down over his forehead.

'Where you goin'? You ain't going up the pub, are you?'

Bert looked awkward. 'Only for a couple of beers.'

'Bert, don't go. Wait for Ma to come in.'

'Vinnie's kickin' his heels doin' nothing, gel.'

Lizzie knew what that meant. Vinnie had returned home in a foul mood that evening and was planning to drown his sorrows.

'What will I tell Ma when she comes back?'

'You'll just 'ave ter say we won't be late.'

'Don't go,' Lizzie pleaded. 'You'll only get into trouble.'

'Not on yer Nellie,' Bert replied with a wink. 'Leave Vin to me. I'll see 'e comes to no harm and that's a promise.'

It was all bravado on Bert's part. But what could she do? She watched him go back down the stairs and heard the front door slam. The house was quiet again. When she returned to the bedroom, Flo was still fast asleep. Lizzie sat on the edge of the bed.

She couldn't knock on Pa's door. He wouldn't want to know. There was nothing she could do except wait till Ma came in from Lil's.

Chapter Four

Chalk wharf was silent, save for the belly rumble of a foghorn somewhere on the river. The fog was yellow and visibility was poor. A walk on the dockside was as perilous as crossing the river in a boat. The smell of oil, spices, wood and chemicals permeated the air. It clung to the two solitary figures that walked, with shoulders hunched, through the murky night.

'Don't look like anyone's about,' Bert muttered, his teeth chattering.

Vinnie narrowed his eyes under the brim of his homburg. 'They'll be here all right. Mik said they was in a hurry to move the stuff. All we gotta do is see the china is gen. Mik'll send the boys to pick it up later.'

'Why don't Mik come 'imself,' Bert asked doubtfully, 'instead of sending you?'

''Cos this is the way 'e does business,' growled Vinnie, wishing he hadn't brought Bert along. He needed a bit of muscle, not a bloody gramophone. And lately Bert was stuck in the same groove, a right whinger.

However, Bert had a point. Why had Mik sent him on this job? Vinnie didn't like to think about it. You didn't argue if you wanted to stay healthy. Vinnie clearly recalled his recent reminder to toe the line; Mik's boys had really gone to town on him that night at the Quarry. In a way, he understood. There were rules and you obeyed them. If you didn't, you took your punishment. He'd got himself nicked and Mik had to square it with the law; Vinnie knew another mistake like that and it would be his last.

'Mik Ferreter ain't into china, is he?' Bert asked, puzzled.

'I told you. He's bought a job lot to flog up West, to the posh shops that sells antiques to the nobs.'

'You're sure it's legit?' Bert asked once more.

'Course I am.'

'Then why ain't we doin' this in daylight?'

Vinnie was getting angry. 'Blimey, Bert, your memory's like a bloody sieve lately. Look, watch me lips.' He pushed his face into Bert's. 'The bloke who's sold the stuff to Mik wants it out of the way. The timber yard's only agreed to store it till tomorrow. It's all gotta be gone by the morning. All right?'

Bert was really getting on his nerves. He used to do as he was told. But lately he never stopped asking questions, and Vinnie was fed up having to answer them. Not that he ever told Bert the truth. Take tonight, for instance. The warehouse was a doddle. All he had to do was make contact. See the booze was all there: twenty crates of gin destined for illegal gaming clubs. But Bert wasn't going to get near enough to the crates to see what was in them. It would all be over and done with in ten minutes. By nine, he'd be in the Quarry drinking with his mates.

Suddenly Bert's six foot four frame stiffened beside him. Vinnie swung round. They peered through the fog and saw an eerie light. The halo wavered, sending out a glow that lit up the structure around it.

'It's the timber yard,' said Vinnie on a slow breath. 'Someone's hung a lamp out for us. See all that wood piled up?'

'I gotta funny feeling about this, Vin.'

'You and your funny feelings.'

Vinnie sighed to himself. It was at times like this he told himself life could only get better. He wasn't going to be a bookie's runner for ever. He wouldn't always be a messenger boy, sent out on piddling little jobs like this. One day, he'd settle the score. Do things his own way, see some real money.

'See anyone yet?' Bert whispered as they moved forward.

'Nah.' The lamplight flickered around the rafter it was attached to and the wood gave out a warm, comforting glow. The notice behind it was now visible, *Bennet's Timber Merchants*.

'You sure this is legit?' Bert grunted.

'For cryin' out loud!' Vinnie closed his eyes.

'It just don't feel right, Vin.'

'It's your daft 'ead that don't' feel right. You don't use it, that's your problem. And when you do, it 'urts. Vicious circle, that's what they call it. Might as well stick a bag over it. Be less painful and it wouldn't make no difference to yer lifestyle.'

Bert dropped his big chin on his chest. Vinnie felt a

wave of satisfaction. He revelled in humiliating people. It wasn't often he got the chance. Mostly it was Mik humiliating him. But Bert was a soft touch, a good target. Vinnie poked his brother in the shoulder. 'I'll tell you once more what we're going to do. We're walking in there, bold as brass. You stay in the background, that's all you've gotta do. I'll do the all the talking. Just act the part. Flex yer muscles and look ugly.'

Vinnie turned to the door. He had a feeling he was going to enjoy this. He was glad he had worn his new overcoat. They would see he had style.

'Door's open,' said Bert cautiously.

'Yeah. Safe as 'ouses.'

They advanced into the dimly lit warehouse. High piles of wooden planks rose to the rafters and wood shavings littered the floor. Down at the end there was a light, another oil lamp hanging from a beam.

'What's that stink?' Bert asked hoarsely.

'Tar,' said Vinnie over his shoulder. 'Don't you know tar when you smell it? They use it on the wood.'

They walked slowly down the aisle. Vinnie's heart was thumping. All he could see was the silhouettes of woodpiles and shadowy corners. When they came to the last stack of wood, he stood still and craned his neck to look round it. He couldn't believe his eyes. It was just like Mik had said it would be. In the light of the lamp, he could see the large wooden crates marked FRAGILE. How many bottles of booze did that lot contain, he wondered? His pulse raced as he savoured the adrenaline rush.

He stepped forward slowly. Bert was right on his heels.

Vinnie groaned and turned, hissing, 'I told you, stay in the background.'

Bert stood with his jaw sagging. Vinnie gave his brother a long, hard glare. Then a movement in the shadows caught his eye.

Out of the gloom stepped three figures. They were dressed in overcoats and hats and none of their faces was visible. Two were tall, broad and muscular. The third and smallest figure walked slowly towards the crates.

A potent mixture of fear and excitement filled Vinnie's veins. His throat was dry, his palms sweaty. He told himself to stay calm. Mik's instructions were to make certain the booze was in the crates; Vinnie intended to follow them to the letter.

'State yer business,' the small figure said.

Vinnie swallowed. 'Mik sent me. To inspect the goods.'

Vinnie wondered if Bert could handle the two goons. More importantly, could he himself match this man in front of him? This was the big league. The real McCoy. Mik had sent him on a serious errand. If he lost face on this one he'd never live it down.

In silence, the overcoated figure leaned across one of the crates and lifted the top. Vinnie moved forward and looked into it. All he could see were bottle tops. He felt a flood of relief. He moved to the next crate. His fingers clamped round the top. He felt the rough edge of the wood prickle his skin. The feeling of power was intoxicating. The smell, the atmosphere, the high he was getting from doing the deal. This was what he was made for.

He jerked up the top. Dozens more bottles. He needn't have worried. Everything was perfect. 'How many crates?' he demanded, his confidence returning.

'Twenty.'

The crates behind were stacked in twos. Too high to reach the top ones. He looked around. No ladders. Nothing on which to climb. Odd for a timber yard. A jolt of suspicion went through him. He tried to calm himself. If he panicked, he'd blow it. 'Open them all,' he said.

There was a long pause. 'You ain't very trusting.'

'Why should I be?'

'You saying them crates ain't full?'

'I ain't sayin' nothing. Not till I've had a butcher's.' Vinnie was getting nervous. He squared his shoulders. 'Me boss is very particular.'

'Your boss wants a bit bloody much,' came the reply. 'Ain't you gonna take me word?'

'I dunno who you are,' Vinnie gulped. 'Why should I do that?'

'Seems to me you ain't got much choice.'

'Oh yes I have,' Vinnie answered in a bolshie tone. He didn't like this one bit.

'Oh no you ain't.' The small figure stepped forward and Vinnie gasped audibly as his lapels were clenched. He stared into a pair of dark, dangerous eyes.

'If you think I'm climbing over twenty bloody crates and taking off all them tops just for you, sonny boy, then you got another think coming.'

'Get your 'ands off,' Vinnie sputtered, intending to brazen it out. He had to keep his head. But already he was struggling with his natural instinct to smash his fist into the unpleasant face in front of him.

'You're a big mouth, you are,' growled his assailant as he thrust Vinnie back against the wood. 'Personally, I don't like the look of you or your mate.'

'That makes two of us.' Vinnie tried to force down his anger. 'How do I know the other eighteen boxes ain't full of bricks and not booze?'

The moment he said it, Vinnie knew he'd dropped a clanger. Out of the corner of his eye he saw Bert. 'You said it was china,' Bert mumbled in a stupid voice. 'For them posh shops up West.'

Vinnie wanted to throttle Bert. Now he would look a right amateur.

'Hark at it,' laughed the little man. 'He thinks it's *china*!' There was a chorus of loud laughter. Directed at him, it made Vinnie cringe. He had been made a laughing stock and it was all Bert's fault.

'You thick 'eaded numbskull, Bert.' Vinnie turned angrily. 'I told you to keep that bleedin' big gob of yours shut, you silly bastard.'

'You told me it was china,' Bert said again. His big lapdog eyes stared forlornly at his brother.

'Course it's not bloody china.' Vinnie pulled his lapels back into shape. 'Don't you see I'm trying to do a deal here? Don't you understand we're on to a winner? And all you can do is stand there and look at me like a—' But Vinnie never finished his sentence because Bert was turning and walking away.

Vinnie couldn't believe his eyes. What was Bert doing?

He gulped down his shock. Bert was leaving him. Dependable, trustworthy, thick as two planks Bert was abandoning him. But Vinnie realized Bert wasn't going very far. The two other men had stopped laughing and were blocking Bert's path.

Vinnie knew then they were trapped. They weren't going anywhere, either of them. Something made him turn. A crowbar was poised above his head. The iron claw came down. It sank into the fabric of his hat, missing his skull by a fraction.

'Bastard!' he screamed as he fell back, unharmed but shocked. The crowbar came down again. He dodged it. This time it lodged in the wood. Vinnie looked into the small man's surprised eyes. He lifted his boot and kicked hard. It was a real pleasure to see the agony; he continued the kicking, enjoying every moment of it.

Without his muscle, the little tosser was nothing. It was he, Vinnie, who would call the tune. When he'd taught him a lesson, he'd make him open up the crates. He'd return to Mik triumphant. Either way, booze or no booze, he'd have followed instructions and saved Mik an embarrassment.

Then suddenly everything went black. Vinnie stared, bewildered, into the darkness. He kicked out, but his boot found only thin air. There was a lot of shuffling and Vinnie stumbled back against the woodpile. He kicked out again, but this time in self-defence. He swung his arms violently, his knuckles grazing the wood. The darkness was pitch. He could hear his own breathing and things going on around him. Movement. Hushed voices. And smells.

Where was everyone? Where was Bert? His heart felt as though it was trying to get out of his chest. He felt his way along the wood, sweat dripping from his forehead. His wet palms found a wall. Why hadn't they come after him?

He flattened his back to it, his eyes searching the darkness. There were outlines shapes, noises. Where the fuck was everyone?

He soon got his answer.

A flicker of light broke the darkness. A thin tongue of orange licked upward, caressing the wood gently. Vinnie stared at it, not understanding at first. Then a cold terror filled him. The inside of the warehouse flickered into light.

They had torched the place. The bastards. They intended to burn them alive. They would die here. This stinking yard was to be their tomb. Nothing would ever be found of them. The warehouse was a perfect incinerator.

He panicked. Coughing and spluttering, his lungs filled with thick grey smoke. Tears streamed down his cheeks. He stumbled along blindly, grabbing at anything he could find. He was going to die here. A slow and terrible death. He was sobbing like a baby and he didn't care.

Suddenly his vision cleared. The smoke parted like a curtain and he rubbed his eyes. He blinked and blinked once more. In front of him was the door they had entered by. He couldn't believe his luck.

For one brief second he thought he heard Bert's voice.

But he convinced himself he hadn't. There was nothing that would persuade him to retrace his steps. And it was Bert's bloody fault anyway. He thought he heard the voice again and ignored it. He stumbled towards the door and wrenched it open. A gust of air poured in. He fell out into the night, not stopping to look back at the burning warehouse as he ran as fast as his shaking legs would carry him.

Chapter Five

'Look at this, bread pudding, still warm from Lil's oven,' Kate told Lizzie as she came in the back door carrying an enamel dish. 'Ain't she a good mate? You smell that mixed spice. Me mouth is watering already. Oh, what a treat!' Carefully, Kate lowered the pudding to the table.

'It looks smashing.' Lizzie went to the table. 'Ma, there's something—'

'Babs'll be in soon,' Kate continued as she filled the kettle with water. 'I told her she could have ten minutes more. Ethel and her two kids are over from Blackheath, so we had to be polite and stay for a bit.'

'That's nice, but—'

'Them two kids are lovely,' Kate sighed, taking off her coat and hanging it on the peg behind the door. 'Really growing up quick. Rosie's just like her mother, all blonde hair and big brown eyes, and for two she's ever so bright.' She turned to Lizzie, her face flushed and smiling. 'Flo all right, love?'

Lizzie nodded. 'She's asleep.'

'And young Timmy!' Kate exclaimed as she put on her

pinny. 'What a little monkey! Into everything he is, but lovable with it. Dunno where he got his blue eyes from, though. None to speak of in the family, certainly not on Ethel's side. Now, go and tell yer brothers I'm doing supper. I'll slice this up thinly. It'll be just like old times, all sitting round the table together having supper.'

'Ma,' Lizzie said, waiting for the eruption when she broke the news, 'Bert and Vinnie went out.'

Kate turned to stare at her. 'Went out? When?'

'Just after you went to Lil's.' Lizzie added quickly, 'Bert said they wouldn't be long.'

Kate stood still, her thin body stiffening. 'Did he say where they were going?'

Lizzie shook her head. She didn't want to tell Kate they had gone down the pub, even though it was obvious to one and all that they had.

Kate walked slowly to the rocker and sank down. 'I should have known better than to go out. I might have guessed the buggers would 'op it the moment I turned me back.'

'Don't worry, Ma.' Lizzie sat on one of the wooden chairs. 'Bert said he'd keep an eye on Vinnie.'

Kate laughed mirthlessly. 'Yeah, I've heard that one before an' all. He can't keep an eye on himself, let alone his brother.'

'Would you like me to cut you a nice piece of Lil's bread pudding?'

'No thanks, ducks.' Kate gazed into space. All the colour had drained from her face.

Silently Lizzie rose and took the boiling kettle from

the hob. Automatically she went through the motions of making tea, trying to think of a way to distract Kate. When she'd poured the hot brown liquid into two mugs, she sat down again, passing one mug to her mother.

'Thanks, love.'

'Shall I take one in to Pa?'

Kate glanced at her. 'No, I hope he'll be asleep by now. If he isn't, he'll let us know all right.'

'Tell me one of yer stories, Ma.' Lizzie pulled her skirt over her knees and tucked her feet up under her bottom. 'The one about poor Granny Allen.'

Kate did smile then. 'Lizzie Allen, you've heard all those stories before. Fact is, I reckon you could tell them to me.'

'No I couldn't.' Lizzie sipped her tea. 'You always make them sound different each time you tell them.'

Kate laughed. 'I do, do I? Oh well, I'll have to remember me lies, won't I?

They both laughed, then Kate sighed. 'Well, Granny Allen was a beauty and famed for it. But Grandfather Allen was a drunk, I'm sorry to say. Yer father saw 'is mother dragged down the stairs by her hair, and yer grandfather let her lie in her own blood. It wasn't the first beating she ever took in drink, and it wasn't the last. When we started to walk out, your father promised me that I'd never have a drunkard for a husband. He kept his promise and never touched a drop since.' For a moment Kate paused, then she glanced at Lizzie. 'You sure Bert gave no indication of where they was going?'

Lizzie shook her head, trying to think of another distraction.

Kate reclined in the chair.

'Tell me about when Pa was at sea and you was in service with that rich lady,' Lizzie said quickly.

'You just told it yerself, you silly moo,' Kate sighed. 'You know the story word for word by now.'

'Not the way you tell it, I don't.' Lizzie really did love hearing all the old family stories. There was only Kate to learn from.

Kate looked down at her mug of tea. After a while she sat back, smiling to herself. 'I met your father whilst I was in service – as you well know. He was at sea and, like hundreds of young women of my time, I was in the employ of a very wealthy family. Occasionally, I got a weekend off from Lord and Lady Arnott's. Then I would come back to the island from Surrey to visit yer gran.

'And that's when you met Pa?' Lizzie prompted, eager for the flow to continue

Kate looked at Lizzie with a frown. 'I dunno why I'm repeating meself like this. I must have told you a hundred times before.' Lizzie was relieved to hear her mother continue despite raising her eyebrows and sighing again. 'Anyway, Granny Watts knew Granny Allen, who lived at the back of this house on March Street, so it was only natural I should bump into yer father when he was home on leave. Well, I left the Arnotts at the same time as yer father come off the merchant boats and transferred to the Port of London Authority. That was when he asked me ter marry 'im.'

'And you said yes.'

'And I said yes.'

'And what happened then?'

'Blimey, gel, I'll get an 'oarse throat at this rate!'

'I'll pour you another cuppa—'

Kate reached out and took her arm. 'Sit down, gel. I ain't finished this one yet.' Kate took a long slow gulp of tea and licked her lips. 'We lived with Granny Watts, who was a widow – me dad died whilst I was in service. I had a bit of training that 'elped me to keep a clean house and yer father worked hard, never losing sight of 'is promise not to drink.'

'He must have loved you, Ma.'

Kate nodded slowly. 'Yes, my love, he did. And I loved him too.' The smile slowly faded and was replaced by an expression of sadness. 'Anyway, the war came along and knocked all the romance out of our 'eads.'

Kate closed her eyes and rested her head against the high wooden back of the rocking chair.

'Why don't you go to bed, Ma?' Lizzie whispered. 'I'll wait up for the boys.'

Kate opened her weary eyes. 'I dunno. The buggers might roll in pissed. I don't want yer father disturbed again.' She rubbed her chest slowly. 'But me indigestion is playing up a bit. I could do with an early night.'

'I'll wait up for them,' Lizzie assured her mother.

'You're a good girl, Lizzie Allen. A real treasure.' Kate kissed her on the forehead. 'Tell those two when they come in, if they make so much as a squeak I'll have their guts for garters in the morning.'

Lizzie watched her mother go slowly along the passage. The door of the front room opened and closed gently.

It was half an hour later when Babs came in. Lizzie put a finger to her mouth. 'Shh! Ma's gone to bed.'

'Shush yerself,' said Babs with a scowl. 'I got eyes in me head, ain't I?'

'You'd better get upstairs to bed.'

'You ain't me mother.' Babs swept out of the kitchen, tossing back her auburn curls. Lizzie sighed. Babs was getting worse. One day, it wouldn't stop at words.

Lizzie sat up in the rocking chair. She must have fallen asleep. The wooden clock on the kitchen shelf said it was almost eleven. She heard a noise at the front door and got up to see who it was. A hand came through the letterbox and pulled up the string. Two figures entered. She thought she was dreaming when she saw who was with Bert.

'Danny! What are you doing here?'

They all went into the kitchen. Danny shut the passage door behind him.

His voice was hushed. 'I'll tell you in a minute.'

Bert asked anxiously, 'Vinnie back yet?'

'No, he ain't. I thought he was with you. You said you were going up the pub.'

'Is everyone in bed?' Danny asked.

She nodded, looking from one to the other. 'Bert, you're filthy! What's that over your jacket?'

Danny nudged him. 'You'd better go and wash yer

hands and face, Bert. I'll have a word with yer sister.' His big shoulders drooping, Bert walked out into the yard. 'Don't be too hard on him,' Danny said quietly. 'He ain't quite himself.'

'I can see that, Danny. What's going on?'

'You'd better sit down. I'll tell you all I know. But it ain't very much, I'm afraid.'

They pulled out the chairs and sat next to each other. 'There was a fire at a timber yard up at Limehouse tonight,' Danny told her. 'As far as I can make out, Bert and Vinnie was in it.'

'Oh, no!' Lizzie jumped up again, her hand clamped to her mouth.

Danny pulled her down gently. 'Hold your horses, gel. Bert thinks Vinnie must have got out.'

'He *thinks*?' Lizzie closed her eyes. When she opened them, Danny was squeezing her arm. 'You all right, gel?'

She nodded. 'I don't understand. What were they doing at a timber yard?'

'Beats me. I found Bert up Poplar. I'd done a few late deliveries for me dad. It was dark, and when I spotted Bert . . . thought he'd had one over the eight. He was sort of stumbling along. I told him to hop up on the cart. He looked bloody awful, all dazed, like. And he stunk of smoke. He kept saying there had been a fire at this timber yard, that he couldn't find Vin.'

Bert came back in, then. His face and hands were cleaner, but his clothes were still filthy. 'Well, whatever your excuse is, Bert Allen, you'd better not let Ma see that jacket,' Lizzie said, her voice shaky. Why couldn't

Bert stay out of trouble? She had warned him enough times. And where was Vinnie? If he had got out of the fire, why hadn't he come home?

Bert slowly took off his jacket and rolled it up. 'I'll give it a scrub in a minute.'

Lizzie couldn't be angry with him for long. He did look in a state. 'Sit down,' she told him, 'and I'll make you a cup of tea. You'd better tell me what happened.'

Bert poured it all out. Chalk Wharf, the timber yard, the crates of booze which he'd thought were china and the three men. Finally he told them how things had gone wrong and the warehouse had caught alight.

'What makes you think Vinnie got out?' Lizzie asked as she pushed a mug of steaming tea towards Bert.

'He was standing by the crates. Someone bashed me over the head and I was out cold for a bit, but when I came to there was smoke everywhere. I crawled on me hands and knees until I found the crates. I'd stake me life he wasn't there. Nor was the other geezer with the crowbar.'

'You got a lump on yer head the size of an egg,' Danny said.

Bert lifted his hand and rubbed his scalp. 'I don't remember much.'

'What happened to the other blokes? Do you remember that?' asked Danny.

'Nah. Only that I lost me temper when I saw the crowbar. I tried to get to Vin. Then it felt like the place was coming down round me ears.' Bert looked at Lizzie. 'I didn't want to come 'ome without our Vin, gel. I swear, I looked everywhere. I went back in but the 'eat and smoke was too much.'

'Bert, that was dangerous!'

'I 'ad to 'ave another look.'

'You shouldn't have gone out in the first place,' Lizzie said sharply. 'And you lied to me, Bert, you said you was going up the pub.'

'To give Bert his due,' Danny intervened, 'I think you'll find Vin didn't give him much of a choice.' Danny glanced at Bert. 'Ain't that so, Bert?'

Bert said nothing, loyal to the end.

'What are we going to do?' Lizzie asked. 'What if Vinnie doesn't come home?'

Danny looked at Bert. 'We'll give him another hour, then we'll go up to Limehouse. We'll take a gander at the wharf, see what's happening.'

Bert nodded, but Lizzie knew they were all thinking the same. That Vinnie wouldn't turn up in an hour. That he might never turn up at all.

Chapter Six

Lizzie glanced at the clock. It was one o'clock in the morning. For the last two hours they had been drinking tea and talking in whispers.

Danny stood up and drew his cap from his pocket. 'Well, Bert. No sense in hanging round any longer. We'd better get up to Limehouse.'

Bert looked crestfallen. Lizzie had tried to wash the stains from his jacket but the rough tweed had turned a muddy colour. There was a ring of black round his neck and his hair was singed.

But Lizzie opened the kitchen door just as four filthy fingers poked through the letterbox. The string was drawn up, a key inserted and the front door opened.

'Where the 'ell 'ave you been?' Bert gasped as he stared at Vinnie.

For one moment Vinnie looked shocked to see Bert. Then he strode down the passage and into the kitchen. 'I might ask you the same.'

'Danny and Bert were just coming to look for you,' Lizzie said.

Vinnie took off his hat and threw it on the table. It

and his overcoat were streaked with black marks. 'Well they won't have to bother now, will they? I s'pose you've heard all about tonight from him.' He nodded at Bert.

'I been looking for you everywhere,' Bert replied slowly. 'Where 'ave you been all this time?'

'Where do you think? Someone had to go and tell Mik, didn't they?'

'But we've been worried,' Lizzie told him. 'We didn't know if you'd got out of the fire—'

'No thanks to him I did.' Vinnie glared at Bert.

'What do you mean?' Bert said hollowly.

'You were the silly bugger who started the trouble,' Vinnie accused angrily. 'I was handling the deal until you did a bunk.'

'You said what was in those crates was legit china,' Bert replied in a hurt voice. 'But it was all knocked off.'

'And you wouldn't have known a bloody thing about it,' Vinnie returned quickly, 'if you'd kept yer big nose out of me business. I told you to keep quiet, but you couldn't, could you? One thing I know for sure is I won't be taking you with me again.'

'Bert did his best to look for you,' Lizzie intervened. 'The least you could have done was come straight home and tell him you were safe.'

Vinnie's dark eyes narrowed. 'Who asked you for an opinion? This ain't got nothin' to do with you, it's between me an 'im.'

'I found yer brother up Poplar,' Danny said, walking

round the table. 'He went back in that warehouse when he couldn't find you outside. Goin' back into a furnace like that takes some doing.'

'Trust you to stick yer oar in,' Vinnie snapped. 'Look, I just told her to mind her own business. Now I'm tellin' you to do the same.'

'No problem,' Danny said evenly. 'I don't think any of us want to know what was in them crates, Vin.' The two men stared at one another, dislike in their eyes.

'Ain't it about time you were leavin'?' Vinnie muttered.

Danny nodded. 'I'm going all right. I don't intend to wear out me welcome.'

Lizzie caught his sleeve. 'Come on, Danny. I'll see you out.'

'Just you keep what you heard tonight to yerself, Flowers,' Vinnie yelled after them.

Lizzie quietly opened the front door. She was worried that her parents would hear. Outside in the street, the fog had cleared. A deep blue sky was full of stars and a white frost touched the windows and roofs of the houses in Langley Street. Danny put his hands gently on her arms. 'He's right, you know. What he gets up to is his own affair and no one else's. He ain't a kid any longer.'

'But what if he'd been caught tonight with all that drink?'

'There ain't nothing you can do, gel. You probably don't know the half of what's goin' on, either. At least there wasn't no life lost in the fire.' He tipped up her chin. 'You gonna be all right? Vinnie ain't likely to cause you trouble?'

She shook her head. 'I just hope no one wakes up.'

'Well, if you need me, you know where I am.'

It was wonderful to be cared about, Lizzie thought as he took her in his arms. Under the starry sky he kissed her. It was the most wonderful thing that had ever happened to her – like the wings of a butterfly softly touching her lips.

He grinned. 'You can slap me face if you want.'

She didn't want to slap his face, she wanted to be kissed again. When his lips had touched hers, all her troubles had melted away.

'See you up the market on Saturday?'

She nodded. 'Danny, thanks for everything.'

'Better get a move on, or Benji'll be frozen stiff, poor bugger.'

She watched him hurry across the road to where the scruffy old grey horse stood. Benji raised his head as he saw Danny approach. In the silence of the night, Danny clicked his tongue as he jumped up on the cart. Only the sound of Benji's horseshoes rang out in the early hours of the winter morning.

'What time did you two roll in last night?' Kate Allen bawled at her sons the following morning.

Bert and Vinnie sat at the breakfast table with long faces. Neither was speaking to the other. Kate knew there was something going on. But this morning she felt so queasy she realized she didn't want to know what.

She had slept deeply and only woken once when she thought she'd heard voices. It must have been the boys coming in, she realized. Thank the Lord Tom hadn't woken.

'Lost yer tongues have you?' She wagged the bread knife at her sons. 'Well, from now on if you both want to live down the pub and drink yerselves to death then go ahead, but don't think yer coming home to this house afterwards. From tonight onwards, that front door's locked after ten. The string's coming off and you'll have to kip on the doorstep.' She looked hard at them both. 'Understood?'

Bert and Vinnie stared at their bread and dripping as if hypnotized.

'Understood?' she said again, louder.

Her sons nodded slowly. As they ate their bread in silence, Kate made a vow to herself. Things were going to be different from now on. If the rest of the household could keep decent hours, then so could these two lazy buggers.

Bert and Vinnie ate their bread and drank their tea. They left the kitchen in silence. Not one word between them. Kate turned to Lizzie as they cleared the dishes. 'What's up with them two?'

'Dunno, Ma.'

Kate raised her eyebrows. 'Something's up.'

'They'll be as right as rain tonight. Don't think early mornings suit them.'

'Well, they'll have to get used to it,' Kate said firmly. 'If Flo can get herself off to school and Babs up to the House by eight o'clock in the morning, then they can too. 'And tonight they can clean out their room. Smells like a bloody match factory up there.' Kate dried her hands, went to the cupboard under the stairs and took out the boots.

'Now, I've something I want you to do for me, gel,' she said, placing the boots in her shopping bag.

Lizzie turned from the sink. 'It ain't the boots, is it, Ma?'

'See if you can get fifteen shillings from old Bloome for them.'

'But, Ma—'

'You remind the tight old sod that I bought 'em 'specially for your Pa to wear when he came home from the war.'

'But they ain't new anymore, Ma. Mr Bloome told me last time, don't you remember? I got ten and six and he was hard pushed to give me that.'

'I know you don't like going to Mr Bloome's, ducks,' Kate sighed. 'But I gotta put something in everyone's stomach. I ain't goin' down that cocoa tin, not if it kills me. Your father don't approve, I know, but it's either me washing that goes to the pawnbroker or the boots. Anyway, he won't find out, if no one tells him.' She laid a cloth over the top of the boots in the basket. 'I don't like asking you to do it for me, you know that, but I'll have a nice piece of hot bread pudding waiting for you when you get back. Now go and get yer coat on, there's a good girl.'

Kate wished she didn't have to send Lizzie, but there was no other way. Just then Vinnie walked down the stairs. 'Where do you think you're off to?' she demanded as he came into the kitchen, dressed in his cap and outdoor jacket.

'To work, Ma.'

'You call what you do *work*?' Kate hated the thought of her son as a bookie's runner. It was never mentioned in the house, but she knew for a fact it was what he did. 'One of these days you're going to run up against the wrath of the law, my son.'

'No chance, mother. I keep on me toes. See you tonight.'

'Just you be careful.' Kate called after him.

When he'd gone out the front door, Kate went to the bottom of the stairs. 'Ain't it about time you were off an' all, Bert? There's gotta be a job going somewhere on this bloody island.'

'Yeah all right, Ma. Just comin.'

Kate was about to tell him to get a move on when the indigestion struck. She swallowed, coming out in a cold sweat. That was all she needed. The bloody pain back again.

Lizzie came down the stairs in her coat and scarf. 'Bye, Ma. I'll be back soon.'

Kate opened the front door. 'Keep yer collar done up, love.' She watched her daughter walk down Langley Street until she was out of sight . . . the daughter whom she loved beyond words, her first girl child.

Bert was next down the stairs. 'Blimey, what's happened to yer jacket?' Kate gasped. 'Looks like you put it through me wringer.'

'Yeah, well, I tried to give it a bit of a clean up.' Bert was going red.

Kate raised her eyes and sighed once more. 'I'll have to see if I can get you something up the market. The sleeves are too short on that one, anyway.'

Bert leaned forward and kissed her on the cheek. 'Cheerio, Ma.'

She inhaled a strange smell. 'I don't know how long ago it was you had a wash, me boy, but you ain't going to win any prizes smelling like that. Tonight we'll bring the bath in. You and Vinnie can have a bloody good soak.'

'Yeah, all right, Ma.'

When Bert had turned the corner Kate closed the door slowly. Her heart was fluttering as though a bird was trapped in her chest. It was happening a lot lately. She'd had a funny five minutes when she'd got up and then again as she'd seen Flo off to school this morning. Usually it wore off by the time she was getting Tom ready. But it was a real bugger this morning.

She went back to the kitchen. What would she buy with the boot money? Very likely a nice mutton stew with lentils or split peas. She might even run to a sixpenny bar of milk chocolate. She loved seeing the kids' expressions if she left a piece by each of their mugs at supper time.

Kids, she thought to herself as she put the kettle on to boil. Hardly kids any longer. Only Flo really. Oh, if only she could get Tom to come out of that blessed bedroom and join in a bit more with the family! It might even help

Vinnie to settle down if he did. Boys needed a father. A visible one.

Vinnie was going to have to change his tune. Bert was going to have to find a job. Sods, the pair of them, doing a bunk last night.

Kate pulled back her shoulders. She intended to iron out a few creases in this family. First off, today, she'd push Tom out just as soon as Lizzie got back. He wouldn't like it. He wanted to sit and sulk in the bedroom all day. Well, if he was well enough to go up the market on Mondays, Wednesdays and Saturdays, he could come up the park with her for a breath of fresh air of a Tuesday.

From now on . . .

Kate took a breath and stood still. Her hand went up to her breast. A pain shot across her chest and down her arm. For a moment she smiled at the irony. A bout of indigestion just as she was going to put her family to rights. Well, indigestion or no, this was a day they were all going to remember.

The smile was still on Kate's lips as she reached out for the kettle, but somehow it slipped through her fingers, the heavy weight tumbling to the floor and bouncing on the stone. The water trickled out and carved a curving passage towards the door, collecting the dirt and fluff on its journey that she had yet to sweep up. Kate's eyes closed and a band of iron encircled her chest.

This time, it didn't go away.

Lizzie stood on the steps of Mr Bloome's shop. Two women from Langley Street were coming up the road.

She went back in and waited for them to go by. When the coast was clear she walked out again and turned in the opposite direction. Mr Bloome had at first offered her eight shillings for the boots. They had finally agreed on ten.

When she reached Westferry Road, she saw Lil Sharpe. Lil was wearing her outdoor coat and flowery turban. That was unusual for Lil. She never came out of the house without her hair done.

Lizzie waved. Lil was in a rush and she wasn't wearing her lipstick. That was a one off, too.

'Lizzie . . . !' Lil's hand went up to her neck, holding the flap of her coat. Lizzie's fingers tightened round the ten shillings buried deep in her pocket. 'It's yer Ma, Lizzie. She's 'ad an accident. You better come quick.'

'What sort of accident?' Lizzie asked anxiously, her heart thumping.

Lil chewed her lip. 'Let's get back to the house, love.'

Neither of them spoke as they hurried back to Langley Street. Outside the house stood Dr Tapper's pony and trap. Dr Tapper, a grey-haired man in a black frock coat, sat at the kitchen table, his black top hat and Gladstone bag beside him. Lizzie knew him well. He had brought all the Allen children into the world and a good many more in the neighbourhood.

He looked up as Lizzie came in. 'Sit down, child.'

She sat beside him. 'Where's Ma?'

'Lizzie, I have some bad news.'

Lil squeezed her shoulder, but Lizzie didn't sit down.

'Did you know your mother had a bad heart?' the doctor asked.

Lizzie shook her head. 'No, but she has indigestion.'

Dr Tapper paused, glancing quickly at Lil. 'I'm afraid it wasn't indigestion, my dear. She was very sick. This morning she suffered a heart attack.'

Lizzie stared at him. She still couldn't take it in. 'Me Ma ain't—' she began as the doctor nodded slowly.

'I'm afraid she didn't recover.'

Lizzie felt sick as she looked into the doctor's sad eyes. He said quietly, 'I'm very sorry, Lizzie.'

''Ere, gel, drink this.' Lil pushed a mug of tea into her hands, but she couldn't drink it. 'Yer Ma's in the front room and yer Pa's in there too.'

Dr Tapper's thick grey eyebrows arched. 'There was nothing you could have done, Lizzie, if you'd been here. And I know this is of no comfort to you now, but she suffered very little.' Dr Tapper's lined face was sympathetic. 'I advised her a few weeks ago to rest, but I'm inclined to believe that it was advice she would have found hard to follow.'

'She came to see you?' Lizzie was unable to believe what she was being told.

'I warned her it could be serious but she didn't want to believe it could be her heart.'

'I should have been here,' Lizzie whispered, almost to herself. 'Why did I go out?'

Lil clasped her shoulder. 'You heard what the doctor said. You couldn't have done anything. She wouldn't want you blaming youself. You was the best daughter a mother could ever have. And she knew it.'

'What happened?' Lizzie asked in a small voice. 'Who found her?'

'I came in about half nine,' Lil sniffed. 'You must have just gone. Thought it was funny when I tapped. There wasn't no answer. I came in and found her here on the floor. Lucky Doug was home. He went round for Dr Tapper.'

Lizzie stared down at the cold floor. She couldn't bear to think of Kate lying on it. If only she hadn't gone up to Mr Bloome's.

'Will your mother remain here or do you want the undertaker to take her?' Dr Tapper wanted to know.

'I don't know.' Lizzie looked up at Lil. 'What would she have wanted, Lil?'

'Think she'd want to stay here,' Lil said quietly. 'I'll help you to lay her out.' Lil's long nose was red where she had been blowing it. 'She was my friend for over twenty years. It's the least I can do.'

'We've only got the front room,' Lizzie said in a daze.

'Your father will have to stay with us. We'll take down the bed and get Doug and Bert to bring the mattress into our front room.'

'Bert ain't home yet is he?' Lizzie asked.

Lil shook her head. 'That'll be the next thing, telling everyone. Think it's best when Flo and Babs come home if you tell 'em with Doug and me, gel. It's up to you, but it'll be a rotten job on yer own.'

Lizzie couldn't think ahead. All she could think of was this morning, when Kate had told her to wrap up and that there would be a nice piece of bread pudding waiting when she got home. None of this seemed real. Any minute now, she would appear and ask about the boots. Lizzie couldn't cry because she didn't believe her mother was dead.

Dr Tapper broke the long silence. 'Before I leave there are one or two points . . .' He glanced at Lil.

Her thin eyebrows rose. 'I'll make meself scarce for a bit. Call me when you need me, love.' She scraped back her chair and, with a nod to the doctor, left.

Dr Tapper wrote out the death certificate, signed it and handed the sheet of paper to Lizzie. Then he reached into his bag and took out an envelope. 'Lizzie, this is for you. Use it to help with the funeral.'

She looked inside the envelope. 'I can't take all this,' she said bewilderedly.

'You'll find five pounds won't go very far,' he told her. 'You have the family to look after and bills to pay. Life won't be easy, my dear. A head start might prove useful.' The doctor rose. 'I'll call on the undertaker and ask him to come as soon as he can. Will Mrs Sharpe be with you today?'

Lizzie nodded.

He put on his top hat, patting it well down on his head before leaving. After he had gone, Lizzie stood outside the front room. She couldn't go in there yet. She couldn't bear to look into her father's face and see his pain. Instead, she went into the kitchen and looked at her mother's pots and pans hanging from the walls. Kate would never use them again. Tears filled Lizzie's eyes. As she wiped them on her sleeve, she heard her mother's voice, saying, 'No time for tears, there's work to be done.'

Lizzie sat down at the table and wept.

Bert stood looking up the passage, his big eyes glistening with tears. 'It ain't possible,' he mumbled when he heard that Kate was dead. 'She was all right when I left. She 'ad indigestion. That was all.'

'It was her heart, Bert. Dr Tapper said so,' Lizzie told him.

'But she never said she had a bad heart.'

'Ma wasn't like that. She never complained.'

Bert wiped his eyes on his sleeve.

There was a tap on the back door, and it opened. Lil and Doug walked in. When Lil saw Bert she pulled a handkerchief from her sleeve. 'Here you are, love. It's one of Doug's and it's clean.'

Bert took it and went out into the yard.

'Give him a minute to take it in and then we'll wheel yer dad next door,' Doug said softly.

'We've got a couple of hours till the family comes home,' Lil said after a while. I've brought a white nightgown with me. It's got lace around the neck. Kate always liked good linen and a bit of a ruffle.'

They had a cup of tea, then Doug and Bert wheeled Tom Allen into number eighty-four. Lizzie was shocked when she saw her mother lying on the bed. Her face was white and thin, the skin on her cheeks hollowed out over the bone. She lay fully dressed, her eyes closed, her arms by her side.

'You all right, gel?' Lil asked gently.

Lizzie nodded. She felt even more as if she was dreaming. She kept thinking that Kate would wake up, get up off the bed and smile.

'It takes a bit of getting used to, the first time.'

Lizzie knew that Lil had done the work before, helping other people in the street.

They undressed Kate, and Lil drew the nightgown on. She looked very small. Lil arranged the long grey plait and folded Kate's hands over her breasts. Lizzie knew then her mother would never come back.

Lil touched her shoulder. 'Leave me to finish, if you like.'

Lizzie shook her head, swallowing hard. 'I can't believe she's gone, Lil.'

'Me neither,' Lil admitted, her voice low. 'Thank God she didn't suffer, love. That's what I think to meself.'

Dr Tapper was as good as his word. The undertaker arrived in the afternoon. He brought the coffin on a hearse drawn by a jet black horse. The iron bedstead was dismantled and Bert and Doug took the mattress next door. Two men carried the empty coffin into the front room and stood it on wooden plinths.

Kate was laid in the coffin. It had been a long, distressing day, and both Lizzie and Lil shed tears. 'She looks at peace, love,' Lil said when they stood alone beside the coffin.

But Lizzie didn't think so. She thought the body looked like a stranger lying there.

Lizzie did as Lil had suggested, and when Flo and Babs

came home she took them next door. There was no easy way to tell them and they were soon in tears. Her father sat in his wheelchair, his head bowed on his chest. Flo clung to her, sobbing, unable to understand, and Babs sat beside Lil, her eyes red and puffy with weeping.

'I don't believe you,' Vinnie yelled when he came home that evening. He ran into the front room.

'It was her heart,' Lizzie told him as he stood staring at the coffin. She tried to comfort him, as she had the others, but he shrugged her off. She knew he didn't want her there and she left him alone. Later she heard the front door slam.

'He'll come home when he's ready,' Lil said when she came in the back door and found Lizzie crying. 'Listen, you've still got to eat. I've got a bit of supper going next door. Have a bite to eat. Keep yer strength up, at least.'

'No, thanks,' Lizzie said gratefully. 'I'd rather stay with Ma.'

'No doubt you'll have a few callers,' Lil told her. 'People paying their respects and all. Would you like the girls to sleep in me spare room?'

'Thanks, Lil.' Lizzie blew her nose and wiped her sore eyes. 'I'd never have got through this without you.'

Lil sighed softly. 'She was me best mate, your mum.'

When she was on her own again, Lizzie sat beside the coffin. She wished she could talk to Vinnie. She needed his support. She wanted to tell him that they all had to stick together now, as Ma would have wanted. But she thought Lil was right. Vinnie had to grieve. He wouldn't be back tonight.

Only she and Bert slept in the house that night. It seemed empty and strange without everyone. Lizzie tried not to think of the coffin downstairs and the cold and lifeless body inside it. But she didn't sleep well.

Next morning she was pleased to see Kate's friends and neighbours, who came to pay their respects. She wasn't so happy, though, to see an official from the council. He had been gone ten minutes when Lil tapped on the kitchen door. Lil was dolled up this morning, her brown hair in tight, shiny curls, her make-up plastered on. A cigarette dangled from her red lips. Doug followed after her. For once he wasn't smoking his pipe. His round, tired face broke into a smile. ''Ello, love. How you feeling this morning?'

'All right, thanks, Doug.'

Lil patted her arm. 'The girls are still sleeping. Thought I'd let 'em have a lay in.'

Lizzie put on the kettle. 'A man from the council's just been round.'

'Blimey, that was quick! What did he want?' Lil asked suspiciously.

'He wanted to know who was gonna look after Flo,' Lizzie explained, pouring out three mugs of tea. 'I think someone from round here must have told them about Ma.'

'What did you tell him?'

'I said I was looking after Flo. Then he said I was too young. I said I'd be sixteen in December and then he said that still made me fifteen.'

'Nit-picking old sod,' muttered Lil. 'Ain't got nothin' to do all day, I s'pose, 'cept sit on his arse.'

'He said it wasn't him personally what makes the laws.'

'No, but he can see Flo's being looked out for,' cried Lil angrily. 'You've got two strapping great brothers living in this house. That not good enough for the council? Bloody do-gooders. I wish I'd been here, I'd have put him straight.'

'And caused more trouble for the girl, no doubt.' Doug glanced sternly at his wife before turning back to Lizzie. 'Go on, love, what else did he say?'

'Not much. He told me he'd come again after the funeral. See how we're managing.'

'How do they *think* you going to manage?' Lil couldn't keep quiet for long. 'Same way you've been trying to manage ever since your dad come home from the war. Same as you do every day. The authorities didn't offer no help when yer mother could 'ave done with it. Now they want to break up a family! Who do they think they are?'

'Powerful people, that's who they are,' said Doug darkly.

'Well, I'd like to see them try—'

'Shut up a minute, love.' Doug put up his hand. 'You're only making this worse.' He said after a pause, 'Lizzie, how do you feel about looking after the family?'

'Course I'll look after them, Doug. That's what Ma would expect.'

'You are still only fifteen—'

'Sixteen in December,' Lizzie reminded him.

He smiled. 'You're a brave lass.'

'How's Pa this morning?' It was to Doug her father usually turned in times of trouble, but Doug shook his head.

'Early days yet,' he told her, not quite meeting her eyes. 'I'll keep him company for the next few days. Me boss has given me the week off. I was due an 'oliday anyway.' Doug was a white collar worker at the docks. He had worked in the offices of the PLA all his life. At fifty-five, he was ten years older than his wife and he looked it. Doug smiled as he rose. 'Well, now I've seen you all right, I'll leave you to it.'

'Did Vinnie come home?' Lil asked when Doug had gone.

'No, it was only me and Bert here last night,' Lizzie answered quietly. She hadn't told Lil about the fire or the events that had led up to it. It didn't seem to be important now. Kate's death overshadowed everything.

Lil was silent for a few moments. Between puffs on her cigarette, she asked, 'How are you fixed for money, gel? We'd like to lend you some. I know Kate was a bit short,' she added tactfully.

Lizzie took the envelope from her pocket and showed Lil the five pound note and Mr Bloome's ten shillings.

'Christ,' Lil gasped. 'Where did you get that from?'

Lizzie told her what Dr Tapper had said.

'Bless his cotton socks,' Lil said, tears in her eyes as she stubbed out her cigarette in the saucer. 'Well, that solves the immediate problem. It's the future you got to think of. What are the chances, do you think, of Babs being taken on at Hailing House, as paid staff?'

'Don't have a clue, Lil.' Lizzie couldn't think beyond the moment. Somehow they would manage, but Lil was always practical, wanting answers before the questions.

'Well, you'll have to find out. Babs acting the Lady Bountiful ain't gonna put food on the table. And what about Bert?'

'Gone for a walk,' Lizzie told her, knowing that Bert and Vinnie still hadn't spoken and she was beginning to wonder if they ever would. 'Said he needed a bit of fresh air.'

A silence fell then as they sat with their thoughts, until, sometime later, there was a knock at the door. 'I'll shoot out the back way,' Lil said quickly. 'It's probably someone to see yer mother. I'll call in later.'

But when Lizzie opened the front door it was Danny who stood there. ''Ello, love,' he said softly. 'I only heard this morning or I would have come sooner.' He handed her a bunch of white lilies. 'Thought I'd bring these and pay me respects.'

She was close to tears. It was only the night before last that he had stood on the doorstep and kissed her. Kate had been alive then.

'Come in, Danny.' She showed him into the front room and they stood in silence, gazing at the coffin. Danny reached for her hand and squeezed it.

'Are you all right?' Danny asked in the kitchen afterwards.

'Not so bad.'

They sat down at the table. 'What a rotten shock. Who'd have thought she had a bad heart?'

Lizzie held back the tears and nodded.

'Tell you what, I'll bring you some fruit and veg over on the cart.'

She knew Danny was trying to cheer her up. 'That'd be nice.'

'When's the funeral?'

'Friday,' Lizzie told him. 'The undertaker said it was the earliest he could fit us in, because of Armistice Day.'

'Would you like me to take the family on the cart?' Danny asked, squeezing her hand again. 'We can lift the wheelchair in the back. Benji ain't like one of them posh black horses with the feathers but it would save a few quid.'

'That'll be lovely.' There was another knock on the front door and Lizzie knew their time was over. 'It's someone to see Ma, I expect.'

He kissed her cheek. 'Send Bert to the shop to let me know the arrangements.'

When they got to the front door, Vi was there. 'Not disturbin' anything, am I?' she asked curiously, giving Danny the once over as he walked out.

'Danny was just leaving,' Lizzie said as she caught his glance. She wanted him to know how much he meant to her, and hoped that he could read the message in her eyes.

'Couldn't believe it when I heard,' Vi was saying as Lizzie closed the door. 'She never said nothing to no one about her heart. What a bloody awful shock it must have been for you.'

Lizzie showed her into the front room and even Vi stopped speaking for a moment in order to shed a tear.

Chapter Seven

Kate Allen was buried two days later. It was the day after Armistice Day, a bitterly cold November Friday. Lizzie was frozen to the bone under her old green coat. Babs wore a navy coat that the ladies of Hailing House had given her and Flo was in her gabardine school coat. They were all shivering.

Tom Allen sat in his Bath chair. He was covered by a thick rug. Vinnie, who had returned home that morning, was dressed in a brand new suit. Bert stood beside him, shoulders hunched under his shabby tweed jacket. It was a pauper's funeral and it showed.

Earlier that morning, Lil had delivered three large homemade cakes. The wake afterwards was to be divided between the two houses: the food at Lizzie's, the drink at Lil's.

'I 'ope we've made enough.' Lil had frowned at the spread on the kitchen table. 'Most of the street's coming. And there'll be a few more besides.'

'I'd never have done it on me own, Lil.'

'That fiver came in bloody handy, I can tell you,' Lil sighed. 'Have you paid the undertaker yet?'

Lizzie nodded. 'We only needed the hearse. I've got three bob left over.'

'It costs you to come into this world,' Lil muttered grimly, 'and costs to go out.' She took her mirror from her handbag. Running her tongue over her teeth, she examined her reflection. 'Ah well, could be worse.' She tilted her small black hat over to one side. 'That's better, ain't it?'

'You always look nice, Lil.' Lizzie covered the cakes with a cloth.

'Thanks. I do me best. This little suit goes back before the war. I turned up the hem and let the skirt out. It's done me a good turn one way and another.' She glanced sideways at Lizzie. 'How is everyone?'

'Vinnie ain't said a word about where he's been,' Lizzie shrugged. 'And I can't do nothing right in Babs' book.'

'You'll have to make allowances. She don't like you stepping into you mother's shoes. What about Bert?'

Lizzie smiled softly. 'Least you know where you are with Bert. He's worn the Blakies off his boots with all them long walks of his.'

'Getting it out of his system.' Lil nodded slowly. 'And Flo ain't stopped crying, poor kid.'

Lizzie went over the conversation in her mind as she gazed down into the deep hole. Reverend Green, dressed in a black cape, intoned from the prayer book. 'Go forth, O Christian soul, out of this world, to Him who has created you, and in the name of Jesus and all his angels, archangels, thrones and denominations, in the name of the patriarchs and prophets . . .'

Kate wouldn't have appreciated a long-winded rigmarole, Lizzie reflected sadly. She hadn't been one for patriarchs and prophets. She had her own kind of faith. It revolved around her family. But she was grateful for the presence of Reverend Michael Green. Not only had the ladies of Hailing House found a clergyman, but they had acquired a plot for Kate at the cemetery too. A rare privilege for a working class family.

Lil Sharpe nudged Lizzie's arm. ''Ere's yer roses, love. You'd better throw them in.'

'Ma would've had kittens wasting such lovely flowers.'

The stems were brittle but the blooms were perfectly formed. Six small buds of red velvet that curled around like a ballerina's skirt.

'Come on, love, you've done famously so far, don't let her down now.'

'Why did she have to die, Lil? She never done anyone any wrong.' Lizzie choked back a sob.

'No one knows the answer to that. Don't torment youself with questions. Just try to accept it. Let's get today over and done with.' The cold made Lil's long nose shiny as she sniffed, delving in her pocket for a handkerchief. Lizzie knew that, like everyone else, she was frozen to the bone.

The Reverend coughed politely. He was eager to be out of the cold, away from people with whom he had no connection.

Lizzie threw in the roses. Finally, it was over. The gravedigger picked up his spade and began his work. Lizzie led the way down the wet, mossy path to the gravel track. At the end, through the railings, she could see Benji. They would now make the journey through Poplar to Cubitt Town, her and Lil sitting beside Danny up on the seat of the cart, the family in the back.

It still all seemed like a bad dream. At least now she wouldn't have to think of an excuse for not going to the Beggar's Opera. But the thought was of no comfort at all.

'There's a good bit of ham in those, love, all sliced nice and thin,' commented Lil Sharpe. She pointed to six large white plates overflowing with sandwiches. 'We'll take them in first, shall we?' Lizzie lifted one of the plates as Lil said in an anxious voice, 'How you feeling? You warmer now?'

'Yes thanks, Lil. I dunno what came over me at the cemetery. Sorry about that.' Curls of ebony fell over her white face. She felt as if the blood had drained right out of her.

'No need to apologize. You 'andled youself well.' Lil looked Lizzie up and down, her eyebrows raised. 'That frock of Ethel's looks really nice on you. Goes with yer green eyes. Did you have to alter it much?'

'I just took up the hem and a bit at the sides.'

'Did you do it on the treadle?'

'No, by hand. The treadle's in the front room.'

Lil realized her mistake. 'Blimey, course it is. Trust me to put me foot in it. Well, you've done lovely repairs. Turn around and let's have a look.' Lil pushed Lizzie round in a circle, holding her by the shoulders as she inspected the dress. 'You're so tiny, love – well, I suppose the word is dainty.' She laughed. 'Ethel's a dirty great lump compared to you – you'd never have believed she once took your size. I bought her the dress for her thirteenth birthday. She only wore it a couple of times before she'd grown out of it.'

Lizzie glanced down at the blue dress. It wasn't very fashionable but it did fit her nicely. Her dream was to buy herself something new one day. A good quality dress or coat that was the height of fashion. She knew she had taste, and she loved clothes. Kate had seen this in her and encouraged her to use the treadle machine. Mending and altering was second nature to her. But one day, when she'd saved up and there were no bills to pay, she'd treat herself.

'It could have been made for you,' Lil was saying as Lizzie tuned back in. 'That long knitted top and pleated skirt with the dark blue collar, and them wide cuffs with the fancy stitching . . .'

Lizzie smiled gratefully. Lil's idea of fashion was to keep everything in mothballs year after year. But Lil was right about this dress. Even though her eyes were a deep green, the blue complemented them.

'Everything ready in the front room?'

Lizzie nodded. The dismantled iron bedstead was hidden under a cover. The wooden chairs were placed in a circle round the room ready for the guests.

'I don't know how many will come,' Lizzie said as she glanced at the sandwiches and cakes, 'but I think we've made enough.'

Lil placed her hands on her hips. 'Well, there's enough

here to feed the five thousand. Langley Street are a greedy lot. They ate and drank themselves silly at the street party after the war. If we run short I can always pop next door and knock out a few more sandwiches. Flo can give us a hand. It helps to take her mind off things.'

Lizzie nodded. 'She helped me set out the table and she's done a bit of dusting. She even cleaned the front room window.'

'Yeah, she ain't done badly – in between bawlin' her head off.'

Lizzie smiled. 'Even Babs said she'd offer round the plates and do the teas. So all in all, it's not bad going.'

Lil nodded. 'No, it ain't, gel.'

There was a long pause before Lizzie said, 'Lil, I hope I'm not gonna get upset when everyone comes. I dunno what come over me at the cemetery.'

'I do,' replied Lil briskly. 'It's called a whopping great shock. I had the same when our two boys died at the beginning of the war, one so quick after the other. Me and Doug didn't know what hit us.' For a moment Lil looked older than her forty-five years. Her face was sad despite her make-up. 'I couldn't believe it for weeks. Didn't eat, didn't sleep, wouldn't speak to Doug. Your mother was the one who helped me then. If it wasn't for her I dunno what I would have done. I just wanted to curl up and die.'

Lizzie remembered. She had been nine at the time. Her mother had called in to see Lil each day, trying to encourage her to eat. She'd made soup and hot bread and finally convinced Lil that life was worth living.

'You're gonna do just fine, gel,' Lil said. 'Now call Babs and Flo to give us a hand and we'll do the honours. Doug and your two boys are seeing to the drink next door in my place. Front door's open. The men can have a good piss-up.'

'I dread to think what state your place will be in.' Lizzie lifted a plate.

'Don't you go worrying about that,' Lil cackled. 'They can get as sozzled as they like without us having to watch 'em do it, silly buggers. They'll not stint on the booze, that's for sure. So off you go and keep yer pecker up. And when everyone's gone, it'll be the living you 'ave to think about, not the dead.'

'Ta, love. Very nice, too.' Violet Catcher from number seventy-nine was squeezed into the old chair that had been pulled out from the cupboard under the stairs. Her fat arms wobbled as she pounced on the sandwiches. 'Lovely bit of 'am. Shame about yer poor mum. We always got on. Unlike some others in this road I could mention.' Lizzie moved swiftly by. Vi was looking for an audience.

Babs and Flo were sitting on the floor beside Ethel Sharpe and her two children, Tim, three and Rosie, two. Lizzie held the plate whilst they all dipped in.

Babs turned up her nose. 'Ain't we got no egg and cress?'

'It's ham or cheese,' Lizzie told her.

'Don't like either.'

'Well, that's the first I've heard of it.' Lizzie reflected

that Babs doing charity work at Hailing House had its disadvantages. Airs and graces in Langley Street were given short shrift and Babs was pushing her luck.

Babs straightened her back. 'Miss Hailing tells Alice – that's the maid – to tell cook to make cucumber sandwiches thin and cut off the crusts. Miss Hailing'd never have big thick slices with the crusts left on. That ain't proper.'

'Well, the motto in this house is waste not want not.'

Babs jumped to her feet. 'Pardon me for opening me mouth.'

The two little children giggled as Babs stalked off.

Ethel laughed. 'Rosie and Tim like the ham. Here you are kids, eat up.'

'How's life in Blackheath?' Lizzie sat down beside Ethel. She got on well with Lil's twenty-one-year-old daughter. Apart from having all Ethel's cast-offs, they both liked fashion. Ethel worked in a haberdashers two days a week.

'Not so bad, Lizzie. I was sorry to hear about yer Ma.'

'Thanks, Ethel. It was a bit of a shock.'

'How you coping?' She poked Timmy in the ribs. 'You eat up that crust young man.'

Lizzie smiled at the little boy. 'Me biggest worry is the school inspector coming round.'

'What's he want?'

'To keep an eye on Flo.'

'Silly old busybody.' Ethel sounded like her mother. 'Don't take no notice. He'll soon get fed up. I'm putting Timmy's name down for school soon. There's one just around the corner. Trouble is, Richard thinks it's a bit rough.'

'Is Richard still working for Greenwich Council?' Lizzie asked, recalling that Lil always said her son-in-law was a stuffed shirt.

'Yes. And he's due promotion soon.'

'Does his mother still look after the kids whilst you're at work?'

Ethel looked up to the ceiling. 'Yeah, and still trying to teach them the king's English – at their age!'

They laughed as Ethel pulled two-year-old Rosie on to her lap and wiped the crumbs off her mouth. Lizzie knew that on the quiet Lil thought Ethel's mother-in-law was a snob.

'You gonna have some more kids, Ethel?' Lizzie asked.

'You must be joking!' Ethel threw back her blonde head. 'One kid at eighteen, the other at nineteen. Sometimes I wonder where me brains were when I married so young. But there you are. I was bowled over by me fella's good looks and extreme wealth.' Both girls laughed again. 'Oh, I'm not being rotten,' Ethel smiled. 'I'm happy with me lot, really. I like working at Rickards. All the lovely materials and that. I like bringing in a wage.'

'Rickards is a lovely shop.' Lizzie felt a moment's pang of envy. Ethel not only had her kids but a good job, too. She'd been to Rickards once, a long time ago, when Ethel had put aside some cheap lace for Kate. Shelves overflowing with roll upon roll of materials, trimmings, buttons, zips and fastenings.

'You'd do well in a shop,' Ethel commented. 'You was

good at figures at school, I remember me mum saying. And you've had a fair bit of training now, selling stuff with your pa.'

'I couldn't do a job as well as look after the family,' Lizzie sighed. 'I have to consider Flo.'

'Yes, but it would have been nice to have the choice, I 'spect.' Ethel blushed. 'Sorry Lizzie, I didn't mean to put me foot in it. Just seems a lot for you to take on, that's all.'

Lizzie changed the subject quickly. She looked down at her dress. 'Recognize this?'

Ethel frowned. 'I think I do . . .'

'Your mum give it to her, Ethel,' Flo interrupted, arriving on the scene in time to hear the last of the conversation. 'It was yours.'

Ethel and Lizzie grinned. Lizzie pushed the plate of sandwiches under Flo's nose.

'I'll have one of each.' Flo reached out to grab a handful.

'No you won't, you'll have one at a time.' Lizzie pulled the plate back.

Flo muttered, 'bossy boots' under her breath. Lizzie ignored it. There would be no family row today. She thought of Lil's words earlier. 'You've got to be mother to your lot now and put food in their mouths and clothes on their backs. You ain't got time to cry, gel, not if you're gonna keep the family together, you need to lay your own rules down, 'cos believe me, those girls will need 'em.'

Another fleeting pang of envy went through her as she looked at Ethel. Lovely kids, a nice job and a new house in a posh part of London. Lizzie pulled herself up short. Ethel's life wasn't hers and she mustn't wish for it.

Flo grabbed hold of Rosie's hand. 'Does she wanna come out in the yard, Ethel?'

Timmy piped up. 'I do.'

'You be a good boy, then,' Ethel said and gave him a wink.

'I'd better go and hand these round,' Lizzie said. 'See you in a minute, kids.'

In the passage there was chaos. The market traders had arrived. Fat Freda, Boston Brown, Dickie Potts and Elfie Goldblum stood squashed together, trying to assess where the drinks had disappeared to.

'Sorry we couldn't get to the cemetery, Lizzie.' Dickie grabbed the last sandwich with his black nails. 'But better late than never, eh?'

'Thanks for coming, Dickie.'

'Wouldn't 'ave missed it for the world. Where's yer dad?'

'Next door. Lil's putting him up till we get sorted. The beer's in there too.'

Dickie pushed Elfie towards the front door. 'We'll be having ourselves a pint or two, then. Where's Danny and the 'orse gorn?'

She hadn't seen Danny since they'd arrived back from the cemetery. After helping to get the drinks ready he'd driven Benji back to the shop. 'Bert said he's gone back to fetch Mr Flowers and Frank.'

'Frank coming, eh?' Dickie nodded slowly. 'Oh well, see you in a bit, gel.'

Lizzie knew Frank wasn't popular amongst the tradespeople. He hadn't joined up in the war. Instead he'd got a job in the docks as security. People never trusted him after that. But the war had been over two years. Frank was always polite and had a civil word for her when she went in the shop.

As the traders left, a big black car stopped outside Vi's. A man in uniform got out and opened the back door. Miss Hailing and another girl climbed out.

'I'm so sorry we are late, Elizabeth.' Miss Hailing extended a gloved hand. Tall and slim, she always looked very regal, despite the hard work she did in the soup kitchens. Kate had taken Lizzie up to the House for sewing classes, held once monthly. It was there that Lizzie had learned to sew properly.

'Thank you for coming,' Lizzie said quietly, feeling the soft, expensive leather in her palm.

'There were delays in the city. The traffic was diverted from Westminster and James couldn't find a short cut.' Felicity Hailing gestured to the girl beside her. 'This is my younger sister Annabelle. She's helping me at the House.'

'We are very sorry to hear about your mother,' Annabelle said. Two large grey eyes stared into Lizzie's. She had soft, light brown hair cut into a fashionable bob and a friendly smile.

'Thank you for arranging for Reverend Green to take Ma's service,' Lizzie said. 'And for the grave in the cemetery,' she added quickly.

'It was the least we could do.' Felicity's accent was cut glass. 'You mother was well regarded at the House. We are eternally grateful to her for Babs' help. Your sister is proving a very valuable member of staff.'

Lizzie stood back for them to enter. Undaunted by the noisy crowd, the Hailing sisters made their entrance. It was odd what Miss Hailing had said about Babs being a valuable member of staff. It was only charity work she did.

Lizzie found Lil and Ethel sitting in the kitchen. 'Royalty arrived, has it?' Lil smirked.

Ethel laughed. 'Come on, Mum, they do a lot of good.'

'So would I, if I had their money.' Lil shrugged, flicking ash from her cigarette into a saucer. 'You want to imagine them sitting on the lavvy. That brings 'em down to size.'

'Can't take you anywhere,' Ethel giggled.

For a moment Lizzie felt sad. She missed Kate as Lil and Ethel joked together.

'You all right, Lizzie?' Ethel asked.

Lizzie sat down at the table. 'I was just thinking how much Ma would have loved all this.'

Suddenly they all saw the funny side. 'Now *that*'s what Kate would have liked,' Lil remarked, wiping the tears of mirth from her eyes. 'A bloody good laugh.'

They all nodded, remembering old times.

'Mind you,' Lil took a deep gulp of smoke, 'we could do with a bit of class round here. When I was a girl the only way to see a bit of life was to go into service. Lizzie's mother was a lady's maid, you know, in her younger day. Had very high values did Kate Allen. Kept her house really nice till that bloody war made her pawn everything she treasured.'

Lizzie nodded slowly. 'Even those bloody boots.'

The other two women looked at Lizzie in surprise. They all burst into laughter again and were still laughing when Flo came running into the kitchen.

'What you all laughing at?'

'Nothing,' said Lizzie, sniffing. 'What's up?'

'Vi Catcher says she's leaving if there ain't no more food.'

'Lippy old mare!' Lil rose and removed a tea towel from a plate of cheese sandwiches. 'Go on, Flo, take her these. Then come back for the cheese biscuits.'

'I wonder how they're doing next door?' Lizzie said as Flo went out.

'I'll go and find out.' Lil took her lipstick from her bag and smoothed it on. 'I'll leave you two to talk about yer blokes,' she said with a wink.

Lizzie went red as she looked at Ethel.

'Don't forget to offer the cake round,' called Lil from the yard. 'And don't forget to tell the Hailings who made it.'

The two girls looked at each other and giggled. Lizzie pulled the large iced fruit cake across the table. 'Would Rosie and Timmy like some?'

'No, but I will. Mum's cakes are lovely.'

'Don't I know it,' Lizzie said as she put a slice on a plate for Ethel.

Ethel licked the icing. 'Where's your Danny got to, then?'

Lizzie went very red. 'Who says he's my Danny?'

'Well, isn't he?'

'Who told you?'

Ethel grinned mischievously. 'Your mum told my mum and mum told me. You can't keep anything secret round here.'

'I never really thought Ma knew.' Lizzie had another pang. Now she would never be able to talk to Kate about Danny.

'Well, she had a bloody good guess then.' It was unusual to hear Ethel swear and Lizzie grinned.

'Has he asked to take you out?'

Lizzie nodded.

Ethel's eyes widened. 'Never! Where? When?

Lizzie told Ethel the story.

'The Lyric! Oh, Lizzie, are you going?'

'No. Course not. How could I?'

Ethel shrugged, nibbling at her cake. 'Never mind, there will be other times.'

Lizzie smiled. 'I never thought of that.'

Ethel roared with laughter. 'You wouldn't.'

Just then Timmy appeared. 'She pinched me!' he cried, pointing to Rosie. 'She's always pinchin' me!'

'I never!' gurgled Rosie, all innocent blue eyes.

'So much for a bit of peace and quiet.' Ethel hauled her little blonde daughter on to her lap. Timmy looked daggers. 'Happy families,' Ethel muttered, grabbing hold of his collar. 'At times like this I could happily trade the kids in for a nice barrow-boy meself.'

Once more they ended up laughing. Lizzie's spirits had

lifted. What her friend had said about there being other times with Danny had cheered her up. Life hadn't ended today even though it felt like it.

Once more the peace was shattered. Flo returned, tears streaming down her face.

'What's the matter now?' Lizzie sighed.

'Our Babs said I was a fat little cow. She said I've been pinching all the sandwiches, but it ain't me. It's her what's been stuffing them on the quiet.'

Lizzie and Ethel looked at each other. It was back to the real world with a bump.

At four o'clock that afternoon, Violet Catcher and Beryl Sweet were the last to leave. Next door, the booze-up was still in progress.

'Oh well, time to clear up,' Lizzie said to herself, as for a moment she saw her mother at the sink, head bent over the washing-up. 'Fetch in the glasses first,' Kate would be telling her, since glass was never washed with china. Everything was done according to how she had learned in service. Each glass would have to be washed carefully, then placed upside down on the wooden draining board.

'Stack the china in piles on the table and throw all the fags in the pig bin.' There weren't any pigs, but the bin was tipped on Doug's vegetables, the only fertilizer his beans ever saw.

'Then, when we've finished the washing up, you and me will have a nice cuppa, love, before we get started on the clearing up.' Her mother's voice drifted from the kitchen.

Tears were close when a figure appeared. Danny strode down the passage. Lizzie quickly blinked them away. Danny stood opposite her and stuck his finger down the neck of his starched white collar. He lifted his chin and stretched his neck.

'I'll undo the studs,' she offered, reaching up. Her hands brushed against his warm skin.

He looked into her eyes. 'Never was one for suits.' He smoothed the dark hair from her cheek, then drew her against him. 'Listen, I want to tell you something.' He held her gently in his arms. 'I'll be here to help you out for a bit, at least for a month or two. As far as money goes, Bert can work in the shop. Me dad needs someone to cart the boxes around. It'll mean a few extra bob for the kitty. But . . . but there's other things I've been mullin' over lately . . . a decision I have to make soon. I don't wanna burden you with it today. With your Ma just gone, it don't seem right.'

'What is it?' she whispered anxiously. 'Tell me.'

He paused. 'Well, we're close, gel, ain't we? No point in denyin' it, is there? You and me . . . I ain't imaginin' it, am I?'

She nodded slowly. What was he going to tell her?

'You see, I've been thinking about travelling and putting it off for a while. Putting it to the back of me mind, like. But, I want to do something with me life. The barrow will never make me rich, but I've always had a yen for Australia—'

'Australia!' She looked at him in astonishment.

He nodded. 'There's gold there, free to anyone who'll

stake his claim. All a man needs is his health and strength. I've got plenty of both. I'll make meself a fortune.'

'But Australia's on the other side of the world. How you gonna get there?'

'I'll work me passage. There are ships out of Liverpool that'll take a man on if he's willing and able.'

'But it's so far away. You might never come back.'

He laughed. 'Don't be daft.' He gazed into her eyes. 'But there's another way.' He bent his head slowly. His breath was warm on her cheek as he whispered, 'You could come with me.'

'Me? Go with you?'

'Why not? It ain't such a bad idea. I've a bit of savings put by. That'd pay your passage. When we got to the other side, we'd soon find our feet.'

'Danny . . . I couldn't . . .' She pulled back. 'How could I, with the family?'

He shrugged. 'Babs is fourteen. She'll have to do what you did when you was her age. When we're rich we'll come back and take care of 'em all.'

'Danny, I can't. It just ain't possible . . .'

'Don't turn me down now. Think about it. I shouldn't have opened me big mouth today. I dunno what come over me.'

The front door slammed and men's voices drifted down the passage. Danny let her go. Vinnie strode into the kitchen. Falling against the table, he laughed. 'Oh, ain't that a shame, looks like we're disturbing the 'appy couple.'

Lizzie saw Danny and Vinnie look at one another. The

bad feeling between them was evident. She knew that after the fire, they disliked each other intensely. Vinnie had no time for law-abiding folk like Danny and Danny wouldn't tolerate Vinnie's behaviour.

'Sit down,' Lizzie said quickly to her brother. 'I'll make you some tea.'

'I don't want no tea.' Vinnie swayed against the wall.

'Sit down, Vinnie, before you fall down,' Danny muttered.

Vinnie's face darkened. 'Don't think I ain't got you sussed out, Flowers. A bloody coster, that's all you are – and ever will be. Well, let me tell you this. There ain't no way you'll be gettin' your feet under this family's table and that's a promise.'

'Vinnie!' Lizzie stepped forward.

Danny stretched out an arm to stop her. 'You've had a skinful, Vin. Go and sleep it off before you do yerself some damage.'

'You got a bloody big gob on you, that's your trouble,' Vinnie hissed. 'How do you fancy comin' outside?'

Danny smiled. 'I wouldn't take advantage of you, mate. Not in the condition you're in.'

The punch that was aimed at Danny was easily avoided. Danny stepped to one side and Vinnie collapsed on the floor.

'Vinnie!' Lizzie ran to her brother.

'Leave him, gel. He's out cold now. I'll get him upstairs to bed.'

'He don't know what he's doing when he's drunk, Danny. He don't mean it.'

'Anything I can do to help?' The voice came from the passage and they looked round. Frank Flowers smiled at them, his eyebrows raised. ''Ello, Lizzie. Sorry to hear about yer mother.'

'Thanks, Frank.' Lizzie looked away from his gaze. It always made her feel uncomfortable. The Flowers boys looked a lot like one another, but Frank was shorter than Danny. They both had blond hair and bright blue eyes, but in character the two brothers were chalk to cheese. Danny was always joking. He never took himself seriously. Frank was quieter, a dark horse, most people said.

'Silly bugger took a swipe at me.' Danny rolled Vinnie over and lifted his arms. 'Grab his feet, Frank.'

Lizzie watched them carry Vinnie upstairs. She never knew what to say to Frank. That intense blue gaze of his always made her shiver.

She placed the dirty dishes on the draining board. She couldn't go to Australia, could she? What would happen to the family if she left them? She knew the answer to that. Pa couldn't look after Flo and Babs wouldn't want to. Vinnie was on his way to a future in crime. Bert was like a big kid still. He needed her. They all did. Yet she would follow Danny to the ends of the earth if the choice was hers.

The thought that Danny wanted her with him filled her with joy. He had even offered to pay her passage. In her wildest dreams she had never imagined that her prayer would come true.

Dear God, make Danny Flowers love me.

Chapter Eight

'You poor cow!' Violet Catcher's exclamation echoed across Langley Street. On the day before Christmas Eve, the neighbourhood gossip stood outside her front door and folded her fat arms across her shuddering bosoms. 'How the 'eck are you going to manage this Christmas with your lot to feed and no money coming into the house now yer Dad's not flogging stuff at the market?'

Lizzie had been wondering the same herself. She had tried to dodge her neighbour opposite as she returned from the corner shop. How did Violet manage to spot her every time she passed? It was too much of a coincidence to have happened three times on the trot this week.

'We'll manage,' she told Vi.

'You know you can apply for parish relief, don't you? I mean you'd get some groceries at least fer the 'oliday. Just pay a visit to the council and tell them you're at the end of your tether. After all, who could blame you, gel, after all you've been through.'

Parish relief was just what the authorities needed to confirm their suspicions that she couldn't look after the family.

'Truth is, we're doing nicely, thank you, Vi. Parish relief wasn't Ma's cup of tea and it ain't mine.'

'Oh, you stick to yer principles, love.' Violet Catcher nodded. 'It was just that I saw Flo playing out in the street in nothing but a flimsy little pinafore. Thought to meself then, that child'll be catching her death if she's not careful. Your mother was always so particular about you kids, always kept you nice despite having to buy secondhand from Cox Street.'

'Matter of fact I ain't shopping up Cox Street this winter.' Lizzie was determined to maintain the family pride. No matter what the cost, she would keep the family together as her mother had done. 'Ethel's given me a nice bit of cloth from Blackheath and I'll run up the girls some clothes on the machine, so don't you go worrying yourself needlessly over us, Vi.' Any cloth from Ethel's place of work was bound to be quality and Vi would know it. 'Anyway, must go. Got to get the tea on.'

'Call in any time over Christmas, love,' shouted Vi as she walked away.

Lizzie kept her basket closed, hiding the parcel of scrag-end that was buried at the bottom. As it was Christmas, Reg Barnes had given her a lean piece. But if Vi knew scrag end was what she was cooking for Christmas dinner, she'd have a field day.

'That you?' She barely had the key out of the lock before she heard her father's voice. He sounded upset and she took a deep breath for the next hurdle.

'Only me, Pa.'

'Where the 'ell have you been?' he yelled from the kitchen.

She hurried down the passage. 'Up the market. I called out I was going, but you were asleep.'

'Trying to sleep you mean. That bloody bloke from the council's been again,' complained Tom as he strained to push the wheels of the Bath chair.

'What did he want?' Lizzie asked anxiously.

'Asked me all these questions, wanted to know where you were, where Flo and Babs were. Said he was going to have to write a report.'

'On what?'

'How should I know? I told him to clear off.'

Her heart sank. 'Oh, you didn't, Pa.'

'Little squirt. What does 'e keep comin' round here for?'

'He has to make sure that . . .that everything's all right after Ma's gone.' She put the kettle on the stove, her mind in turmoil. Had the authorities heard Vinnie had been in trouble? Or was it one of the neighbours reporting that the Allen girls were neglected – someone like Vi Catcher?

'Did you bring me any baccy?' her father asked. 'It comes to something when there ain't even a roll-up in the house.'

'Bert'll have some when he comes in. Bill Flowers has given him a bonus for Christmas.'

'Christmas?' Tom repeated slowly. 'What a bloody waste of time Christmas is. The sooner it's over the better. Don't speak to me of it again. I'll not sit at a table without yer mother and that's a fact. Make what you like of it for all I care. Now get me coat and push me in the yard.'

'Pa, it's cold out there. You'll catch yer death.'

He looked up at her and nodded slowly. 'Aye, if only I could. Now do as I tell you, gel. I ain't got the energy to argue.'

Resigning herself, she went to the bedroom and took the coat and cap from the hook on the door. Outside, the sun shone down on the rows of washing and smoke covered roofs.

Tom gazed sightlessly over the dilapidated fences, head buried in the collar of his greatcoat. Beryl Sweet's fence was propped up by an old pram. Only Doug's fence had seen a repair or two. His vegetable garden was the only fertile patch, filled in summer by runner beans.

In the kitchen, Lizzie unwrapped the seven portions of scrag-end. They would cook up nicely with pearl barley and a few onions, and Danny had brought carrots and potatoes. A stew would last until Sunday. In the larder she found a fragment of suet. Placing this under the gauze cover that was used for meat, she satisfied herself that the wolf was kept from the door.

Just then Flo and Babs came in the back door.

'I'm hungry,' said Flo looking at the empty table.

Lizzie shut the larder door. 'Where have you been? It's late.'

'Up the baths,' said Flo airily.

'You know Ma didn't like you going up there. You're too young to muck about with the boys.'

'Oh, leave her alone.' Babs took off her coat. 'Everyone else goes up the baths.'

'Not at her age they don't,' Lizzie replied shortly.

'Me friends do,' Flo said truculently. 'I dunno what all the fuss is about.'

'The fuss was because you should have been at school. You told Miss Evans that because Ma was dead you had to help at home.' Lizzie put her hands on her hips. 'I got the shock of me life when Miss Evans stopped me at the school gates. She even asked what sort of work I made you do. I had to tell a lie, say you 'elped me out, or she would have told the authorities.'

'I don't reckon they'd do anything,' Babs shrugged. 'You're just havin' a go at everyone. I'd like to see you do some real work, like me. Working up at the House with the ladies is a proper job and Ma was really proud of me for doin' it.'

'Yeah, she was an' all.' Flo threw a glance at Lizzie. 'She always said our Babs would do all right for 'erself and she 'as.'

Lizzie fought back the urge to do as Lil had advised – give Flo a clip round the ear when she was cheeky. Well, she'd tried it. The result had been outright rebellion. Flo was a bright girl, Miss Evans had said so, but she wasn't making the most of her talents.

Lizzie looked at Babs. 'If you're so certain that the authorities won't do anything, then the next time they come round, I'll tell them to speak to you. I'm sure they'd like to have a little chat – seein' as how yer only fourteen yerself. Matter of fact, I'll offer to walk right up there with them to Hailing House. Then we can both have a look at all this marvellous work you're doing for the ladies.'

Babs glared at Lizzie.

'And as for you, young lady,' Lizzie said, turning to Flo, 'I ain't lying any more on your account. The next time you decide not to go to school, you know what's in store for you.'

Flo's eyes filled with tears. 'I hate you!' She ran up the stairs.

Babs tossed back her head and flounced after Flo. The bang of the bedroom door said it all. Lizzie knew that Flo was falling under Babs' bad influence. She went to the sink and gazed out over the cold grey yard. At least this afternoon she had won a battle if not the war.

Christmas Eve and Lizzie and Flo had smiles on their faces. 'Look what Lil give us. A cake with a snowman on it.' Flo ceremoniously carried the white cake into the kitchen and lowered it to the table. 'She stuck currants on for eyes and a slice of carrot for 'is mouth. She said we ain't to eat it before tomorrow but it wouldn't matter if we 'ad just a little of the icing now. She made a bit extra on the side, see?'

'Well I'm off to work,' announced Babs, who had walked into the kitchen at that moment. Lizzie noted that her sister was dressed in the new grey coat that she had been given at Hailing House. It had a grey velvet collar and little velvet flaps over the small pockets. On her head she wore a beret of the same colour.

'Look at Lil's cake, Babs,' Flo said. 'Ain't it smashing?'

'It's all right, I s'pose. But you want to see the cake Miss Hailing had made. It's for the Christmas party this afternoon. It ain't made with carrot and currants neither. It's real marzipan inside, not just a bit of white icin' on top.'

'How d'you know that?' Flo asked, frowning.

'Miss Hailing told me so herself.'

Flo's dark brown gaze went to Lizzie. 'Why ain't we going to this party, then?'

'Because you're not invited,' Babs put in with a toss of her head.

'But Miss 'Ailin' knows us, don't she? She came 'ere to our house.'

'Flo's right, Babs,' Lizzie agreed. 'Why didn't we get an invitation too?'

'Dunno, search me.'

'I don't 'ave no parties to go to,' Flo sniffed. 'It ain't fair.'

'Have some icing from the cake.' Lizzie tried to distract Flo.

'Don't want any now. Gone right off it.'

'Well, go back in to Lil and tell her thank you for the cake. I'll be in later to see her meself.'

Flo went reluctantly out of the back door, shoulders drooping. Lizzie looked at Babs. 'Couldn't you have taken her to the party? After all, it's Christmas and she's only a kid.'

'I told you, she ain't got an invitation.'

'If she was with you they wouldn't turn her away.'

'You must be joking.' Babs' deep red hair seemed to glow around her face. 'Flo? At Miss Hailing's party? She'd pee her drawers and pick her nose and I ain't having Miss Hailing see that, I can tell you!'

'She's your sister. If Ma was here she'd tell you to take her, peed drawers or not.'

Babs looked murderous. 'Well, Ma ain't here. You are. And you ain't doing a very good job of taking her place if you ask me. We ain't got no Christmas decorations or presents or anything that we used to have when Ma was here. Just 'cos you're the oldest you think you've got the right to tell us what to do. Well, I'll tell you this for nothin', I'm not havin' it. Don't you ever try to tell me what to do again!'

'Come back here, you little madam!' Lizzie yelled as Babs swept out of the kitchen.

Lizzie knew Babs was right. She hadn't managed to buy decorations or presents. She had wrapped up one small gift each for the dinner table on Christmas Day, but that was all. Bert's wage from the shop bought the food. Vinnie's contribution paid the rent. But since the funeral, Vinnie was staying away a lot. Lizzie knew she couldn't count on his money anymore. If it hadn't been for Lil making them a Christmas cake, they would have had to make do with jam roly poly.

Carefully she lifted the cake from the table. She put it in the larder, moving Danny's vegetables to one side. By the time she returned to the kitchen, she had made up her mind. She would ask Vinnie for a regular contribution. He always had new clothes when he came home.

Australia . . . she thought wistfully. Some hope!

That evening, Vinnie was done up to the nines. Lizzie watched him in the passage, gazing at himself in the cracked mirror. If he was in trouble with the law, she thought as she stared at his new clothes, at least it hadn't come knocking on the door – yet. The hat and the double breasted jacket with the wide lapels and striped collar attached to his shirt by gold studs made him look every inch the villain.

Seeming satisfied with his appearance he turned to Lizzie. 'Ain't you never seen a decent suit before, gel?'

'You look very nice, Vinnie.'

He nodded. 'If I say so meself, I do.'

'Vinnie, old Symons called and I paid him the rent. We've got nothing left in the tin.'

'You've got Bert's extra money, ain't you?'

'Bert's money bought the baccy and the groceries,' she tried to explain. 'We didn't have anything left over.'

'Look 'ere, I give you a fair whack, don't I? You got to admit it's me that keeps a roof over our heads.'

'I know that, Vin. And I'm grateful. Ma couldn't have managed without what you gave her and neither can I. It's just that it's Christmas. And with me not taking Pa up the market there ain't enough money to buy presents.'

'Presents?' His thin eyebrows shot up. 'Now presents ain't nothin' to do with me, gel, and you know it. If you want presents then it's up to you to buy 'em.'

'I would if I had the money.' She knew she was pushing her luck.

Vinnie looked at her coldly. 'You're a fine one to talk. Blimey, you'd have thought we was royalty the way we entertained half the bloody street after the funeral and that's a fact.'

She was about to remind him that it had been Dr Tapper's money that had paid for the funeral and the wake when he pulled the brim of his hat over his eyes, signalling the end of the conversation.

'Anyway, can't stop,' he told her as he opened the front door. 'Mik and me are doing some business tonight. Gonna see a man about a dog.'

The only dogs that Vinnie ever saw, Lizzie reflected, were ones with numbers on their backs. She wondered what had happened to the brother whom she had grown up with, the brother who, before the war, had been a happy go lucky eleven-year-old. The Vinnie who hadn't acted the villain in order to gain people's respect. Even his narrow escape from the fire hadn't made him change his ways. Though he and Bert were now on speaking terms, they no longer went to the pub together. Bert had learned his lesson over Mik Ferreter. Vinnie hadn't.

He didn't look back to say goodbye. So much for her grand plan, Lizzie thought, as she closed the door. Vinnie wasn't going to help her. She glanced at Pa's door. If only she could talk to him. But she knew he didn't want to talk. He wanted to bury himself away and ignore the world.

Lizzie looked up the stairs. Flo stood at the top in her nightgown. 'Flo, what are you doing up?'

'Listenin' to you rowing with Vin.'

'We wasn't rowing. We was just talking.'

'Is Babs at that party?'

'No. She's gone next door to give Lil her Christmas card.'

'What about Pa? Has he still got the hump?'

'No, and it ain't the hump he's got. He's just getting over Ma in his own way.' They both knew he was probably sitting in his chair and staring out of the window.

Flo came down the stairs. 'I brought 'ome some coloured paper from school.'

'You mean you pinched it?'

Flo went red. 'We could make some decorations.'

Lizzie smiled. She didn't have the heart to send her back to bed. It was Christmas after all. 'Come in the kitchen then, where it's warm.'

They sat at the kitchen table and cut out shapes from the crêpe paper. 'I dunno if we was really allowed to take the paper,' Flo confessed, her brown eyes twinkling, 'but I knew we didn't have nothing at home.' Flo held out her blue and red paper chain. 'Pretty, ain't it?'

'I'll hang it up here.' Lizzie took down two saucepans. She stretched the paper chain between the nails. 'There. What do you think?'

'I'm hungry.' Flo looked at the larder door. 'Seein' as it's Christmas, could we have a bit of Lil's cake?'

Lizzie grinned. 'Give you an inch and you take a mile.'

But five minutes later Flo was smacking her lips. 'Don't suppose I could 'ave another bit, could I?'

'You supposed right.' Lizzie shut the larder door firmly.

'Can we play actors and actresses, then?'

'Just for ten minutes.'

Flo jumped on to the chair. 'I'll do me Charlie Chaplin. You watch me and I'll make you laugh.'

Lizzie sat down as Flo swung her imaginary cane and doffed her bowler hat. She was Charlie Chaplin to a T. Trust Flo to bring tears to me eyes, she thought, laughing and crying at the same time.

'Pretend I'm on a real stage,' Flo shouted, climbing on the table.

Lizzie thought of Danny. They had never gone to the Queens or the Lyric. Suddenly her longing to see him was a physical pain.

'Now it's your turn, Lizzie.' Flo collapsed into a chair. 'Sing a carol or something.'

'I don't want to wake Pa.' Lizzie didn't feel like singing. She felt sad and lonely.

'Sing it quietly then.'

'When we're upstairs.'

'Will you sit with me till I get to sleep?' Flo asked, coming to sit beside Lizzie.

Lizzie took Flo's hand. 'You ain't a baby anymore.'

'Wish I was,' giggled Flo, leaning her head on Lizzie's shoulder. 'Then I wouldn't have to go to school.'

That night Lizzie tucked Flo in the big double bed and sat on the covers beside her. She sang 'Silent Night' and by the time she had finished Flo was fast asleep. Lizzie tucked the blanket around her little face and bent to kiss her. She smelled of Christmas cake.

The house was very still.

Now there really was the breathless hush of Christmas at number eighty-two Langley Street.

Chapter Nine

Christmas morning 1920 and the bells of Christ Church pealed merrily across the island. Lizzie woke early, pulling her coat over her nightgown. Babs and Flo slept soundly, curled together for warmth. Babs still had a ribbon in her hair from the party.

There was no time to waste. Lizzie had to lay the table and prepare dinner. At seven in the morning the house was silent. She peeped into the boys' bedroom. Only Bert lay there, fully dressed, sprawled over the bed.

'Merry Christmas one and all,' Lizzie murmured, smiling at the sight. Well, at least Bert had managed to find his way home. It wouldn't do to wonder what Vinnie had got up to last night or where he was. With or without Vinnie, it was Christmas Day.

Lizzie washed and dressed in the blue frock Lil had given her. Next she placed the scrag end into a saucepan and boiled it. Straining the meat and saving the stock she added the peas and pearl barley that had been soaking overnight. The kitchen was warm and cosy. It was beginning to feel like Christmas.

Making herself a cup of tea, she decorated the table.

First she laid down a red curtain, placing Lil's cake in the middle and hiding Flo's nibbling with a holly leaf. There was a small gift for each of the family. A pair of braces each for the boys, pink and white coconut squares for Flo and two shiny green hair ribbons for Babs. Last but not least was a handkerchief for her father, the initials T.A. embroidered in red. Each gift was wrapped in brown paper, a name written over it. With a few sprigs of holly that Bert had brought home from the shop, the kitchen looked festive.

Outside, the sun was shining in a clear blue sky. The shed glistened, its roof spangled with frost. All the chimney pots billowed smoke. A ginger cat leaped from the hedge, leaving tiny paw prints on the white ground. A sense of wonder filled her. Kate had always made Christmas special and somehow she would find a way to make the day special too.

'You coming out for dinner, Pa?' Lizzie stood outside his door at one o'clock.

'No. I told you I wasn't.'

'Well, we ain't going to eat without you. It's Christmas Day.'

Tom Allen finally opened the door. 'You lot are better off eating by youselves.'

'We ain't starting,' Lizzie said grabbing hold of the Bath chair, 'till you sit down with us.'

He made no protest as she pushed him into the kitchen. Soon she had everyone gathered at the table. Boiled potatoes, carrots and dumplings filled each plate to the brim. There were more potatoes than meat but

Lizzie knew they'd satisfy the gap in six hungry stomachs.

'Can we open them brown parcels now?' Flo wanted know.

'After dinner,' said Lizzie. All eyes regarded the small, neat objects lying by their forks. She wanted to make sure there was a surprise to end with. She pushed back her dark hair from her face, her cheeks flushed and her green eyes sparkling.

Everyone ate rapidly except Tom. Lizzie knew he was thinking of Kate. His pale gaze lingered on the space she once filled.

They all missed her.

'You should 'ave been down the Quarry last night,' blustered Bert in an effort to cheer everyone. 'The landlord's old mother drank everyone under the table. Eighty-two and she was still on 'er feet when time was called and it didn't look like she was gonna stop, neither.'

Flo, as usual, had bolted her dinner. 'Can we open our presents now?'

'After the cake.' Lizzie winked at Flo as she cut it. No one had noticed the missing bit. 'It's lucky to make a wish on Christmas Day, so make sure your wishes are ones you want to come true.'

'I'll wish for a doll like Rosie Ryde 'ad for her birthday,' Flo announced. 'Only I want one with yellow 'air, not black.'

Lizzie put her fingers to her lips. 'Shh. You mustn't tell your wish.'

'Why not? It might 'elp.'

'No it won't. It'll take away the magic.'

'You ain't never gonna get a doll like Rosie Ryde's in a small parcel like that,' declared Babs.

'Might,' disagreed Flo. ''Ow would you know what I've got?'

Babs tossed her red head. 'Anyway, who'd want a doll? They're soppy.'

'They ain't!' Flo was indignant.

Bert belched. 'Ain't any seconds is there, gel?'

To the sounds of Babs and Flo arguing, Tom Allen pushed himself away from the table. Lizzie didn't try to persuade him to stay. It was Christmas, but that made no difference to the Allen family. A good row was on the menu even if turkey wasn't.

It was four o'clock and beginning to get dark.

Lizzie answered a knock at the front door. 'Merry Christmas.' Danny carried a large box of fruit in his arms. Apples and oranges were balanced on top of one another in a pyramid, grapes and bananas sticking out at odd angles. At the top was a sprig of mistletoe. 'Are you goin' to ask me in, then?' His fair hair fell over his face in a thick wave as he walked into the passage. 'There's more to come,' he called over his shoulder as she followed him to the kitchen and he lowered the box to the table.

'Danny, this ain't all for us, is it?'

'This is yer Christmas present. Now I'm going to collect mine.'

'How do you know I've got you one?'

He laughed as he drew her against him. 'Let's say

there's something I've wanted to do that'll count as me present.' He picked up the mistletoe and held it above their heads. 'Now close yer eyes and don't peep.'

Her heart beat fast as she closed her eyes and her lips tingled in anticipation. He kissed her, sending little shivers across her skin.

'You look lovely,' he whispered. 'A sight for sore eyes.'

'You were the last person I expected to see today.'

'Then you don't know me as well as I thought you did. Didn't think I'd let Christmas pass without giving you that kiss, did you? Now, here's what we're going to do. Have you got any plans for the rest of the day?'

She laughed. 'Chance'd be a fine thing, Danny Flowers.'

'Good. 'Cos I'm invitin' you all to a party.'

She stared at him, moving back a step, her eyes wide. 'A party? Where?'

'Don't look so surprised. I'd say we were well overdue for a bit of fun. If we can't have a bit of a knees-up on Christmas Day, when can we 'ave it?'

'You're not joking?' she asked breathlessly. 'You really mean it?'

'Course I mean it. Now go and get them girls ready.'

'But where are we going?'

'You'll have to wait and see, won't you? Tell Bert to wake himself up. Him and me will lift yer Pa and his chair on the back of the cart.'

'But I don't have anything to wear for a party.'

'Lizzie Allen, you're a stubborn woman, that's for sure.

But you won't get the better of me today.' He grabbed hold of her hand and pushed her gently to one side. Lifting the box of fruit from the table he lowered it to the long wooden bench. Sweeping the red curtain from the table, he placed it round her shoulders and tied the corners under her chin. Taking the sprig of mistletoe he tucked it in her dark hair. 'Why, with a cape like this you could be a princess.' He lifted her chin with his hand. 'You are my princess.'

Suddenly she was laughing. 'I suppose next thing is you'll take the lace down for the girls.'

'Why not? That's exactly what we'll do.'

He pulled her along the passage and tugged her up the stairs as the girls came running out of the bedroom. 'What's going on?' cried Babs.

'I'm taking you all to a party,' Danny informed her. 'A Christmas party.'

'A party? A party!' Flo cried. 'Lizzie, 'e ain't 'avin' us on, is 'e?'

'Take all the lace curtains down,' laughed Danny. 'You'll all look like snowflakes.'

'We're gonna dress up, we're gonna dress up!' cried Flo dancing round the landing.

'I'll put a nosebag on Benji. Don't be too long, because me guts is grumbling something awful and there's plenty to eat where we're going. So get on with you, fast as you can.'

Lizzie couldn't believe it. Christmas was going to be special after all.

*

Langley Street had never seen such a sight as the late afternoon parade on Christmas Day 1920. A sweating grey horse towed the Allen family, laughing and singing, across the length of the island. The girls sitting in the cart were dressed in white lace, bunches of holly and long tails of ivy threaded through hats and scarves.

With her cape round her shoulders, Lizzie sat beside Danny on the driver's seat. Bert sat in the back with his sisters, his hair flattened by cold water, a parting neatly scraped in the middle. He roared out every carol under the sun. Babs and Flo joined in, every now and then clouting their brother for singing off key. Their white lace smocks gleamed in the late light, like busy candles lighting up the dusk. People emerged from their houses to investigate the racket. Some waved from their doors, and Violet Catcher nearly fell out of hers.

Lizzie wished she could have waved at Lil and Doug, but they were spending the day at Blackheath with Ethel. The horse and cart progressed sedately up Westferry Road and into Manchester Road. A small group of ragged children joined them, singing and dancing in their wake. A few tried to climb aboard but Bert's ugly face soon deterred them.

The laughter went on, as did the singing, until Danny twitched the reigns. Benji turned, his nose leading him as it had many times before to the stable behind the costermonger's shop. At the junction of Ebondale Street and William Road the laughter faded to whispers. Their faces peered over the side of the cart.

The terraced houses, all with three floors, each had an

airey. Each airey was railed with long iron posts, rusted and peeling. Lizzie knew that Bill Flowers lived above his shop, his sons below it. By day the doors were thrown open, the front extended across the paving stones. Fruit and vegetables were displayed in boxes that only hours before had been sold at Covent Garden.

'We're going in *there*?' Lizzie gasped. 'In your house?'

Danny pulled in the reins. 'A costermonger's party not good enough for you, then?' He jumped from his seat and lifted her down.

'I hope you got something nice to eat at this party,' Flo shouted, trailing lace behind her. ''Cos we ain't had nothing since Lizzie's stew and that bit of cake afterwards.'

Danny laughed. 'You'd better go and see for yourselves, hadn't you? If there ain't no ice cream, it won't be a party, will it?'

'We ain't had ice cream for so long I can't even remember what it tastes like.'

The Allen family made their way in single file down to the basement of the corner shop. Danny and Lizzie were the last to enter, a girl dressed in a red cape and a young man, tall and handsome, with his arm lying lightly round her waist.

Chapter Ten

'Go steady, Lizzie Allen, or you'll fall and break your neck if you don't watch where you put your pretty feet.' The narrow steps turned at a sharp right angle. 'Go on in, Bert, the door's on the latch,' called Danny as they descended, and Bert and the girls pushed open a door that gave way to a spacious room, at the end of which was a big coal fire burning brightly in the grate.

'Who lives 'ere?' asked Flo as they walked in.

'Just Frank and me. Dad lives upstairs above the shop. Make yourselves at home, everyone. Flo, gel, you go over and sit by the fire and get yourself warm.'

'Ain't it big?' Flo stared around her.

'It's a lovely fire.' Flo kneeled in front of it, raising her palms towards the heat. A large brass coal scuttle filled with coal stood by the fender and a pair. of tongs and a brass shovel hung beside it.

Lizzie admired the surroundings that made up Danny's life. The heavily draped window gave little light from the street, but the gas lamps filled the room with a warm glow. The floor was covered in duckboards, planks of wood preventing the dampness from seeping into the carpet above.

Two comfortable easy chairs stood either side of the fire, tufts of horsehair poking out of their backs. A dresser spanned half of one wall, its pillared cupboards and thick shelves filled with china and curios, and next to it a grandfather clock chimed the hour, its deep chords filling the air. At the far end of the room was a chiffonier, raised up on four bulbous feet, but it was the upright piano beside it with two ornate brass candlesticks fixed to its front that caught Lizzie's eye.

'Ma always wanted a piano,' Lizzie said wistfully as she walked over and touched its shiny surface.

'Me and Frank ain't musical,' Danny told her. 'Mum used to play it, though. She had a lovely voice, so me Dad says. Course I never 'eard it, but sometimes I think I know what her voice sounded like . . . almost as though I've got the sound of it in me head.'

She knew that feeling too. Sometimes Kate's voice would ring in her ears as though she were standing right beside her. 'Ethel used to have lessons when Doug was in regular work and afterwards we'd have a bit of fun, mucking about on the piano together. Ethel would teach me a few tunes, though I'd sort of know which keys to put me fingers on.'

'We'll have a good old sing-song later and you can give us a tune.'

'Oh, I'd probably be a bit rusty.'

''Spect it's like riding a bike, ain't it? Sort of natural, like.'

She laughed. 'Yes, I 'spect so.'

'Here, you two,' he called to Babs and Flo, who were inspecting the china ornaments on the dresser, 'there's lemonade, ginger beer or ice cream soda – who wants a drink?' He walked to the sideboard by the kitchen door where bottles of drink were lined up by the glasses.

'It ain't real lemonade, is it?' called Flo.

'Is it real?' He looked back at Lizzie and winked. Course it's real. Absolutely kosher.'

'What are we 'aving to eat? Is there any jellies?' Flo hurried over to watch Danny pour the sparkling lemonade.

'Flo, it ain't polite to ask,' Lizzie said quickly.

'Have a gander in there.' Danny gave Flo her drink, tilting his head towards the kitchen. 'Help yerself.'

'She will an' all,' Lizzie giggled as Danny took her arm and led her towards the fire.

'Ah well, she won't make much impression on what's out there. Gertie came over this morning and done us proud. Me old man, Frank and Gertie will be putting in an appearance later.' Danny glanced at Bert, who had made himself comfy in one of the chairs beside the fire. 'Beer, Bert? Help yerself, mate, there's bottled brown on the sideboard or there's a barrel up in the storeroom.'

Bert grinned and reached for the nearest bottle. 'Think I'll 'ave a brown for now.'

Lizzie looked around in admiration. 'It's a big airey, Danny.'

'S'pose it is. There's the sitting room, the kitchen, the

scullery, then Frank's room and mine. The glory hole's full of junk. Come and have a look.'

The first bedroom was Frank's. The pictures on the walls displayed men who looked stiffly at the camera. They were dressed in the rough working clothes of the costers: thick trousers and jackets, caps discreetly removed from their heads for the benefit of the photographer. 'Rogue's gallery,' Danny chuckled.

'Are they all your family?'

'Unfortunately, yes. Grandad Flowers is the old bloke in the middle there. I don't remember much about him, only that when he was alive he had a blooming great voice that scared me and Frank half to death. That's Uncle Charlie and Uncle Fred, me dad's two brothers.' Danny pointed to two young boys standing by a horse and cart. 'Uncle Fred got scarlet fever and died young. Uncle Charlie ran away to sea and me dad ain't seen or heard of him since.'

Lizzie's gaze went to the photograph of a young woman wearing a long dark dress with a high collar. She was seated formally on a chair, her hands in her lap.

'That's me mum,' Danny said quietly. 'Puts the others to shame, don't she?'

'She's beautiful.'

Danny nodded and was silent for a moment. 'Still, it wasn't meant to be and that's that,' he sighed, shrugging back his shoulders. 'Dad and Gertie rub along well enough together. Gertie's a good sort. She was the closest thing to a mother we ever had . . .though Frank don't really see it that way.' A frown on his forehead, Danny sighed. 'When Mum died having me, well, I think Frank felt sort of cheated. He never took to Gertie like I did. It was easier for me. I hadn't had three years of a mother's love, so I didn't know any better. Me dad said Frank never spoke much till he was four or five. As for me, I ain't stopped rabbiting since I was born.' He laughed softly. 'As you well know, gel.'

Lizzie smiled at Danny's joke, but she was curious about Frank, who everyone said was a dark horse. The two brothers were so different yet looked so much alike. She wondered if Frank resented Danny for the death of their mother, just as he had resented Gertie Spooner for taking her place.

Lizzie gazed at the big brass bed, the old-fashioned wardrobe and bulky set of drawers. An oil lamp stood on the corner of a marble-topped washstand and above this hung a glass case in which there was a large stuffed fish. She thought the room resembled Frank, dark and brooding.

The next room was the glory hole, as Danny called it, so full of furniture you couldn't walk inside. But Danny's room was light and cheerful, having a window, which Frank's didn't. Under the window was a desk on which stood a silver-framed photograph of Danny's mother. Unlike Frank's room, there were no photographs on the walls, but there was a large coloured map of the world.

'Mum painted it,' Danny told her. Each continent was a different colour. The oceans were dark blue with tiny white eyelashes denoting waves. 'She was clever like that.

Dad said she finished it just before I was born. Look, that's Australia – where I'm going to make me fortune.'

Lizzie stared at the tiny green island of England and the huge red continent of Australia. 'It's so far away, Danny. And what about your dad? Who's going to help him with the shop?'

Danny shrugged. 'Dad ain't that struck on me going, but he's not the sort to hold me back. And he's got Frank to help him with the business. It ain't as if I was leaving him on his jack.' He gazed at the map, then turned slowly towards Lizzie. 'I've never been out of this country except to war, when I was sixteen. I saw action for twelve short months but it seemed like a lifetime. They said the war was important for the world. Maybe it was, maybe it wasn't. But I found meself thinking if I survived, I'd live every day like I never lived before. I made meself a vow. If ever I got out alive, I wouldn't waste a moment.'

Lizzie wanted to be at his side, to go to Australia too. But how could she leave the family?

'Well, now you know,' he said gently. 'It's me dream, you see, one that I'll have to follow whilst I'm still young enough.'

'It a wonderful dream, Danny.'

'I'd like to share it with you, you know that, Lizzie.'

She knew it, but as he took her in his arms and she waited for his kiss, she didn't reply. He lowered his head and his lips touched her waiting mouth, then softly nuzzled her hair. She leaned against him as pleasure and pain swept through her, mixed emotions that she could not understand.

*

Bert snored in one of the armchairs beside the fire. Babs and Flo, as usual, were in the middle of a disagreement.

'You're making an 'orrible din,' said Babs as she tried to push Flo from the piano stool.

'I ain't!' Flo glared at her sister. 'No worse than you, anyway.'

'Miss Hailing taught me to play "Silent Night",' Babs retorted, unable to dislodge Flo from the keyboard.

Flo's cheeks went bright pink. 'Yeah, with one finger I expect.'

Lizzie intervened. 'Flo, let Babs play a tune and then you can have a go.'

Flo jumped up, pulling the lace curtain from her shoulders. 'She'll sit there for ever, making an 'orrible row. She can't play no better than I can.'

Danny took Lizzie's arm. 'Leave 'em to it,' he chuckled.

He guided her across the room, down the two steps into the kitchen. It was a long, thin room with a high ceiling. Over the cooking range were copper pans, skillets, spoons and ladles, all crammed on to the shelves. The big wooden table down the middle was overflowing with sandwiches, pies, tarts, trifles, cold meats, saveloys and sardines.

'It's a banquet,' Lizzie gasped as she stared at the feast.

'There's more in here if we run short.' Danny opened the pantry door. All kinds of delicious smells oozed out. She had never seen a hock of ham so large, or bacon so mouth wateringly pink. Big jars of pickles, fruit and fish all stood on the bottom shelf, their contents squashed tantalizingly against the glass. A crusty cottage loaf as big as the bread board occupied the middle shelf. Above this was a tin of Clarnico confections and a wedge of yellow cheese covered in muslin. On the top shelf was a hessian sack full of biscuits, a plate of muffins and a large china pot of jam.

'I ain't never seen so much food in all me life!'

'Well, it's Christmas, ain't it?' Danny closed the pantry door and nodded to the turkey. It stood, as brown as toffee, on an oval dish in the centre of the table, its legs decorated with fluted white caps. 'Hope you didn't eat too much dinner. Should be a tender bit of meat. We kept old Kaiser out the back with Benji. That bloomin' bird ate as much as the 'orse did.'

Just then, Babs came into the kitchen, a glass in her hand. 'Everyone's arriving,' she said, her face flushed. 'Frank says to come and tell you.'

'What are you drinking?' Lizzie asked.

'Port and lemon.' Babs tossed back her hair and smiled at Danny. 'Frank said he'd pour me a shandy if I wanted, but that port and lemon was a lady's drink.' She gave a little toss of her head. 'Well, are you two coming or not?'

'Hold yer horses,' said Danny, grinning.

'I don't like Babs drinking,' Lizzie said as they followed her out. Babs was walking towards Frank, swaying her hips and giggling.

'Aw, she's just having a bit of fun,' Danny assured her, sliding his arm round her waist. 'Come on, stop worrying about Babs. You're meant to enjoy yourself tonight. And I'm gonna see that you do.'

But Lizzie was worried about Babs. She was flirting with Frank Flowers and looked much older than her years. It wasn't just the port and lemon that had gone to her head, Lizzie realized. It was in Babs' character to tease. And without Ma to keep her in check, Babs' bad behaviour knew no limits.

Boston Brown, all six feet and seventeen stone of him, had an arm round tiny Elfie Goldblum's shoulders. They stood beside the piano singing to Fat Freda's rendition of 'Won't You Come Home, Bill Bailey?' Elfie's cloth-capped head barely came up to Boston's swelling chest. But it was, surprisingly, the tenor of the tiny jeweller's voice that outshone the fishmonger's bass.

The room was full of laughter, beer flowed freely. Empty brown bottles and froth-stained glasses jiggled on table tops. Every now and then a hand came over and replenished a glass. People moved to and fro, laughing and joking. Some of the women were dancing, garters and pink flannelette drawers shamelessly exposed. Fat Freda played a medley of tunes as the men drank steadily.

Dickie Potts and his friends argued politics. Lizzie thought of her father, recalling how once he would have enjoyed the discussion. Now he was all alone at home grieving over Ma. Should she have left him on Christmas night?

'Penny for yer thoughts?' Frank Flowers smiled down at her. She hadn't realized he was standing there. She had been leaning against the dresser, listening to Dickie and his friends, absorbed in her thoughts of Pa.

'Oh,' she said, a little embarrassed. 'Hello, Frank.'

'You looked a long way away. Can I get you a drink?'

'No thank you. Speaking of which, I'd prefer it if you didn't give Babs any more alcohol.'

'Oh, did I do wrong?'

'She's only fourteen.'

'She don't give that impression, does she?' Frank said in a tone that Lizzie didn't like. 'But I won't give her any more, not if you're against it.'

'Where's Danny?' She didn't like being alone with Frank.

'He's gone upstairs to get Dad and Gertie. Now, if you ain't drinking, would you like a cup of tea, instead?' He smiled again, and she had to admit he did have a nice smile.

'All right, a cup of tea,' she agreed, hoping Danny would be back soon.

Frank pushed his way through the crowd, disappearing into the kitchen. For a minute she was cross with herself for being suspicious of him, he was Danny's brother after all. Nevertheless, she felt uncomfortable in his company.

'Making his play, is he, gel?' chuckled big Reg Barnes, the meat man, coming to stand beside her.

'What do you mean, Reg?'

'Why, I mean old Casanova himself,' Reg murmured, gulping his beer and looking a little tipsy. You watch that lad – he's got a reputation to maintain. 'Owever, the same can't be said for his brother.' Reg gave her a conspiratorial wink. 'Young Danny only has eyes for you, gel, getting himself up to the market every Saturday and never wanting to miss, even when there was much better business up the Embankment or Covent Garden.'

Lizzie went pink. Was it true what Reg said?

Reg nodded, as if guessing her thoughts. 'You can take my word for it, Lizzie gel.'

Lizzie felt a warmth run through her as she lowered her eyes.

'I'd better 'op it,' Reg said suddenly and nodded towards the kitchen. Frank was coming back.

'What was that all about?' Frank asked as he arrived beside her carrying a cup of tea. He glanced disparragingly at Reg's departing figure.

'Oh, you know Reg,' Lizzie answered, blushing even deeper. 'He was just chatting.'

'A right old windbag is Reg,' muttered Frank. 'You don't want to believe a word he says.' He set the cup down on the table and stared into her eyes. 'Listen, Lizzie. You're me brother's girl, I know that. But I'll tell you this for nothing. If Danny was out of the picture, I'd set me cap at you, and that's a fact.'

Lizzie stared into the pale blue gaze and a shiver went through her. She was unable to look away as Frank's gaze burned down on her. Just then Fat Freda yelled from the piano. 'Lizzie, how about you and young Flo giving us a song?'

Flo ran up and grabbed her hand. 'Come on, Lizzie!'

'What about yer tea?' Frank asked sullenly.

'I'll drink it later.'

Knowing that Frank's eyes were following her, Lizzie went with Flo to the piano. Fat Freda leaned forward. 'Well, my lovelies, what is it to be?'

'Do you know "A Beautiful Picture", Freda?'

Fat Freda nodded. She took a swig from her tumbler and began to play. The front door opened and Danny, his father and Gertie Spooner walked in. Lizzie felt safe again. When she gazed into Danny's eyes she forgot about Frank; no one else in the room mattered. It was just her and Danny.

The room was still as Freda's fingers paused over the keys. Lizzie and Flo began to sing, their soft voices floating across the room and weaving a tender magic.

If those lips could only speak, if those eyes could only see, if those beautiful golden tresses were there in reality. If I could only take your hand as I did when I took your name, but it's only a beautiful picture in a beautiful golden frame.

Book Two

Chapter Eleven

It was 1 January 1921. Lizzie put on a new brown hat with a gathered crown and upturned brim. The hat was a present from Ethel at Christmas, one of Rickard's display models.

Lizzie hadn't been able to afford a present for Ethel. But she'd sent over some oranges and apples that Bert had brought home from the shop. She'd written that she planned to wear the hat on New Year's Day, when Danny called for her.

As Lizzie was wishing that she had some nice shoes to match the hat, Flo came down the stairs. She had put on a clean dress and brushed her short brown hair ready to go to Lil's.

'When's Danny coming, then?' Flo asked as she came into the kitchen. She frowned at the old black boots that Lizzie was trying to breathe life into.

'Ten o'clock.' Lizzie rubbed hard at the leather with a rag.

'Where are you going?'

'Just for a walk.' Lizzie slipped on the boots and did up

the laces. 'Now don't go getting in Lil's way and no arguments with Babs.'

'Lil said we can 'elp her make a cake.'

'That should keep you out of trouble.' Lizzie hoped Babs and Flo would be on their best behaviour. She was nervous enough about going out with Danny. She hadn't slept a wink thinking about it and was grateful to Lil for having the girls. 'You be good till I get back.'

Flo giggled. Her large brown eyes were mischievous. 'That's what Ma used to say.'

Lizzie put her arms round Flo. It was the first day of the New Year and there was a big gap in it for them all without Ma. 'Happy New Year, in case you've forgotten,' she whispered.

'Happy New Year, Lizzie.'

Lizzie held Flo at arm's length. 'Don't forget to wish Lil and Doug a happy New Year.'

Flo skipped to the back door, then stopped. 'Has he kissed you yet?'

Lizzie's green eyes opened wide. 'Has who kissed me?'

Flo giggled. 'Danny, of course.'

'You cheeky little devil—'

'Bet he has. Bet he's given you a big one right on the lips.' Laughing, Flo ran out into the yard and squeezed through the fence.

Lizzie smiled to herself. She hadn't seen Danny since Christmas night, when he'd brought them home on the cart. She had missed him so much, counting the days – and nights – until she saw him again on New Year's Day.

'I'll be back this afternoon, Pa,' she called out as she slipped on her coat.

As usual, no reply. If only Ma was here, Lizzie thought sadly. The house seemed so empty, especially with Vinnie staying away. Lizzie sighed. If Ma was alive, things would be different . . .

A knock on the door brought Lizzie up sharply.

'Happy New Year,' Danny grinned as she opened it. He smiled, showing lovely white teeth.

'Happy New Year, Danny.'

He slipped off his cap and stuck out his elbow. Lizzie slid her hand through his arm. He made her feel like a princess as she stood beside him. Her wavy black hair fell over her shoulders, brushed so much it was gleaming under Ethel's hat.

'Eyes left,' Danny grinned as they passed Vi Catcher's. The lace curtain shook and Danny squeezed her arm. 'Now everyone will know Lizzie Allen is my girl.'

Danny's girl. She said it over and over again in her mind. Danny's girl. She felt as if she was walking on air. She didn't know when she had ever felt so happy. She wished the feeling could go on for ever. Everywhere looked bathed in a glow of sunshine, though in reality it was a cold and rather grey day.

They walked down Westferry Road and into Manchester Road towards Island Gardens. The mist was clearing from the river. A few boats chugged along, mostly barges, empty of goods, mooring quietly on the cold, dark waters lapping up to the wharves. There were no tall ships sailing by. The river was calm and uncluttered. Later in the day, when the mist had cleared, bigger vessels would cut through the water. A strange quiet lay over the river. A few early risers passed by, nodding and smiling.

They sat on a wooden bench under a shelter. The park spread out before them, a little piece of green heaven amongst the drab factories. There were swings and even a sandpit. No one had buckets or spades, but they all loved to play in it when they were younger. Lizzie sighed. Those days were gone. Not even Flo played here now. It was the open air baths that took her fancy, and the older kids hanging round it.

'Well, we never did get to the Queens or the Lyric,' Danny said suddenly, rubbing her cold hands between his. He asked her the question she had been dreading. 'Have you thought any more about Australia?'

'Danny, I can't the leave the family.'

'Why not?'

'Flo needs me – she's only a kid. And there's Pa. Who'd look after him?'

'Babs. She'd have to if you wasn't there.'

'But she's only fourteen. They'd take Flo away, put her in an orphanage or something. And Pa would—'

'But you've got yer own life to lead, gel. Like I told you, it wouldn't be for ever. We'll come back when we're rich and look after them all.'

Lizzie looked away.

'You don't believe I'll make me fortune, do you?'

Lizzie didn't know what she thought about Australia. It was too far away to have an opinion on, another world.

But she knew that Australia was causing them to argue. They sat in silence, until Danny said suddenly, 'Well, I'm going to prove I can do it!'

Tears sprang to Lizzie's eyes. 'You don't need to prove anything to me, Danny. I like you just the way you are.'

He bent close to her ear and whispered, 'I hoped you'd say that.'

'Oh . . . you!' Lizzie couldn't be angry with him for long. She loved him so much. He could always make her laugh, even when she was on the point of tears.

'Think of it as if I'm just going on ahead,' he said softly as he drew her close. 'I'll write and tell you what it's like. Tell you all the things about Australia that you never knew. Then, in a year or two's time, if you want, you can follow me out.'

She knew he meant what he said but she couldn't see herself leaving Flo, at least not till she was fifteen. She gave a little sniff. Danny took her chin in his hand.

'And if all else fails, I'll come home for my girl.'

'Would you really?'

'Cross me heart and hope to d—' He didn't finish. Lizzie put her hand on his lips.

'Shh. Don't say it,' she told him quickly.

He took hold of her hand and kissed it, murmuring softly, 'I've got to go soon, gel, or else I'll never get there.'

He slipped his hand round her waist and she knew that she would go on loving him for ever, across all the oceans and continents that seemed a world away.

That night in bed she couldn't sleep. As Flo and Babs

snored softly beside her, she thought of Danny. Even though she loved him, she couldn't leave the family. She prayed that if she never got to Australia her Danny would come home again to find her.

'We'll have to celebrate on the fifth,' Lil said one morning at the end of January. They were sitting in Lil's kitchen and the topic of conversation was Lizzie's birthday in February. 'I'll make a lovely big cake. Ethel and the kids will come over. Your Danny too. You're only sixteen once, gel.'

Lizzie wasn't sure she felt like celebrating. Ma wasn't there and Danny was going away. He might even have sailed before the fifth of February. But she knew Lil wanted to do it and she couldn't refuse. There was enough money in the cocoa tin to put on a little spread. Bert's wage at the shop was regular. And now he was away from Vinnie's influence, he didn't spend so much money down the Quarry. There was always fresh fruit and vegetables, too, provided by Danny.

'Vinnie might bring you a present,' Lil said sarcastically. 'Where's he living now?'

Lizzie shrugged. 'Up Poplar, near the bookie, he said.'

'Well, I hope he doesn't forget the roof he was born under.'

'He always leaves a bit of money when he comes,' she said in her brother's defence. But the reality was that Vinnie hardly ever called now and when he did it was only to look prosperous and flash. Lizzie hoped Lil would never bump into him. She would fire questions and the answers wouldn't be what she wanted to hear.

Lil flicked her ash into a saucer. The subject of Vinnie was dropped.

'What about the authorities?' she asked. 'Still checking on you, are they?'

Lizzie grinned. 'Flo is behaving herself and I haven't let us all sink into ruin, so I think we're in the clear.'

They sat together until Lil stubbed her cigarette out and stood up. 'Well, that's settled then. I'll start yer cake today. Do you want fruit or sponge?'

'Fruit would be nice.'

'Fruit it is then, gel. And we'll buy a few bottles of beer for the blokes. Your Pa won't drink, but Doug and Danny'll have a tipple.'

'*If* Danny's still here,' Lizzie sighed.

'He will be, love, you mark my words.'

It was a hope Lizzie clung to as the week went by.

'Ethel, it's beautiful!' Lizzie gazed in wonder at the miniature chest of drawers on the table. She opened the top drawer full of cottons and threads, and the next one, brimming with thimbles, sewing needles and buttons. The bottom drawer was filled with darning wools and skeins of pretty embroidery silks; she had never been given a present like it.

'Happy birthday, Lizzie,' Ethel said, giving her a hug. Ethel was wearing a soft green frock and had her fair hair pinned back from her face, accentuating her big blue eyes.

'Ethel, this must have cost a fortune!'

'No, it didn't. To be honest I got the box separately and filled it with stuff from Rickards.'

'Well, it's lovely.'

'I'm glad you like it.' Ethel glanced at Lizzie. 'Is Danny coming this afternoon?'

They were sitting on the chairs in Lil's front room, and Rosie and Timmy, Ethel's two, were in the backyard with Flo and Babs, playing hopscotch. Doug had taken his beer into next door with Tom, and Lil was in the kitchen preparing tea.

'He's coming over about five. Bill said he could knock off a bit early if Bert stayed on to help.'

'I bet you're glad he's here for your birthday.'

Lizzie smiled. 'Yeah, I am, Ethel.'

'It's a shame you can't go with him, you know.'

'Well, I can't and that's that.'

'What about Babs? Why can't she stay at home? You had to do it when you was her age.'

This had been Danny's suggestion, but Lizzie couldn't see Babs washing the clothes and scrubbing the floor, let alone looking after Pa and Flo. 'I don't think she'd give up Hailing House. The ladies count on her.'

Ethel gave a sharp tut. She looked up from under her lashes like Lil did. 'Well, charity starts at home, Lizzie. Why shouldn't Babs take her turn? I mean, it's not like she's indispensable to Hailing House. They'd soon find someone else to fill her place. But Danny ain't going to find someone to fill yours, is he?'

Lizzie had been trying not to think like that. Inside her

there was always a niggling little voice whispering that she was missing her opportunity. Absently Lizzie smoothed the soft blue pleats of her dress. Ethel's cast-off had been brought out once again. Deep in her heart she wanted to have nice new clothes and look beautiful for Danny. To live a life that wasn't always overshadowed by poverty. It seemed all this was possible in Australia.

She suddenly heard Ethel's voice again. '. . . so I said I'd mention it, Lizzie. At first you'd just be keeping check of the stock in the warehouse, but that would lead to a job in the shop. Our manager has a keen eye for a good worker.'

Lizzie blinked, hearing Ethel's last words. 'You mean there's a job going at Rickards?'

'In a month's time when someone retires. They'll want a person who's good at sewing and can sell to people. Just up your street, I thought, but as Mum pointed out, Blackheath is on the other side of the river, a blooming long way to go. Still, I thought I'd mention it, as I could put a word in for you.'

'Is it full time?' Lizzie asked curiously.

'Yes, Monday to Saturday.'

'I appreciate you thinking of me, Ethel, but—'

Just then there was a scream from outside. Both girls jumped to their feet and a moment later they were in the yard staring down at Flo. She was squirming on the ground, holding her knee. Babs was standing over her, hands on her hips. Lil was bending down examining the wound. Rosie and Timmy peered over their granny's shoulder.

'What happened?' Lizzie demanded, looking at Babs.

'She was showing off,' Babs declared. 'I told her not to jump off the wall but she did, right on Doug's spade.'

'She pushed me!' yelled Flo in tears.

'Liar!' Babs' face went scarlet. 'I never touched you.'

'Yes you did. When no one was looking.'

'You little—'

'That's enough!' Lizzie bent down beside Flo.

Lil raised her eyes. Her handkerchief was soaked with blood. 'I reckon it'll need a stitch or two. It's a deep cut . . . caught the sharp edge of the spade.'

Flo began to bawl even louder. Lizzie stood up and looked at Babs. 'You'll have to run round for Dr Tap.'

'I get the blame for everything round 'ere,' she screeched. 'Go and get the doctor yourself.'

At this, Timmy and Rosie started crying. Ethel took their hands and led them indoors, as Lil furiously mopped up the mess. Lizzie tried to decide whether she should make Babs go or run for old Tap herself.

The problem was solved by Ethel. 'Danny's arrived, Lizzie,' she shouted from the kitchen. 'And Frank.'

'What's up?' Danny hurried across to where Flo was lying. 'Blimey, Flo, how did you do that?' Flo sobbed, piling on the agony, and Danny glanced at Lizzie. 'Don't think that little lot will stop by itself.'

'I know.' Lizzie sighed, giving Babs a black look. 'We – I was just going for the doctor. She can't walk round to his place like that.'

'Well, that ain't no problem, I'll take her,' Danny said,

giving Flo a big grin. 'We've got the cart outside. Come on, young miss.'

But as Danny bent down, Frank stopped him. 'I'll do the honours,' he said quickly, jerking his head towards Lizzie. 'It's your girl's birthday, ain't it?'

Danny grinned, his blue eyes meeting Lizzie's. 'And I ain't said happy birthday yet, have I?'

Frank slipped his hands under Flo and lifted her up. 'Right, young lady, let's get you round to the old quack. You'll be as right as ninepence soon.'

'I'll help, Frank,' a sweet voice suddenly said. Babs went to stand beside Frank, looking up at him with a smile. Lizzie was speechless. She could hear everyone talking at once as they followed Frank, Flo and Babs out to the cart. But nothing was registering. Lizzie's fingers were itching to throttle Babs!

'Happy birthday, gel,' Lil said as she cut the fruit cake covered in pink icing and handed it out.

'Happy birthday.' Danny gave her a lovely brown pair of woollen gloves.

'Just what I wanted,' Lizzie gasped.

'I know, don't I?' he grinned. 'Can't have my girl going around with frozen fingers.'

Everyone had been so kind. Lil had given her a long woollen scarf that smelled faintly of mothballs but was very warm, Ethel the sewing box and Danny the gloves. Flo had made a special card at school, with a pretty lace edging. Even Babs had given her a navy blue hair ribbon. Earlier that day her father had given her a photograph of

Kate. Her mother looked very young, dressed in a white cap and apron and a long black dress, the uniform of service. The date on the back was 1895. Her mother had been fourteen. With tears in her eyes, Lizzie had hugged him. She knew the photograph was precious and hadn't been given away lightly.

When Flo returned, she hobbled in and showed off her bandaged knee. 'Dr Tapper said it wouldn't 'urt, but it did,' she proudly told Rosie and Timmy. The little kids squealed in horror.

Babs tried to catch Lizzie's eye. She went to sit beside Frank in the front room. Lizzie ignored the little display of airs and graces. She wasn't going to let anything upset the apple-cart tonight. Not even Vinnie's absence. Bert arrived at seven with a box of fruit and pushed it into her arms. The apples and pears were polished like marbles. It made the perfect end to her day.

'Don't forget to think about the job,' Ethel said at nine o'clock when she pushed the kids up the stairs to bed. They were staying at Lil's overnight and still full of beans.

'Yeah, thanks Ethel. I'll let you know.'

'I'll wait on the cart,' Frank told Danny as everyone filed out of Lil's house. Frank bent down to kiss Lizzie. She quickly turned her cheek. She felt a bit guilty as she moved sharply away; after all, he had been kind enough to take Flo to the doctor's.

'Thanks, Lil. I had a lovely time.' Lizzie gave Lil a big hug.

'You're worth it, gel.'

When Lizzie and Danny were alone on the doorstep of

number eighty-two, he took her in his arms. 'I love you, sweetheart,' he murmured.

'I love you too, Danny.' Lizzie looked up at him. In the darkness, she tried to read his expression, but when Benji moved outside Vi's he let her go.

She watched him turn then and stride across the road. One agile spring and he was up on the cart. She heard Frank urge Benji on and soon they were vanishing into the darkness. Lizzie swallowed. She was trying very hard not to let the tears fall in case any of the kids was still up.

Chapter Twelve

Seven days later, there was a tap on the door.

'Mornin', Lizzie.' Frank stood there in his overcoat.

'What's wrong?' Lizzie's heart was beating fast. 'It's Danny, isn't it?'

Frank nodded as he stepped in. 'He went to sign on a boat this morning and told me to give you this.' Frank took an envelope from his pocket. 'He's loading coal to pay for his passage, but he don't know how far he's gonna get on this city vessel. Italy, he hopes. Then he'll board another ship. Soon as he lands he'll cable you.'

Lizzie slipped the letter in her pocket. She didn't want to read it in front of Frank. 'Do you want a cup of tea?' she asked.

'If it ain't no trouble.' Frank followed her to the kitchen.

He sat down and Lizzie put two enamel mugs on the table. She was trying to ignore the panic growing inside her. Danny had gone. She had been dreading this day and now it had come.

'I dunno what to say,' Frank muttered. 'Is there anything I can do?'

'No, thanks all the same.'

'Are you all right for veg? I've got some nice King Edwards coming in tomorrow. Dad's bringing a load back from Covent Garden on the cart. Guaranteed no frost bite. Bert can fetch a few home for you.'

She knew Frank was making conversation, trying to take her mind off Danny. He leaned his arms on the table. 'Danny said I should ask you if you wanted a job in the shop.'

She sat down quickly. 'Danny said that?'

Frank nodded. 'Dad needs someone on Monday, Wednesday and Saturday, 'cos I'm gonna take the barrow up the market.'

'But Bert will be at the shop, won't he?'

Frank moved uncomfortably. 'Yeah . . . well, that's the point, really. I don't like to say it, but the truth is, Bert ain't no brain of Britain. He's all right when it comes to humping stuff, but a dead loss at figures. Me dad'll wants someone a bit quick at totting up.'

Lizzie didn't know what to say. She had been thinking about the job at Rickards, but it was too far. She couldn't look after the family and hold down a responsible job, whereas three days a week in a greengrocer's would be just right. She could do with the extra bit of money, too.

'Anyway,' said Frank when she gave no reply, 'think about it. No rush.' He gulped his tea and stood up.

In silence she accompanied him to the door. 'Well, cheerio, gel. See you soon.'

'Bye, Frank.' She watched him walk down the street. A deep sense of loneliness filled her. When would she see Danny again?

Up in the bedroom, she took out the letter. 'My Darling Lizzie,' he wrote, and her heart fluttered. 'I wish that I could say goodbye, but I've heard news of a ship wanting a crew and I'm going to try to sign on. If I'm successful, by the time you read this I shall be on my way, missing you with all my heart. But I intend to strike it rich in Australia and save enough money to come home a wealthy man. You know I had to do this. The shop is not my line, Frank is the man for that. Be assured that I leave England with one regret, that you are not by my side. I'll write and I hope you will write to me, and if things change for you then tell me and somehow I will make it possible for you to join me. Meanwhile, I'll prove to you that a costermonger's son is worth his weight in gold. Until I write again, all my love, Danny.'

She read the letter again and again. He hadn't mentioned anything about her working in the shop. Perhaps there wasn't the time. She tried to take comfort from his words, but what comfort was there in a separation that might last many years? Tears brimmed at the corners of her eyes. She thought of the days when she went to market with Pa, eager for the sight of the barrow and Danny. How he could make her laugh and forget her worries. Tell her jokes and give her hot roasted chestnuts to eat. And how, that day, when he asked her to go out with him, she had imagined sitting in the Lyric way up in the gods.

She folded the letter slowly. 'Oh, Danny,' she sighed, 'what am I going to do without you?'

And then she seemed to hear Ma's voice again. The soft voice always came to her when she felt low. A voice that told her there was only one thing she could do. Dry her tears and start all over again.

Two weeks later, Lizzie was pegging out the washing. The air had a bite to it that still recalled winter, yet a wide blue sky and the occasional sparrow hopping from tree stump to gutter and flirting with a twig or two indicated the beginning of spring.

'Hello, ducks,' Lil called over the fence. 'Saw you out here, so I thought I'd come and say hello. A bit parky, ain't it?'

'It's freezing, Lil. Doubt if the washing will dry.' Lizzie pushed a peg over the steaming sheet and joined Lil at the fence. Their hot breath billowed up in the frosty air.

'I popped in last week, like I said I would, to chat to yer Pa,' Lil commented. 'Dunno that he was too pleased to see me though.'

'Thanks, Lil. It puts me mind at rest when I'm at the shop. And I really appreciate you keeping an eye on Flo for me till I come home.'

'Does yer dad go out at all these days?'

'Last time was weeks ago, with Bert, up Island Gardens. He won't even let me clean his room properly. And he don't like me helping him to dress no more, or clean his stumps.'

'Well, anything I can do to help, let me know. By the

way . . .' Lil lowered her voice and leaned over the fence. 'I saw your Vinnie the other day, up Poplar High Street. He was with that Mik Ferreter. A shifty looking bugger if ever I saw one. To be honest, love, your brother was always a magnet for trouble, even as a kid. I remember when he started to mix with that bunch from Limehouse. Worried the life out of your poor Ma. Even my two lads, who I'll admit were no angels, wouldn't knock around with them.'

Lizzie nodded. 'Ma must have been really worried.'

'It was that bloody war,' Lil remarked acidly. 'Vinnie might have stood a chance if yer Pa had been at home and told them all to piss off.' They stood in silence for a moment until Lil shrugged her shoulders. 'Anyway, how's the job going? Do you see much of Frank?'

'No. He goes up the market with the barrow.'

'Don't suppose he sells half as many chestnuts as Danny,' Lil grinned. 'What's it like in the shop?'

'I was a bit nervous but Bill's very kind. And I like meeting the customers.'

'Yeah, and the money comes in handy.'

Lizzie nodded. 'With me and Bert working I can put a bit aside for emergencies.'

'What about Babs? Is she earning yet?'

'No, but I might go up to the House and speak to the ladies. Babs is fifteen next month.'

'And not before time,' Lil agreed. 'It's up to them to give the girl a fair wage. And if Babs don't ask, then you'll have to ask for her.' Lil touched Lizzie's arm. 'Ain't heard nothing from your Danny yet, I suppose?'

'No. But he said he'd write.'

'Yeah, he won't let you down, gel, not Danny.'

Every morning, as soon as she woke, Lizzie wondered where Danny was and what he was doing. Had the boat got to Italy? Had he managed to find another one to Australia?

'Well, I'd better get cracking,' Lil sighed. 'Ethel's coming over with Tim and Rosie for tea. I'll pop in and say hello to yer Pa tomorrow whilst yer at the shop.'

Lizzie watched Lil go. A deep pang went through her for Ma. She missed the quiet chats they used to have and the stories Ma would tell her. She missed not being able to confide her feelings about Danny. She wished that she could walk right back in and find Kate standing at the sink, telling her the kettle was on and it would soon be time for a cuppa.

Lizzie had plans for the afternoon. She was going up to the ladies at the House to ask about a wage for Babs. Talking to Lil had made up her mind. She wasn't going to put it off any longer.

Before she left, she took a tray of food in to her father. 'I think Babs should be paid a wage,' she told him. 'I'm going up to have a word with the ladies.'

'Take the key off the string,' he told her. 'I don't want no one coming in.'

'Why don't you come with me, then?'

'Me legs are giving me gyp,' he muttered, turning his chair to face the window.

Well, it was up to him, she told herself as she plaited

her thick black hair, put on Ethel's hat and combed out the curls on her forehead.

It was bright and breezy outside; all the washing would be dry when she got back. What would Miss Hailing say when she asked for money, she wondered? She wasn't asking for charity. It was a puzzle as to why the ladies hadn't offered to pay Babs before. Lizzie felt within her rights to ask, but even so, she didn't like having to.

The gates of the rope factory were closed. A queue of men stood at the entrance waiting for work. Times were hard and the poor and hungry waited days on end for work. Bert was lucky to have the job at the shop. Would she rather see Vinnie lined up here or working for the bookie? Ma had always said you couldn't feed a family or pay the rent on principles. Was that why she had always accepted Vinnie's money?

Hailing House was a large red-brick property set back from the road. Twice weekly it opened its doors to the community. Men, women and children queued on the pavement outside for their bowl of soup. 'The Slummers', as the ladies were known, returned to their country seats at the weekend, having done their good work.

Lizzie had gone to the House with Ma, to attend the sewing classes. It was a treat to be welcomed by Alice the maid and escorted to the sewing room at the back of the House, where all the women of the island would gather for the busy sessions.

Lizzie walked up the wide, spotlessly clean steps. She gave two sharp raps on the brass knocker. When the door opened Babs stood there.

'What are you doing here?' Babs demanded. She wore a blue corduroy dress and a pair of shiny black patent shoes. Her red hair was pulled neatly back from her face and tied in a ribbon.

'I thought you helped in the kitchens,' Lizzie burst out. "Why are you dressed like that?'

'None of yer business,' Babs retorted. 'What do you want?'

'I've come to see Miss Hailing.'

'Well you can't. The ladies are very busy.'

'Well then I'll wait.'

'You can't do that either. Not looking like that.'

'What did you just say?' Lizzie stared at her sister.

'You're a disgrace coming here,' Babs hissed. 'Look at the state of you. I could lose me job over this, you selfish cow.'

'Elizabeth, is that you?' A voice called from inside.

Babs spun round. 'Miss Annabelle!'

Annabelle Hailing appeared, dressed in a fluffy grey jumper and cardigan. A row of pearls hung round her neck. She wore an elegant wool skirt over silk stockings and fashionable leather shoes.

'Lizzie ain't stopping, Miss Annabelle,' Babs said quickly. 'She was just passin'. I happened to see her from the window and thought I'd say hello.'

'I'm sure you've time for a cup of tea, Lizzie,' Annabelle said, opening the door wide. 'Please come in and leave your coat with Barbara.'

'Oh, I won't stop long.'

'Barbara, tell Alice we have a guest. A pot of tea for

two would be very welcome. Oh yes, and some of Cook's excellent sponge cake, I think. We'll sit in the drawing room by the fire.'

Lizzie followed Annabelle, ignoring the look of horror on Babs' face. Why had Babs said she had seen her outside? And what was she doing all dressed up in uniform?

The drawing room had high white ceilings and long, elegant windows. A red velvet couch stood in one corner. The deep red material was the same colour as the drapes. A rose-coloured rug lay over the floor, its edges laced with a fringe. Lizzie thought it looked as though someone had carefully combed it out each day. The antique furniture was all highly polished and sparkling.

'How is the family?' Annabelle asked as they sat down in the large fireside chairs.

Lizzie explained about Pa's depression and a little bit about Danny sailing for Australia and finally leading to her job at Flowers.

'Oh, I can understand now why you and Flo didn't come to the Christmas party,' she said. 'You must have been very busy indeed.'

Lizzie stared at Annabelle. They had never been invited to the party. Or had they?

'Ah, here's tea.' Annabelle smiled. Though Alice had grey hair, she had a fresh, round face. On the tray were white bone china cups, saucers and side plates, silver forks and spoons wrapped in napkins. On the silver stand was a delicious looking sponge cake.

When Alice had gone, Annabelle cut the cake. 'I can

assure you, Cook's recipe won't come anywhere near the high standards of your friend Lil.'

Lizzie wasn't thinking about cake. She was furiously planning what she was going to say to Babs. It was because of Babs they hadn't gone to the Christmas party. But what came next was the biggest shock of all, as she heard Annabelle continuing, 'As you know, Barbara has been asked if she would like to replace Alice, who is retiring. And because Barbara has taken so well to the job, Felicity and I thought it only fair to increase her wage . . . perhaps another two shillings, to four shillings a week?'

Chapter Thirteen

'James will drive you home,' Annabelle insisted.

Lizzie tried to smile but she was furious. Babs had been earning two shillings a week since Ma died. And she had never said a word. The devious cow.

'I've two parcels for you,' Annabelle was telling her. 'My young nieces have grown out of their clothes. I thought they might be of some use.' She rang the bell and Alice appeared. 'Tell James to bring the car to the front of the house, please, Alice.'

They walked to the front door. 'James will carry the parcels for you.'

'Thank you,' Lizzie said as she left. James was waiting by the big black motor car. He opened the door and she climbed in.

Lizzie had never been in a car before, let alone one driven by a chauffeur. If she could stop being so angry, she told herself, she might enjoy it.

The seat was real leather. The windows were gleaming. The car didn't seem to be moving it was so smooth. The streets went whizzing by. Everything smelled new.

'Are you comfortable, Miss?' James looked in the driving mirror.

'Yes, thank you.'

'If you want to open the window, you just turn that handle on the door.'

She wound down the window but soon closed it as the smell of the pickle factory poured in. The dock gates flashed by, then row upon row of dirty houses. When James brought the car to a halt Lizzie glanced at the neighbours' windows to see if anyone was watching.

James opened the car door and helped her out. 'Where would you like the parcels?' he asked.

'Inside the front door, thank you.'

Just then Flo rushed out from the house. 'Lizzie, who's that? What's he got? What's in them parcels?'

Lizzie put her hands on Flo's shoulders. 'Some new clothes from the ladies.'

'Did you have a ride in that car?' Flo squeaked. 'Can I have one too?'

'No, you can't.'

'Oh, I think we could manage once round the block,' James said with shrug.

Flo jumped up and down, clapping her hands.

'Behave yourself, now. Sit nice and quietly. James don't want a chatterbox putting him off his driving.'

James extended his hand and Flo went scarlet as he helped her into the rear of the car. Lizzie's mind was on Babs as she waved to Flo. What if she had asked Annabelle about paying Babs a wage? It would have been embarrassment all round.

'Whose car is that?' her father shouted as she walked in.

'The ladies', Pa. James gave me a ride home.' Lizzie put her ear to the door. 'Can I come in?' She wanted to talk to him about Babs.

'No, I'm trying to have a kip.'

She knew it was useless. It would be up to her to have it out with Babs. When the big black car came round the corner, Vi's curtains were twitching and all the kids in the road were staring.

'How fast did you go, Lizzie? We went twenty miles an hour. We could have gone faster. But we didn't case we ran someone over.'

'Did you wave to everyone?' They were up in the bedroom with the parcels and Flo's cheeks were pink.

'Yeah. Sammy Baker blew me a raspberry.'

'Cheeky devil.'

'I bet old Vi's eyes popped out of her head when she saw me getting out of a posh car like that. When I grow up I'm gonna marry a sh . . . sho . . .'

'Chauffeur,' smiled Lizzie.

'When he opened the door, he said, "Hup you go, miss." I ain't never been spoken to like that before. And nobody ain't ever bowed to me. His eyes went all sort of funny under that hat. Look, I'll show you!' Flo strode round the bedroom with stiff arms and legs.

'You're a card, Flo Allen.' Lizzie laughed. 'You should be on the stage.'

'I'm gonna be.' Flo threw herself on the bed. 'I'm gonna be an actress, or a singer or a dancer.'

'And don't forget to marry a chauffeur too.'

'Yeah. And I'm gonna have a car like that one day. When I get as famous as Charlie Chaplin, I'm gonna buy a house of me own. Over the water in Blackheath where Tim and Rosie live. You and Babs can come for the 'olidays. Just as long as you all mind yer ps and qs.' Flo bounced up and down beside the parcels. 'Go on, open it quick, Lizzie.'

Lizzie untied the string, and dresses, jerseys, skirts, underwear, stockings and blouses spilled out. The next half hour was spent trying them on. A blue dress with a lace collar and a party frock of white linen with leg of mutton sleeves and a wide blue cummerbund were both Flo's size. Two warm winter jerseys, a long skirt of blue serge and a grey wool coat fitted Lizzie. She undid the row of grey buttons down the front. The smooth black velvet collar matched the turned back cuffs.

'Look what I've found,' cried Flo. 'Just what I always wanted. Shoes with straps.' She kicked off her boots and slid on the black patent shoes. 'They'll fit perfect with a bit of newspaper down the front.'

Lizzie shook out a yellow dress. 'This will fit Babs.'

'She don't like yellow,' Flo said darkly. 'It don't go with red hair.'

'Well, it's the right size.'

'Look at all these,' Flo gasped as she pulled out knickers, pink flannel stays and long woollen stockings.

'Just what we could do with.' Lizzie held up a cotton petticoat. 'All washed and ironed, too.'

'I ain't bothered what I got on underneath, no one sees

me drawers.' Flo pranced around the bedroom in her party dress, tossing back her hair and wiggling her bottom. They were laughing so much, no one noticed the door open.

'What's going on here?' Babs came in, her face flushed. 'Who do all those clothes belong to?'

'Do you like me party dress?' Flo shouted. 'Miss Hailing gave 'em to us.'

Babs glared at Lizzie. 'So, that's what you turned up for today!'

'It wasn't,' Lizzie said angrily. 'It was to ask the ladies about giving you a wage.' Lizzie didn't mention the party, not whilst Flo was there.

Babs' face went red. 'You what?'

'You heard. And then I find out they've been giving you two bob a week since Ma died.'

Babs lifted her chin. 'And what if they do! You don't go short. Bert and Vinnie give you all that money.' Babs' eyes narrowed as she stepped forward. 'You even got yerself a job at the shop. Danny ain't been gone five minutes and yer makin' up to Frank.'

'That ain't true and you know it,' Lizzie shouted. 'Frank offered me the job. Danny told him to.'

'Well you would say that, wouldn't you?'

'It's the truth—'

'I see Frank looking at you,' Babs yelled. 'And you make the most of it.'

Lizzie stepped forward, dropping the petticoat. 'You're a liar, that's what, Babs Allen.'

Flo grabbed her clothes and ran from the room.

'Now look what you've gone and done,' Lizzie cried angrily. 'Why didn't you tell Flo and me about being invited to the Christmas party?'

'I would have thought that was obvious,' Babs said coldly. 'It was about time I had something nice to meself. When Ma was alive I was always getting ticked off and you was the goody goody. Well all that's changed now. I'm keeping what I earn for meself.'

Lizzie shook her head slowly. 'Oh no you're not. You'll pay your way like everyone else.'

Babs smiled. 'Not if I'm not here I won't.'

'What do you mean by that?'

'Exactly what I said. Soon as I get the chance, I'm off.' Babs shouted as she turned and ran down the stairs.

Lizzie rushed after her, leaning over the banister. 'Where are you going?'

Babs glared up at her. 'Somewhere me company is appreciated.' The door slammed and the house was silent.

Lizzie went back into the bedroom. Where was Babs going? Did she really mean what she said about leaving? Feeling sick, she sat down on the bed in a daze.

Chapter Fourteen

Five o'clock had just passed and Lizzie was taking the tray to her father's room. What could she cook for tomorrow, Good Friday, she wondered, to make the day a bit special? A cake would go down well for tea, but for dinner she could cook a meat pie. There was some mince left over from last night's meal. That, and a thick gravy with roast potatoes.

She glanced down at the tray she was carrying. Apple dumplings. They were tender and juicy, made from the cooking apples that Bert brought home from the shop. There were two slices of bread beside this and a scraping of jam. It didn't look much, but it was filling and apple dumplings were Pa's favourite.

She knocked first before pushing open the door. He was sitting by the window in his chair. 'Tea's up, Pa.'

'Leave it on the cupboard.'

She went over and lowered the tray. 'Don't let it get cold, Pa. It's your favourite, apple dumplings.'

He turned to frown at her. 'Who was that who called this morning?'

'It was Reverend Green. He was only here a few minutes.' She had hoped the visit had gone unnoticed.

'What did he want?'

'Miss Hailing asked him to call because it was Easter.'

Her father pushed his chair from the window. 'Well, you can give him his marching orders if he comes again. I don't want no holy Joes coming round this house and trying it on.'

'He was just being friendly. Giving us all a blessing.'

'Let him go and bless the poor buggers waiting at the dock gates. We don't want the likes of him round here. They're only interested in one thing. Telling you how to live your life and charging you for it.'

Lizzie looked at her father. The light shone on his hard, set face. There was no reasoning with him lately; he suspected everyone and trusted no one. Leaving the room, she stood in the passage and blinked back a tear. As she stood there, Flo came slowly down the stairs.

'I'll get you something to eat,' Lizzie said.

'I'm not hungry.'

'That's not like you.' Lizzie went towards her. 'What's the matter?'

Flo burst into tears. 'I dunno. I got a sore throat and these . . .' There were tiny red spots covering Flo's neck. When Lizzie undid her blouse, Flo's chest was covered in them.

The ambulance had just left as Bert and Frank pulled up in the cart. 'What's goin' on?' Bert shouted as he jumped down. 'What's the ambulance round 'ere for?'

Dr Tapper said quietly, 'You'd better take your sister inside, young man.'

'What's wrong?' Bert asked again as Frank joined them.

'Go in,' Lil told him firmly, 'and she'll tell you.'

'I'll be on my way, then.' Dr Tapper clutched his Gladstone bag and pulled at the brim of his top hat.

'Give us a shout if I can help,' Lil called as she disappeared through her front door.

Lizzie went to the kitchen and sat down. She looked up at Frank and Bert, who stood hesitantly in the doorway. 'Dr Tap says Flo's got scarlet fever.'

''Struth,' breathed Frank, moving towards her. 'Poor kid.'

'How did she get it?' Bert asked bewilderedly as Frank ushered them along the passage.

'I don't know, Bert. She was covered in spots. She might have got it at school. Miss Evans said there was one girl in Flo's class who had it.'

'Where have they taken her?' Frank asked quickly.

'To the Mile End Road hospital. There's a special place there for people with infectious illness.'

'Mile End,' muttered Bert. 'How are we gonna get up there?'

'I'll walk up to Poplar and catch a tram,' Lizzie told him. 'I've packed a few clothes, but she's only got one good nightdress. I'll have to get her another one from Cox Street.'

'I expect they've got plenty at the hospital,' Frank murmured.

'Do you think so?' Lizzie bit down on her lip. 'She won't like being away from home . . .' Tears welled up in her eyes.

'Hey, come on, now.' Frank sat down beside her at the table, patting her arm. 'She's gonna be all right. You wait and see. I'll take you over on the cart.'

'Would you?' She looked up at him. 'But ain't it a long way?'

Frank shrugged. 'I'll give Benji a nosebag while you're gettin' ready.' He stood up and went out to cart.

'Do you want me to come too?' Bert asked.

'No, I'd rather you stay with Pa. He still ain't come out of his room, though he must have heard all the commotion.'

Bert nodded slowly. 'I'll tell him what's happened.'

Leaving Bert she went upstairs to the bedroom. The evening sunshine spilled through the window. Gathering Flo's few possessions and putting on her coat, she went back downstairs.

'Got everything?' Frank asked as he came in the front door, rubbing the oats from his hands.

'Yes.' She looked up at Bert. 'Look after Pa, won't you? Lil's next door if you need her.'

'Yeah. Don't you worry, gel.'

They went out to the cart and Frank helped her up on to the seat. Taking his place beside her, he picked up the reigns. 'Get on there!' he shouted, shaking the reins.

All the lights went on in the houses as the cart trundled along. When would Flo return home? she wondered. Could she be cured?

Benji began to trot faster, the shadows settling over their path as they clattered along the empty street.

Frank went the quickest way, through Limehouse. The last of the sun had disappeared and a yellow fog filled the streets. Even the gas lamps were indistinct as the mist crept around them, giving them an eerie glow. Frank stopped the cart and pulled a potato sack up from the back. 'Put this over yer legs, gel. It'll keep you warm.'

Lizzie was grateful for the rough protection. She was shivering, though more from nerves than cold. Frank told her not to worry, that everything was going to be all right, and though the journey seemed endless they finally reached the hospital. Frank drew the cart up outside the front entrance of the big Victorian building. Light spilled out of the many windows. An ambulance was parked by the doors.

'I don't know if I'd ever have found it.' Lizzie held on to his shoulders as he lifted her down. 'Thanks, Frank.'

He smiled at her, holding her gently. 'Might clear up a bit by the time we go home.' He took her arm and they walked up the stone steps.

Inside it was warmer and the high ceilings gave off a clear, bright light. 'Can I help you?' A nurse came towards them along the corridor. She wore a white cap and a high, starched collar. Her long blue dress was almost entirely covered by a white apron.

'My name is Lizzie Allen. My sister was brought in by ambulance at tea time.' Lizzie glanced down the long corridor hopefully.

'Was she involved in an accident?' the nurse asked, looking them up and down.

'No, she's got scarlet fever.' There was a tremble in Lizzie's voice. 'Her name's Florence, but we call her Flo. The ambulance men said it would be better for me to wait till tomorrow to come over. But Flo don't like being away from home.' Lizzie clutched her small bag of possessions.

The nurse, who had very dark, piercing eyes, glanced at Frank. 'Are you a relative too?'

'No.'

'Frank brought me here,' Lizzie said quickly.

'Well, I'm afraid I'll have to ask you to wait in the waiting room, sir. We have very strict rules for visitors. Especially for those patients who are being assessed.'

Frank shrugged. 'Fair enough. I'll have to go out to the horse anyway.'

'The horse?' The nurse frowned. 'You came on a *horse*?'

'Horse and cart,' clarified Frank in a brisk tone. 'It's a long way from Langley Street, 'specially at night.'

The nurse's voice softened. 'Well, in that case, perhaps we'll be able to find you a cup of tea. Come into the waiting room when you've seen to the horse.'

Frank smiled at Lizzie. 'See you later. Give Flo me love.'

When Frank had gone, the nurse crooked her finger. 'Come along. We're quite a way from the isolation wards. But as we go you can tell me what happened.'

As they walked, Lizzie explained about Flo's spots and

sore throat, then Lil going round for the doctor and his diagnosis. Part of her was hoping the nurse would tell her it was wrong and that Flo was sitting up in bed, well again. But instead, the nurse, who was a sister, explained that all infectious cases were assessed in a special ward.

The long, echoing corridors seemed never-ending. Some of the people they passed looked very sick. They huddled on benches and chairs and sometimes in Bath chairs, like her father's. She saw several men missing their limbs and she thought of how Pa must have suffered during the long months in different hospitals.

'Has Flo been ill for long?' the sister asked as she pushed open an outside door and a gust of foggy air blew in.

'She's been a bit off-colour for a week,' Lizzie told her as they walked across to another building and up a ramp. Inside, a gust of heat and strong disinfectant enveloped them. 'She wouldn't eat tonight and I knew something was wrong. She loves her food. Then I saw the spots.'

'Does Flo take any medicine?' They turned into a brightly lit room where a secretary sat at a desk piled high with papers.

'Ma used to give us Galloway's lung syrup and sometimes camphorated oil or wintergreen.'

'Is that all? Cough medicine and balms?'

Lizzie stiffened. 'They always did us good. Ma was very particular about medicines.'

'I'm sure,' said the sister, quickly patting her arm.

'It costs a shilling every time the doctor calls,' Lizzie felt impelled to explain. 'And there's five of us kids.'

The sister smiled kindly. 'It must be very expensive for your mother.'

'She died last year,' Lizzie told her. 'It's me that looks after everyone now.'

'Oh dear. I'm sorry.' The sister was quiet for a moment as they entered a small, warm room. 'And your father?'

'He lost his legs in the war.' Lizzie was afraid to tell this woman too much, but in the circumstances what could she do?

'Mary,' said the sister to a girl sitting behind a desk. 'A young girl by the name of Florence Allen was admitted this afternoon. Do you think we could arrange for her sister to see her? She's come all the way from the island in this dreadful weather.'

'I'll ask the doctor,' the secretary replied and hurried out of the room, her leather soles squeaking on the lino.

There were six wooden chairs lined along the wall. The sister gestured to one of them. 'Take your coat off and sit down, Lizzie. If they allow you to see Florence, you'll have to wear some very peculiar clothes to protect against germs coming in or going out of the hospital.'

Lizzie took off her coat. 'Will Flo get better?'

'She will have very good treatment here,' the sister replied, adding quickly, 'Is there an inside toilet or bathroom in your house?'

Lizzie shook her head. 'No, but we've got the shed. Me grandmother used to call it the closet. We wash out there and bring the tin bath in for a good soak.'

'I see. Well, one of the things that we do to fight

infectious diseases is to look at the problem of overcrowding. Some houses can also be insanitary—'

'Ma always kept a clean house,' Lizzie protested at once. 'She made certain we all kept clean too.'

'Yes, I'm sure she did. But the doctors ask a lot about their patients' circumstances. As you are in charge of your family, I'm afraid you'll have to be prepared for questions of this nature.'

Lizzie sniffed. 'Yes, I suppose so.'

'You have a lot of responsibility on those young shoulders,' sighed the sister, shaking her head slowly. 'And the expense can be no easier for you than it was for your mother.'

'Except that I've got a job now.' Lizzie didn't want the authorities to think she couldn't afford to look after Flo.

'What kind of job?'

'I work in a greengrocer's four days a week. And me two older brothers bring in a wage.' She didn't mention Babs, who had been staying out a lot and had refused to give any money.

'Well, that must certainly be a help.' The sister nodded.

'How long will Flo have to stay here?'

'Well, if possible, the doctor will keep her under observation here in this ward. But depending on her recovery he might transfer her to the children's ward of the New Cross Isolation Hospital.'

'New Cross? That's miles away.' She would have to go through the Blackwall Tunnel under the river and then walk or catch a bus to Greenwich and Deptford.

'Let's wait and see,' said the sister with a reassuring smile. 'Now, here's Mary.'

The secretary was carrying a neat pile of starched white linen. 'The doctor said you may spend a few minutes with your sister,' she told Lizzie. 'You must change into these and wash your hands and face before going in.'

The sister laughed at the expression on Lizzie' s face. 'You'll get used to our funny ways. You'll see lots of other 'ghosts' floating about too.'

Lizzie was shocked. Flo lay with her eyes closed in a bed with iron rails. Her spots were bright red and seemed to have increased. They had cut all her hair very short and Lizzie was grateful to be hidden behind the mask, hood and gown. She could hide her expression of shock at everything she saw: the small room containing only the bed, a chair and a wooden locker; the brick walls were painted cream and brown and the window was very small.

'Just a few minutes,' said another nurse who had brought her from the cubicle where she had washed and changed her clothes.

Lizzie walked to the bed and Flo opened her eyes.

'Lizzie?' Flo spoke weakly, her lips trembling. 'Why are you dressed up like that?'

'We have to wear this to keep the germs away.' Lizzie wanted to give Flo a hug but she wasn't allowed to touch her.

'I don't want to stay here, Lizzie.'

'It won't be for long. As soon as you're better you can come home.'

'Will I get better?'

'Course you will, you daft 'a'p'orth!' Lizzie tried to joke.

Flo sniffed back her tears. 'They put me in a bath that smelled funny and then they cut off all me hair.'

'They have to do that,' Lizzie assured her gently. 'And your hair will soon grow again. It needed a good cut anyway.'

'The doctor said I've got to eat grapes. I don't even know what they taste like.'

'They're nice. I'll bring you some from the shop.'

A big shiny tear rolled down Flo's cheek.

'I'll be back tomorrow,' Lizzie whispered as the nurse came in and told her it was time to leave. 'Now try to sleep and dream of them lovely grapes I'm going to bring you.'

'You're shaking like a leaf, gel.' Frank urged Benji on, slapping the reins and clucking his tongue. 'Put the sack across yer knees.' He reached behind the seat and threw the potato sack across her legs. She huddled underneath it. She wasn't really cold even though the fog was still thick. She felt so tired she could go to sleep sitting up. To keep herself awake she told Frank all about Flo.

The fog swirled in patches, then cleared suddenly. The dirty streets of Limehouse were scattered with drunks and street women and a few cabs braving the weather. Lizzie was glad she hadn't had to make this journey on her own.

Frank had lit two oil lamps and hung them on the side

of the cart. Bill used them in the mornings when he drove the cart back from Covent Garden or Spitalfields. A few Salvation Army officers stood outside the Seamen's Mission, the ex-servicemen's hostel. Frank told her there had been a big Easter service there. But Lizzie couldn't stop thinking about Flo all alone in the hospital.

'She's in the best place,' Frank told her as the cart clattered over the cobbles.

'But she might have to go over the water to New Cross.' Lizzie didn't realize she was speaking her thoughts aloud. 'How am I going to get there?'

'I'll take you,' Frank said with a shrug as he shook the reins. 'It won't be no trouble.'

'No,' said Lizzie quickly. 'I wouldn't want that.'

'Don't be daft,' Frank muttered crossly, glancing at her. 'I told you, I'll take you. It ain't no bother.'

They sat in silence for a while and Lizzie wished she hadn't argued with Frank. He had been kind to her tonight and she should be grateful. But she didn't know how long Flo was going to be in hospital. And she didn't want to be in Frank's debt.

'Do you want a cup of tea before you go home?' Lizzie asked politely as Benji came to a halt in Langley Street.

'Nah, thanks all the same. Better get home.' He jumped off the cart and came round to her side. He helped her down and she leaned on him, her body tired and weak. They stood by the door as the fog cleared and the bright moon shone down on the slippery pavement.

'It's Good Friday tomorrow – we're closed for the

day,' Frank said, his silhouette tall in the moonlight. 'I'll take you to the hospital.'

'No,' Lizzie replied quickly. 'I'll catch a tram.' She didn't want to seem ungrateful, so she added quickly, 'You've done enough. I wouldn't have been able to get to the hospital tonight if it wasn't for you.'

He pulled his cap down over his forehead. 'I ain't never met anyone at stubborn as you, Lizzie Allen.' He hesitated as he left her. 'Night, then.'

'Night, Frank. And thanks.'

She watched him jump back up on the cart. In the darkness, his broad shoulders looked like Danny's. For a moment her heart ached so much she let out a moan. If only Danny were with her now to share her troubles.

The horse and cart and Frank melted into the mist. She really didn't want him to take her to the hospital again. She would get up bright and early and ask Lil to keep an eye on Pa. Luckily she wasn't at the shop tomorrow.

As she pulled the string up and slid the key in the latch, her mind was working quickly. Tomorrow she would find out about the trams going to hospital. She was determined to visit Flo without asking help from Frank.

Chapter Fifteen

Violet Catcher sat outside her front door on a wooden chair, her legs protruding from her skirt like pink balloons. The August heat had caused her to roll down her stockings and hold her pinny out, away from her body. She flapped it up and down, inducing a small breeze. Her face was red, her frizzed hair covered by a multicoloured turban. She watched everyone and everything, the heat having no effect whatsoever on her eyesight.

Lizzie let the lace curtain that covered the small window by the front door fall back into place. How was she to leave the house unnoticed? Other than a murder taking place in the house next to Vi's, it looked as though her neighbour was there for the duration.

'Off to the shop, then, ducks?' would be Vi's first question, as Lizzie walked past, followed swiftly by, 'Does the old 'eart good to see you better off, gel, 'specially with your Flo being sick all this time. No one deserves a bit of luck more than you, that's what I says.' Lizzie mimicked Violet's coarse tones. ''Spect you get a nice bit o' fruit and veg on the side? That Frank

Flowers is sure to look after you. Strapping great fella like him.'

Lizzie smiled to herself as she prepared for work. No one considered Bill Flowers a suitable subject for gossip and, officially, it was Bill who was her boss. Sixty years old and hard of hearing, the old coster didn't qualify for juicy bits of scandal. No, Lizzie thought wryly, the truth didn't fetch much attention these days, not like a good bit of tittle-tattle.

She slipped on a pale green summer frock with a pretty scooped neckline and short sleeves. It was her favourite dress from Anne Hailing's parcel. She smoothed down the soft cotton, aware that a little more weight suited her. Her hair was pinned up neatly for work at the shop. The sun had spattered freckles over her nose. She liked to look smart for the shop nowadays. At first she had worn a coarse grey overall, as weighing up the fruit and veg was a filthy job. But as trade became brisker, she left this to Bert. Now she did the books and shared the ordering with Bill. She had come to know the business well and now worked four days each week.

At home things had also improved. She had brought the rent up to date and redeemed the sewing machine. Flo, too, had benefited. Frank provided a regular supply of large, juicy black grapes for her diet. Lizzie took a bunch from Covent Garden each time she visited. And instead of transferring her to New Cross they had moved Flo to a convalescent home near the hospital, an easy trip by bus and tram.

If only Danny was here, Lizzie thought as she picked

up her bag from the chair. If only she knew where he was. Why hadn't he written? 'What's happened, Danny?' she whispered aloud. 'Where are you?'

Five months had passed. Frank had said that a letter from Australia might take months to arrive in England. Where was Danny? In Australia or in some other country? What could have prevented him from writing?

She caught the sad expression on her face in the mirror. What was she miserable for? She had a job to go to, one that had made a difference to their lives, providing security. And it was a job she liked and was good at. Pulling back her shoulders she called out, 'I'm off now, Pa. Lil will be in with your tray at dinner time.'

'Tell her not to bother.'

'It ain't no bother. She likes coming in for a chat.'

Lil always came in at midday. She sometimes brought him a hot meal, or Lizzie would leave cheese and pickles in the kitchen. Lil would add a mug of tea to it, stopping for a few minutes, though it was she who did all the chatting.

'Stubborn as a mule, that father of yours,' she complained good naturedly. 'Tells me to clear off, the daft old bugger. So I tell him he can starve for all I care but I ain't about to let good food go to waste. Then he calls me a nosy parker and tells me I should mind me own business. Silly old sod.'

Lizzie opened the front door and stepped out into a warm summer's day. Vi Catcher gave her a wave. Sighing softly, Lizzie closed the front door and walked across to number seventy-nine.

'You look a smasher today, gel.' Vi nodded at her green dress.

'Thanks, Vi.'

'Nice to see you all done up. You've filled out a bit since you been at that shop. Must be all the fruit and veg doing you good.'

Lizzie smiled. 'Was the cauli I brought you last week all right?'

'Did me a real treat, that. Put a bit of cheese with it and baked it in the oven. Made it last for three days. But you shouldn't have troubled, love. You can't afford to spend yer money on me.'

'It didn't cost me a penny, Vi. They were left over from Saturday. I gave one to Lil and thought you'd like the other.'

'Too true. Anything you got left over I'll have off you,' Vi said eagerly.

Lizzie felt sorry for Vi even though she was an old gossip. She never had any visitors and no one knew if she had any family. She'd lived alone in the house for as long as Lizzie could remember.

Vi put up her fat hand to shield her eyes from the morning sun. 'How's your Flo doing, then? Last time I saw you she was being shifted to that convalescent 'ome.'

'She likes it there,' Lizzie told her. 'They've got nice gardens and when it's sunny she can go outside if she's well wrapped up.'

'If me legs was up to it, I'd go over and see her meself. Dunno how you keep making all them bus journeys.' Vi raised her eyebrows. 'Old Tap given you all the once over, has he? That fever has a nasty habit of spreading.'

'Dr Tap tests us regularly and we're all clear.' Lizzie knew Vi was afraid of catching diseases.

'Nasty disease, that is,' Vi sighed. 'Your mum used to say to me she was more worried about health than money and I reckon she was right. As I was saying to Mrs B down the road whose uncle had a touch of it last year—'

Lizzie began to move away. 'I'd better go. I'm late already.'

'Give Flo me love!' Vi boomed out.

As Lizzie walked the sun bathed her in its soft early glow. It was a glorious morning. All the scents of the island whirled into her nose. They brought back childhood, the hot summers spent in Island Gardens under the trees. Flo, as plump as a puppy, Babs sitting on the edge of the pond with the boys, catching minnows. And when it was time to come home, there was tea to look forward to, a rich fruit cake and sometimes a treat of toffee apples.

She closed her eyes for a moment. Her long dark lashes flickered down on her cheeks. They were all so happy then. What had happened to Babs and Vinnie? She had long since stopped asking either of them for money and none was forthcoming. They were like strangers, coming and going without speaking. What could she do to make it right again?

Twenty minutes later and she had arrived at Ebondale Street. The fruit and veg were already laid out in their boxes. Bill would have brought all the fresh stock on the cart from the city early this morning. By the looks of it Bert had finished the display and he had drawn the blind up in the shop window. The sun glinted off the freshly cleaned glass and the white price tickets she had made for the bargains stood up straight in their boxes. Each piece of fruit would be fresh and shiny. Attention to detail helped to boost turnover, and low prices enticed the customers.

This was her future, here, at the shop. She must stop dwelling on the past. Tonight she would catch a bus to see Flo. Perhaps they could sit out in the garden and enjoy the summer evening. Flo had been very ill but now she was recovering.

There was a lot to be grateful for.

The bell over the shop door tinkled as Lizzie walked in. Frank came out from the back room and smiled when he saw her.

'Hello, Frank,' she said, surprised to see him dressed in a suit and tie. 'Where you off to, then?'

'As a matter of fact, I'm taking the day off to go up West,' he told her.

'What's happening to the barrow?'

Frank shrugged. 'Well, going up to Cox Street ain't a matter of life and death, is it? I've more important business to attend to.'

Lizzie didn't say what she was thinking. That Bill relied on his son to take the barrow up to the market. The money Frank took at market wasn't a great deal, but together with the takings at the shop it paid all the bills and wages.

When Lizzie tried to pass Frank, he took hold of her

arm. 'Ain't you gonna ask me what the business is?'

'No, Frank. That's your concern. Now, is there anything you want me to do here? And where's Bert? I didn't see him out the front.'

'He's gone down to make himself a cup of tea.'

She frowned. 'Bert usually has his break at eleven.'

Frank nodded. 'I told him to nip off early. I've left everything priced up. King Edwards at sixpence for eight pounds, parsnips at tuppence a pound and the other veg at a penny a pound for a good mixture. There's leeks, onions and shallots all weighed up in bags and ready for the customer. See? I had it all done early this morning, before breakfast.'

'So you have.' She gazed around the shop. 'But why? I would have prepared them before doing the books. That's what you pay me for.'

'Truth is, I thought you might like to come up West with me. Get the experience. Me business today is with a new supplier.'

'A new supplier? Who?' she asked in surprise.

'Well, that's what I've got to find out, haven't I? This bloke I met at the market said they're setting up a new line in fruit and veg. From what he said, I thought we might be interested.'

Lizzie looked at Frank, unable to dismiss the growing suspicion that sometimes he resembled Vinnie. The way he talked and his manner suggested something a little underhand. Although she didn't want to think it, she wondered if Frank had the same attraction to easy money as her brother.

'Your father brings our stock from market,' Lizzie said quickly. 'It's fresh and cheap. Why should we want another supplier?'

Frank's eyebrows shot up. 'Ain't you ever thought about the day the old man will retire? I mean, he's sixty-one now and fitter than most. But there will come a time when he'll want to ease up.'

'Couldn't Bert take over the horse and cart?' Lizzie suggested.

'What, can you see Bert pittin' his brains against them Covent Garden traders?' Frank gave a disparaging laugh. 'I don't think so. Don't even know if he could find his way there, come to think of it.'

Lizzie knew Frank was right. But perhaps Bert had never really been given the chance to prove himself. She wanted to say as much, but didn't. She and Bert were lucky to have jobs. She couldn't tell Frank how to run his own business.

'Anyway,' Frank said, shrugging back his shoulders, 'this bloke has got one of them new fangled motor vans. Reckons he can deliver the goods instead of us having to fetch them.'

'You mean do away with the horse and cart?' Lizzie asked in a shocked tone.

'No. Not at first. But we've got to move with the times. Think of the future.'

'But delivery would cost money wouldn't it?' Lizzie asked, forgetting herself. 'It would cut down our profits and—'

Frank broke in with an impatient sigh. 'It occurred to

me that as you were going over to Flo, after seeing this bloke, we could go to the hospital together. Thought a big bunch of flowers wouldn't go amiss, something a bit special. We could choose some nice ones at Ludgate Circus, all the colours of the rainbow.' Softening his voice he added, 'I reckon your little sister deserves a bit of a treat once in a while, don't you? Buck her up a bit.'

Perhaps she had misjudged Frank? Sometimes she was surprised at how thoughtful he could be. Also, he was Danny's brother. She had to remember that.

'That's kind of you, Frank . . .' she said doubtfully.

'The answer is no, right?' He gave her a wide grin. 'Well, I won't force you into anything you don't want,' he said easily. 'And I won't go running before I can walk, either. I'll keep in mind all you've said. But, in the interests of business, I can't turn a deaf ear to a good proposition, now can I?'

'No, course not, Frank. I wish you luck.'

'Thanks. I 'ope I won't need it.'

Frank walked out of the shop, his broad shoulders swaying, and Lizzie wondered if she had done right. She enjoyed the business so much. It would have been exciting to learn about a new supplier and whether or not it would benefit them. It would also have been wonderful to see Flo's face as they gave her a big bunch of flowers, fresh from Ludgate Circus. However, she couldn't change her mind now.

She went out to the back room where Bill was stacking potatoes. The small room was like an oven. He had sweat dripping from his lined forehead and he was passing a filthy rag over it, groaning and wheezing.

'Mornin', Lizzie,' he mumbled, putting his hands on his hips and stretching.

'Morning, Bill. What's happened?' There was veg all over the floor.

'Had an accident with the taters,' he groaned. 'I ain't no 'ercules any more.'

'Let me help.' Lizzie put on her overall and tied back her hair.

Bill sighed as he prodded a large, dirty potato with the tip of his boot. 'Me blooming back is giving me gyp.'

'This won't take a moment. You make yourself a cuppa,' she told him, reaching for the brush and pan and wondering if Frank's prediction wasn't nearer to coming true than any of them had supposed.

Chapter Sixteen

It was early in September when Frank Flowers gave himself the once over in the chipped shop mirror. He was preparing to meet Vinnie Allen. The knocked-off suit with the wide lapels was just the right fit. A shade large on the shoulders, but he liked that. The blue serge made him look taller, too.

'And where do you think you're off to again?' demanded Bill Flowers as he stood in the doorway of the storeroom in his grimy apron, tatty cloth cap and scruffy boots. 'You're supposed to be down the market with the barra.'

Frank hadn't realized his father was there.

'The barra ain't lucrative, old man. I ain't wasting me time on it no more.' Frank continued to inspect himself in the mirror above the till.

'You must be jokin'. That barra's a little goldmine.'

'No it ain't. It's just a lot of hard work for a pittance.'

'At this rate, you ain't ever going to die of overwork are you?' scoffed Bill Flowers as he shuffled towards his son.

'No, and I don't intend to neither.' Frank tugged

lightly at his tie. It was navy blue, discreet yet jaunty. He reckoned the plain dark suit and white shirt was spot on. He and Vinnie had a nice little deal going on suits. Through their contact up West they made a tidy little profit.

'Where you goin', all dressed up like that? You look a real dandy.'

Frank combed back his hair carefully. 'Why don't you shut yer trap and give us all a rest.'

'Who's gonna 'elp me in the shop?' the old man demanded. 'Lizzie ain't in today.'

Frank stopped combing his hair. 'No, and don't you know it. Look at this place. It's a bloomin' tip.'

'It's a storeroom. It ain't supposed to be tidy.'

'And it ain't supposed to be waist deep in rotting veg, either.'

'Why don't you clean it up yerself, then? I got a bad back and you do bugger all.'

Frank told himself he wasn't going to get into a row this morning. 'I got more important matters to see to. It's your mess. You clean up. I'm off.'

Bill Flowers blew his dripping nose loudly, stuffing the rag into the sleeve of his cardigan. 'Well you ain't takin' my money with you and that's a fact.'

'I'll take what's owing to me, you stingy old sod,' Frank muttered contemptuously. 'Look at you. No wonder we've been losing trade all these years. Who wants their fruit and veg served up by a flea-ridden old coster?'

The old man narrowed his eyes. 'I put clothes on yer back and fed you and if it wasn't for me you'd have nothing. They'd have taken you away and put you in an orphanage if I hadn't stopped 'em.'

'Yeah, well maybe I'd have done better if they had,' Frank growled as he turned and walked over to the till.

Bill Flowers hurried after him. 'You keep away from that till!'

Frank's eyes darkened. 'Stay out of me way or—'

'Or what?' sneered the old man. 'I warn you. I'll blow the whistle if you lay a finger on me. I know all about them scams you pull.'

'You do that and you'll be the first to suffer,' Frank snarled. 'If I go down, you'll go with me, old man. I'll make sure of that.'

'I ain't done nothin' wrong!'

In one swift movement Frank reached his father and thrust him against the wall. The old man let out a startled yelp as a fist tightened round his throat. 'If you know what's good for you,' hissed Frank through his teeth, 'you won't breathe a word about what you think you know. And if ever the coppers come round when I'm not here, you just think of a good story to send them on their way. After all,' Frank continued as he increased the pressure round his father's scrawny neck, 'you'd have trouble explaining youself to the Old Bill if they found half a bloody gents outfitters down in the airey, wouldn't you?'

'Y . . . you threatenin' me?'

'Yeah, that's exactly what I'm doing.' Frank pushed his face up to his father's. 'Savvy?'

Bill Flowers spluttered, gasping for breath. 'I . . . I'll bet you ain't told *her* about that letter yet, neither!'

Frank stared into the watery old eyes that were bulging out of their sockets. He wasn't going to let the old devil see how much that last remark troubled him. Slowly he released his grasp. 'What letter?' he asked evenly.

'The one our Danny sent her from Australia,' came the spluttered reply. 'The one her sister brought round here.'

'How do you know about that?' Frank curbed the urge to throw the old man across the room.

'I . . . I 'eard her – that Babs. She come in the shop, didn't she, the silly cow. Pinchin' someone else's letters for you, she is. That's thievin' in my book.'

'So you was listening, were you, you nosy old devil?' Frank laughed, despite his anger. Carefully he shrugged his jacket back into place. 'Well, let's you and me get one thing clear. It's in your interest that the girl stays here at the shop. Without her, you and the shop would be in a right state. She's brought in the custom and worked like a bloody slave to clean this place up. If you open your big mouth, it's you who'll lose out, not me.' Frank smiled nastily as he walked to the cash register and pressed one of the keys. The drawer sprung open. He grabbed at a handful of notes and pushed them into his breast pocket.

'You're me own son,' Bill Flowers wheezed as he leaned against the wall, 'but by God, you're a bastard.'

Frank laughed again as he walked slowly to the store-room door. 'I'm glad we had our little talk. Clears the air a bit. Cheerio, Dad.'

Once out in the fresh September breeze, Frank took a deep, satisfied breath, inhaling the oxygen deep into his lungs. He walked along Ebondale Street with a spring in his step. What his father had said about Danny's letters had caught him off guard. It was a bit of bad luck, the old bugger overhearing Babs when she'd brought the letter into the shop. She was supposed to go to Ferreter's place at Poplar. Still, he was on to a winner there. That letter had given him the break he needed. He'd written to Danny himself and made certain that what he said would stop him from ever writing again. Mind, he'd told Babs to watch for more letters, just in case. He'd have to keep Babs happy, the flighty little piece. She really fancied her chances with him and he saw no harm in stringing her along.

Frank whistled a little tune, pleased with himself. The old man had come to depend on Lizzie. They all had. She was a nice little earner. She was bright, quick and she wasn't bad looking. Business had never been better.

Frank laughed to himself. Life was looking up. Things, at last, were going his way.

A screech of brakes brought the open top bus to a halt. They stepped down on to the pavement and Lizzie paused, turning to stare at the vehicle.

'I've never been on one of them open top buses before. It was wonderful,' she told Frank.

They watched the bus move off, staring at the large number nine displayed next to its stated route: Kensington Road, Piccadilly, the Strand and Charing Cross. Now they were at Ludgate Hill and the magnificent dome of Saint Paul's filled the skyline. A late-September haze softened the purple-blue crown of the most famous church in London.

'You could see everything from up there,' Lizzie gasped as the bus disappeared. 'All those shop windows and the people dressed up so nicely . . .'

'That's the city for you, gel. 'Specially up this way. This is where it's all happening.'

'I've never seen so many motor cars.'

'As I said,' Frank told her with a shrug, 'we gotta keep up with the times.'

Lizzie nodded thoughtfully. She had finally agreed to meet Mr Cole, the fruit and veg supplier Frank had been talking about for weeks. Perhaps Frank was right and the horse and cart were outdated. She knew Bill was dead set against any change, but she had slowly come round to Frank's way of thinking. Not that it was up to her to give an opinion, but she was flattered that Frank wanted it.

Lizzie stared at a big motor car full of top hats. 'I wonder if it's anyone famous,' she gasped, her eyes riveted as it passed by.

'Look, there's the king.' Frank pointed to the passenger in the rear seat, a well-dressed man with a small beard.

'Oh, now you're having me on.'

'Well, I can't help it, can I?' Laughing, Frank took her arm. 'Come on, let's eat.'

'Won't it cost a lot up here?'

'This is a business meeting. I told you.'

She looked doubtfully at him. 'Are you sure?'

'Course.' They strolled down Fleet Street and turned

off at Shoe Lane. Frank was easy company and he made her laugh. He told her a lot about London. About how on Sundays, if she wanted to see anyone famous, she should go to Hyde Park. He told her it was full of carriages and horse riders, and that just watching them parade up and down could fill up a whole day.

'See that little place with the bow windows?' Frank said suddenly. 'That's where we're headed.'

'It looks ever so posh, Frank. I don't feel dressed up enough.'

'You're the prettiest girl I've seen all day,' he told her quietly. 'Mr Cole will be very impressed.'

What was this Mr Cole like, she wondered? She was very nervous. What would she say? What questions should she ask? Frank had told her he would do most of the talking, but when she had a question she should speak up and ask it.

It was quieter down this road. There were no buses and only a few motor cars. Everyone's clothes looked very expensive and rather heavy. The suits with long jackets looked elegant and smart. Would she look out of place in her green summer frock? Frank didn't seem to notice. And now she was too excited to worry about what she was wearing.

The sign above the shop with the bow window said 'Batsford's Fine Food Restaurant'.

'It's not like your Savoy,' apologized Frank as he pushed open the door and the bell tinkled. 'But the food is good.'

All the couples at the tables looked well dressed. The

young men wore suits and the women had fashionable hairstyles. There was a pleasant haze of smoke in the room and the aroma of cooking.

'Well?' whispered Frank as they stood there. 'What's the verdict?'

She could feel herself blushing. 'It's lovely, Frank. I just ain't been in a place like this before.'

'No one would guess it. I'll bet all the girls are envious of you.' She looked up at him. He was staring straight into her eyes. 'You look beautiful.'

'Hello, Mr Flowers,' a voice said, and Lizzie jumped.

'Hello, Rose. Is our table free?'

The waitress nodded. 'Just give me a minute to clear it.'

Before Lizzie could ask anything, Rose was leading them to a corner table. Covered in a starched white cloth, it looked very impressive.

Frank pulled out a chair. Lizzie sat down and he sat next to her.

'When will Mr Cole be here?' she whispered.

Frank looked towards the door. 'We'll give him ten minutes before we order.' He passed her the menu. 'Let's choose what we're gonna have.'

She read aloud, 'Beef soup, sausages, mash and onions, steak and onion pie, baked potatoes, fish and chips, roast lamb—'

Frank grinned. 'You reckon you can eat all that lot in one go?'

She giggled. 'I'll have what you have.'

'That's me girl,' he laughed. "We'll order the biggest lamb chops they've got.'

'Lamb!' She had only eaten scrag-end since the war.

'Then we'll have apple pie and custard that melts on your tongue.'

'I couldn't eat afters as well.'

'You don't know till you try.'

Lizzie felt very special, sitting in a restaurant and being part of everything that was going on. She couldn't help liking the feeling. Frank's blue eyes met hers and she blushed.

'What about Mr Cole?' she asked quickly.

Frank shrugged. 'We'll give our order. They won't wait all day.'

'Your usual, Mr Flowers?' asked the waitress with a smile.

'Yeah, thank you, Rose. And the same for the young lady. Oh, and two lemonades please. And, er . . . we're expecting someone only he ain't shown up yet.'

Rose gave Lizzie a quick glance. 'I'll put your orders through anyway.'

'She's very pretty.' Lizzie wondered if Rose was one of the conquests that Reg Barnes had alluded to at the Christmas party when he had called Frank a Casanova?

'Is she? Can't say as I'd noticed.'

The two tall glasses of lemonade arrived, a thin slice of lemon floating on the fizzy tops. 'To us!' Frank lifted his glass and chinked it against hers.

Rose brought their meals. Succulent lamb chops with gravy running over them, crisp brown baked potatoes and mint sauce served in a little glass dish with a silver spoon. Frank served her a portion. Her knife slipped through the tender meat like butter; she had never tasted anything so delicious. In no time at all she had eaten every scrap.

Frank glanced at her plate. 'Pretty good for someone with a small appetite.'

She giggled. 'I can't believe I've eaten all that.'

'And you ain't finished yet.' Frank nodded to the puddings that Rose brought to the table. The pie and custard disappeared as quickly as the chops. After their empty dishes were removed, Lizzie gasped. 'I forgot. Mr Cole ain't turned up!'

'No, he ain't, has he?' Frank frowned. 'All I can say is, I'm sorry I dragged you up here. It's a bit embarrassing, actually.'

'If Mr Cole can't be bothered to turn up on time for an appointment like this,' she said as they stared at the door, 'I wouldn't like to depend on his delivery service.'

Frank looked at her for a long while before replying. Arching one eyebrow he nodded slowly. 'You got a point there, gel. You ain't even met the bloke and you've sussed him out already.'

'Oh, I shouldn't have said that.' Lizzie wished she'd kept quiet.

'Yes you should,' Frank said at once. 'He's stood us up, ain't he?' Frank glanced at her quickly. 'That's not to say I ain't enjoyed every minute of yer company.'

Lizzie blushed. They were silent for a moment, then Frank got up and went to the till to pay. When he came back, he pulled out her chair and she stood up.

'Sorry you come for nothin',' he said gruffly.

They stood outside on the pavement and Frank rubbed his chin. 'Tell you what, let's take a walk back up to Saint Paul's – should see a few nice carriages on a day like this. Then we can catch a bus from Cannon Street to the convalescent home. Take Flo that big bunch of flowers.'

'Well . . . I don't know . . .'

'A bit of exercise to walk off our dinner won't go amiss.'

She didn't argue. She wanted to see Flo. Going across the city now would mean she wouldn't have to get a bus later. They turned the corner of Shoe Lane and Frank pointed up at Saint Paul's. 'Looks like a picture postcard, don't it? A real work of art.'

Lizzie nodded, enthralled. 'Miss Evans taught us there's six hundred steps to the Whispering Gallery.' She laughed. 'After them lamb chops I dunno if I'd even get up the first few.'

'Blimey, you wouldn't catch me trying it,' Frank chuckled. 'Come on, let's get them flowers for Flo.'

She chose chrysanthemums, lilies and sweet Williams from a stall on Cannon Street. Frank insisted on paying for them.

'This is the new K type,' Frank told her as they jumped on the bus and sat down. 'The driver sits behind that shield over the engine. Gives him a bit of protection. Pretty smart contraptions ain't they?'

Lizzie felt as though she was on holiday, though as she'd never had one she could only guess at what that felt like. She gazed out at the bustling streets. 'Oh, Frank, I love London. I reckon we live in the best city in the world.'

'It would take something to beat it,' Frank agreed, sliding his arm along the back of the seat. 'I wouldn't give you a shilling for the likes of Sydney.'

For a moment Lizzie continued to look out of the window, then slowly she turned to stare at him. 'Sydney? What made you say Sydney?'

Frank blinked his fair lashes. 'Did I say Sydney?'

'Yes . . . you did. Have you heard from Danny?' Her heart started to beat very fast.

'No, course not. Sydney just tripped off me tongue. Dunno what I said that for.' Frank drew his arm from the back of the seat and loosened his tie. 'I said it 'cos it was the first place I thought of, seeing as how our Danny's there, or so we hope.' He shrugged. 'I suppose me little brother's on me mind, not hearing from him. Blimey, gel, don't you think I'd tell you if I'd heard? In fact, I'd bet me last bob that it would be you he'd write to first, not me or the old man. After all, you are his girl, aren't you?'

She nodded sadly, hope quickly turning to despair. She felt suddenly empty, as if all the joy had gone out of the day. For one moment she had thought Frank may have heard something – anything – about Danny.

'Hey, come on, cheer up.' Frank nudged her. 'He'll be writing to you soon. It can't be much longer now.'

She managed a smile. Then, looking out of the window, she blinked back the tears. It wouldn't do to let Frank see her upset. After all, he was trying to cheer her up. She didn't want to seem ungrateful.

*

The old Victorian manor house loomed out of the trees. Grange Mount was used as a convalescent home for patients discharged from hospital but still recovering from infectious diseases. The corridors were dark and gloomy, the dormitories austere. Lizzie always tried to make her visits bright. Last time she had come she'd brought a cover for Flo's bed. Comprising odd pieces of material stitched together to form a quilt of many colours, she had hemmed it round in blue stitching.

In Flo's dormitory there were six beds, three on each side of the room. Flo was reading a book on one of them as Lizzie entered.

She looked up. 'Oh, Lizzie, you've come!'

Lizzie went to hug her. 'Course I've come. Don't I always?'

'Yes, but I always think you might not.'

'That's daft.' Lizzie held Flo away to inspect her. She had lost all her puppy fat and her cheeks were pinched, but her lank brown hair had grown and had a nice shine to it.

'Do you think they'll let me out soon?' Flo asked miserably.

Lizzie sat on the bed. 'The doctor said you're nearly better. It won't be long before you're home.' She didn't want to raise Flo's hopes. The matron had been very non-committal when asked about Flo's release date.

'They ain't said nothing to me.' Flo looked belligerent and Lizzie smiled. That was more like the old Flo.

'Dr Tap has told me I've got to feed you up when you come home. And you'll have to take yer medicine.'

'But we ain't got no money for medicine.'

'We'll manage,' Lizzie assured her. 'I'm working five days a week at the shop now. Trade's really picked up. Next time you even so much as sneeze, day or night, I'm going to send Bert round for old Tap.'

They laughed, sending a happy echo around the drab room. 'I don't think Dr Tap would like seeing Bert in the middle of the night,' giggled Flo. 'Bert would scare 'im to death.'

''Specially in his long johns.' Lizzie wiped the tears from her eyes. It was so good to laugh again.

'Where's that little girl you made friends with?' Lizzie glanced at the next bed. There was no pillow, only a blanket draped over it.

'Louise?' Flo bit down on her lip. 'One night they came and took her away. The nurses and doctors were wearing them 'orrible white clothes. They all looked like ghosts.'

Lizzie remembered what the sister had said at the hospital about seeing 'ghosts'. Her mind went back to Flo lying in that narrow bed, with the fever raging through her. She realized now that she was one of the lucky ones that the 'ghosts' had never spirited away.

'Let's go in the garden.' Lizzie changed the subject quickly. 'I've brought someone with me who wants to see you.'

'Is it Bert?' Flo asked excitedly as she pulled on her coat.

'No . . . no, it ain't Bert. It's Frank. He's got a present for you.'

'Oh.' Flo looked away.

'Ain't you pleased?'

'Why has he come to visit me?'

''Cos he likes you, that's why.'

'How can he like me, if he don't know me?'

'But he does know you. He always gives me the grapes – he's been very kind.' Lizzie linked her arm through Flo's 'He's bought you a big bunch of flowers to cheer you up.'

At the door, Flo stopped, tears in her eyes. 'I can't wait to come home.'

'It won't be long now.'

'Can we go down Island Gardens again? Like we used to when we were kids.'

Lizzie laughed. 'Course we can.'

'And buy sherbet dips and play on the swings?'

They were laughing and crying together now. Lizzie hugged her, closing her eyes. 'Oh, Flo. I've missed you.' When she pulled away, she sniffed back the tears. 'We're a daft pair, ain't we?'

They held hands as they walked along the corridor, singing, 'All of our troubles and cares of the day, like silver bubbles drifting away. Just a cosy nest, sweet and Heaven blessed, like a bluebird's nest in Sleepy Valley.'

Chapter Seventeen

'When's young Flo coming home?' Vi Catcher asked in a curious voice.

Lil was waiting for Reg Barnes to trim the fat from the mince. She intended to cook it for Doug tonight, with a few fried onions. She hoped Reg wouldn't take long. If she got talking to Vi she'd be standing here till dusk. 'Sometime today,' she told Vi, who was next in line at the meat stall. It was Wednesday at Cox Street market and trade was brisk.

'They ain't sending her home on a bus are they?'

'Course not. The ladies up Hailing House offered to fetch her in their motor car.'

'Only right they should an' all. A blooming great vehicle like that just standing idle waiting for—'

'Yeah, it was a nice gesture,' Lil said before Vi got into her stride. 'That'll do nicely Reg,' she called hurriedly to the butcher. 'Doug don't mind a bit of fat here and there.'

'I been meaning to call,' Vi continued, 'but I don't want to intrude.'

'There ain't much Lizzie can't cope with,' Lil said

briskly, wishing Reg would get a move on. He was trimming the meat and gassing with the customers at the same time. 'Needless to say she's over the moon about Flo.'

'She was lucky, that little 'un, she could 'ave had an 'emorrhage. Wonder if Reg has got any more of that mince going cheap.' Vi glanced at Lil. 'You still got to eat, ain't you, no matter what happens.'

Lil nodded. 'You'd better catch his eye quick.'

But Vi was not to be rushed. 'Unlucky house, number eighty-two. I've had my share of misfortune, but what with Tom losing his legs, then Kate going and that Vinnie turning out such a bug—'

Lil swung round, her dark eyes flashing. 'Well, you could look at it like that,' she told Vi crisply, 'or you could say the Allens were past the worst. At least Tom came home from the bloody war and Flo beat the fever. And if I know Lizzie, she won't let the grass grow under her feet when it comes to keeping the family together!'

'Yeah, yeah,' Vi agreed hurriedly. 'I just meant they had a bit of bad luck, that's all.'

'Well, looks like it's changed to good now,' Lil added tartly as she turned back to Reg Barnes and reached over for the parcel of meat wrapped in newspaper.

Reg winked at Lil. He raised his thick dark eyebrows at Vi. 'Now what can I do for you, young lady?'

'None of yer lip, you cheeky sod. I want what she had only cheaper. And trim off the fat. I like mine lean.'

'Cows don't fall off trees, you know,' called the butcher, passing Lil her change.

'No, they fall straight into your bloody lap!' shouted Vi, and the women round the stall all laughed.

'Well, I'd better be on me way,' said Lil quickly. 'I'll tell Lizzie you asked after her.'

'You do that. And tell her if she wants anything—'

'I'll tell her. And watch him with that mince,' Lil grinned. 'You never know what comes out of that mincer.'

'Only the best for you ladies,' shouted Reg, enjoying the joke. 'Cross me 'eart and 'ope to fly.'

'It's not you 'eart you'll want crossing,' bawled Vi. 'It'll be that big greasy palm of yours that you keeps shoving under our noses!'

Lil hurried off, pushing the meat deep into her shopping bag. She could still hear Vi's voice bellowing out. Vi was all right, but feed her a titbit and it would be headlines by tea time.

Lil made her way across to the fish stall.

'Yer looking glam as usual,' cried Boston, twirling his handlebar moustache under his straw boater. 'Must be the quality of all me fish that keeps you looking so blooming healthy.'

'It ain't yer fish, you saucy bugger,' smiled Lil. 'Got me heads and tails?'

Boston reached under the stall and brought out a package. 'That cat of yours must catch rats the size of elephants on what you gives it to eat.'

'As long it don't start bringing elephants to the back door, I ain't complaining.' Lil tucked the parcel on top of the meat. 'While I'm here I might as well have a bit of rock salmon for tomorrow. I'm gonna do me neighbour a nice fish pie for supper.'

'You mean Lizzie?' Boston asked quietly.

'Yeah,' Lil nodded. 'Flo's comin' home today.'

'The fever well and truly cleared up has it?'

'Well, the kid wouldn't be coming home if it wasn't, would she? Now concentrate on what you're cutting up on that slate of yours. I don't want no bones.'

The fishmonger grinned. 'Trust me, gel.'

'That's what they all say,' smirked Lil. 'I'd trust you just as far as I could throw you, cock.'

Lil liked shopping at the market. All right, none of the traders were saints. Everyone knew that Reg Barnes had a bit on the side and Elfie Goldblum would flog you brass for gold if he could get away with it. Fat Freda had been known to slip you the wrong change – to her advantage, of course – and Boston Brown's fish hadn't always come straight from Billingsgate. But they were a good laugh and took all the insults with a smile.

Lil walked back through the market, but just as she came to the second-hand clothes stall she caught sight of Frank Flowers. He was leaning on a lamppost, talking to a girl. Lil picked up a navy blue jumper and examined it, looking up every so often. A third person joined them. She wasn't surprised to see it was Vinnie Allen. They all stood talking for a while, then walked off in different directions.

Lil dropped the jumper and made her way out of the market. It was none of her business – Doug would say – what that little trio was up to. Doug always told her she'd sniff out a gnat's fart at a mile. He'd also reminded her that the Flowerses had been good to Lizzie and she'd have to agree. There was no denying that life was a lot rosier now for the Allens than when poor old Kate was alive.

As she headed home, Lil decided not to tell Lizzie what she'd seen. It would serve no purpose to upset the girl. But that Vinnie mixed with a rough bunch! Last time she had bumped into him, it had been up Poplar High Street with the bookie. Was Frank also involved with Mik Ferreter?

By the time Lil reached Langley Street she felt proud of herself for making the decision to resist temptation. She would button her lip for once.

But resisting one temptation didn't mean she had to resist another, did it?

As soon as Doug got in, she'd tell him.

Lizzie had made the bed with clean sheets and washed all Flo's clothes. The wardrobe, cupboard and floor were scrubbed and disinfected. And the stairs and passage were as clean as a new pin. The boiler had been going non-stop since the weekend. Taking four days off from the shop meant that she could be with Flo until Sunday. Then Lil said Flo could stay with her until half term whilst Lizzie was at the shop, and, if Flo felt better, she could go back to school before Christmas. Flo said she would like that. She missed her friends and it would break the ice before the New Year.

Just as Lizzie came down the stairs, a small hand came through the letterbox and grabbed the string. Lizzie's heart hammered in her chest. She stopped still as the door slowly opened.

There stood Flo, eyes wide as saucers in her pale, gaunt face. Behind her was James, carrying a big brown paper parcel tied up with string. Her mind flashed back to the day he had brought her home from Hailing House. That had turned out a dreadful day, but Lizzie knew this was going to be one of the happiest in her life.

Flo was home.

Bursting with joy, Lizzie ran down the rest of the stairs. They were soon in each other's arms, laughing and crying at the same time.

'Flo, Flo,' was all Lizzie could mumble, sniffing back her tears. She looked at James and went red.

'I've 'ad a lovely ride,' Flo said wheezily. 'We went really fast this time.'

'No too fast,' said James with a wink at Flo. She giggled as he handed her belongings to Lizzie.

'Thank you for bringing her home,' Lizzie said quietly. There was a tremble in her voice. 'Will you thank the ladies for me?'

'Indeed I will,' said James in a deep voice. 'Is there anything else?'

Flo giggled again.

'No thank you.'

James touched his hat and returned to the big black car. They watched it move off slowly.

When Lizzie closed the door she looked Flo up and down. 'Well, miss, we've got to put some weight on you.'

Flo looked at her with big brown eyes that seemed almost too large for her face. She was wearing her old gabardine mac that was now too small, the sleeves stopping half way down her arms. Lizzie had put a bit by for a new coat and was saving the excursion to the market for a surprise.

'Where is everyone?' Flo asked looking round.

'Babs is at the House and Bert's at the shop.'

'Ain't you supposed to be there too?'

'I've got the rest of the week off.'

Flo pouted in her old fashion. 'You ain't gonna be around all the time tellin' me what to do?'

Lizzie kept a straight face. 'Oh yes I am. I got it all planned out. It's yer medicine three times a day, sitting nice and quiet till tea time, then early to bed.'

Flo's face dropped. 'Ain't I allowed out to see me friends?'

Lizzie shook her head.

'I thought you said I could go back to school for Christmas.'

'I thought you didn't like school.'

'Well I've changed me mind, ain't I?' Flo said belligerently.

At this, Lizzie couldn't keep from laughing. 'That got you going, miss, didn't it?'

Flo looked cross for a moment, then burst into laughter. Suddenly the door of the front room opened. Lizzie and Flo turned to stare at their father sitting in his wheelchair. He pushed the wheels forward and moved out into the passage. He looked clean and shaved and his grey hair was neatly combed back from his face. Lizzie couldn't believe her eyes. She had asked him a dozen times if she could help him wash and tidy up before Flo came home. Each time he had refused. Now she knew why. He wanted to surprise them – and he had.

The girls stared at him. Slowly he raised his arms to Flo. She fell into them, hugging him gently. Lizzie saw tears in his pale eyes and she guessed there were big ones in Flo's.

All three of them were silent. Then Flo broke away, sniffing.

'You look a bit thin, me girl,' Tom said huskily, taking out a handkerchief and blowing his nose. Lizzie was pleased to see it was one that she had boiled and ironed yesterday for him.

'Yeah, well, the food at the 'ome wasn't like Lizzie's.' Flo held on to her father's hand, her cheeks flushed.

Tom Allen smiled, his gaze going up to his eldest daughter as he said softly, 'You ain't ever said a truer thing, Florence Allen. Next to yer mother's cooking, yer sister's is the best you'll get anywhere.'

Lizzie was so surprised she didn't know what to say. A lovely warm feeling was melting inside her and she didn't want the moment to end. By the time she had got her breath back, Tom was pushing his chair towards the kitchen and Flo was talking ten to the dozen, giving him a running commentary on the time she had spent away.

Then the front door burst open again. Babs hurried in, breathless and panting. 'Is she home yet?'

Lizzie nodded. 'She's just arrived.'

'The ladies let me come home early,' Babs gasped, dragging off her coat and flinging it on the stair rail. 'I got some sherbet dabs in me pocket.' Delving into her coat, Babs pulled out a brown paper bag. 'Can she have 'em?'

'Course she can,' Lizzie replied. 'And I've got a cake in the pantry. We'll have a nice bit of tea. Pa's in the kitchen too.'

It was Babs' turn to look surprised. 'Blimey,' she grinned, widening her pretty brown eyes. 'That's a first, ain't it?'

Lizzie's heart was beating very fast as she walked down the passage with Babs. They were on speaking terms again. Flo was safely home and Pa had come out from his room to have tea with them in the kitchen. Life felt wonderful.

Lizzie couldn't sleep. She wasn't used to Flo in the bed again, squeezed between her and Babs. There was less room but the extra warmth was lovely. Lizzie tossed and turned. Her mind was still whirling. The family was united once more. She hoped it would always be like this. Pa, Babs, Bert, Flo and her all sitting round the table at supper time as Flo caught up on the news. Only Vinnie had been absent, the family's fly in the ointment.

Lizzie got out of bed, unable to rest. She pulled her coat over her nightdress and went downstairs. The house was silent, except for Bert's snoring, which bounced off every wall.

In the kitchen, Lizzie lit the oil lamp. Bill had given it to her as a little perk of the job when she had first started at the shop. It was like one of the lamps off the cart that Frank had lit the night they came home from hospital in the fog.

Lizzie made herself a cup of tea and sat by the lamp's warm glow. Her thoughts turned to Danny as they always did at night. Whilst she had been visiting Flo in hospital she had been too tired to lie awake for long. A picture of Danny's face would flash up in her mind and she would soon be asleep.

But today, a day of celebration, had left her wide awake, the questions going round and round in her head. Why hadn't Danny written? Where was he? Why had he broken his promise? Did he ever think of her? Could he imagine the depth of sadness in her heart? Did he know that she was still waiting for him?

Lizzie sighed as she stared into the flickering shadows of the kitchen. Suddenly there were shapes and figures filling the chairs and reflected on the walls. Ma was sitting in the rocking chair talking to Granny Watts and Granny Allen, who were perched on the hard wooden seats in their long skirts and shawls. They were all laughing and gossiping about their men and families, every now and then lowering their voices for the best bit of gossip. Other figures crowded round them, ones Lizzie didn't recognize but knew were family too, men, women and children who made up the generations of the Allens and the Wattses.

She felt a deep, tranquil sense of love and security. Her ancestors were there to remind her that life was a drop in a vast ocean.

The figures began to fade, leaving the kitchen quiet

and still again. But the feeling of love and peace remained. Lizzie knew that help had come at the time in her life when she most needed it.

She stood up and extinguished the lamp.

As she went quietly up the stairs, she squared her shoulders. She had to forget about Danny and move on, making the best of everything she had.

Book Three

Chapter Eighteen

1924

'That lets me out,' grunted Frank Flowers. He threw down his cards and raised his arms above his head in a long stretch. The room was filled with smoke; the gambling, drinking and philandering that had gone on in the airey over the Friday night and into the early hours of Saturday had made the air pungent. With his shirtsleeves rolled up and collar removed, Frank scratched the top of his chest. The blond, bristly stubble on his chin had formed into a light beard, unlike that of the man sitting next to him.

The gypsy's dark hair was greased and combed away from his narrow face. Yawning loudly, Mik Ferreter grinned slowly through uneven teeth. 'Well, Frankie boy, I'm gonna have to clean you out. No wonder your old man don't trust you with the takings. You've given it all to me.'

'You ain't kidding, Mik.' Frank laughed nervously. 'It'd pay me to stick to Lena – a whole night with her is a damn sight cheaper than a round of poker with you.'

'Yeah, well, no one comes cheaper than Lena,' muttered Vinnie, who sat on Frank's other side, his elbows resting on the table. His braces hung loosely round his hips as he leaned forward on his chair. A dark blue Homburg was tilted over his forehead and a cigarette dangled from his lips.

Vinnie was getting on Frank's nerves. In fact, Ferreter was too. The luck that had won the bookie the pot on the table was highly suspect, but Frank kept his mouth shut. Ferreter didn't play by the rules. He made them up as he went along.

'Lena ain't a bad looker,' Frank said in mild defence of the woman who had spent the night in his bed.

Vinnie laughed. 'Yeah, but only if you're desperate.'

If that little toerag pushes his luck much further . . . thought Frank angrily, then told himself to calm down. Vinnie was baiting him. He wanted a reaction. Well he wasn't going to get one.

Vinnie nodded to the bedroom, which had not long been vacated. 'Gave her a right good seeing to, did you, Frankie? Let her know who was boss?'

Frank swigged his beer. 'Yeah, well, why not? Might as well enjoy me last days of being single.'

The bookie threw his head back and laughed. 'Now that takes the biscuit, that does.'

'What do you mean?' Frank bristled.

'You ain't gonna be any different when you're hitched, you randy old sod,' said Mik Ferreter gruffly. 'You ain't stopped taking your Johnny out since I've known you. Hardly likely to keep it in there just 'cos you've got a ring on yer finger.'

Frank regarded this as flattery. He grinned. 'Nah, I'm gonna turn over a new leaf. You see if I don't. Anyway, I got me girl's big brother over there to keep an eye out for me.'

The bookie sneered. 'He can't keep an eye out for himself, let alone you.'

Vinnie's close-set eyes slid towards Ferreter. Frank felt a wave of satisfaction. Vinnie had sold his soul to the devil years ago, but Ferreter treated him with no greater respect.

'Dunno about that,' Vinnie objected in a surly voice. 'I ain't done so badly for meself.'

Ferreter's eyes flashed. 'Oh yeah? Is that a fact, now?'

'I mean, I ain't in a lot of shit,' Vinnie corrected himself quickly, 'not like I used to be.'

'And who got you out of the shit?' The black-eyed gypsy tilted his head, his dark eyes menacing.

'Well, course . . . you did, boss.' A hush fell on the room. Frank was glad he wasn't in Vinnie's shoes. 'It's all down to you, boss, all me luck, everything what you done for me,' Vinnie spluttered.

'Say it again, Vincent. Louder this time.'

Vinnie licked his dry lips. 'I owe it all to you, boss. Everything. I owe it all to you.'

'Put money in yer pocket and clothes on yer back, did I?'

Vinnie was sweating, the beads of fearful moisture standing out on his brow. 'You've always seen me right, Mik.'

'And kept the law off yer back. And paid all yer fines.'

'That too . . . that too.' Vinnie nodded hard.

Frank smiled to himself. Vinnie had got too big for his boots, ever since he took over the house in Poplar. Not that a whore house was much of a feather in anyone's cap. All Vinnie had to do was set up a few girls and half a dozen games of poker each week. Poker and tarts – well, even Vinnie couldn't go far wrong with that.

Ferreter narrowed his eyes. He paused, his tongue flicking out to curve slowly round his thin lips. 'And o' course, there was that job a few years back. I hear the Old Bill is still looking for the bloke who done over that poor sod – night watchman, wasn't it? A jeweller's up West?'

Frank turned to stare at Vinnie. Now *this* was interesting.

'I dunno nothing about a jeweller's,' Vinnie blurted, going white. 'I . . . I . . . never went near the place.'

'You and me know that, don't we, old son? But does the law?'

'Y . . . you said you told them . . .'

Ferreter grinned. 'Oh yeah, I told them you was with me.'

'Well then . . .'

'But me memory ain't so good – sometimes. See what I mean? It varies according to me mood.'

Frank felt a pulse throbbing in his temple. His eyes were riveted on Vinnie, whose face had drained of colour.

The bookie nodded slowly. 'Memory's a funny thing, ain't it? Now sometimes I recall that night clear as a bell. You were round my place at Poplar and so were you,

Frank. Yeah . . .' Ferreter gave a chuckle, turning his gaze on Frank. 'You was all dolled up to the nines in one of them flash new suits.'

Frank swallowed. He didn't remember that. And hinting at a flash suit – did Ferreter know about the deals with Vinnie?

The bookie's smile widened. He stroked his cards lightly with the tip of his finger. 'There now, Vincent. Ain't you the lucky one? You got real mates sitting at this table. Mates that'll look out for you whenever the law pays a call. And you, Frank, out the goodness of yer heart, you'd remember that evening 'cos you was wearing that new suit of yours.'

Frank remained silent. A cold sensation was creeping down his spine. Mik Ferreter leaned forward. He laid down three aces. His gaze met Frank's stare then drifted towards Vinnie. 'Reckon I just hit the jackpot.' He counted the notes piled in the middle of the table and stuffed them in his pocket before rising to his feet. Steadily he surveyed the two men watching him. 'We'll have to do this more often. Nice place you got here, Frankie boy.' He swung his jacket from the back of the chair. Pushing the wad of notes into the breast pocket, he playfully punched Vinnie on the jaw. 'Gotta see a man about a dog. Don't bother seeing me out. I know me way.'

The airey door closed. A gust of March wind blew into the room, freshening the foul air. Vinnie slumped over the table, dropping his head in his hands. 'Bastard,' he muttered.

Frank stared at him. 'What was all that about?'

Vinnie didn't reply. It wasn't until Frank poured him another drink and pushed it against his arm that he looked up.

'What's he mean about the jeweller's up West?' Frank was oblivious to the melting pot of anger sitting next to him.

Vinnie downed the beer with a vengeance. 'Use your head, you idiot! What do you think he means?'

Frank half laughed, a nervous, light laugh. 'You were in on that job?'

The younger man closed his eyes. 'At last he susses it.' When he opened them, a look of disdain spread across his face. 'It's all about alibis. He's knitted us together like a bloody jumper.'

Frank's mind had gone blank. 'That job was years ago, anyway.'

'Exactly. That's what I'm saying. Mik hoards things. Keeps it all up here.' Vinnie jabbed a finger at his forehead. 'Like that bloody fire at Chalk Wharf.'

Frank looked at Vinnie blankly. 'Yeah, but that was an accident. You said so yerself.'

Vinnie looked exasperated. 'Mik sent me on that little job because them blokes from over the water were a bit suspect. I was expendable if things went wrong. And they did, didn't they?'

A chill went down Frank's spine as the truth began to dawn. 'Christ almighty, Vinnie, why didn't you get the hell out of it after that?'

Vinnie laughed mirthlessly. 'When are you gonna wake up, you silly sod? No one walks out on Mik

Ferreter, not unless they're tired of breathin' and fancy a swim at the bottom of the river. Mik's in the information business. He collects it, puts it on the back burner till he needs it. Then when he's ready, he'll give you a nice little reminder. Like he did tonight.'

'But I . . . I ain't in his pay!'

'You don't have to be. You're in it up to your neck without a bloody penny in yer palm.' Vinnie half snarled, half laughed. 'For instance, your future old lady ain't gonna be too impressed with your track record, if someone was to tell her. She'd drop you like a hot brick.'

'But I ain't married her yet. I ain't even asked her. I'm a free man still.'

Vinnie arched an eyebrow. 'Married or not, do you fancy that straight-arsed sister of mine will give you a pat on the back for bedding Lena and them other whores?'

Frank felt his neck shrinking down in his shirt. Lizzie wouldn't touch him with a bargepole if she were to find out.

Vinnie chuckled. 'And what about that little deal you cooked up with our Babs? Conveniently forgotten, have you?' He dragged the air noisily through his teeth, his eyes challenging. 'How you got her to pinch Danny's letter from Australia and give it to you? And when she'd done that how you got her to keep a lookout for anything more that might turn up in the post?'

'I did it for Lizzic's own good,' Frank pleaded desperately. 'It turncd out that me brother was seeing someone himself, had a kid by her an' all.'

'Yeah, but you weren't to know that then, were you? You don't know when he hitched up with his missus.'

'But that was three years back. Who's to remember it now?'

Vinnie muttered, 'I'll bet you a pony Mik does.'

'But I ain't never told him.'

Vinnie stood up. He pulled on his coat and straightened his hat. 'You really are a stupid sod. Ferreter knows everything about everyone. He goes for your soft spots. What you're most afraid of losing. Your freedom, your money – or your woman. Whatever it is that hurts most. Don't you know that our Babs has been kipping with him these last two years? Or did you think you was laying her all on your own?'

Frank's mouth fell open. He couldn't believe it. He wouldn't believe it. 'You mean to say you'd let your sister – no more than a kid – sleep with a piece of shite like Ferreter?'

Vinnie shrugged. 'She's been sleeping with you, ain't she? And anyway, I told you, he's got me by the balls. Whatever Ferreter wants, he takes. The only thing he ain't been able to talk between the sheets is your intended. God help you if you think she's gonna let you anywhere near her just 'cos you've put a ring on her finger. All she's after is the shop. She'll have you worn out with all that carrying and lugging and you'll be too knackered to get it up at all.'

Frank jumped to his feet. ''Ere, you watch it, Vin. That's my girl you're talking about!'

Vinnie laughed. 'Yeah, right. Pull the other one. She'd

drop you like a ton of bricks if yer brother come back.'

The mention of Danny was too much for Frank. He lunged at the departing figure and they toppled together against the wall, falling on the sideboard and sending the china crashing. Suddenly a blade flashed in the light. Cold steel pricked Frank's throat as the tip of the knife licked his gullet.

'Don't you ever lay a finger on me again,' Vinnie rasped furiously as he held him down, ''cos if you do, I ain't gonna think twice about giving them ugly tonsils of yours a tweak.'

'T . . . Take it easy,' Frank spluttered, going red in the face. 'I shouldn't have done that. Sorry, mate.'

Vinnie relaxed his grip slowly and slid the knife back into his pocket. 'You keep yer paws to yerself, understand?'

Frank nodded. Vinnie had boasted that he carried a knife, but he hadn't thought anything of it, fancied it was just a bit of bull. But tonight his eyes had been opened.

Vinnie paused at the door. 'Give me sister me best,' he drawled contemptuously. 'Ain't been home much lately – due to the pressure of work.' He patted the pocket of his jacket, his fingers lying briefly on the hard shape beneath the cloth. 'Oh yeah, before I forget. All those deals you're doing on the side . . . we'll have a chat about them soon. Mik wants a piece of the action, thinks you might need a helping hand shifting all them fags and bottles of booze.'

Frank stared incredulously after him. How did Ferreter know about his fag and booze sideline? Vinnie departed and Frank felt sick to his stomach. He slumped down at the table and drank a beer. He felt no better when he'd drunk it so he poured himself another. Then he turned his attention to the bottle of Scotch in the sideboard. Crunching over the broken china, he swore under his breath.

There was only one alternative as far as he could see. Wed Lizzie and go kosher. What if she did want the shop? That was fine by him. Perfect in fact. He no more wanted to work in a greengrocer's than fly to the moon. What he did want was a wife he could trust to run the business, cook his meals and be there in his bed. And, by God, that's what he was going to have.

Chapter Nineteen

Lizzie closed the shop door and shivered as the bell tinkled. She pulled her coat tightly round her. She hadn't noticed the cold until now. Serving the customers kept her warm, but at six trade had dropped off.

Christmas was just two weeks away. She was pleased with the new lines she had added for the festive season. The cakes, sweets and home-made bread were selling well, thanks to the bakery that supplied fresh goods for the shelves. It was as Lizzie was bundling up the last of the fairy cakes into bags for late customers, that Frank appeared. He was wearing his cap, thick jacket and hard-wearing trousers, a scarf tucked warmly round his neck. 'Just put the horse in the stable,' he told her, his breath fanning out in the freezing air. 'Given him a few oats to keep out the cold.'

Lizzie smiled. 'All the deliveries done, Frank?'

'Every last one of them.'

'Well, I think I'll close up now. Bert's just gone and your dad's upstairs. He was feeling the cold today, you know. I wish he would take it a bit easy.'

'Yeah, I know. He worries me an' all.'

'I've told him I can manage in the shop. With Bert in the storeroom and you out on the cart, there's really no need—' Lizzie stopped as she realized he wasn't listening. 'Are you all right, Frank?'

'Oh, er, yeah.' He nodded, removing his cap and folding it up in his mittened hands. 'Except that . . . well,' he looked at her and lifted his shoulders. 'Lizzie, could you and me have a word, d'you think?'

'What, now?'

Frank nodded. 'I'd prefer it if we went downstairs. It's a bit cold in here to talk.'

Lizzie felt her heart sink. She knew by Frank's expression there was something wrong.

'The books are up to date,' she said quickly, resting the broom against the counter. She had already recorded the week's takings. Sometimes on a Saturday she worked on the books down in the airey. Frank always made her a cup of tea, watching in silence as she spread out the books on the big oak table in the front room. With the increase in turnover, she had paid off the shop debts. She hadn't found the bookkeeping difficult. It gave her a thrill to see the rows of figures written down neatly and to know there was nothing owing.

'It's not the books,' Frank told her edgily. 'It's something else.'

Lizzie couldn't think what it could be. Her secret fear was always that now she had accomplished so much at the shop it would all end. She knew Frank was content for her to run the business. He had told her so many times.

But she always wondered if Bill might do something unexpected, like selling up.

'All right,' she said hesitantly. 'I'll lock up.'

But Frank moved towards her, restraining her gently. 'You go on down and put the kettle on. I'll see to everything up here.'

Lizzie handed him the keys. His eyes didn't quite meet hers. She had a sinking feeling. Was Frank going to tell her she wasn't wanted anymore? What would she do if she had to leave the shop? She loved the work now and relied on the regular wage. Would Bert have to leave too? Where would he get another job? Disturbed thoughts hurtled through her mind as she left the shop and walked into the cold December air.

The door to Frank's airey was open as always. Inside the big front room a fire was burning in the grate. There were a few sprigs of holly on the dresser and in the hearth. The room looked festive, Christmas paper chains hanging from one corner to another.

The airey was very familiar now. She almost took it for granted. From the first day she had come here with Danny for the Christmas party, it had felt like a second home. Even when Danny had first gone to Australia she had derived some comfort from it, knowing that it had once been Danny's home too.

Lizzie sat in the chair and gazed at the hot black coals. So much had happened in the three years he had been away. If she concentrated hard, she could almost see his face in the flames . . .

Suddenly there was a click and she jumped. The front

door opened and closed. Frank crossed the room, then took the chair opposite. 'I built up the fire before I went out. Thought it would be nice,' he said, looking uneasy.

She nodded. What was he trying to tell her? She waited, her heart beginning to hammer, but still Frank said nothing.

'Frank, it's nice sitting here but—'

'Did you put the kettle on?'

'No.'

'I'll do it then.' He got up and was about to hurry off when Lizzie stood up too.

'Frank. I don't want a cup of tea. Just tell me what the trouble is.'

He turned and stared at her. For a moment, in the light of the flickering flames, she thought it could be Danny standing there, with his wide blue eyes and thick curly blond hair. Her heart gave a painful clench as Frank moved towards her. 'Oh, there ain't no trouble,' he told her. 'At least, not yet.'

Lizzie frowned. 'What do you mean?'

'Sit down again, gel.'

'But Frank—'

'It'll only take a minute.'

Reluctantly Lizzie sat down again. Frank took the other chair. He cleared his throat and, heaving a sigh, looked directly at her. 'I've got to ask you something.'

'Yes, you said so in the shop.' She waited. She didn't understand. It was not like Frank to act this way.

'You ain't gonna get all upset, are you?'

'How can I answer that, Frank, when I don't know what it is?'

Frank coughed once more. 'It's about . . . well, you and me.'

Lizzie stared at him. 'You and me?'

'Yeah.' Frank took a breath. 'You know how I feel about you?'

'Frank, I don't want to—'

'You're the light of me life, gel. I ain't never overstepped the mark, 'cos I know you was Danny's girl. But he's been gone three years and he's . . . he's got a family of his own now, ain't he?'

Lizzie had tried to forget the day last year when Bill had received a letter from the other side of the world. Its contents had finally put an end to all her dreams. Danny had written to his father telling him he had married a girl in Australia and they had a baby son. When Bill had read it out, Lizzie felt as though the ground had opened up and she was falling into it. Even though Danny hadn't written, the flicker of hope had never died. But the day the letter had come the tiny light was extinguished for ever.

As she sat there, a fist grabbed hold of her heart, sending the pain of betrayal shooting through her body once more.

'I ain't getting any younger . . .' Frank's voice broke into her thoughts. 'I'm twenty-six.' He struggled with his collar, releasing it under his jacket as he added in a rush, 'What I'm trying to say is, will you . . . will you marry me, gel?'

She thought she hadn't heard properly. Her heart and mind had been filled with an agony that had removed her from the present. But as she looked up, she saw that Frank was staring at her, his mouth slightly trembling.

'What did you say, Frank?'

'I asked you to wed me, Lizzie. I love you, that's what I'm trying to say. I always have.'

'But . . . I . . . Lizzie knew she was shaking her head, but she couldn't speak, feeling a deep pity for the man who was sitting on the edge of his seat, looking in great distress.

Frank stood up. He reached into his pocket and brought out a small box.

'Open it,' he told her.

Lizzie's shaking fingers slipped off the top. Inside the box, on a bed of soft blue velvet, sparkled a ring.

'Frank,' she breathed in astonishment. 'What's this?'

'Your Christmas present.'

'But, Frank, I can't accept this.'

'Lizzie, ever since Dad got that letter from Danny, I've waited for this day. I know you was cut up about the news – him finding himself a wife in Australia – so I kept me feelings to meself. Till now.'

Frank lifted the ring and it glittered in the firelight. He took hold of Lizzie's hand and slipped it on to her finger. 'See them little stones? Lovely ain't they? Diamond, emerald, amethyst, ruby, another emerald, sapphire and topaz.'

'Frank,' Lizzie gasped, unable to contain herself, 'it's a dearest ring!'

'Blimey, is it?' Frank mumbled, looking vague.

'Ma told me about them. It was one of her stories. She worked in service when she was a girl. The lady of the house wore a Dearest ring. See? D-E-A-R-E-S-T. It's the first letters of each stone. D – diamond, E – emerald, A – amethyst, R – ruby, E – emerald again, S – sapphire and T – topaz.'

Frank stared blankly at the ring. 'Well, fancy that.'

'It must have cost a fortune.'

Frank shrugged. 'Only the best for my gel.' Realizing what he had said, he added quickly, 'That is, if you'll be my gel.'

Lizzie slid the ring off slowly. The bridge of tiny stones sparkled brightly as she replaced it in the box. 'I . . . I don't know what to say, Frank. You caught me by surprise.'

'I'd look after you,' Frank said hurriedly. 'And Flo. And yer Pa. They could all move into the airey. There's plenty of room. And you could run the shop, have it all the way you wa—'

'Frank,' Lizzie interrupted softly, 'marrying me and taking care of the family . . . well, I don't know if you've considered it properly.'

Frank stared at her, this time, his eyes holding hers determinedly. 'I've had two years to think about what I just said. But I kept me distance 'cos I knew you two were, well . . . planning a future and I didn't have no right to make me feelings known. But now I reckon I'm in with a chance.'

Lizzie was in shock. She couldn't think straight.

'Think about it,' he said huskily. 'Don't answer me yet. Lizzie Allen, I love you with all me heart.'

The following afternoon, Sunday, Flo had gone to Lil's to see Ethel, Rosie and Timmy. Pa was in his room and Bert was fast asleep upstairs after the big roast dinner.

Lizzie was putting away the dinner things, thinking about Frank, and didn't hear the knock on the back door.

'Got a minute?' Ethel asked as she walked in.

'Ethel! I was popping in to see you after I'd cleared away.'

'I'm only over for a couple of hours. Richard's mum's coming tonight. We're going to discuss Christmas.' Ethel rolled her eyes. 'Whoopee.'

The two girls giggled. 'Got time for a cuppa?' Lizzie asked.

'Lovely.' Ethel pulled out a chair and sat down at the kitchen table. Her wavy fair hair was styled neatly and she wore a stylish tweed suit. Lizzie really admired Ethel's taste in clothes. One day, when she was a bit more flush, she was going to splash out on a suit for herself – a thought which sent her mind back to Frank again.

Lizzie made the tea, listening with one ear to all Ethel's news about Rickards. The boss was a bit of a tartar, very strict about punctuality, ticking Ethel off for being just five minutes late. Lizzie was glad she hadn't gone to work there. Bill never minded what time she turned up, though Lizzie always made a point of arriving well before eight.

'Well, are you going to tell me?' Ethel asked with a twinkle in her blue eyes as they sipped their tea.

Lizzie frowned. 'Tell you what?'

'I could have come in here and walked out with the cocoa tin and you wouldn't have noticed.'

Lizzie giggled. 'Trust you, Ethel Ryde. As a matter of fact, I would have noticed if you'd taken the cocoa tin.'

Ethel's blue eyes widened. 'What do you mean?'

Lizzie got up, reached for the cocoa tin on the shelf and brought it down. A second or two later, Ethel was holding the ring in her fingers and looking stunned as Lizzie told her the whole story.

'I know,' said Lizzie with a sigh, 'that's how I felt.'

'What are you going to say?'

'Well, either yes or no.'

Ethel spluttered. 'Course you are. But which one?'

Lizzie stared at the beautiful, dainty ring. The bridge of tiny stones twinkled hypnotically, red, blue and green in the afternoon light. 'I haven't made up my mind.'

Ethel's eyes were coming out of their sockets. 'Talk about making the poor bloke suffer.'

'He only asked me last night. He said the ring was me Christmas present.'

'Well, I know what I would have said.'

'What?'

'How soon can we set the date?'

Both girls burst into laughter. Lizzie wondered if she was being foolish in not accepting Frank immediately. There was security in the shop. Lizzie knew she could make the business pay. She could do a great deal more to add to the profits. As for the family moving to the airey, it would be an answer to a prayer. She wouldn't have to pay the rent or gas and she could make certain that Flo behaved herself. As for Pa, he could have Danny's room with the lovely big window.

Lizzie blushed. She was already planning it in her mind. Had she really come to a decision? Perhaps talking it over with Ethel had helped.

As Ethel studied the ring, Lizzie's fingers played with the pleats of her cream-coloured linen dress. It was one she had made herself, with a fashionable loose bodice and pleated skirt. Her thick, black hair was curled up around her ears and a few stray curls fell across her cheek. Her green eyes were misted as she looked up and murmured, 'Ethel, are you happy?'

Ethel shrugged. 'What's happiness, Lizzie? If it's having a nice home, two healthy kids and a husband that doesn't fool around with other women, then yes, I'm ecstatic.' Ethel laughed quickly. 'Mind you, the happiness soon wears thin at six o'clock tonight when his mother walks over the threshold.'

Lizzie was inclined to believe Ethel never really told her the absolute truth. Richard was a bit of a stuffed shirt. There seemed to be a distinct lack of humour in their lives.

'Did you love Richard when you married him?'

Ethel's cheeks flushed. 'Blimey, that's a leading question.'

'Sorry. I just wondered.'

'Well, yes . . . and no,' Ethel said hesitantly, looking from under her lashes. 'It's not quite what you think when . . .' she giggled, '. . . you know.'

Lizzie stared at her friend. Suddenly she understood Ethel's embarrassed grin. It wasn't long before they were both crying with laughter again and wiping the tears from their cheeks. Lizzie knew that the moment for intimacy had passed – as usual, with a joke.

'Go on,' Ethel spluttered at last, 'put it on.'

Lizzie frowned at the ring in Ethel's fingers, then slowly took it and slid on her left hand.

'It fits perfectly,' Ethel whispered in surprise.

'Yes. Funny that.'

'And funny it's a Dearest ring. Bet it cost a bit, you know.'

'That's what I said.'

'He must think a lot of you. What's he going to do if you say no?'

Lizzie looked up and grinned. 'Give it to someone else, I 'spect.'

Ethel snorted. 'Well, that would be a crying shame now, wouldn't it?'

Lizzie nodded as she stretched out her fingers and the little lights flashed again, making her heart skip a beat.

They sat in silence staring at the ring, a thousand questions pouring through Lizzie's mind, one of which Ethel voiced.

'What about Danny?'

'He's married ain't he?' Lizzie replied rather sharply. 'They've got a baby son. The only thing he said about me in his letter to Bill was to send me his best regards.'

'You didn't write back?'

'No, I thought it was better to leave it at that.'

'I'd never have thought Danny would—'

'Well, he did,' Lizzie interrupted crisply. 'And that's that.'

'Does that mean you're going to accept Frank?'

'I dunno, Ethel.'

'You could do a lot worse.'

'I know.'

'Lizzie. Do you love him?'

Lizzie had asked herself the same question, always wanting the answer to be yes. Frank was kind and he could give them all the security they needed. What was more, he said he loved her. Not quite looking at Ethel, Lizzie said carefully, 'I'm very grateful to him.'

Ethel raised her eyebrows. 'If Danny had asked you to marry him, and you had accepted, would your reason for marrying have been the same?'

Lizzie smiled sadly. 'Danny never asked me to marry him. Frank has.'

Once more they sat in silence, gazing at the ring. Lizzie thought over the questions that Ethel had asked her. Was it fair to marry Frank if she didn't love him in the same way she loved Danny? She knew that Danny would never return for her. He had a wife and family of his own now.

'Funny how that ring fits so well,' Ethel murmured suddenly, and Lizzie's gaze went to the ring sitting snugly on her finger. It *was* strange how it fitted so well. It was almost . . . almost . . . as though it was meant to be. Like an omen, really, if there were such things.

Chapter Twenty

'I now pronounce thee man and wife.' Reverend Green had whistled away the service in less than half an hour. 'You may kiss the bride.'

The slim gold band on her third finger glinted in the sunlight. It was Wednesday 24 September 1925, Lizzie's wedding day. Nine months after Frank's Christmas proposal.

Lizzie had given her answer in the New Year and Frank had booked the church in February. Now she placed her hands on her husband's shoulders and he grasped her ivory veil, turning it over the garland of pink rosebuds pinned to her hair. His warm lips pressed down hard and hungry over hers.

'Thank you, er . . . Mr and Mrs Flowers?' Reverend Green's embarrassed tones caused Lizzie to pull away, blushing as she caught the look in his eye. 'We'll go along and sign the register now. Come this way.'

Lizzie thought how much it had pleased her to marry in church. St Peter's wasn't known for its beauty, rather its practicality. The sharp stone, unpainted ceilings and draughty aisles were sombre and grey. But Lizzie didn't care. In her long cream silk wedding dress and three-quarter veil she felt beautiful. She'd always dreamed of a church wedding. Today her dream had been fulfilled.

She looked down at her dress. The bodice was embroidered with tiny pearls and the skirt flared down to the floor, showing the tips of her cream satin shoes. She had made the dress herself and carefully sewn on the small pearl buttons. The material had come from Ethel's shop, but the ivory lace veil was Lil's. The tiara of pink rosebuds, also made of satin, was over three decades old, but Lil had preserved it in tissue paper. The intricate little rosebuds looked real as they pressed close to one another on top of her head.

Frank extended his arm. They walked to the vestry and signed the documents with Reverend Green. Flo, wearing her pale pink bridesmaid's dress with an ivory sash, was waiting beside Doug and Bert to follow them down the aisle.

The organist played the Wedding March. The church was full. All the traders from the market were there, her neighbours from Langley Street, Frank's family, Dr Tapper and his wife and the Hailing sisters.

Frank squeezed her arm as they went. 'You look beautiful,' he whispered.

The gathering turned to follow. Once outside, people threw confetti and it floated down on the warm September breeze. The sun shone brightly as the photographs were taken. Frank had thought of everything, Lizzie realized. Even her posy of roses had been delivered before she left the house.

Doug Sharpe stood beside her in his hired suit. Lil and Bert stood on the other side. Bert was dressed in a new brown suit especially bought for the occasion. For once the sleeves and trouser bottoms fitted. Lil looked lovely, Lizzie thought. Her blue woollen day dress, the one bought for Ethel's wedding during the war, peeped out under her coat, her brown hair was tucked up into a wide brimmed hat.

'Congratulations, love,' Doug whispered, proud to have been chosen to give her away. He puffed out his chest as the photographer lifted his hand and the camera flashed.

'You look a cracker, ducks,' whispered Lil with a wink, leaning forward. 'Really lovely.' Lizzie had managed to bring Lil round to her way of thinking over the last two months that marriage to Frank wasn't such a bad idea, after all.

'Thanks, Lil, so do you.'

'One more,' shouted the photographer, and everyone stood to attention.

Frank looked down at her. 'How do you feel then, Mrs Flowers?'

She laughed softly. 'Wonderful, Frank.'

'Lizzie!' Ethel called. Her face was hidden under the wave of smooth fair hair that curved from an apricot hat. She wore a matching dress and coat in ruched wool, its yoke trimmed with narrow tucks of a deeper shade. Richard stood beside her in his grey suit, looking very proper, whilst Rosie and Timmy played in between everyone's legs. 'Don't forget to throw your posy.'

Lizzie threw her posy into the air. A roar went up as Flo caught it. Her cheeks were flushed with pleasure as she laughed shyly.

'Come on, time we went,' said Frank, leading her along the path. The horse-drawn carriage waited in the road. He tucked the veil in carefully, before jumping up beside her.

They waved as they went, leaving everyone to follow to the Methodist hall. Frank slipped his hand around her waist. He looked very handsome in his formal dress, with a blue silk tie and top hat.

Lizzie looked back at the crowd and waved.

She was now, officially, Mrs Frank Flowers.

The Reverend soon departed from the Methodist hall and the atmosphere lightened. Now the serious drinking was underway along with a knees-up.

By nine o'clock Bert had consumed his fill. A trickle of guests began to leave the hall. Most of them were travelling back to their homes on foot. They stumbled into the night, arms joined and singing, reluctant to end the evening.

Bert smiled to himself as he puffed on his cigarette, sitting on the brick wall, breathing in the crisp night air. He'd been a bit miffed about Doug giving Lizzie away, but Doug was a good mate. Lizzie looked on him like a father. Seeing as their own father couldn't or wouldn't attend the wedding, perhaps things had worked out for the best.

A bank of thick grey cloud drifted across the moonlit

sky. Bert finished his cigarette and put in an appearance. The market lot were the last to leave. Sitting at a table in one corner were Elfie Goldblum, Bill Flowers and Dickie Potts, all three with waistcoats exposed and ties removed.

Bert pulled out a chair and sat down. A little sorrowfully he said, 'It ain't gonna seem right without our Lizzie at 'ome.' He had to raise his voice; Fat Freda was belting out the tunes on the hall piano.

'Ain't she going on 'oneymoon?' Elfie leaned forward, his wrinkled brown face close to Bert's.

'Nah.' Bill Flowers wiped the froth of the ale from his mouth. 'The bastard would have none of it. Said he'd take her away when we weren't so busy at the shop. But the God's truth is he wanted to get her down them airey steps before the gel could change her mind.'

'They make an 'andsome couple,' Dickie remarked, changing the subject.

'Going up in the world is our Frank.' Bill took another gulp of his beer. He looked quickly at Bert as he smacked his lips. 'If it weren't for your sister, the sod would've had me out on the street without a farthing, as skint as the poor beggars down the Sally Army.' He nodded slowly. 'But give him time and he'll undo all the good now he's got her where he wants her.'

Bert hadn't realized how much the old man disliked his son. He wasn't surprised. Frank was an easy man to dislike. That's why he was staying with Pa at number eighty two and not going to live at Ebondale Street. Better than being around Frank all the time. Not that he'd admitted as much to Lizzie. He was relieved when

Pa had dug his heels in over the move. Bert thought of all the times Frank made him work in the storeroom for hours on end or out the back unloading the cart in the pouring rain. When Lizzie was around it was a different matter, he'd be allowed in the shop or given a mug of tea. As soon as she had gone, though, Frank would send him out again, telling him to keep his ugly mug out of sight.

Suddenly Fat Freda stopped playing. A hush descended on the room. All three men cast a look of disbelief at the two women who had just entered the hall.

'Ain't that your Babs standing at the door, Bert?' Elfie muttered.

Bert nodded in astonishment.

'Bit late to arrive, this time of night, ain't it?'

Under their crêpey folds of skin, Bill's eyes looked like a lizard's. His usually straggly grey hair was plastered back over his head and disappeared under his grubby collar. 'Now we'll see the sparks fly,' he mumbled. 'You know who the other bit of stuff is, don't you?'

Elfie Goldblum nodded. 'Lena from Limehouse.'

Bert stared at the two women. Babs had piled on the make-up. Her red hair was short and frizzy. The other woman, whom Bert had seen hanging around the airey, wore a tight red skirt and was laughing loudly.

'Would you believe it,' muttered Bill, 'Frank's tarts coming here! Bloody cheek.' Bill shook his head slowly. 'Just look at that, will you?'

Babs, striding over to the table where some of the other men were sitting, linked her arms round Frank's neck. She sat on his lap, her purple dress sliding up over her knees.

'There's trouble there, my friends,' said Elfie darkly.

The old coster nodded. 'I'm sorry to have to say it, Elfie, but you're right. Lizzie don't know what she's let 'erself in for. I always thought she had her head screwed on right and she'd suss the smarmy bugger. But I was wrong. And whatever else you might say about him, he's finally pulled it off.'

'So he has, William,' Elfie agreed. 'The signs are not good, my boy.'

Bert looked for Lizzie. She was nowhere to be seen. Perhaps she was with the other women in the room out the back. He didn't know what to do. Should he find her and warn her? Or should he wait in the hope that trouble would go away? But he couldn't believe that. Why should Babs come here tonight? Why had she brought Lena with her? Was what Bill had said true? Looking at Frank now, laughing and joking with the two women, Bert feared it was.

Lil appeared from the side door, her arms full of crockery, her gaze landing on the drunken party. The look of horror on her face added to the weight of misery that filled Bert's stomach as Lizzie came to stand beside her.

Lizzie stood in the bedroom, her body stiff, her fear and confusion mounting. Doubts cancelled out the hope as the pictures revolved in her mind of Frank and Babs and the other woman.

She closed her eyes and put her hands over her mouth. She mustn't cry. That would only bring Frank into the room. And she needed time to think, to put right in her mind what was wrong.

But the door opened and Frank stood there. 'Well then, gel, what's up?' His shirt was open at the neck and his feet were bare. They had arrived back from the hall and while he had poured himself a drink she had come to the bedroom.

'I'm not undressed yet, Frank.'

'No need. I'll do that for you.' He stared at her, his eyes roving hungrily over her wedding gown, the pale silk glowing like a candle in the gaslight. She had removed the rosebuds from her hair and it fell loosely around her shoulders in long rippling waves. He walked towards her and took her in his arms.

'Frank, no . . .'

'I'm burning for you, don't you know that?'

'We . . . we have to talk.'

'There ain't nothing to talk about as far as I'm concerned,' he breathed heavily. 'All this time, all this time . . . I've waited.' He pushed his fingers roughly into her hair. 'What's this, then? You're my wife now.'

'Why did you behave the way you did tonight? Frank, it was our wedding day!'

'What way?'

She pushed her hands against his chest. 'You humiliated me.'

He laughed loudly. 'If you mean that bit of horseplay with your sister – what else was I supposed to do? She came over and sat on me lap. We was just mucking about, that's all, having a joke.'

'It didn't seem like it was a joke to Babs.'

He stopped laughing then, his eyes hardening. 'What the bloody hell are you going on about? You should be thanking me for patching up things between you and yer sister. You've done enough whining to me about never seeing her – then when I do me best to make her feel at home, I get this.'

'It wasn't just that, Frank, it was that other woman too. She wasn't invited to the wedding – I didn't know her . . . but you did. Who was she?'

'I dunno, do I? Just a friend of Babs', I s'pose. Didn't stop to ask her for particulars, did I? Blimey, I was just enjoying meself, gel, that's all. It don't mean nothing, giving someone a peck on the cheek when you're merry. I was only being friendly. What the 'ell you getting so worked up for?'

'Because I saw—'

'Saw what?' he demanded angrily. 'Me and me mates having a few drinks and a good time? What's there wrong in that? I was celebrating. I'm a married man now and you're me wife. It's that bloody Lil, ain't it? You been talking to her. She puts all these ideas into yer head. Now, you can tell her from me to piss off.'

He took her face in his hands and pulled her lips close to his. She smelled the drink, and for a moment she swayed as his mouth came down on hers. His kiss was long and hard, his hands going down over her shoulders, pulling her against him. She felt the roughness of his beard against her skin as he lifted her in his arms and carried her to the bed.

Perhaps she was wrong to condemn him for what happened tonight? But she had been shocked when she had watched him with Babs and that other woman. Was she jealous? Seeing Babs kissing him had been bad enough, but when he had danced with that girl, her arms all over him, she hadn't been able to watch any longer. She'd fled into the small garden at the back of the hall and burst into tears. Lil was close behind and, taking her wrist, she had told her not to be a silly cow. Though Frank had suggested it was Lil who had put ideas into her head, it wasn't. Lil had said that the blokes were all drunk and it was just a bit of rough and tumble. Lizzie had never seen Frank drunk before and she wondered if Lil was right. In which case, she had been jealous for no reason and, if Lil and now Frank were to be believed, there had been no real harm in what had gone on.

Frank's hands were going over her dress trying to find the buttons. She heard them snap from the material. Suddenly she was terrified. Then he was astride her, his hard palms pushing down on her shoulders.

Somewhere in the back of her mind she recalled her conversation with Ethel. Was gratitude reason enough to marry? And now, looking up into her husband's face, she knew it wasn't. But she had chosen to marry him. This was now her life.

He loosened himself above her.

'Please, Frank,' she begged, 'not like this, not our first time . . .'

He stared at her damp hair spread out over the bed-spread, at her flushed cheeks and the look of terror in her eyes. As he took her, she watched the veins at his temple stand out like tiny threads of silver, like the cotton she had used to sew the pearl buttons on to her wedding dress.

Chapter Twenty-One

May 1926

Flo grimaced at the tray of freshly made brandy balls placed in the centre of the table. 'It's Saturday,' she complained as she stood in her nightclothes. 'I don't want to work in the shop. I want to go swimming.'

Drawing her arm over her hot forehead, Lizzie pushed the copper-lined pan that had contained the boiling toffee sugar back on to the range. 'One day a week helping me isn't much to ask, Flo.' She lifted a tray of freshly coated apples with sticks piercing their cores from the wooden draining board and placed them on the table. 'I rely on your help on Saturdays.'

'But I go to school all week. Saturday's me only day off.'

'It's only for a few hours—'

'I don't see why I have to stay at school,' Flo interrupted grumpily, 'just so you can get twenty-five bob every month.'

Lizzie lifted each toffee apple with a spatula, easing

them from the tin tray as the toffee hardened. 'The twenty-five bob is an allowance to help with your education. You passed your exams – you've a brain on you, Flo. When you leave at Christmas you'll get a nice job. In an office, with good pay.'

'I don't want to work in an office.'

'Well, you're going to and that's the end of it.'

'Me friends from me old school ain't done too bad for themselves.' Flo pushed back her short brown bob and turned the kiss curl of fringe with her finger. 'They're earning good money.'

'What, peeling and bottling onions all day?' Looking up from her work, Lizzie said, as she had many times before, 'That ain't a proper job and you know it.'

'Yes it is. I could start now if you let me. They took Jane Skinner on last week and she's only fourteen.'

'Listen, Flo, I'm not arguing with you. You are not going to work in a pickle factory and that's that. Now, get dressed and help me with these.'

'I don't want to,' cried Flo, almost in tears. 'I don't get any time off, 'cept Sundays and then I have to go back to Langley Street with you to see Pa and Bert. It ain't no fun anymore, I have to help you cook the dinner and make all the beds.'

At six thirty in the morning, Lizzie had been up since four, cooking. She was in no mood for an argument with Flo. 'We don't go back ho—' she began, stopping abruptly as she avoided referring to the old house as 'home'. Eight months after their move from Langley Street and Flo was still complaining. She hadn't really wanted to move into the airey. She maintained that if Pa and Bert were staying put, so could she.

'We don't go back to Langley Street every Sunday,' Lizzie answered shortly. 'We haven't visited for a fortnight. Now put on your clothes.'

But Flo remained where she was, her brown kiss-curl looped over her forehead. 'I suppose you're taking it out on me 'cos *he* didn't come home again last night.'

Lizzie almost dropped the spatula. 'What did you just say?'

'Well, it's true ain't it?' Flo cried as tears plopped over her lashes.

'It's no concern of yours what time Frank comes home,' Lizzie snapped. 'Now get dressed.'

'Bet you don't know where he is, though.' Flo's tears had vanished.

'And neither do you, so don't start.'

'You don't want me to enjoy myself. You hate my friends.'

'I don't like one or two. And you know who they are.'

'Sydney Miller's all right. He isn't a bit like what you think.' Flo's cheeks were red. 'He ain't a hooligan like everyone says, he's a—'

Lizzie's mouth fell open. 'So you are seeing him, then?'

Flo's expression was defiant.

'He tried to set fire to the school, Flo.'

'It wasn't him, it was someone else,' cried Flo indignantly.

'And how would you know?' Lizzie demanded. 'I've forbidden you to see him.'

'He ain't no worse than Frank! He ain't done half what Frank's done!'

Lizzie swallowed hard. 'Don't talk rubbish—'

'It ain't rubbish, it's true. He walloped you the other night. And don't say he didn't, 'cos I heard everythin'.'

'Flo—'

'And it ain't the first time neither,' Flo spluttered. 'I hate him!' Flo was shaking, her white flanelette nightdress clutched in her hands.

Lizzie walked round the table. She wanted to put her arms round Flo and tell her everything was all right. But everything wasn't all right and Flo knew that. She must have heard all that had gone on when Frank came home drunk. Nothing that Lizzie had been able to do or say had prevented the quarrels. She couldn't lie to Flo. Instead she said quietly, 'Flo, listen to me. Frank has provided us with a home, food in our stomachs and decent clothes. We want for nothing. You go to school dressed properly in a uniform, unlike some of your friends. Yet you mix with the likes of Sydney Miller—'

'Now I know why Babs left home,' Flo yelled. 'You drove her out, that's what you did. You turned into a right bossy cow after Ma died. Babs couldn't stand it and neither can I.'

'Stop it.' Lizzie wasn't going to let Flo see how much her accusations had hurt. 'You're growing up and there are rules to obey. Ma would have told you the same. Sydney Miller is trouble.'

'Vinnie says he ain't,' burst out Flo, her tone defiant.

Lizzie stared into Flo's face. 'Vinnie? When did he say that?'

'I dunno. I can't remember. But he said it.'

'When did you see him?'

'It . . . it was one day – on the street . . .'

'You didn't tell me.'

'Why should I?' Flo turned away, but Lizzie pulled her back.

'When did you see Vinnie?' she demanded.

'You don't understand,' Flo sobbed miserably. 'But Vinnie does.'

'All right, I don't understand.' Lizzie was loosing patience. 'Now, are you going to tell me the truth?'

'I went up his house – a real nice one in Poplar,' Flo admitted spitefully. 'He took me there. He said I could take Sydney too.'

'You mean that bookie's place?' She couldn't believe it. Flo had gone inside a brothel. 'Flo, don't you know what kind of house that is?'

'Our Vin and Babs live there,' Flo hurled at her. 'Me brother and me sister. And they don't treat me like a kid, neither.'

'I don't want you going there again.'

Tears of frustration slid down Flo's cheeks. She ran out of the kitchen and the bedroom door slammed.

Lizzie sank down at the table. Flo – at the house in Poplar! She closed her eyes, trying to block out the thought. How could she stop Flo going there?

For the first time she felt a real dislike for her brother

and sister. The determination she had always had to hold the family together was now gone; it was Flo who mattered – whom she must protect. Vinnie and Babs had gone their own way.

Lil Sharpe stood in the shop with her shopping bag open, four fruit cakes inside it. 'How many do you want?' she asked Lizzie, lifting them out one by one on to the counter.

The Saturday morning frenzy was over. Boxes of fresh fruit and vegetables had been rummaged over, bargained for and nearly all sold. Bert was sorting the remainder. His big hands turned over the apples and pears, the cauliflowers and cabbages, dropping the damaged ones into a box at his feet for halfpenny bundles.

Lil's homemade cakes were always popular. Together with the brandy balls and toffee apples, they were displayed in the glass-fronted cabinet at the back of the shop.

'I'll take all four, Lil.' Lizzie inspected the cakes, which were carefully wrapped in greased paper. 'Can't seem to get enough of these fruit ones.'

'You're welcome, gel. How much are you charging for each slice?' Lil's frown was speculative.

'Tuppence. I keep the prices down. The kids can buy chocolate bars at a penny from the sweet shop up Manchester Road. But you get more with the cake.'

Lil chuckled. 'There ain't no flies on you, Lizzie Allen.'

'Nor on the stock!' Lizzie laughed.

'Lizzie, I was thinking of sponges. They'd go off

quicker with cream. But jam ones would be all right, wouldn't they?'

'Make one and we'll try it out.'

'How big?"

'The same size as the fruit cakes. I'll get twelve good slices out of it.'

'Done,' said Lil as she closed her bag. 'Business good?'

'Got nothing to complain about, Lil.' Lizzie set the cakes on big white china plates. She cut each one into triangles of twelve. As the fruit fell out, they scooped up the left overs with the tips of their fingers and ate them.

'You'd better put the price up, gel,' Lil said, smacking her lips. 'Though I say it meself, tuppence is too cheap.'

Lizzie placed the cakes on the shelves. 'I want the customers coming in regular first. Then I'll add a bit on. Now, how much do I owe you?'

Lil's eyes grew wide in mock horror. 'You ain't gonna chisel me down again, are you?'

They both laughed until Lizzie wiped her eyes on the corner of her apron. 'Lil, would I do that?'

Lil's husky laughter crackled in her throat. 'You probably will one day. But I don't blame you. You've got a business head, I'll give you that. No one can beat your prices. Lil glanced around the shop, at the shining windows and decorated boxes of fruit. 'You've turned this place round, gel, there's no denying it.'

Lizzie took three silver coins from the till. Lil grabbed them with a wink and tipped them in her purse. 'Ta, love.'

'I'd like to sell more lines,' Lizzie murmured as she

removed her apron, hanging it on the hook behind the door. 'More confectionery. Sweets are popular. They don't go off like the fruit and veg. But I can't do it all, not unless I find another shop.'

'Blimey, that's a bit ambitious, ain't it?' Lil looked impressed.

'Maybe. But not impossible.'

'I said to Doug you'd go far.'

Now it was Lizzie's turn to laugh. 'As far as Ebondale Street!'

'Gertie still running the barra?' Lil asked curiously.

Lizzie nodded. 'Bill drops off the chestnuts and lights up the brazier on his way back from Spitalfields. Gertie loves it.'

'Well, I hope me cakes go as well. It's a real little earner for me,' Lil confessed. She seemed hesitant to leave. 'You coming over to Langley Street tomorrow?'

Lizzie frowned. 'Yes. Why?'

'Oh, nothing.' Lil sighed, her shoulders drooping. 'Don't suppose you've seen your Vinnie lately?'

Lizzie wondered how many more times Vinnie's name was going to be mentioned this morning. 'No. But Flo has.' Reluctantly she added, 'She went up the house in Poplar.'

'What? Without telling you?'

'Lil, what were you going to say?' Lizzie didn't want to talk about the brothel. Lil would only make her feel worse.

Lil paused. 'Vinnie's been at your house—'

'At number eighty-two?' Lizzie yelped.

'Calm down, now, love. I knew you'd be upset.'

'What did he want?' Lizzie felt her stomach churn.

'Ain't Bert said nothing?'

'No. Not a word lately. I've been worried about him. He's, well, not shaving or washing. I don't know why.' Lizzie glanced at Bert outside the shop, looking the worse for wear.

'Well it ain't my place to say, really—'

'What, Lil?'

Lil lifted her hands to the scarf that was loosely folded round her neck. 'For the last couple of weeks your Pa has been in with us. A couple of Vinnie's, er, friends has been staying at the house.'

'What?' Lizzie screamed. 'Why didn't you tell me?'

'Keep yer hair on,' Lil said, glancing at the queue. 'We don't want half the neighbourhood knowing do we?'

'Oh, Lil, why didn't you say about the blokes before?' Lizzie had begged her father to move to Ebondale Street, but he had stubbornly refused. Bert said he didn't want to come either. She knew something would happen to them if she left them on their own. Now it had.

Lil's brown eyes travelled up slowly. 'They ain't blokes, love, they're women.'

'Women?' Lizzie stared at Lil.

'One of them is that Lena person, the tart that caused trouble at your wedding. She's bedded in your room at the back. The other bit of skirt's livin' in Bert and Vinnie's room by the looks of it. Gawd knows where Bert's disappeared to. I ain't seen him there at all. I think this cow must have kicked him out, because she hangs out of his window all day smoking fags. And she's . . . she's . . . well, she ain't dressed in nothing proper, that's for sure.'

Lizzie's hand went over her mouth. 'How can this have happened, Lil? What's going on? I should never have left. I knew something awful would happen if I did.'

''Ere, don't let me hear you talking like that. You had the chance of getting married and you took it.'

Lizzie saw that Lil was watching her. 'I just meant I was feeling bad about leaving Pa and Bert.'

'Well, Bert is twenty-four, love.'

'Yeah, but he's like a big kid.'

'You never know, it might be all right. The house might be empty tomorrow. Doug said you would never have to know if I didn't open me gob. But I was afraid someone like Vi would come in the shop and blab it all out. And you'd think why ain't Lil told me? And it would be an even bigger shock for you then. And we might fall out, 'cos you know how these things happen . . .' Lil took a deep breath, her lips twitching as she sighed. 'At least you know I ain't kept you in the dark. I didn't mean to upset you.'

'You haven't, Lil. But me temper is a bit short today.'

'See you tomorrow then?'

Lizzie nodded.

'Your dad will be in with us, don't forget,' Lil told her as she gathered her bags together. 'We've got him on the mattress in the front room.'

'Oh, Lil, what a mess this all is!'

'It ain't no trouble for us, love. But there's none more

sorry than me – for you.' Lil sighed again as she tucked the handles of her big bag over her arm and left.

'I thought marrying Frank was for the best,' Lizzie whispered to herself as she watched Lil's thin figure hurry down the road. She looked about her, at the once dilapidated shop that she had built up into a thriving business. Success had come at a high price. A price she had been willing to pay.

Chapter Twenty-Two

Benji plodded towards the kerb and Bert drew in the reigns. Number eighty-two looked much the same. The front door was shut and the windows were closed, the lace curtains drawn across them.

The street was deserted. The men were in the pubs and their women busy cooking Sunday dinner. Lizzie had a plan: if she couldn't gain entrance, she would call the police. Bert had objected to this during their quarrel last night. It was their first real quarrel in years and neither of them had recovered from it. They sat stiffly beside one another on the cart. Was Bert right in suggesting they wait, Lizzie wondered?

Wiping his forehead with a grubby cloth, Bert eased the rim of his cap from his head. 'Probably down the boozer,' he muttered.

'All the more reason to go in.'

'The front door's shut. There ain't no key on the string now. I tried it the other night. Someone must've took it off.'

'I've got me spare key,' Lizzie said determinedly. 'You'd better move the cart up a bit, Bert, because you'll be seeing that top window open shortly and whatever I find in our house that don't belong there, it's shooting right out of it.'

'Aw, Lizzie, you'll only cause more trouble.'

'It's them that's caused the trouble, not me.' She lowered her legs and slid to the pavement, firmly brushing down her coat.

Bert jumped down beside her. 'I reckon you should see Vin first.'

'What good would that do?' She looked at her brother and sighed. 'Vin moved them in here. And I'm moving them out.'

Bert lowered his eyes. 'I wish you'd wait a bit, gel, that's all.'

'For how long? It's our house, Bert. Whatever were you thinking of, to be driven out of it by strangers.'

He looked at her sadly, his great head drooping. 'They . . . they said things about me. So I went down Island Gardens and slept on a bench. Me mind was all confused. Then they took away the string and wouldn't let me in.'

'And you came into the shop each day, not saying a word?' Lizzie stared up at her brother.

'I didn't want no trouble.'

'So you keep telling me. Well, we've got trouble whether we want it or not.' She squared her shoulders. 'Now, are you coming?'

Bert nodded gloomily.

Lizzie nodded at Lil's house. 'We'd better tell Lil we've arrived.'

Lil's door was on the latch. They walked into the

passage. An aspidistra filled the space under the stairs. In number eighty-two there was a cupboard in the same place. A narrow carpet with a triangular design of mustard and black ran down the hallway, and shiny brown linoleum covered the boards. By comparison to their house it was a palace.

'Lil?' Lizzie shouted.

In the front room a striped mattress was rolled up and pushed behind the gateleg table. Light shone through Lil's white Nottingham lace curtains and reflected on the couch. It was a surprise not to see Doug there. He always read his newspaper on Sunday morning as the dinner was cooking.

'No one's in,' Bert grunted.

'Lil knew I was coming over.'

'I ain't looked outside,' said Bert. 'P'raps Doug's having a jimmy riddle. Maybe Pa's in the yard too.' He turned and walked down the hallway and out through the kitchen.

Lizzie heard the back door open and, a few moments later, close. Bert walked back into the room and shook his head. 'Not a soul.'

In the quiet hallway the summer breeze floated gently around them from the open door. Lizzie shivered. Lil had been expecting her. Only something important would have caused her to be absent. And where was Pa? He couldn't go far in his wheelchair.

'Look who's coming over.' Bert nodded across the street. 'She must have seen the cart.'

Vi Catcher was running across the road. Her great

bosoms bounced up and down under her pinny. A mountain of fat propelled itself over the threshold, shaking and shuddering. 'Oh my God, gel, oh dear, oh dear! I bin in such a state,' wheezed Vi, red in the face. 'I should never have thought I would live to see this happen. First them tarts driving out your poor Pa and Bert and then making themselves at home like they have! That house was sacred to your mother. Like a brothel it's been! Yes, that's the word for it – I can't say less – like a brothel' – she took a breath, her head nodding and twitching – 'and with all this – I never thought I'd hear the like. Never!'

They watched as she stumbled breathlessly into the front room. Her eyes went from side to side as she took out a handkerchief and gave her big nose a blow.

'What's happened, Vi? Where is everyone?'

'Oh, love, I don't know how to tell you.' Vi collapsed on a chair. 'Lil . . . told me to say . . . she said "Tell Lizzie we don't know nothing for sure. Tell her we're down at Barrel Wharf, tell her that's where the chair was found."'

Lizzie's stomach churned. 'Chair? What chair?'

'Your father's, love. It was early this morning. He never slept on the mattress, never bedded down in the sheets, from what Lil could tell. He'd got out somehow – just gone – gone! And then someone came knocking at the door and said they'd found a chair down by Barrel Wharf. But there weren't no one in it, gel. No one.'

Vi took in a breath that whistled down the tunnel of her throat. She looked up at them. 'They think he's gone off the side, love. They think he went down in the water.'

Each day for five days a Port of London police boat was tied alongside the jetty of Barrel Wharf. A small crew prepared a diver for his search on the river bed.

For each of those days Lizzie watched and waited. The diver sank below the water in his rubber suit and weighted boots, his large brass helmet disappearing into the blackness. A stream of bubbles gurgled upwards as the air line trailed in his wake. The search was slow. The diver's task was hindered by the rotting timber that fouled the thin tubing of the air line, his only means of survival.

On the last day, Saturday, the market traders joined her. By now, the police said, a body would have washed away with the current. Unless it was snagged deep down on the river bed.

Lizzie stared into its depths. She had loved the river all her life. The sun was setting, the surface spangled gently in its light. Here, on the mossy steps, many summers ago, she had sat with Babs and Flo, their toes dangling in the water.

She couldn't believe Pa was down there. She couldn't accept it, that he'd thrown himself in. No one knew what to say to her. What other answer was there than that Tom Allen had ended his life?

The diver was hauled up for the last time. When the helmet came off he shook his head. A policeman came over to Lizzie. 'I'm sorry,' he told her. 'We've found nothing.'

'Ain't you gonna search tomorrow?' Lizzie begged.

'We'll search by boat along the river.' He spoke quietly, as though it was all over. 'Go home now. We'll send a constable to your house if we find anything.'

Darkness began to fall. The river turned into a lake of ink. Lizzie shivered. It was May, but the nights were still cold. The coming of spring deepened her grief. Spring was when life blossomed, not died.

'Looking back,' said Dickie, trying to be of comfort as he stood beside her, 'we didn't realize what a bad way he was in.'

'If only he'd come to live at Ebondale Street.'

'And leave his little patch?'

'So I left him.' The thought had been tormenting her night and day.

'Don't talk daft,' Dickie told her sharply. 'He could've moved in with you and Frank if he wanted. But he was a stubborn old sod. Langley Street was his home.'

She leaned forward, gazing into the dark water. Nothing anyone could say would make her feel better.

'Listen,' Dickie told her sternly. 'Your Pa pushed himself all the way down here. He let himself out the house in the dead of night. He knew Lil and Doug wouldn't discover him gone for hours. He planned it, gel, for whatever reason. This is what he wanted. His choice. And to tell you the truth, that's the way I'd want it too, only I dunno if I'd have the courage. Your father was a brave man. You'll always have that to remember him by.'

The police launch chugged by in the darkness. Dickie put his arm round her shoulders. 'I'll walk you home.'

They turned away from the river. It felt as though all

its coldness had seeped into her bones. What must it be like down there, under the surface? What if the police never found a body? If Pa was alive somewhere, why had he abandoned his chair? He couldn't go far without it. How long would it be before she would know what had happened to him?

At Lil's house, Dickie said goodbye and hurried away, a small, bent figure in a tatty old mac. Even Dickie, her father's oldest friend, couldn't believe that Tom was still alive.

Lil, Doug and Bert were waiting in the front room.

Lizzie shook her head. 'No news.'

'Take off yer coat, gel. Sit down and warm yerself up.'

'I won't stay long. Flo's at home.'

'How's she taken it?'

Lizzie shrugged. 'I don't think it's dawned on her yet.'

'I'll make a quick cuppa.' Lil patted her arm and hurried out to the kitchen.

'What did the police say?' Doug asked as she sat down on a chair, warming herself in front of the fire.

'The boat is still searching, but the diver's stopped.' Tears filled her eyes and ran down her cheeks.

Doug pulled a handkerchief out of his pocket and gave it to her. She mopped her eyes and blew her nose. In silence Bert stood up and put his big arm round her.

'I know he wasn't happy, Bert,' she sobbed. 'But to do this!'

'Yeah,' mumbled Bert. 'I know.'

'He wasn't the old Tom Allen,' Doug reminded them gently.

'If I hadn't have moved to Ebondale Street, he might be alive today.'

'You can put that idea out of yer mind,' Lil interrupted as she came back from the kitchen with a tray of tea. 'Your father wasn't himself long before you left that house. I know what yer going through. Doug and me both felt responsible when that kid came knocking to tell us they found his chair down the wharf. All sorts of things go through yer mind. But in the end it boils down to one thing, and that is it was yer dad's choice to do what he did.'

Lizzie knew what Lil was saying was true. She hadn't thought much about how Lil and Doug felt. What it must have been like for them on that awful morning. Her only thought had been to turf out those women next door; she hadn't dreamed something much worse was about to happen. After Vi's appearance she had been in a kind of stupor. Then she'd seen Lil and Doug in the middle of a crowd with white, anguished faces. The disbelief she had felt when she'd looked at the empty chair – it all seemed like a bad dream that she couldn't wake up from.

'Drink yer tea, gel.' Lil sighed. 'No one's to blame. It's just one of them terrible things that happen in life.'

They drank in silence. Even Lil had run out of conversation. Lizzie noticed that Doug didn't bother to light his pipe, just held it limply in his hand. They were all still in shock.

There was a knock, and with a sigh Lil got up to answer it. A few minutes later she was back. Dr Tapper removed his black hat as he walked into the room.

'What's wrong?' Lizzie sprang to her feet. She thought the police might have found her father.

'There's nothing to be alarmed about.'

Bert and Doug looked up anxiously. The doctor went over to the hard wooden dining chair by the window. 'Is there any news from the wharf today?' he asked as he sat down rather breathlessly.

'No. None.'

'Are they continuing the search?'

'Only with the boat, down river,' Lizzie explained.

'I see.' When they were all seated, he spoke again. 'As there is no news, I think I must share some information – confidential information – with you. Your father, Lizzie, was insistent I reveal this to no one. But now that the likelihood is . . .' He held up his hands in a gesture of resignation, 'I think what I have to say might help ease your minds.'

Everyone stared at the old man. Lizzie's heart began to pound heavily.

'Do you want me and Doug to go, if it's personal?' Lil asked.

Lizzie shook her head. 'No, Lil, course not.'

'Very well.' Dr Tapper drew himself up and looked straight at Bert. 'You recall, Bert, some months ago, you came to the surgery on your father's behalf?'

'Yeah,' Bert said in an unusually quiet voice.

'You didn't tell me.' Lizzie frowned at her brother.

She wondered how many other things Bert had hidden from her.

'Pa said not to bother,' he stammered, going red. 'It were only for his rheumatism pills.'

'He may have told you they were for rheumatism,' said Dr Tapper slowly, 'but the medication I prescribed him was for the alleviation of pain.'

Once more everyone was silent, until Lizzie burst out, 'Pa was in pain?'

'I'm afraid the gangrene had . . . accelerated.'

'Oh, Gawd,' gasped Lil, her hand going up to her mouth.

'You mean . . . you mean . . .' Lizzie began, her words tumbling out, 'it was his stumps . . . they were . . .'

'Lizzie, your father requested that I keep his condition – and treatment – secret. As his physician, I had to comply.'

'You mean . . .' Lizzie tried again, forcing herself to ask, 'he was . . . he was . . . dying?' Lizzie swallowed as a big tear rolled down her cheek and fell on to her hand.

Again the doctor paused, then nodded slowly. 'Laudanum appeared to provide the only relief.'

Lizzie put her hands over her face. As she sat there, sobbing, Lil put her arm round her. 'I didn't have no idea it was that bad,' Lil said in a shocked voice.

'Poor old Tom.' Doug had tears in his eyes.

Lil pressed a clean handkerchief into Lizzie's hands.

'I'm sorry if I have upset you, my dear.' Dr Tapper lifted his drooping shoulders. 'But doubtless you have questions as to why your father might have taken his own life.'

'And you think he might have gone down the river that morning to . . . to . . .?' Lil didn't finish.

'It's quite likely, quite likely.'

Lizzie could hardly bear it. Something was being ripped out of her. It felt like her soul, pulled out of her body by some dreadful force. She couldn't get the terrible words from her mind. Pa had been dying and in pain. And she hadn't known. She hid her face, fighting against the misery inside her. Oh, Pa, she wailed in her head, if only you had told me. I would have stayed with you.

'Lizzie, there was nothing you could have done. Nothing anyone could have done,' the doctor assured her.

'Will the police want to know?' Lil asked him in a shaky voice.

'Yes, it may help with the investigation.' Dr Tapper added softly, 'There were many times when I thought it would have been kinder to everyone concerned to know the truth. But the last thing he wanted was pity. You must remember that, Lizzie. It will help.'

Somewhere at the back of her mind she had always known Pa had locked himself away from the gaze of others to avoid their pitying glances. But, even so, it was like a knife plunged into her heart that his life had ended in this way.

When Doctor Tapper had left, Lizzie went into Lil's kitchen and blew her nose. Lil followed, sitting beside her at the table.

'At least there's a reason now, gel,' Lil said in an empty voice.

'It don't seem to help much,' Lizzie sniffed.

'Your dad wouldn't have wanted . . . well, if the stuff old Tap was giving him hadn't helped . . . he would have done what he did whilst he was able to. Sorry to be blunt, but it all adds up, don't it?'

'He could have told me, though.'

'Yeah, and worried the life out of you.'

'Do you think that's what he thought?'

'He loved you, gel. I know he had a bloody funny way of showing it, but he did.'

Lizzie didn't want to talk about it anymore or the tears would never stop. She scrubbed the mugs in the sink, then the teapot. She could hardly see what she was doing for the tears welling in her eyes.

Lil dried the china in silence, then suddenly said, 'What you gonna do about next door?'

Lizzie shrugged. 'I ain't thought much about it lately.'

'Does old Symons still come to the shop each week for the rent?

Lizzie nodded, placing the shining teapot upside down on the draining board. 'It used to be regular as clockwork on a Friday. Funny thing is, I ain't seem him since the end of March. I got the rent waiting for him in me bag.'

'That's queer. He never missed a week with yer poor old mum. She never let him down, neither. The rent was always there in the cocoa tin, come rain or shine.' Lil dropped the towel to the draining board, her intake of breath loud. 'Blimey, you know the answer, don't you? He's been paid already!'

Lizzie looked round at Lil. She didn't understand. 'What do you mean, Lil?'

'Vinnie's paid him, ain't he?'

'But I've got the rent book.'

'But you're not living there.'

'Neither is Vinnie,' Lizzie spluttered.

'Yeah, but it's only your word against his. With yer Pa gone and you up Ebondale Street . . .' Lil's face was white. 'No wonder we seen a bit of Vinnie round here lately. He's staking his claim, ain't he?'

Lizzie sank down on a chair. It all felt too much, as though her brain was going to burst. 'But why would he do that?'

Lil bit her lip. 'Saw a business opportunity, I 'spect.'

Lizzie knew what Lil really meant. That Vinnie trampled over anything and anyone, even his own family, if there was money at the end of it. 'We're only guessing,' Lizzie said vaguely.

'We ain't far wrong, and you know it,' Lil said with a sigh.

'What about Bert?' Lizzie asked faintly.

'The poor sod is terrified of them women. He won't go back whilst they're there.'

'But it's his home, not theirs.'

'It was,' Lil said sharply.

'Maybe I should tell the police.'

'What good's that gonna do if your Vinnie's paid the rent and got a rent book? You can bet yer life he's bunged old Symons a few extra quid to back him up, otherwise you'd have had the old skinflint on yer doorstep a month ago.'

Lizzie tried to think, but grief kept getting in the way. She was feeling so many conflicting emotions. She was beyond tears. A terrible emptiness had taken hold of her. She knew she should fight for the house, but she didn't have the conviction.

'Come on, gel, it'll all work out,' Lil said, patting her shoulder. 'Bert's welcome to kip on the mattress in the front room, like yer Pa did, till everything's sorted out. He's no trouble. In fact, Doug likes the company.'

'You sure, Lil?'

'Wouldn't say if I didn't mean it, would I?' Lil got up and put on the kettle, resorting to another cup of tea to bolster them, before telling the men.

Chapter Twenty-Three

The months passed slowly by and there was no news from the police. It was December once more and the nights were closing in. Hundreds of chimneys puffed out smoke, mixing with the mist that rose from the river. A damp yellow fog spread over the houses. It was Saturday evening and Lizzie was in the storeroom with Bill.

'Bert doing the last of them deliveries?' Bill wheezed as he spat on the big brass scale and polished it with his elbow.

Lizzie nodded, her back beginning to ache. She was glad it was the end of the week. Tomorrow was bath night. The old tin bath was filled with kettles of hot water in front of the open fire.

'He should be back soon. Then we'll close up.'

'Ain't seen that son of mine around for a while,' Bill muttered. He glanced at her sharply.

Lizzie hadn't seen Frank all week. She knew he would turn up when he was hungry or needed money.

'You all right, gel?' Bill Flowers' gruff voice broke into her thoughts.

She nodded, reaching for the broom.

'You looked a bit like my Daisy, then,' he told her. 'She was always sweepin' up. A good little worker, she was. You two would have got on like a house on fire.'

It was the first time Bill had spoken intimately of his dead wife. 'How did you manage after she died, Bill?'

He shrugged. 'Gertie came in to 'elp, didn't she? Give the baby his milk and keep an eye on Frank. Trouble was, Frank never took to her. He missed his mother. The doctor told Daisy she shouldn't have no more after Frank. But it weren't no good telling Daisy about kids. She had it in her mind to have a clutch of 'em.' The old man stared into space, his lips trembling. 'Frank was four when it happened. He somehow thought that Danny was responsible for Daisy going.'

'But she died in childbirth,' Lizzie protested. 'Danny couldn't help that.'

'Frank never saw it that way. Felt bitter, even as a kid. And his nature ain't improved. You know that better than anyone.'

Lizzie knew. Frank had been a different person before their marriage, kind and caring. Why had he changed? Or had he changed? Had she just thought he was someone else?

'Still,' Bill changed the subject quickly, 'this won't get the work done. He bent to lift a sack of potatoes on to his back, a slow and painful process.

'I wish you'd leave that to Bert,' Lizzie said anxiously.

'The day I can't pick up a sack of spuds I'm finished.'

Bill humped the sack to the back of the storeroom and dropped it beside the others.

Knowing she couldn't stop him, Lizzie finished sweeping the floor. Then she put on her coat and went to the till and rang up the day's takings. The books on the shelf below were all up to date. Although business was good, more money was going out than coming in. The shop was up fifty per cent up on last year. So was Frank's spending. A fact neither she nor Bill had the power to change.

It was half past six when Lizzie locked up. Bert and Bill went off to the pub. Lizzie hurried down to the airey, wondering if Flo was in. She had left school in August and found work as an office clerk. Since the office was in the pickle factory it was a kind of compromise. Saturday was Flo's half day.

When Lizzie walked in, Flo and Sydney Miller were standing in the middle of the room. They broke apart quickly.

'Hello, Mrs Flowers.' Sydney Miller wasn't tall, standing just an inch above Flo, but he was well built and upright. His cap was stuffed in his pocket and his brown hair was cut neatly, short back and sides. His boots were shining, a fact that didn't escape Lizzie's quick eyes.

'Hello, Sydney.' Lizzie took off her coat, wondering what to do. She knew that, whether she liked Sydney or not, Flo was going to have her own way.

'Sydney walked me home,' Flo said hurriedly, going bright pink.

'Where have you been?'

'For a walk. Over Blackheath. We passed Rickards and waved to Ethel.'

'So what are you doing now?' Lizzie looked at Sydney, who didn't seem like a ruffian. In fact, she couldn't fault his clean trousers and jacket.

'We thought we'd . . . er, just say hello.' Flo still had her coat on. Sydney shuffled his feet, looking awkward.

At least Flo had brought him home, Lizzie thought. They hadn't gone to the house in Poplar as Flo had once threatened, an outcome Lizzie had always dreaded.

'Would Sydney like to stay to tea?' she asked.

She didn't have to ask twice. Flo was at her side in the kitchen, talking ten the dozen. Sydney sat by the fire, contemplating the shine on his boots.

'Thanks, sis,' Flo whispered, as Lizzie fried bubble and squeak from Thursday's leftover mash. She gave Lizzie a peck on the cheek.

'What was that for?' Lizzie hid her amusement.

'You know, having Sydney home.'

'Don't think I'm gonna do this every week.' Lizzie fried sausages, adding an extra two to the pan for Sydney.

'No,' murmured Flo with a giggle. 'I'll do the cooking next time.'

Sydney left at eight. He thanked Lizzie for the lovely meal and grinned at Flo. The young man had surprised Lizzie. He hadn't said much. Maybe it was because Flo nudged him hard when he opened his mouth. But he always called her Mrs Flowers and said ta or thank you. He was eighteen, two years older than Flo, but he had a young, fresh face with a big smile plastered permanently over it.

No one brought up the subject of the Millers' reputation. Lizzie didn't know if Sydney took after his six notorious brothers. But since Flo was determined to go out with him, she was prepared to give him a chance.

'Well, what do you think?' Flo asked as they sat by the fire before bed.

'What do I think about what?' Lizzie knew what Flo wanted her to say.

'About Sydney, of course.'

'Has he got a job?'

Flo looked disappointed. 'I knew you'd ask that.'

'Well, has he?'

'Would you like him any the less if he didn't?'

'So he has, then?' Lizzie smiled.

Flo sat back in the armchair and nodded. 'Up Billingsgate. Portering. Didn't you smell the fish?'

Lizzie ignored that one. 'Are you two serious?'

'What does that mean?' Flo cried indignantly. 'We're just . . . enjoying ourselves, that's all.'

'Not too much, I hope.'

Flo grinned. 'You sound just like Ma.'

'Yeah, well, I've got to keep my eye on you.' Lizzie knew that Flo would have what she wanted in the end. But there had to be some rules defined.

Flo snuggled into the chair and yawned. 'He ain't half a laugh, is Sydney.'

'Well, you could have fooled me. He hardly said two words tonight.'

'Yeah, well, he was nervous, wasn't he?'

'What of?' Lizzie kept her smile hidden.

'You. He didn't know what reception he'd get.'

'Well, he didn't have anything to complain about when he left, not with that full stomach.'

Flo burst into laughter. 'Blimey, that *is* Ma talking.'

They were both laughing then and Lizzie leaned forward to poke an ember of coal back into the grate. 'Well, time for bed,' she sighed. For a moment a pang of loneliness went through her. She would sleep alone without her man. Frank always collapsed on the couch when he came home, too drunk to take his clothes off. He rarely came to bed. She knew that he didn't want to talk to her. There had been too many bitter quarrels and, worse, fights. His answer was to use the airey as somewhere to eat and fill his wallet.

Lizzie sat back in the chair. She gazed proudly at Flo. She had turned into a lovely young woman, her health and weight regained. Her brown hair was no longer straight and lank, but shining and fashionably waved. Flo took care with her appearance and Lizzie knew why.

'What you lookin' at?' Flo asked, yawning. 'Me hair's all right ain't it?'

'You know it is.'

'He ain't bad, is he, Lizzie?'

Lizzie smiled. 'If you say so. But you two – behave youselves. You're only young.'

'I know,' grinned Flo, rising to her feet and yawning again. 'As soon as I get as old as you I reckon I'll 'ave had all me fun.'

Lizzie snorted. 'You cheeky blighter!' Flo was taller than her now. She couldn't clip her round the ear anymore.

'Night, then.' Flo bent and kissed her cheek. She ran down the passage giggling. Lizzie knew that for the next ten minutes Flo would be painstakingly winding papers around her hair to curl it, attempting to look like Mary Pickford, her favourite film star.

Lizzie cleared away in the kitchen. Then she undressed and washed, pouring warm water from the jug into the bedroom bowl. When all was done, she brushed her long black hair. Drawing it on to her left shoulder to plait, she looked into the mirror. Two large green eyes stared wistfully back at her from under the ebony tumble of hair. Was Pa's body ever going to be found? Would they ever know what happened to him?

Lizzie shuddered. She had tried to share her worries with Flo, but Flo refused to talk about Pa. She was only sixteen. Lizzie knew she wanted to block the bad memory out and she didn't blame her.

Lizzie slipped on her nightgown and went to lock the front door. Before she reached it, she heard noises outside. It couldn't be Flo. She would be asleep by now. The voices got louder, laughing and singing. Her heart started to race. She hadn't locked the door yet. She reached out, was almost there . . .

It swung open. Frank, Vinnie and Babs all staggered in. Frank had his arm round Vinnie's shoulders. They were laughing and falling over themselves.

'Well, look who it ain't,' Babs screeched, her voice

high and piercing. Her eyes were puffy and her red hair was so frizzy it looked like a mop. Lizzie stared at her sister's swollen stomach.

'What do you want?' Lizzie faltered, hiding her shock.

Babs laughed loudly. 'Now that ain't much of a welcome, staring at us like we was strangers! There was I, thinking you and me could have a couple of drinks and chat over old times.' She paused, her red painted mouth quivering. 'You know what I think? I think you should show a little more hospitality to yer family, that's what I think.'

Lizzie's heart sank. 'Do you know what time it is?'

Babs shrugged, unconcerned. 'So what? There ain't no hurry.'

Lizzie went to the passage door and closed it. She didn't want Flo to hear all the commotion.

'Where's me little sister?' demanded Babs as though reading her mind.

'Asleep, of course.' Lizzie was panic stricken. She didn't want Flo to see Babs or Vinnie in this state. Why had Frank brought them here? Babs shouldn't be drinking like that with a child in her belly.

'You act like you're her mother,' Babs sneered. Her old coat and thin dress were stained; she looked as though she hadn't washed in months.

'This isn't the time—' Lizzie began, but Vinnie butted in, his sly face in a snarl.

'Bleedin' cheek, telling us what to do. Frank, get yer old girl into order,' he yelled, falling into the armchair by the fire.

Frank staggered towards Lizzie. She tried to back away; the fumes on his breath make her feel sick. He looked dreadful. Unshaven and dirty, like Babs. She felt she was looking at a stranger.

'What you going to do, then?' he demanded, grasping a beer bottle that Babs thrust into his hand. He drank noisily from it, dragging his sleeve across his mouth.

Babs cackled loudly. ''Ere, lover boy, your missus ain't half got an opinion of herself. Always did have, the stuck up little cow. Ma never had chance to notice us. It was always Lizzie this, Lizzie that. A right little goody two shoes she was.'

Frank swayed, his bloodshot eyes trying to focus.

'She says she ain't gonna let me see Flo, and I'm 'er sister,' Babs continued in a cajoling tone. 'Who does she think she is?'

Frank grabbed Lizzie's wrist and dragged her towards him. 'Want to come to bed, eh?' he muttered, his foul breath in her face. 'No, course you don't. Oh, no, all these years and you've been pleased to see the back of me. Well, maybe I should make you do your wifely duty tonight. Now what do you say to that?' When she didn't reply, he yelled, 'Did you hear that, Vin? Not a word. Not a bloody word!'

'Always told you she was a cool one,' Vinnie muttered.

Frank let the bottle fall to the floor as he pulled her against him. She moved her head but he grabbed hold of her chin, jerking it round. 'We'll see about that.'

Lizzie lifted her eyes. She gazed calmly into her

husband's face. There was nothing Frank could do to her that he hadn't done before. She wasn't going to let him see she was afraid now.

Frank gurgled in his throat. 'God above, what a bloody fool I was in wedding you.'

'Send them away,' she whispered. 'Please.'

'Watch her, Frankie,' Babs hissed, coming close. 'Tomorrow you'll wake up and she'll have you eating out of her hand.'

'Yeah, and ain't that the truth!' Vinnie jeered. 'Don't let her fool you, Frankie boy. Reckon she's still sweet on yer brother.'

Frank's eyes blazed. 'Don't listen to them, Frank,' Lizzie begged. 'Send them away. It ain't none of their business.'

'That's what you'd like, admit it!' Frank demanded. 'Me out of this house and *him* back in it.'

'No, Frank—'

'You lying cow.' He slapped her hard. His face swam in front of her. She almost fainted. He threw her against the wall with a bone-jarring thud. All the air was knocked out of her as she struggled to stand up.

'I know what you need,' Babs grinned, walking towards Frank, swaying her belly. She reached up and kissed him on the lips.

Lizzie stared up at them. Frank put his arms around Babs and kissed her back.

Lizzie felt the tears rush into her eyes. Although her body ached it was nothing to the pain in her heart. Now she knew she was alive. Now she felt all the emotions.

Hate, loathing, disgust, betrayal. Her husband and her sister. And the baby? Was it Frank's?

Lizzie forced herself to look, watching Frank's hands travel over Babs' swollen breasts, over the huge mound of her stomach, his fingers pulling at her skirt.

Lizzie forced herself to watch. She would remember this night all her life.

Suddenly Babs stiffened, her fingers grasping Frank's shoulders. Her broken nails dug into the cloth of his suit. He stared at her, his mouth open. For a minute Babs was silent, her eyes blank, her body still. Lizzie watched breathlessly as slowly she began to tremble. A long, piercing cry came from her mouth and filled the room. It seemed to echo round and round until Lizzie thought it wouldn't ever stop.

When it did, Babs was on her knees. Frank was staring down, his jaw sagging open as the stain spread over the rug.

Chapter Twenty-Four

'Christ! What's 'appening?' Frank yelled, staring down at Babs. The pool on the floor spread out beneath her.

Vinnie sprang up from the chair. He stared down at his sister as she rocked on her knees. 'She ain't having it, is she?'

Lizzie rushed to Babs. She couldn't make Babs hear her, she was screaming too much. Just then the passage door opened. Flo stood in her nightgown, her eyes full of sleep. Her hair was tied up in paper curlers. She saw Babs on the floor. 'Babs!' she screamed, and ran to Lizzie. 'What's happening? What's – she ain't—'

Lizzie nodded. 'Her water's broken.'

Flo gasped. 'A baby? I didn't even know she was having one.'

'We need the doctor. There's blood in the water.'

'She ain't supposed to have it now.' Vinnie's black eyes narrowed as he came to stand over Babs. 'She said she wasn't due till January.'

'Well, it's started.' Lizzie felt Babs' nails dig into her arm. Another contraction came and Babs screamed louder, tears rolling down her cheeks. 'Run for Dr Tap,' Lizzie shouted at the two men, but they stood still, fear written over their faces.

Frank staggered to the sideboard. He poured a whisky and gulped it down. He turned to Vinnie. 'She's your sister. You go.'

Vinnie dragged on his coat. 'I ain't getting involved.'

'Help us!' Lizzie pleaded with him as Babs clung to her. 'Go for the doctor, please!'

Vinnie's face was white. 'Ain't there some old girl that comes out who'll know what to do?'

Lizzie shook her head. 'Not when someone's bleeding like this. Look at her. Vinnie, she's your sister. She needs the doctor.'

He gave a low curse but muttered his assent. Then he looked slowly at Frank. 'You bugger!' he growled before turning and leaving.

'Hurry, please hurry!' Lizzie yelled after him. She was terrified for Babs, who looked almost unconscious. Her eyes had rolled back in their sockets. Lizzie knew it was only Dr Tapper who could save her. Was the baby still alive? Why had it come so early?

She looked up at Frank. He poured more whisky and drank it. 'Help me get her to the bedroom,' she begged, wondering how a grown man could act in such a way. 'If you don't help me, she'll have the baby here.'

He stumbled over, clumsily dragging up Babs' arm and pulling it round his shoulder. Lizzie took her other arm. Together they carried her down the passage.

In the bedroom, Flo stammered, 'What shall I do?'

'Lay an old cloth over my bed. Then boil some water. And towels – plenty of clean ones.' Lizzie knew the doctor would want them.

Flo ran out to the linen cupboard. She was soon back with an old sheet, which she spread over the bed.

Frank dropped Babs on to the bed, almost falling down beside her. Lizzie managed to lift up Babs' cold, blood-stained legs and push them over the sheet. 'Don't forget the water and towels,' she told Flo, giving her a little shove. She knew Flo was terrified, her eyes wide as she stared at Babs moaning on the bed. 'The doctor will be here soon.'

Flo went, but Frank gazed down at Babs as though stunned. Her face was drained of blood under the tear-stained make-up.

Lizzie stared at her husband, her heart pounding. What was he thinking? Was he the baby's father? Slowly he turned and staggered from the room. Lizzie knew that the questions she had just asked herself would not be answered tonight. Frank was a liar. He was also a cheat and a coward. He had no interest in anyone under this roof except himself. He cared nothing for Babs in her distress. For a moment, a deep hatred welled up in her. It filled every inch of her body until she couldn't breathe. Then Babs cried out, twisting on the bed, writhing in agony.

Pity and sadness overwhelmed Lizzie. What a dreadful price to pay for an illegitimate child. Lizzie knew there was worse to come. Suddenly the angry emotions drained away, leaving her strangely calm. She knew she had to remain so for Babs and the child's sake. Taking a breath, she began to remove Babs' pitifully shabby dress. As she whispered words of comfort to her sister, she was praying that Dr Tap would arrive before it was too late.

Dr Tapper prepared for a long night. It went that way with some women – he had delivered enough babies in his time to know the signs. The baby was in distress, and with the way the mother was it would be touch and go. How had she come to be in this state? He had known the Allens all his life, delivered all of the children. Kate Allen would be turning in her grave if she could see her daughter now.

Dr Tapper sighed deeply. Being roused from his bed had done nothing for his temper. The girl's brother had told him to come here, then disappeared. What had happened to the family, he wondered, in the years since Kate had died?

He gazed down on the semi-conscious girl, unwilling to cut her. He was of the old school. He wasn't for butchering, as some of his kind were. He'd not lost many, not when he recalled the hundreds he'd delivered, all sizes, shapes and colours. Some were alive and kicking, a few blue and cold as steel.

He moved the stethoscope slowly over her abdomen. The baby was in distress. He was against the old ways, the backstreet butchers. And there were plenty of those old crones, all of them with their crafty methods. He'd seen enough of their work. The mothers got infected and many never recovered.

He had spent his life amongst these women. It was the poverty that sickened him. And it wouldn't change, not in his lifetime, anyway. The poor little buggers grew up to a living death anyway, sick, wretched and starving. And in the end they went after a few years' miserable existence. Would the same happen to this infant if it survived?

The doctor adjusted his stethoscope, his brow furrowed.

'Can you hear the baby?' Lizzie asked him.

'Yes. And here's another contraction coming.' The doctor cursed softly. The girl's breathing grew laboured, her eyes moving quickly under their lids.

'It's a breach,' the doctor said. 'I'll have to turn it. Hold her still.' He bent to the girl's ear. 'Don't push, wait until I say,' he instructed loudly as the sweat dripped off him. The chances were she couldn't hear him. He spoke automatically, forcefully.

Should he use the knife he wondered? It would be too late for both of them if he didn't. Surely it was better to save one? But he was a stickler for hope. He'd pumped up their little chests with his own mouth, blown into them until he was as blue in the face as the infant. Even now after all these years he didn't want to admit defeat. He took another breath, parted her legs once more and examined the birth canal.

'More hot water and towels,' he shouted.

What was he going to do? He must be softening in his old age.

'Is Babs gonna be all right?' he heard the younger girl ask. She had been waiting outside.

'Doctor's doing his best. Come and help me.'

Dr Tapper shook his head as he heard the door close. He looked down at his young patient, reflecting on the saying that the good and innocent die young. Well, maybe this girl would survive. Whether her child would be as fortunate, he had no way of knowing.

At ten minutes to three in the morning, on Sunday 12 December 1926, Babs' baby girl was born. Her breath was held so tightly from her turbulent passage into this world that she looked quite dead, even to the determined old doctor. But he fought for the tiny scrap, slapping the wrinkled blue skin and scooping away with his fingers the mucus that clogged her minute throat.

Lizzie stood with Flo, watching in terror, as the baby refused to respond. Her eyes were squeezed tight, her starfish fingers bunched into blue metal fists. As she hung upside down in the doctor's hands, he gave a cry that had both Lizzie and Flo jumping in fright. But the words he uttered caused a small miracle. They would live in Lizzie's memory for the rest of her life.

'Live for your grandmother, child, live for Kate Allen!' the old man raved, sweat pouring from his face, his bloody hands and arms shaking as he held the infant aloft.

The scream was instantaneous. A yell of defiance in the face of death. A wail that penetrated Lizzie's trembling body and made Flo gasp aloud. It continued, as Babs' cries had rung out continuously four hours earlier, rebounding from the walls.

Dr Tapper laid the baby beside her mother. He took a damp cloth and cleaned her limbs. Lizzie gave him a clean white towel and he wrapped her in it.

Babs' white face was impassive. She stared at the child and the old man without recognition.

'She needs to suckle,' he said quietly.

Lizzie watched as he turned down the sheet and laid the child at Babs' breast.

The wailing stopped. Greedy sucks replaced it.

'Hold her,' the doctor said, more firmly.

But Babs slowly turned her head. She lay without movement, allowing the doctor to push the child into place with a pillow. They looked on as the baby fed, with no loving arms about it.

The doctor washed his hands in the bowl. He pulled down his shirtsleeves, then replaced his waistcoat. When he looked at Lizzie, his face was that of a very old man. Older than she had ever seen him before.

'Make certain the baby is fed,' he told Lizzie. 'One of you must always be present.'

'Why won't she feed her?' Flo asked, her young face seeming to Lizzie to have also grown older.

'Who knows.' Dr Tapper looked long and hard at them. 'The child's survival will depend on you, until the mother responds.'

'What about Babs?' Lizzie asked. 'Will she be all right?'

'If the bleeding stops, yes, she will recover.'

'What if it doesn't?'

'Just pray it will.' He pulled on his black coat and

picked up his bag. His movements were slow and weary. Lizzie was reminded of Bill and the sack of potatoes.

'Will you come again?' Lizzie asked as they all moved to the door.

He nodded. 'Later today. Yes. Remember, be vigilant with the child.'

As Lizzie went to accompany him from the room, she glanced at Flo. 'Wait here. I won't be long.'

Flo looked nervous. Lizzie squeezed her hand. 'I won't be long.'

In the front room, Frank was lying on his back on the couch, snoring loudly. The doctor looked down at him as he passed, hesitating briefly. At the door, he paused. Stretching out his hand, he laid it on Lizzie's shoulder. 'It will be up to you to guard the child's safety,' he told her quietly.

'I don't know about babies,' she said in confusion.

'Then here is your chance to learn.' He gripped her shoulder tightly. 'It sometimes happens that a woman rejects her baby. For a while at least. Be patient – and circumspect. This baby girl is your mother's first grandchild. She would have looked after her as if she was her own.'

For a few moments they looked at one another. Lizzie felt the weight of his words, understood their meaning. Until Babs had recovered, she must care for the child, see to its needs. Kate would have wanted it. She would have undertaken the duty with love and patience. Lizzie knew what was expected of her.

When the doctor left, she returned to the bedroom, ignoring the figure prone on the couch. Flo was bending over the bed, guiding the baby's hands to her mother's breast. Babs' face was turned away, her eyes closed as though she was sleeping.

Lizzie stood quietly beside Flo. The baby's small mouth sucked at the nipple. It was a miracle they had both survived. A peaceful air spread over the room. The agonizing delivery and the events preceding it seemed distant now. The new life that had resulted from such pain bathed them in its miraculous glow.

'Go and sleep now,' Lizzie whispered.

'I'll stay,' Flo said quickly, her fingers linked with the baby's. 'I'll watch too.'

'We'll take it in turns,' Lizzie agreed. 'But one of us must rest.'

Reluctantly, Flo wriggled her finger free. The baby's eyes flickered open. Lizzie and Flo breathed in sharply.

They were a deep midnight blue.

Chapter Twenty-Five

Lizzie placed the sprig of holly on the shelf beside Lil's sponge cakes and laughed as Ethel made a face behind Lil's back.

'Well?' demanded Lil as she turned quickly to frown at her daughter. 'I'm in demand, ain't I? Why shouldn't I blow me own trumpet?'

'It wouldn't be like you not to, Mum,' Ethel laughed.

It was two days before Christmas. Lizzie, Ethel, Lil and Bill were all in festive mood. Lil had just brought some freshly made cakes, as Lizzie had sold out.

'How many cakes is that this week?' Lil demanded of Lizzie. 'Tell her.'

'Twelve,' admitted Lizzie with a rueful smile. 'You must be putting something in them, Lil.'

'They melt on yer tongue,' Bill said as he came into the shop from serving outside. 'Don't need me choppers in to eat 'em. See?'

The three women screeched as Bill spat out his teeth, stuffed them in his pocket and pushed a slice of sponge cake into his mouth, gulping loudly.

'You'll get indigestion,' Lil cackled loudly, pulling up the collar of her coat.

'Nah,' Bill disagreed smugly. 'Not on your food, Lil. Even old Benji likes your cookin'. And he's right partic'lar, he is.'

Lil's eyes opened wide. 'You ain't been giving me cake to the 'orse!' she cried in alarm. There was so much laughter that the customer outside came in the shop and joined in the merriment. It was whilst everyone was laughing and joking that a soft wail came from the storeroom.

'The baby!' Lizzie turned and hurried away, closely followed by Lil and Ethel.

In the storeroom a big bassinet stood by the sacks of potatoes. The three women peered into it. As they were staring at its contents, Bill poked his head round the door.

'You do the honours, gel. I'll manage out here.'

'You sure, Bill?' Lizzie rocked the pram up and down.

'Bert's due back in a minute. Give the young 'un her grub.'

But Lizzie, Lil and Ethel were too engrossed in the baby to listen.

'You don't feed the poor little blighter in here, do you?' Lil cried as Lizzie lifted the baby, swathed in blankets, and rocked her in her arms.

'Course not, Lil. I take her downstairs. You coming?'

'Wouldn't miss it for the world, ducks.'

'What about you, Ethel. Got time for a cuppa?'

Ethel nodded eagerly. 'What do you think I came over for? Er, is Frank home?'

Lizzie shook her head. 'No, coast's clear.' She knew that neither Ethel, who had a day off from Rickards, nor Lil would want to bump into Frank. There was no chance of that. He didn't want to answer any questions about Babs or the baby. He had dragged himself from the couch the following day and without a word to anyone, left the airey. Lizzie knew it would be some time before he showed his face again.

Soon all three were downstairs in the airey chatting, taking off their coats and fighting over who should hold the baby. Lizzie left Lil and Ethel to decide and went to warm the milk in a pan. When it had boiled, she poured it into the banana-shaped glass bottle and quickly made tea.

The fire roared in the grate, the armchairs pulled up beside it. Lil and Ethel had settled themselves beside the warmth, with the baby on Ethel's lap.

'Blimey, ain't she small!' Lil exclaimed, as Ethel removed the blankets. The long white linen gown that Lizzie had bought from the old girl's stall at Cox Street market was tucked warmly round her.

'She's put on an ounce. Bill weighed her on the shop scales. She's nearly six pounds.'

'Ethel was ten pound eleven ounces,' Lil yelped. 'Like a blooming great baby elephant she was.'

Ethel sighed loudly. 'Yeah, well, tell the world won't you, Mum.'

'Had an appetite to match,' Lil added for good measure.

Ethel rolled her eyes at Lizzie.

'Well, the rate she's feeding, she'll soon beat that,' Lizzie said as she took the baby from Ethel. She nuzzled the teat against the baby's lips. At once the little girl sucked greedily at the teat. 'Look!'

'A right little gannet,' Ethel squeaked

The two women bent close to the baby. Lil heaved a sigh. 'She ain't half lovely. Bald as a badger, but lovely. And them eyes, so blue. Yeah . . . really blue.'

Lizzie looked up. Ethel coughed. 'Where's Babs then?' Lil continued, unaware of what she had just said. 'Why don't she breastfeed?'

Lizzie didn't want to say that Babs disliked feeding the baby. She also didn't want to reveal that Babs was out of the house most of the time. She had stayed in bed for a week, until the bleeding had stopped. But as soon as she was on her feet, she was off out. Lizzie had tried to persuade her to stay in and rest, but on Monday, she had come down from the shop to find the baby screaming and Babs gone. Lizzie'd had a terrible fright. She remembered what Dr Tapper had said about being vigilant. So she'd got Bert to go to the secondhand stall at the market and buy a crib. She made up her mind that she would take the baby into the shop and keep an eye on her there. Bert had returned with a great big old perambulator. Lizzie had managed to squeeze it into the storeroom. Luckily, the baby seemed to like it, almost as though she knew she was safe. She rarely cried.

'What's Babs going to call her?' Ethel asked.

Lizzie shrugged. That, too, was of no interest to Babs. 'Hasn't thought of a name yet.'

'Well, she's got to be registered, ain't she?'

Lizzie nodded. 'I'm going to do it tomorrow.' As soon as Babs came home this evening, she was going to tell her the baby had to have a name.

'Is Babs gonna stay here?' Lil asked curiously as she looked around the airey.

'She's sleeping in my room with the baby. There's plenty of space.'

'What does Frank say about that?

Lizzie had her answer ready. 'He don't mind,' she shrugged. 'He sleeps on the couch.' She didn't add that he was never home to sleep on it now.

'Where do you sleep?' Ethel asked.

'With Flo.' Lizzie grinned. 'A bit like old times.'

'So it's happy families again, is it?' Lil said with a hint of sarcasm.

Lizzie didn't answer. It wasn't happy families, not yet, at any rate. But she hoped it would be. She could offer Babs and the baby a home until they got somewhere. Flo loved the baby as much as she did. They could all live together under one roof like the old days.

Lizzie looked up at Lil. 'I like the name Polly.'

Lil frowned. 'Polly put the kettle on, I suppose.'

Ethel chuckled. 'Well, she'll be doing a lot of that in this house.'

'Yeah, but don't count yer chickens,' Lil said, looking at Lizzie. 'It wouldn't do to get too fond of her. Babs might up and off. You know what she's like.'

'She's got nowhere else to go,' Lizzie replied shortly. Why did Lil always have to put a damper on things?

'She could go back to where she came from.' Lil didn't say the house in Poplar, but they all knew she meant it.

'Why would she do that?' Lizzie put the bottle on the table and lifted the baby on to her shoulder. She patted her back, as she had done at every feed since her birth. She loved the feeling, the sense of calm. She loved everything about the little mite.

'Because she won't want to stay cooped up here.' Lil sniffed. 'Sorry, love, but that's the way I see it.'

'Oh, Mum!' Ethel said, embarrassed. 'Why do you have to go and say that?'

Lil looked at Lizzie, her dark eyes unwavering. 'Because I know Babs, that's why. Leopards don't change their spots.'

Lizzie didn't want to hear any more. She was certain Babs was going to change her ways. How could she want to go back to that life, living amongst women who sold their bodies for money? Babs had been looked after and cared for here. She was amongst family, with no bills to pay and a roof over her head.

'Could I hold her for a minute?' Ethel asked. She met Lizzie's eyes. There was apology written in them for her mother's outspokenness.

Lizzie smiled at her friend and gently laid the baby in her arms.

'Blimey!' shrieked Lil, staring at Ethel. 'Don't you go getting broody again.'

Ethel kissed the baby's forehead. 'Oh, hark at it,' she whispered, tracing her finger over the baby's soft pink skin. 'Your Auntie Lil doesn't half go on.'

Lil was about to reply when the baby gurgled and brought up wind. In doing so, she gave everyone a big smile that spread right up to her deep blue eyes. The three women all screamed in delight, then howled with laughter as wind travelled down the other way to the tradesmen's door – as Lil remarked, holding her nose with her fingers and gasping with laughter at the same time.

Christmas Day 1926 was one of Lizzie's happiest. Flo, Sydney, Bert, Babs and Lizzie all sat round the kitchen table, a feast set out in front of them. Bert and Sydney had carried the big perambulator down from the shop. Polly, as the baby had finally been named, was fast asleep in it.

Bill had spotted Frank going down to the airey the day before. It was Friday, Christmas Eve, and custom was brisk. Polly had been blowing bubbles, staring up at the twirling coloured balls that Bert had fixed on the hood of the perambulator. When Bill hurried in breathlessly to tell Lizzie he had seen his son going down the airey steps, Lizzie's heart had started to beat very fast. She knew Babs was at home, or had been, earlier that day.

Lizzie said nothing to Bill and continued to serve the customers. She didn't want to see or speak to Frank. There was only thing that mattered, Polly's welfare. And whilst the baby was in the storeroom she could guarantee her safety.

Bill had been surprised that Frank hadn't made an appearance in the shop. Lizzie knew why. He didn't want to face her. Though Bill didn't know the truth about the night of Polly's birth – no one did – Lizzie would never forget the scene she had witnessed. She had no forgiveness in her heart for her husband. She hoped that in time the painful memory would fade. But the hurt and anger was still inside her. She tried to put it to one side, for Polly's sake.

In the afternoon she had taken Polly down for her feed. The airey had been strangely silent. Babs wasn't in. Frank had taken some clothes from his wardrobe. The thought crossed Lizzie's mind that they had gone away together. But what about the baby? She had gone back to the shop after Polly's feed, anxious and upset. She realized how much Polly meant to her and Lil's warning words went through her mind.

However, Babs had come back that night, laughing, joking and a little tipsy. She helped Lizzie decorate the Christmas tree and even fed Polly. She said nothing about Frank and Lizzie didn't ask.

Now it was Christmas Day. All the family sat around the table. Sydney had been invited and looked smart in a waistcoat and white shirt, the collar pinned underneath by gold studs. As Lil and Doug had gone to Ethel's, Bert had come over for the day. He too wore his Sunday best, a suit brought out of mothballs for the occasion.

Babs was trying to flirt with Sydney, but hadn't got very far. He blushed very easily. Flo kept giving Babs black looks. Lizzie thought how much like old times it was and for a minute she remembered Pa and Ma. No one had said anything about Pa. No one wanted to remember the bad times on Christmas Day.

Lizzie dished out the roast turkey, stuffing, sausages,

bacon and batter and jugs of rich brown gravy. It all disappeared very quickly, to be followed by Christmas pudding and brandy sauce. The kitchen reeked of it. And right on time, at the end of the meal, little Polly stirred in her perambulator.

Lizzie went and picked her up, bringing her into the kitchen. She was warm as toast with rosy cheeks. Her big blue eyes looked like sparkling little jewels. She rubbed her snub nose with tiny fingers and yawned. Lizzie lowered the baby into Babs' lap.

'Here's to Pol,' Bert said, raising his beer.

Lizzie lifted her glass of ginger wine, as did Flo and Sydney. 'To Pol,' they cried.

Lizzie looked round the table. Everyone was happy, laughing and enjoying themselves. She missed Bill and Gertie but they were over at Gertie's place, no doubt celebrating in style. And she missed Ma and Pa, but she hoped they were together and looking down on the family, happy to see them united.

'Happy Christmas everyone,' she said breathlessly, glancing at Flo and Sydney, then at Bert and Babs and finally, with a tug at the heart, at little Polly.

Even Lil, on Boxing Day, didn't ask after Frank. Lizzie knew no one cared. Lil put on a spread as usual at her house, for friends and neighbours. There was a big knees-up in the afternoon, with the baby's head well and truly wetted.

'The same women next door, are they?' Lizzie asked as she joined Lil in the kitchen to prepare the punch.

'Yeah, but I never speak.' Lil rolled some apples and oranges on to the table. She picked up a sharp knife and began to slice them. 'The blooming front door opens and closes all night. It's a wonder the coppers don't do something about it.'

'I've never heard from old Symons.'

'No, well, you wouldn't would you? I 'spect Vinnie pays him a good whack.'

'Do you see Vinnie at all?'

'Doug saw him the other night. Up at the Quarry. Didn't say two words.'

'I meant does he come next door.'

Lil shrugged. 'Don't look out for him, gel. He ain't worth the trouble.'

Lizzie knew that Lil was angry about what Vinnie had done. They all were. But what could they do? She had turned the problem over and over in her mind, but it always came down to money. As long as the landlord was earning, he didn't care where the money came from.

'Ethel not coming over today?' Lizzie asked, changing the subject.

'No, poor kid,' Lil replied as the noise from the front room grew louder and merrier. 'Richard's old girl is having a do and wanted them all over at her house. Ethel was dreading it. They all sit there like stuffed dummies. The kids have to be on their best behaviour and be quiet.'

'Don't they have a knees-up?'

Lil laughed as she chucked the chopped fruit into the punch bowl, then poured on lemonade. 'You must be jokin'. There ain't a pair of pink flannelette drawers to be seen within miles of the Rydes' front room.'

They were laughing over this when Babs walked in with the baby. Polly was bawling and red in the face. Babs looked fed up. 'I think I'll go for a walk,' she said, passing Polly over to Lizzie. 'She ain't stopped screaming.'

'Why don't you go out in the yard?' Lil said, jabbing the knife at the back door. 'There's Ethel's old pram in the shed. Lay her in it and rock her.'

Babs gave Lil a frown. 'I've got a headache. I need to stretch me legs.'

'She's probably hungry,' Lizzie said as she lay Polly against her shoulder and patted her back. 'Do you want me to feed her?'

Babs shrugged. 'If you want. See you later, then.'

Lil and Lizzie watched Babs sway down the passage, grab her coat from the coatstand and go out the front door. It closed again with a bang. Lizzie knew Lil was bursting to speak her mind. She knew exactly what Lil would say about Babs. Earlier on she had called her 'a moody cow' – but, as Lizzie rocked the baby gently, Lil bit her lip and resumed chopping the fruit.

'She's as good as gold now,' Lil muttered under her breath. 'Knows when she's well off, that baby does.'

Lizzie smiled to herself. She knew Lil would have liked to get to the bottom of Polly's conception and the reason why Babs had suddenly decided to return to the fold, but Lizzie was certain that things were turning out for the best. Even if Babs wasn't a natural mother, she would learn to love little Polly. Who couldn't love the dear little mite? And Lizzie was quite prepared to make up for the lack of affection meanwhile. Between her and Flo, little Polly was showered with attention at home. And when Bert, Bill and Gertie chipped in, Polly was positively adored.

'Right,' said Lil, wiping her hands on her pinny. She lifted the big glass bowl in her rough red hands. 'Doug, get yer poker ready. The punch is coming!'

Holding the baby carefully against her, Lizzie followed Lil into the front room. The heat from the fire nearly knocked her over, as did the noise. The tradition was to place the punch bowl in the hearth, heat the poker and plunge it into the punch.

This year, Doug was ready in advance. He was holding the poker aloft, glowing red from the heat of the fire, his round face beaming. Everyone held their breath. Lil lowered the glass bowl in front of the fire on to the shiny green tiles. When she stepped back, no one said a word, they just waited.

Lizzie propped the baby up in her arms. This was the first Christmas of her young life. These were the rough, kind people of the Isle of Dogs who made up Polly's world. Even though she was not yet a month old, Lizzie wanted her to see all that was going on.

Doug thrust the poker into the punch. The liquid sizzled like a witch's cauldron, froth bubbling over the surface. Everyone clapped and cheered. Lizzie clasped Polly tightly, giving her a hug. Polly stared back at her as if she understood, her dark blue eyes sparkling in the light of the fire. As bright and twinkling as the lights radiating from the stones on Lizzie's Dearest ring.

Bert drove them home at ten o'clock. A sky full of stars lit up the dark streets. Flo and Sydney snuggled against each other in the back of the cart. Polly was sound asleep in her cocoon of blankets, safe in Lizzie's arms.

Babs hadn't returned to Lil's. All the way home, Lizzie wondered what she had been up to. Where had she been all that time? And with whom?

'It was a lovely do,' Flo said from the other side of the cart as she snuggled against Sydney. 'That punch went to me head.'

'Yeah, me too,' said Sydney with a big grin.

'Well, as long as it ain't gone to yer hands,' Flo giggled and they all laughed as she slapped Sydney's hands playfully.

Lizzie knew that Sydney was blushing, even in the dark. She had changed her opinion of Sydney Miller. She just hoped he would stay on the straight and narrow for Flo's sake. She could see them getting hitched one day.

'You lot all right in the back?' Bert shouted over his shoulder.

'Lovely,' the three of them yelled back and started laughing again.

Little Polly remained asleep. She was soothed by the movement of the cart. Though the sacking from the potatoes was rough and prickly, it kept them warm. Lizzie thought of the night long ago when Flo had scarlet fever and Frank had driven her to the hospital. He had seemed so kind and considerate. A different person. But then perhaps she had been different too. Perhaps Frank's jealousy was not unfounded. She had loved Danny dearly. It was a love that had changed her life and sometimes she still couldn't believe that Danny had broken his promise to her.

Under the light of the moon and the stars, Lizzie knew she was becoming maudlin. She didn't allow herself to think of Danny very often. It was a luxury she afforded herself only rarely. A guilty one, because she was still Frank's wife, no matter how he had behaved.

The baby stirred under the blankets. Lizzie hugged her tightly. They would soon be home. It had been a lovely Christmas, the best in years. She just hoped that when they got in Babs would be in a good mood and cuddle Polly for a while. Polly needed to hear her mother's voice – the most important voice in her young life.

When Bert drew the cart up in Ebondale Street, they all climbed out. Their breath curled up in the night air like smoke. It wasn't as cold as it was damp. Lizzie was eager to get Polly inside.

'I'll stable the 'orse and give him something to eat,' Bert told them as they stood at the top of the steps leading down to the airey. He hugged Lizzie and the baby, then Flo. After seeing to Benji, he had to make the long walk back to Langley Street. He jumped back up on the cart and clucked Benji on.

'Go on home, then,' Flo said to Sydney, elbowing him hard in the ribs. 'The party's come to an end in case you haven't noticed.'

Lizzie knew that Flo was embarrassed.

'Goodnight, Sydney.' Lizzie started to make her way down the dark steps. She knew Flo wanted to be kissed goodnight.

'Er, 'night Mrs Flowers,' Sydney called in a strangled voice.

'Won't be a minute,' Flo yelled.

Lizzie smiled to herself. Young love!

She had tied a key on a string for Babs and it hung behind the letterbox. With the baby in the crook of her left arm, she reached in and drew the string out. Turning the key in the lock, she walked into a dark room.

At once, Lizzie knew Babs wasn't home. Her heart gave a little kick. Where was she? Making her way over to the perambulator, just visible in the darkness, she lay Polly inside it. Next she lit the two oil lamps and light filled the room.

Everything was just as it had been when they had left that morning. Suddenly Flo came flying in. She was about to speak when she saw the look on Lizzie's face. Her expression of pleasure from the kiss she had just received from Sydney quickly faded.

'Blimey, where is everyone?' Flo spluttered, walking slowly forward.

'Babs ain't here.' Lizzie looked in the kitchen and came out again.

Still with their coats on, Lizzie and Flo walked down the dark passage, the oil lamp in Lizzie's hands, light and shadow fluttering around them.

At the bedroom door they stopped. 'Can't hear a thing,' Flo whispered. 'Let's go inside.'

Lizzie knew before they went in that the room was empty. It was cold and still. But then Lizzie noticed something else. There was nothing in it, no clothes strewn over the chairs or shoes on the floor. Babs' few possessions, most of them donated to her by Lizzie and Flo, were always scattered untidily everywhere.

Now they were gone.

Lizzie stood still, her heart sinking. Lil's words went through her mind again. 'A leopard doesn't change its spots . . .'

'Look, what's this?' Flo walked over to the dressing table. She picked up a torn piece of paper and read aloud. 'Have found somewhere to live. Will be back for the baby soon. Babs.'

It was then that Lizzie knew what fear was. It travelled like a spear through her body as her mind raced ahead. Where had Babs gone? Who was she with? What was she doing? And most frightening of all, when would she return for Polly?

Book Four

Chapter Twenty-Six

1931

'Take a deep breath, blow out all the candles and make a wish.'

'Will it come true, Auntie Lizzie?'

'One day it will.'

'When I'm grown up?'

'P'raps.'

'I want it to come true now.'

Brushing Polly's dark curls from her face, Lizzie laughed. 'That's a bit of a tall order.'

'Will you help me blow them out if I haven't got enough puff?'

'Everyone will.'

The airey was full of laughter, smoke and happy faces. Though 1931 had been hard for the nation, Lizzie was content. She gazed at her five-year-old niece, dressed in her pale pink party frock, her long curly black hair tumbling over her shoulders. A thrill of pride went through her. Lizzie, at twenty-six, was grateful for the little girl whom she looked upon as her daughter. Today was Polly's birthday party. Officially the day before, the twelfth of December, the celebrations had been moved to Sunday, when the shop was closed.

Lil's pink and white iced sponge was decorated with five tiny pink candles. 'Blow!' everyone cried. Polly blew, extinguishing four. Her small heart-shaped face fell.

Lil laughed. 'Aw, never mind, love. Make yer wish anyway. I'll light 'em all again and we can have another go.'

Polly's bright blue eyes were puzzled. 'Shall I say what my wish is after I've wished it, Auntie Lil?'

'No, keep it all to youself, ducks. Don't tell a soul.'

'But if I don't say what it is, who's gonna know what I want?'

Before Lil could answer, the front door opened. Flo, late home from the factory, came flying in. Her short brown hair was strewn over her face and she was puffing hard. 'Happy birthday, monkey. May all your wishes come true!' She scooped Polly into her arms.

'Put me down, Auntie Flo. I'm just making me wish,' Polly giggled.

Lizzie felt very happy, watching her friends and family. Her green eyes were sparkling, her long black hair drawn back into an elegant clasp and fixed at the nape of her neck. She wore a new beige wool crêpe dress with a V-shaped neckline. The dropped waist and accordion pleats were very fashionable. It was the first dress she had ever bought new and she loved it.

All the guests were spruced up. Lil wore a smart black and white two piece suit. Doug had put on a stiff collar and a silk waistcoat. Bert wore a clean pair of trousers and a set of red braces. Vi Catcher, sitting in the chair beside Fat Freda, sported a new hat with a feather in it. Freda, as usual, made no concession to the occasion. She wore with pride her market overall, a large flowered garment with voluminous pockets.

'Blimey, I ain't got enough wind to blow out me matches lately, let alone all them candles,' puffed Boston Brown as he bent over the table, pursing his lips and pressing his handlebar moustaches out of the way.

'No, but you've still got enough breath to flog that cheap fish of yours to all me customers,' Reg Barnes replied. 'I keep telling them they'll end up looking like 'addocks if they don't eat a bit of beef.'

'You two should worry.' Elfie Goldblum looked up at the two tall men either side of him. 'You should be selling jewellery when the nation is nearly bankrupt!'

'Go on with you,' Fat Freda called from her chair. 'You got all yer pound notes 'idden under yer carpet, Elfie.'

'I wish I had a carpet, my dear. I don't know such a luxury.'

'It's that MacDonald's fault!' cried Reg. 'He don't know what he's doing. Says we've got ourselves in a blooming fix. But who's to blame, that's what I wanna know? Not the ordinary bloke on the street, it ain't. We work bloody hard for a pittance and if I had half the chance I'd tell him so.'

'A chance you'll never have, my friend,' said Elfie darkly.

'It'll mean another coalition if you ask me,' mumbled Doug. 'None of them up in Whitehall knows whether they're on their heads or their heels.'

'You ain't wrong there,' nodded the fishmonger. They're putting up taxes again – wringing the last penny out of us, just like the other lot did after the war.'

'What are you blokes going on about?' cried Lil, hands on hips. 'This ain't a bloody union meeting. Now all of you, let's help our Pol to blow out them candles.'

Lil lit the candles once more. There was a lot of huffing and puffing. All the candles flickered out and Polly was showered with hugs and kisses.

Lizzie smiled at Ethel, who had just brought in a plate of sandwiches from the kitchen. Ethel was dressed in a light grey dress, her fair hair styled short and smart. She was still very attractive, but seemed quieter now. Lizzie put it down to living with the humourless Richard all these years.

'Your two enjoying themselves, are they?' Lizzie asked, glancing at Ethel.

Rosie and Timmy were now thirteen and fourteen. They were happy kids and took after Ethel, or how she used to be. Full of life and laughter.

Ethel nodded. 'You don't have to ask do you? They love coming here.'

'You should bring them more often.'

'Wish I could.' She looked up from under her lashes and sighed. 'We have to visit Richard's mum and pay homage on Saturdays.'

Lizzie couldn't help giggling at the mental picture of

the whole family kneeling at Mrs Ryde's feet. 'Still as bad is she?'

'On a scale of one to ten, I'd say twelve. Next thing is she'll be wearing a tiara and one of them fur capes.'

The two girls laughed together, but Lizzie knew Ethel's mother-in-law took a lot of tolerating. 'Is trade still brisk?' Ethel asked, changing the subject as she always did when it came to Richard's snobby family.

'Not bad. We're turning over, that's the main thing. What about Rickards?'

Ethel frowned. 'Well, the Depression's hit us, no doubt about that. I reckon we should sell cheaper and take a cut on the profits. Encourage new trade.'

'Why don't you suggest it?' Lizzie asked at once. She agreed with Ethel. They had had to bring their prices right down in the shop.

Ethel raised her eyes. 'You know what Rickards are like – real stick in the muds. They've sacked two of the warehouse staff rather than trim the profits. It was a good job you never came to us, Lizzie.'

'Yeah, I s'pose it was.' Lizzie might have regretted her decision to marry Frank, but she loved the shop. It was the best thing that had ever happened to her.

'Seen anything of Frank, dare I ask?' Ethel asked tentatively

'No – and I don't expect to.'

'He's working for the bookie, is he?'

'So I've heard.' Lizzie hadn't seen her husband more than a handful of times since Polly had been born. The fact that he avoided her made her even more certain he was Polly's father. She had accepted her marriage to Frank had failed, but the anger and hurt were still there, locked deeply inside her. He didn't bother Bill for money any longer, working, according to gossip, for Mik Ferreter. It was a fact that surprised no one, least of all Lizzie.

'What about Babs? Still comes to see Pol, does she?' Ethel ventured.

Ethel was the only one, apart from Flo, with whom Lizzie had shared the truth of the terrible night of Polly's birth. Lil had a good idea what had happened, but Lizzie had always kept silent on the subject of Polly's father. Babs had never said who it was and Lizzie hadn't asked.

Lizzie nodded. 'She turns up every now and then. Takes Pol up Island Gardens or the market.'

'What does Pol think of that?'

'She don't say much. When I ask if she has a nice time, she just nods and says yes. But I notice she's never too keen to go.'

Just then Polly came running over. 'When are Bill and Gertie coming, Auntie Lizzie?' she cried excitedly, pink icing round her mouth.

'As soon as they've finished dinner. Come here, young lady, and wipe your mouth.' Lizzie bent down and dabbed Polly's small mouth with a napkin.

'Will Mummy be coming as well?' Polly licked her clean lips.

'She might. We'll have to see.' Lizzie knew that Babs couldn't be relied on to turn up, despite it being Polly's birthday party.

'Thank you for my book, Auntie Ethel,' Polly chattered on, luckily not discouraged by Lizzie's answer. 'I like fairy tales. My favourite's when Beauty kisses the beast. He's not really a beast, but a prince. He had a spell put on him.'

'I hope you enjoy it, darling.' Ethel gave Polly a hug.

Lizzie picked up a knife and began to cut the cake. At the back of her mind there was always the worry that Babs would take Polly away. It wasn't likely. She hadn't wanted to in five years. Why should she change her mind now? She had nowhere to take a child, much less provide for her. But the thought haunted Lizzie. Babs was unpredictable, her mood swings frequent. Lizzie never felt at ease whilst Polly was out with her mother. She always breathed a sigh of relief when they returned home. What would she do if Babs demanded Polly back or just took her?

'Want any help, sis?' Flo came to stand at the table. She had changed into a pale blue dress that showed off her good figure and long legs. Her brown hair curled softly round her face. To Lizzie's relief, the kiss-curl had finally turned into a smooth, glossy wave. The engagement ring on her finger was from Sydney. He'd proposed in the summer and Flo had accepted him. Next year they would be married.

'No, but you could top up the drinks,' Lizzie smiled. She watched Flo go off, happiness radiating from her sister's face. Lizzie's mind flew back across the years to when that expression had filled her own eyes. Her heart gave a painful jerk as she thought of Danny. Did he ever think of her? She could still remember the deep sound of his voice . . .

'You all right, love?' It was Lil.

'Yes. Want a piece of your cake?'

Lil burst into laughter. 'Like taking coals to Newcastle, that is.' Lil wound an apron round her waist. 'I'm gonna start on them dishes in the kitchen whilst everyone's occupied. Fancy a chat?'

Lizzie nodded. A little reluctantly she followed Lil. She never quite knew what Lil would ask during one of her 'chats'. In the kitchen they stood side by side at the sink. Lil ran the water. 'You were deep in thought, gel. Is it that bloody husband of yours again?'

'No, not really.'

'You ain't seen him, I suppose?'

'No.'

'Well you wanna count yerself lucky.'

Lizzie didn't know about that. She missed being cared for as Frank had done before their wedding, his love only to disappear quickly afterwards.

'Good riddance to bad rubbish,' Lil said, her voice hard. 'Sorry, but you know how I've always felt about Frank.'

'Yeah, Lil. I know.' Lizzie pushed back her dark hair that had somehow managed to escape from its clasp.

Lil sighed as she washed the dishes. 'Do you remember the old days? When we had to bring in all the water from a tap in the backyard. You remember how you was up at the break of dawn, getting ready to push yer dad to market. I used to see you sometimes and think, poor little cow. And now look at you. A proper lady – and I mean that.' Lil puffed on a cigarette, somehow managing to keep it dry. 'You've come on a long way since then, love.'

'Do you know Ma's been gone eleven years and Pa five?' Lizzie murmured distractedly. 'Don't reckon we'll ever know what really happened to Pa.'

'No, you're not wrong there.' Lil busily scoured the dishes. At fifty-seven, her brown hair was streaked with grey, her face thinner, but she was still the same old Lil. 'I look at your old house sometimes and wonder where the time's gone.'

'Who's in there now?' Lizzie had lost count of the women moving in and out. There had been so many.

Lil sniffed. 'Well, that brassy bit of stuff, Lena, has stuck her heels in; no one's gonna move that cow in a hurry! The others come and go like bad pennies. Your brother turns up to collect the takings for Ferreter and he pays Symons.'

'How do you know all this?' Lizzie asked in surprise.

Lil smirked. 'When Lena's had a few up the pub she tells everyone her business. She's got a mouth as big as the Blackwall Tunnel.'

'And the police know?' Lizzie always felt angry about this. 'Why don't they do something?'

'Because the coppers get a back hander.' Lil puffed hard on her cigarette. 'The country's in such a state everyone's out for themselves, even the Old Bill.'

There was silence then and Lizzie guessed what was coming.

'Where's Babs today, then?' Lil asked.

Lizzie shrugged. 'Don't know.'

'Dunno how she could show her face.'

'I hope she comes, for Polly's sake.'

'Probably better if the kid never saw her again.'

Lizzie gave a gasp. 'Lil, don't say things like that.'

Lil pulled out the plug with a vengeance. 'Well, she don't treat that kid right, never has.'

'I don't want Polly to ever think she wasn't wanted.'

Lil turned to smile at Lizzie. 'You won't have to worry about that. You've given her all the love of a mother and more.'

'But it's not the real thing, is it? I'm not her mother. And she'll start to ask questions as she gets older.'

'You worry for nothing,' Lil said kindly. 'You know, I used to worry meself sick about our Ethel. There was I fretting over our Rosie and Timmy drifting off and us never seeing them again. But it's all come around the other way. The more hoity-toity the other half of the family gets, the more the two kids wanna come over to see us. You know, they're dead curious when I tell 'em the stories of their mum when she was a little girl and her two brothers who fought in the war. They like to hear about their two uncles who died for their country. They was heroes, our Greg and Neil, and the kids love that.' They stood quietly for a moment, each deep in thought. Then Timmy came running into the kitchen. 'Auntie Lizzie, there's someone at the door.'

'It's probably Bill and Gertie, Tim. Could you let them in?'

Lizzie was thinking about what she and Lil had been talking about when Flo came rushing towards them

'Blimey, gel, whose house is on fire?' Lil joked.

Flo stared at them, her face pink all over.

'What's the matter?' Lizzie asked, her heart racing. 'Is it Babs?'

'No, it ain't,' Flo sputtered. You'll never guess who it is.'

Lizzie glanced over Flo's shoulder. Two figures stood in the doorway; a tall man with his hand resting on a small boy's shoulder. The boy had a mop of sandy coloured hair and huge blue eyes that seemed to fill his face as he looked up. The man beside him stood without smiling, until meeting Lizzie's gaze his lips parted briefly, hesitantly, in a manner that Lizzie had only recalled in her dreams and had never dared hope to see again in reality.

Chapter Twenty-Seven

'I thought you'd have a surprise.' Flo shook Lizzie's arm, getting more excited by the minute. Danny was surrounded, the questions pouring at him from all angles.

'Blimey.' Lil's voice was a shocked whisper.

Polly came running down the kitchen steps. 'Who is that man, Auntie Lizzie? Is he coming to my party? He's got a boy with him—'

Lizzie closed her hand tightly around Polly's.

'Give yer Auntie Lizzie a chance now, love,' said Lil firmly, recovering quickly. 'Let her get her breath.'

'I thought it was a ghost,' Lizzie breathed, staring at Danny, unable to believe what she was seeing.

'No, he's real enough.' Lil nudged her arm, a grin spreading across her lips. 'Handsome bugger still, ain't he?'

Danny wore a suit under the heavy travelling jacket. His hair had turned a golden blond and was brushed back behind his ears. He seemed taller, Lizzie thought, and broader. She tried to tear her eyes away, but she couldn't.

'Shouldn't you go and speak to him?' Lil gave her another nudge.

'I . . . I dunno what to say.'

'You could start with hello,' chuckled Lil.

Everyone was talking at once. Danny was walking towards her. Lizzie stepped forward, Polly at her side.

'Hello, Lizzie.' Danny's voice hadn't changed. It was still deep and warm, and her heart raced up into her throat as she heard it.

'Hello, Danny.' Words failed her. There was a pounding in her ears that seemed to be getting louder.

Boston Brown clapped Danny on the shoulder. 'Where've you been all this time, you rascal? We thought we'd seen the last of you, you know!'

'Been living well by the looks of you,' shouted Reg, joining them. He slapped Danny on the back. 'Must be eating all them Australian cows the size of cartwheels.'

'And who's this?' cried Fat Freda, pushing her way through the men and looking down at the boy. 'Is this yer lad?'

Danny nodded. 'Tom, these are my friends from market, the ones I told you about.'

The boy stared up under his blond fringe, his blue eyes moving slowly over the gathering.

'You're the image of yer old man.' Freda attempted to soften her loud voice. 'How old are you, then?'

'I'm eight,' Tom replied quietly.

'Knew yer dad when he was your age.' Boston bent down and ruffled the boy's hair. 'Blimey, you are his double, mate, aren't you?'

The boy stared at the strange, coarse faces gathered round him. The freckles across his nose were like dots of brown paint sprinkled on his fair skin. He was dressed in a jacket and long trousers and was, Lizzie thought as she gazed at him, as Boston had remarked, the double of Danny.

'It's me party today.' Polly stood in front of Tom, who was a head and shoulders above her. 'I'm five. It was me real birthday yesterday, but the shop was open so I had to have it today. Would you like a piece of me birthday cake?'

Tom nodded slowly, his pale cheeks flushing.

Lizzie looked into Danny's smiling eyes and away again.

In the kitchen, Lizzie pulled out a chair. 'Sit down here, Tom.'

'I'll sit next to you.' Polly scrambled into the chair beside him. 'We've got lemonade or cream soda or ginger beer.' Polly reeled off the drinks.

'Could I have some milk?'

'The milk's in the pantry in a blue jug, Pol. Find a clean glass and fill it up for Tom.'

Whilst Polly went to get milk, Danny sat down at the table, pushing his golden hair back from his face. He looked very tired suddenly.

'It's been a long trip,' he said apologetically. 'We left Freemantle four months ago. Our ship had to pick up passengers at ports along the way. We docked last night, at Tilbury.'

Everyone had gone back into the front room, leaving them alone with the children. Lizzie couldn't stop looking at Danny. His skin was brown and weathered, making his eyes seem even bluer than ever. He wasn't the young boy she had known, but a fully grown and very handsome man. Had he made his fortune as he'd said he would? Why had he returned to England? And, the question she wanted to ask most, where was his wife?

Polly returned to the table, a glass of milk in her hand. 'Where's Fr . . . Fr . . .' she began, frowning at Tom.

'Freemantle.' Tom gulped down the milk. 'It's a town in Australia.'

'Where's Australia?'

'On the other side of the world.'

'Did you live there?'

Tom nodded, glancing at his father. 'But we're going to live in England, aren't we, Dad?'

Danny didn't reply. Lizzie clutched the teapot. They were coming to live in England! But where? And why? Her mind was whirling.

'I've just blown out me candles,' Polly told Tom and Danny in a sing-song voice. 'I made a wish. But Auntie Lil says I can't tell no one what it is.'

'No, course not,' agreed Danny softly. 'That would spoil it.'

'My mummy might come,' Polly continued as though she had known Danny and Tom for years. 'Or she might not.'

Lizzie quickly made the tea. It hadn't taken Polly very long to break the ice.

'Where does she have to come from?' asked Tom.

'Up Poplar. She lives with my Uncle Vinnie. She works a lot. She don't get much time to come round here.'

'Oh.' Tom took another gulp of milk.

Danny looked up at Lizzie. This time she didn't look away, but she didn't offer any explanation either.

'Where's your mummy, then?' Polly was off again.

'She died,' Tom told her, licking the milk from his lips.

Lizzie felt her insides go cold. She turned and stared at the little boy.

Polly leaned her elbows on the table and stared into Tom's face. 'That makes us nearly the same, 'cos I haven't got a daddy.'

'Did he die too?' Tom asked.

Polly nodded. 'Why do you talk that funny way?' Polly asked suddenly.

'It's how we speak in Australia.'

Polly giggled. 'It's nice. I like it.'

Lizzie placed a slice of birthday cake in front of Tom, then picked up the teapot and began washing it. Danny rose from the table. He came to stand beside her and grinned. 'You're going to scrub the pattern off if you're not careful.'

She realized what she was doing and stopped.

'It's a bit of a shock, me turning up, I suppose?' He took the teapot from her hands and dried it with the cloth.

Lizzie nodded. 'I'm sorry to hear about your wife.'

He hesitated as though about to say something, but then was quiet.

'Was she ill?' Lizzie asked.

'Elsa died of pneumonia.'

'Elsa? That's an unusual name.'

'Yes, it's Swedish.' He said no more, continuing to turn the teapot in his hands. After a while he spoke again. 'We didn't mean to interrupt your party. Dad wasn't home. Then we heard all the noise coming from down here.'

Lizzie realized he didn't want to talk of his wife. Perhaps it was still painful to do so. She poured hot water into the teapot. 'Bill's at Gertie's house. They'll be here soon.' She looked up at him, unable to resist a smile as she thought of Bill's reaction to seeing his long lost son. 'Your dad's going to have a shock when he sees you.'

Danny laughed. 'Yeah, I 'spect he will.' His smile faded as he looked into Lizzie's eyes. 'We've got a lot of news to catch up on.'

Lizzie didn't know if he was referring to her or Bill. So many thoughts were milling about in her head. Tom must have been very young when his mother died. Had Danny raised him on his own?

Just then, Lil came into the kitchen. 'As usual, I'm interrupting,' she cackled, coughing on her cigarette. 'Have you got somewhere to stay, yet, ducks?'

'No, we've come straight from Tilbury,' Danny replied with a shrug.

'Well, I've just had a word with Bert.' Lil puffed out a cloud of smoke. 'He said he'll kip on the mattress downstairs if you and Tom want his room for a couple of nights whilst yer looking for a place. Course, you might want to stay with yer dad, but I thought I'd make the offer.'

'Are you sure?' Danny sounded relieved. 'I don't want to put you out.'

'You won't.' Lil chuckled. 'That boy of yours looks as though he's getting on all right with our Pol.'

'Yeah, he does, doesn't he?' Danny was grinning. Turning his back to the two children, he said softly, 'Who does Polly belong to?'

'She's Babs',' Lizzie told him.

Lil raised her eyebrows. 'Yeah, well, that's a matter of opinion,' she muttered under her breath. 'Anyway, if you want to come home to us later, I'll do you a bit of grub and fill the bath up for that boy of yours. He can have a good soak and then have an early night. Strikes me he's about all in.' Lil nodded to the teapot. 'Why don't I make the tea whilst you two have a chat.'

Lizzie blushed. She didn't want everyone watching them; all eyes and ears seemed to be directed towards the kitchen.

'To be honest, Lil,' Danny said softly, 'me and Tom are pretty bushed. I think we'd better leave the chatting to another day. And anyway, this is Polly's party. We ain't going to spoil it for her.'

Lizzie glanced at Danny gratefully.

Lil looked at them both and then at the children. Lighting up another cigarette, she nodded slowly, exhaling on a long breath. Finally she turned back to Danny. 'Well, me and Doug will be leaving before it gets dark. You're welcome to join us.'

Danny smiled. Lizzie saw his chest rise gently in a sigh. 'Thanks, Lil, that'll do fine.'

Lizzie knew it was a sigh of relief, because she felt that way too.

*

Lizzie was feeling very strange the next morning. She dressed quickly and prepared breakfast wondering if she'd dreamed all yesterday's events. But Polly rushed into the kitchen in her nightdress, all her questions confirming it hadn't been a dream.

'Eat your porridge,' Lizzie had told her firmly in the end. 'You'll be late and Flo won't have time to drop you at school.'

'I don't want to go to school.'

'Why?'

'Uncle Danny and Tom might come round.'

'No they won't. They've got lots of other things to do. Now, let's get you dressed.'

Lizzie took Polly into the bedroom. Her mind wasn't on what she was doing. It was going over last night when Lil and Doug had left and Danny and Tom had gone with them. Danny had said very little. She had watched them leave, still unable to believe he was back in England.

Gertie and Bill had turned up late. Bill was overwhelmed when he heard the news. He didn't seem to be able to take it all in. Gertie had poured him a stiff drink but for the next hour he'd been unusually quiet.

Flo took Polly to school and Lizzie washed up the breakfast things. When she went up to the shop, Bill was waiting for her. 'Don't turn the sign on the door yet. Leave it closed,' he muttered. 'I've got a message for you.'

Lizzie stared at the old man. 'Who from?'

Bill led the way into the storeroom. He closed the door firmly. 'Danny.'

'Danny?' Lizzie's heart crashed in her chest. 'When did you speak to him?'

Bill looked weary, a growth of grey stubble on his chin. 'I couldn't rest,' he explained as he sat on a sack of potatoes with a long sigh. 'I went to Lil's late last night after I walked Gertie home. Me and Danny had a long chat.'

Lizzie didn't know what to ask first. 'Is he really coming back to live on the island?'

'He wants to open one of these new fangled garages. When he was in Australia he learned how to mend all them big lorries that the mines own.'

'But I thought he went out to Australia to look for gold.'

'He did, but he never found any. Instead, he met a bloke who taught him all about mechanical engines. That's what he's been doing all these years.' Bill sucked in a deep breath.

'But why didn't he write, why didn't he—'

'I dunno, gel. You'll have to ask him.' Lizzie stared at her father-in-law. He didn't seem to want to look her in the eye. She knew Bill knew something that he wasn't telling her. 'He said he'd see you up Island Gardens at twelve o'clock. You can have a bit of peace and quiet up there, with no one around.'

Lizzie sat down on a sack. Her legs suddenly felt lifeless. She felt as though she was doing something wrong. Going off up the park to meet Danny seemed underhand.

Bill was watching her. 'Now, listen to me, gel, you

don't owe Frank nothing, not after the way he's treated you.'

'He's still me husband.'

Bill shrugged. 'Please yerself, but Frank's gonna find out about Danny coming back. He ain't gonna welcome him with open arms, is he? I tired to tell Danny what a sod Frank is . . . how he's mixed up with a load of villains and, most important of all, that he don't have no time for his brother. But Danny's got a blind spot when it comes to Frank. So that bit's up to you, love, I'm afraid.' Bill stood up. 'Don't forget, twelve o'clock.'

Bill's words went through her mind. She didn't know what to do. She wanted to see Danny again. She wanted to look at him, to listen to his voice, to look into his eyes. And yet how could she feel this way when all those years ago he'd let her down so badly? Besides, for better or worse, she'd married Frank.

Chapter Twenty-Eight

She walked down the path to the river. The breeze blew across the park and a ship's hooter sounded. The sun sprinkled its light on the water, a sun that was more summer than winter. Bill was right. The place was deserted. All the kids were at school. Everyone else had better things to do on a Monday.

Would Danny be there on the bench where they used to sit, she wondered? Pulling the soft fur collar of her coat up to her neck she hurried on. The small path gave way to green and the low well of the sand pit.

The park bench came into view. Her heart leaped. Danny was sitting there dressed in the coat he'd worn the day before. His elbows were on his knees, his head bent. When he heard her footsteps he looked up.

She looked both ways. Still there wasn't a soul about.

'I wasn't sure you'd come,' he greeted her, rising to his feet. 'Sit down, get yer breath back.' His accent was still cockney. It gave her a thrill of pleasure to hear it.

They sat down, saying nothing. Danny's big blue eyes were staring at her. 'You haven't changed.'

'I must have. I was only a girl then.'

'You look the same to me.'

Lizzie turned to stare at the patch of green in front of them. 'Why have you come back, Danny?'

'Why do you think?'

She kept her gaze ahead. 'Did you make your fortune?'

'No. But I learned a lot.'

'Is learning enough to live on?' She looked slowly back at him.

'I'm gonna give it a try. Open a garage. Build up me own business.'

'A garage? You mean for motor vehicles?'

Danny nodded. 'That's me trade now. I learned out there, in Australia. Mending the big lorries that cart the rubble away from the mines. It's big business keeping them monsters going. A good bloke taught me. I'd never have got a trade if it wasn't for him.'

Lizzie looked at the man whom she had known as a boy. She hardly knew this stranger. He had spent eleven long years away. They had changed and they both knew it.

He looked down at his big workworn hands. 'Lil told me a lot last night. Then Dad came round and added his bit. But I'd like to hear it from you.'

'What do you want to know?'

He turned slowly, his eyes full of confusion. 'What are your feelings for Frank?'

She wasn't ready for that question. It was the last thing that she was thinking of. She didn't know if she'd ever loved him. It was a terrible admission, but it was true. She had married him for security and because he had asked her, as she had once confided to Ethel.

'Lil told me something,' Danny went on when she didn't answer. 'She said you never received my letters.'

'What letters?'

'The ones I wrote to you from Australia.'

'Well, none ever came.' Was he telling her the truth? Or was it just an excuse?

'I sent the first one from Sydney. I arranged with the post office to send any that came for me to Adelaide, where I was going.'

'But I . . . I never received any. I waited . . . and waited. Months, years . . . but a letter never came.'

'I kept going back to the post office. The only letter that came was from Frank. He said I shouldn't write again to you. He said I should write to him, that he'd let me know how things were going.'

'Why would he say that?'

'You mean you didn't know?'

She shook her head. 'When was all this?'

'Christmas, nineteen twenty-one. I drove in from the bush to Adelaide and there was this letter from England, waiting for me. I thought – at last – it was one from you. But it was from Frank. He wrote you'd got engaged in the summer, that you were marrying in spring. He said you had asked him to write and tell me. I couldn't believe it. I read it a dozen times over.'

'But it wasn't true,' Lizzie said in bewilderment. 'It was nineteen twenty-five when we married.'

Danny stared at her. 'You mean . . . three years later?'

'And our engagement was only for nine months.'

His face went ashen. 'So . . . Frank lied,' Danny whispered, his breath hushed. 'Me own brother . . . lied to me . . . deceived me. But why – why would he do that? He knew you were my girl, that I was coming back for you . . .'

Lizzie felt sick. The years rolled away. There she was, sitting on a bus beside Frank. It was in London, 1921, and they were on their way to visit Flo. Frank had put his arm along the seat behind her. 'I wouldn't give you a shilling for the likes of Sydney,' he had said. She had asked him why he had said 'Sydney', thinking he might have heard from Danny. And the truth was, he had, only the letter was meant for her and somehow he had got hold of it and—

Lizzie closed her eyes. Oh, why hadn't she known? Why had she allowed herself to be fooled? Frank had lied not only to Danny, but to her, and she had believed his lies. She didn't know what had happened to Danny's letters. But she believed he had written them.

'You waited, then?' Danny murmured, taking hold of her hands. 'You waited all that time?'

She nodded, his warm, strong fingers around hers. Frank had robbed them of a life together. He had done it coldly, calculatingly. In that moment she hated Frank. He had used her. He had never loved her. He had only loved himself.

'You know I named Tom after your dad, don't you?' Danny said softly.

Lizzie had guessed and she nodded, her heart full.

'What are we going to do, gel?' Danny asked her.

'What do you mean?'

'You didn't answer my question.'

'Frank is . . . still my husband.'

'Lil said you ain't lived with him for five years.'

'It won't make no difference. He won't like you coming back.'

'I ain't bothered what he likes. I'm bothered about us.'

'What about Elsa?'

Danny sat back, squaring his shoulders. 'I told you, she died.'

'You haven't said much about her.'

There was a long pause before he replied. 'There's not a lot to know. Like I said, she was from Sweden and trying to make a new life in Australia. A lot of the immigrants suffered because of the heat, especially those from cold countries. She . . . she was . . . not very strong.'

'Is that why she died so young?'

He nodded. 'The climate didn't suit her.'

There were so many things Lizzie didn't understand. Danny seemed reluctant to talk about his life in Australia, especially Elsa. Had he loved her so much that even now he couldn't bear to talk about her death? Then there was the letter. Even if Danny had believed the things Frank had written, he could still have come home to see for himself. If she meant anything to him, wouldn't he do that? But she knew she was blaming Danny for Frank's deception. Why shouldn't he believe Frank? He was his brother, after all. Unlike Frank, Danny had a trusting nature.

'Will you stay with Lil?' she asked after a while.

'Only until I can find a place. Lizzie, it's not too late for us.'

He gripped her small hands in his large ones. She gazed into his deep blue eyes. Frank had robbed them of a past. Danny wanted to claim a future but she couldn't bring herself to deceive Frank the way he had deceived her.

She slid her hands from his fingers. 'I have to go now. I told Bill I wouldn't be long.'

'When will I see you again?'

'I don't know.' She made herself walk away and tears filled her eyes. She still loved him, after all these years.

Lizzie was pleased when Christmas was over. Usually she loved it. But this year she had worried Frank would turn up. She opened the shop on New Year's Day to the familiar sound of her customers' complaints. Unemployment was rife. All day the talk in the shop was of the men threatening to demonstrate. The women were full of it. Yet another government crisis had provoked anger. 'All we want is work,' everyone said, 'and a fair day's wage and what do we get? Sod all!'

Most families on the island hadn't had a shilling for the meter let alone money for Christmas. What little spare there was had been spent in the pub. The first day of January was cold and bleak in more ways than one.

At six o'clock they were closing up and the doorbell went. Lizzie was in the storeroom, sweeping the floor. Bill called out, 'I'll see to it.'

Lizzie was thinking of what she had to prepare for

dinner. There was plenty of bubble and squeak left over from Christmas. She stretched her back, the strain on it from the day's exercise seeming greater than ever. Perhaps it was the bitter cold. She had expected Lil to come by, but she hadn't. Bert had said Danny was out every day looking for a place. Had he met Frank? No, he couldn't have. He would have told Lil or Bert if he had.

Just then she heard Bill enter the storeroom. 'I won't be a minute,' she called over her shoulder. 'I'll just put the broom away—'

'Hello, Auntie Lizzie.'

She swung round, her eyes widening as she saw who it was. 'Tom!' Danny stood beside him, a big smile on his face.

Bill bent down to his grandson. 'Well, this is a surprise, you coming to see yer old Grandad.' The old man ruffled the boy's untidy fair hair.

Lizzie stared at Danny, her heart beating fast. Her aching limbs and the pain in her back was forgotten. This was the Danny she used to know, dressed in working clothes, an open-necked shirt and jacket. There were streaks of dirt across his face and brick dust covered his trousers.

'Happy New Year,' he said softly.

She had almost forgotten what day it was. 'Happy New Year, Danny . . . Tom . . .' She bent down to give Tom a big hug.

'I've found a place at Morley's Wharf,' Danny told her.

'Morley's Wharf by the bridge?' Bill asked.

'That's right. An old warehouse. I'm doing it up. Tom and me moved in today.'

Lizzie glanced at Bill, whose face told her that he, too, was shocked at the news. 'It's cold in here,' she said quickly when she saw Tom shiver. 'Let's go downstairs.'

Bill nodded, looking brighter. 'Right you are. I'll just get me baccy tin.'

'Is Polly home?' Tom asked eagerly as they all left the shop and Bill locked up for the night.

Lizzie nodded. 'She's going to be surprised when she sees you, young man.'

'I want to tell her I'm starting school soon.' Tom looked up at his father as they stood in the cold, dark street. 'Aren't I, Dad?' he said proudly.

Later that evening, Polly and Tom were playing dominoes by the fire. The four adults were sitting at the kitchen table, talking quietly. Lizzie had made a meal of cold meat and crusty slices of white bread. The dirty plates were piled on the draining board. Flo was smoking a Woodbine, her elbows on the table. Danny was sipping his tea. Bill sat next to his son, his gnarled old fingers drumming on his baccy tin.

The talk had been of all that had happened in the years since Danny had left. Danny told them about Australia and his work with the mining company.

'Well, I hope you've considered yer brother,' said Bill at last as he rolled another cigarette. 'He tried to stop you coming home once before. Likely he'll try again.'

'I'll face that problem when I come to it,' Danny replied tightly.

'Frank's in with a rough bunch.'

'This is me home, Dad. And Tom's, too.' Danny looked down at the mug in front of him. 'Frank owes me an explanation.'

'Well, you can talk to 'im,' Bill interrupted again. 'But it won't do you no good. Just watch yer back, son. That's my advice.'

'Is there a place to sleep in this 'ere warehouse?' Flo changed the subject and puffed a cloud of smoke into the air.

'There's an office.'

'What, you'll sleep in an office?' Lizzie exclaimed in horror.

'It'll do us for a bit.'

'Blimey, you ain't joking about all this, are you?' Flo croaked.

'No, I'm not,' Danny replied. 'I've found the right place. There's even a hole in the middle of the floor where they stored the grain. Once we've got rid of the rats, it'll do for an inspection pit.'

'Rats!' shrieked Lizzie and Flo together.

Danny laughed. 'The rat catcher's coming tomorrow. Then Tom and me will make a start on the mending. Some beams need replacing.'

'How are you gonna find business, son?' Bill asked. 'There ain't much doing in the docks.'

'Not on the boats, Dad, but the factories run lorries.' Danny's voice was filled with enthusiasm. Everyone stared at him. 'Tom and me did the rounds. I've talked with the bosses. They send their wagons up to the city or beyond for repair. I've told them I can do the work in half the time, at half the price, once I've bought me tools and got the place set up.'

'Blimey, that was quick work.' Bill spluttered on his cigarette.

'It's what I want, Dad. I know I can make a go of things. I also know what you're all thinking. That I'm asking for trouble. That I should disappear again. Well, I'm sorry you all feel that way. But you don't think I came all the way back from Australia just to leave again, do you?'

Bill gave one of his loud sniffs. 'It's just that things have changed.'

'The island is my home,' Danny replied. 'Now it's Tom's. I've told him all about England since he was old enough to understand. After Elsa died, I promised meself I'd provide him with the two things his mother didn't have, a future and a family. Elsa had no relations in Australia and very few in Sweden. So I decided Tom's future was here, on the island, where I grew up. If he takes a shine to mechanics, he'll come into the business with me. He looked round the table at each one of them.

'I wish it was that simple, son,' Bill sighed.

'Yeah, you don't know yer brother.' Flo stated what they were all thinking.

Lizzie was afraid, not for herself, but for Danny. He didn't know the kind of person Frank had changed into. Just then the two children ran into the kitchen.

'Don't go,' Polly pleaded as Danny got up. 'We ain't finished our dominoes yet.'

He ruffled her dark hair. 'We've got a long walk back.'

'I'll take you on the cart.' Bill rose creakily to his feet.

'You need a motor van, Dad,' Danny grinned. 'I'll fix one up for you.'

'How the 'ell am I gonna drive one of them things!' exclaimed Bill.

'Easy, Grandad,' giggled Tom. 'I'll teach you.'

'Can he drive?' Flo stared at Tom.

Danny laughed. 'You bet he can.'

'Well, I'll be blowed.' Bill grinned, pushing back his cap. 'Tell me, lad, how much hay does one of these 'ere motor vans eat?'

Everyone burst into laughter. Despite her worries, Lizzie joined in. A happy family – the kind that Danny had imagined for Tom – was something she, too, had always dreamed of. She had first stood in this kitchen eleven years ago when Danny had told her he was going to Australia. Now he was back again. But what did the future hold, she wondered anxiously?

It was a freezing cold Sunday at the end of February. Lizzie sat next to Bert on the cart. She was shivering, even though she'd put on her warmest coat, her brown leather gloves and woollen scarf.

'I said we wouldn't be too long,' she shouted at Bert above the clatter of the wheels. 'Flo's keeping an eye on Pol till we get back.'

Bert nodded, his forehead creased in a deep frown. 'Yeah, all right. The old boy ain't so fast these past few weeks, though.'

Lizzie knew Bert was worried. Benji had been off colour, his movements slow and laboured. He refused his nosebags and didn't want to leave his stable in the mornings. 'What's wrong with him?'

'Dunno. Getting old I s'pose. Must be gone seventeen now.'

Lizzie nodded, recalling that Benji had looked ancient even twelve years ago, with his grey-brown shaggy coat and huge ragged hooves.

Last night Bert and Bill had been talking about retiring him. The subject of a motor van had arisen. 'See Danny in the morning,' Bill had decided. Glancing at Lizzie, he had added, 'You'd better go with Bert. He's the one who'll be driving it.'

She hadn't seen Danny since New Year's Day, but she got all the news from Bert. Danny had been teaching him how to drive. Surprisingly, Bert had taken to it like a fish to water.

Lizzie was curious to see what this place of Danny's was like. Even Flo had been over to see it, Lil and Doug, too. But Lizzie was still worried about Frank. No one had seen him for months. She had even wondered if he had gone to prison and no one had told her.

'That's it.' Bert nodded to a large, ramshackle warehouse standing on the wharf. It had a small door set in the wall and a lot of the windows had fallen out. There was a pile of old junk outside.

Bert reined Benji in. ''Old yer breath when you go inside,' he warned Lizzie. 'It stinks a bit.' He helped her down from the cart and pushed open the small door.

Petrol and oil fumes rushed out at her. Lizzie blinked, holding her breath. How could Danny work in that smell all day?

Bert pointed to the pair of legs under a lorry. ''Ello, mate!'

Danny emerged, wiping his face in the crook of his arm. His cheeks, nose and overalls were black with grease. He rested his elbow on his knee, blinking his eyes. He grinned when he saw who it was.

'We come over about the motor van,' Bert told him.

Lizzie tried to hide her embarrassment as she looked at Danny. 'You did offer.'

'Course I did. I've been giving Bert lessons in my old motor car, but I've got an engine that I'm doing up, just right for the shop.'

'Could I drive it too?' Lizzie asked boldly.

Danny scrambled to his feet. 'All you need is a couple of lessons. There ain't nothing to it, is there, Bert?'

Bert shook his big head, looking pleased with himself.

'Well, do you want the grand tour?' Danny asked.

Lizzie nodded. They walked the length of the warehouse, right to the end. 'Those big doors there are where the trucks picked up the sacks deposited from the holds of the ships,' Danny explained. 'They're big enough to let in the kind of lorries I'll be repairing, like the one I'm working on today.'

'What's up there?' Lizzie pointed to a narrow flight of wooden stairs. At the top was a door.

'The office. I lock all me tools in there at night. Tom and me have got lodgings now, a few minutes away.'

'What are you going to call yerself?' Lizzie asked as they walked back down the warehouse.

'Flowers and Son. Repairs and Reconstruction for all Motor Vehicles,' Danny said proudly. 'Got a sign I'm putting up next week.'

'Tell her what that is, Danny.' Bert pointed to a large chain hanging over a rafter. The end had a hook on it that dangled over the lorry.

'It's an engine hoist. Secured to this mechanical wheel, I can raise any size engine without help. And this is my inspection pit.' He kneeled down and began to lift the loose planks that formed a square in the floor. 'The rats have gone now, at least the big ones have.' Below was a dark hole. Lizzie shrank back. She didn't want to see a rat.

He looked up at her and laughed. There was a sparkle in his eye and she smelled the oil and grease on his skin; the heat rose from his warm body under the overalls. His hair was streaked with oil and dirt; he pushed it back from his face with a motion she recalled so well, and her heart missed a beat.

'When are we gonna see the van?' Bert asked, making her jump.

Danny replaced the boards in the floor. 'It's out the back, Bert. Go and have a look.'

Bert hurried off eagerly. Danny rose to his feet. 'I'm glad you came. I was beginning to think you never would.'

'Benji's getting old,' she said, staring after Bert. 'We need to replace him.'

'Was that the reason you came?'

She wanted to say that seeing Danny was the *only* reason she had come. He was looking into her eyes to search for the truth. She knew he could read her thoughts. It hadn't changed between them. It had always been like this. They didn't need words. Slowly he drew her towards him.

'I want to be with you and look after you,' he told her then. 'I want you and Polly to live with me and Tom.'

She was already shaking her head. 'I can't.'

'Why not? What are you going to do when Dad retires? When Flo and Syd get married? Why shouldn't our lives change for the better, too? I want to take care of you and Polly. I love, you, Lizzie, I always have.'

All these years and now he was offering her a future. It was all she had ever dreamed of. It was all she had ever wanted. Even the scandal she could bear if it was just herself. But there were the children to consider; Polly and Tom would be ridiculed, made fun of at school. Winks and nods would follow them.

'I know I could make you happy, Lizzie.'

Could she be happy, a married woman living with another man? Some women attempted it. But for her there was always the guilt, the knowledge that Frank had been right – that she had never stopped loving Danny.

Just then Bert shouted from the top of the warehouse. They broke apart as they heard his footsteps hurrying towards them.

'It's a little cracker, Danny,' Bert shouted as he neared, out of breath. 'Does it go?'

Danny looked away, running his hand through his hair. 'Yeah, it goes, Bert.'

'Can I start it up?'

Lizzie watched Danny pull a bunch of keys from his overall pocket. Then, giving a soft sigh, he nodded towards the door.

Chapter Twenty-Nine

All the bitterness rose up in him. It swelled in his throat, like bile. Frank clenched his hands into fists and let the anger grow.

'I don't like all this hanging around,' Vinnie muttered. 'What we waiting for?'

Frank stared through the windscreen, his pale blue eyes darting from the figure of his brother stooping over the van's engine to the tall, ungainly form of Bert Allen. 'We're waiting for the right moment. I ain't held off all these months just to go and rush things.' Frank wanted to savour his revenge. He wanted the odds in his favour. So far, his plans were going well; it was a bit of luck – *her* coming to Morley's Wharf.

Frank relaxed back on the front seat of the large black car. He had parked it on the waste ground by the bridge. Used as a rubbish tip by the locals, it made the perfect cover.

Frank narrowed his eyes. 'We'll wait till they leave. Then go in.'

'What if the Old Bill show up?'

'Why should they? No one's gonna know what's

happening in there. It's simple. We go in and do the business.'

'Well, I don't like it.'

Frank's eyes were cold as he glanced at his brother-in-law. 'And I ain't liked what you've lumbered me with over the years, either. So we're quits, ain't we?'

'What about Mik, if he finds out.' Vinnie replied. 'Nothin' happens on his patch without his say so.'

'Who's gonna tell him?' Frank demanded angrily.

Vinnie moved restlessly in his seat, his close-set eyes staring at the warehouse.

'Look, they're going.' Frank pointed to his wife and the two men accompanying her round the outside of the warehouse to the horse and cart at the front. He watched with baited breath as his wife climbed up on the cart. All his suspicions were confirmed; sooner or later he knew he'd catch them together. 'Couldn't be better,' he murmured with a satisfied grin. 'Just what I've been waiting for.'

Frank glanced at Vinnie. He didn't trust him further than he could throw him. They both knew what Ferreter was capable of if he discovered they had been conducting business of their own on the island. Vinnie had no choice, though. Frank knew too much about his brother-in-law for Vinnie to refuse to help him.

The cart began to move off. The man Frank hated most in all the world stood alone by the warehouse. Danny had robbed him of a mother and his childhood, did he really think he could now take his wife? Frank's fists tightened.

'Coast's clear,' he growled at Vinnie. 'Now we'll go in.'

Lizzie watched the familiar landmarks pass by as she sat up on the cart, huddled in her coat for warmth. The gas works and Deptford dry docks on the other side of the water, Greenwich hidden in cloud. Only the wind whipping the foam at the quay gave any indication the tide was turning.

She inhaled deeply and the smells of the island filled her nose. Since Danny had come back into her life, colours were brighter, smells sharper; Danny's eyes had seemed bluer, his hair more golden – the evidence of Australia, an English complexion coarsened by sun.

The noise of the bridge traffic drifted over the clattering of the cart. In the distance she could hear the drone of sawmills. Tar and sea salt lay on her lips, a sprinkling of rain fell on her cheeks.

'I'll need a few more lessons,' Bert was saying as he urged the horse along. 'But it won't be long before I get the hang.'

She nodded absently. 'We must pay Danny.'

'He don't want nothin'. Said he got it from up West, from one of them big posh stores that wanted to get rid of it 'cos it had been in an accident. Danny got it going and drove it back. Then he bashed out all the metal to make it look proper again, then mended the engine.'

They talked about the motor van as Benji pulled them

through the streets. The going was slow and suddenly Benji stopped.

'What's the matter?' Lizzie asked.

'Dunno. I'll see.'

Lizzie watched Bert jump down and examine each hoof, then pat the long grey neck as it drooped downward. Bert jumped back on the cart.

'Benji ain't going anywhere today – he's lame. Lost a shoe somewhere.'

'How are we going to get him home?'

'He might make it without the weight of the cart.'

'Might?'

Bert shrugged gloomily. 'Yeah, well, he ain't no spring chicken anymore, is he?'

'What are we going to do, then?'

Bert looked over his shoulder. 'Danny's the closest. I'll take off the harness. It's only a short walk to the workshop.'

Lizzie looked back over her shoulder. Bert was right; it wasn't far back to the wharf. 'I suppose we don't have much choice,' she sighed.

Bert jumped down once more. His big hands uncoupled the horse from the cart, a process hampered by the rain that started to fall heavily. He stuffed the nosebag full of oats under his jacket, then looked up at her as rain streamed down his face. 'Yer gonna get soaked if you stay there. You go on if you like.'

She climbed down, the rain falling harder now. Bert lifted the big harness from the horse and the sweat rose up in the air like a cloud.

'Are you sure, Bert?'

'Course. No sense in us both drowning. I'll get the poor old bugger to the workshop somehow.'

Reluctantly she left them, pulling her coat up over her head, wondering if Benji would make the journey back to the warehouse.

She was soaked by the time she reached the workshop. The sky was black and the rain falling straight and hard. The little door was slightly open. Lifting her wet coat and stepping in, she stared into the darkness, once again inhaling the petrol and oil fumes.

Her eyes were unaccustomed to the shadows. The day had turned very dark and the workshop was unlit. Danny was nowhere to be seen. Perhaps he was out by the motor van at the other end of the warehouse? She began to walk towards it then stopped as she heard a movement.

'Danny?' she called softly, moving towards the big lorry.

A figure stepped in front of her. She stopped, frowning uncertainly. 'Who is it?' she stammered, trying to see in the darkness.

'Who do you think?' Frank emerged from the gloom looking dirty and dishevelled. His eyes glittered as he came towards her, a strange expression in them that made the hairs on the back of her neck stand on end. The man following him was not as tall, dressed in a long overcoat and trilby. She recognized her brother at once.

'Vinnie . . . Frank . . . what are you doing here?' She

stared at them, her eyes going from one to the other. 'What do you want?'

'Well, now, that's no way to greet your husband.' Frank smiled menacingly. 'I think it's about time you and I had a little chat.'

She tried to move back as he stepped towards her, but her body wouldn't respond. Her throat tightened, her legs felt as though they had lead weights attached to them.

Suddenly she heard footsteps. It was Danny, coming towards them from the other end of the warehouse. She wanted to warn him that Frank and Vinnie were there but it was too late. Frank had turned round and was staring at the approaching figure.

'Ah . . . and here's me long lost brother. Arriving just on time.' Frank's voice was filled with contempt. 'Now, ain't that cosy? Me wife and me brother – the two people who I been most wanting to see.'

'What do you want, Frank?' Danny looked at Lizzie, his eyes full of concern. She tried to tell him by her eyes that she was all right.

'What do I want?' Frank laughed loudly. 'Did you hear that, Vin? He wants to know what I want.' Frank moved towards Danny, stopping a few inches in front of him. 'Did you think I didn't know what was going on behind my back? I ain't such a bloody fool as you think!'

'I've never thought you were a fool,' Danny replied evenly. 'A liar and cheat yes, but not a fool.'

Lizzie was terrified. She knew her husband was

dangerous, sometimes a violent man. She didn't want Danny to say anything to provoke him.

'I only had to wait,' Frank continued as though he hadn't heard Danny, 'and it was odds on she'd come running to you.'

'Your wife has nothing to do with you and me,' Danny replied calmly. 'It was down to you, Frank, if you felt a grudge, to come and talk to me, man to man.'

Lizzie stared at her husband and brother. What did they want? What were they going to do to Danny?

Frank's eyes slowly narrowed. 'The time for talking's over. I'm going to put an end to your games with my wife. I'm going to give you a little souvenir to remember me by.'

'What happened to the letters I wrote, Frank? What did you do with them?' Danny demanded, ignoring Frank's threat. He pulled himself upright. Taller and leaner than Frank, he was still no match for two, Lizzie thought, terrified now.

'I burned them,' Frank growled bitterly. 'Like the bloody rubbish they were.' There was no remorse in his tone. Lizzie felt sick. Frank had destroyed those letters – letters that would have changed the course of her life.

Tears welled in her eyes. 'Was it Babs who gave them to you?' she heard herself demanding as she stepped forward. 'The only way you could have stolen them was through someone at home. It wasn't Bert . . . and it wasn't Flo . . . and Pa would never have done such a thing . . .' She broke off as Frank wheeled round to face her.

He laughed again, shaking his head slowly. 'Took you long enough to work that one out, didn't it?'

'But that was a terrible thing to do!'

'Listen, you was ditched eleven years ago,' Frank yelled, moving closer. 'It was left to me to put a roof over yer head. Casanova here was off gallivanting, making his fortune. Picked up a woman the moment he set foot on land. Gave her a kid, too—'

'It wasn't like that,' Danny shouted, stepping forward. 'And you damn well know it.'

Frank's eyes were gleaming. A pulse throbbed at his temple. 'You got what you wanted, lover boy. You always did. But not anymore. You should have stayed away. But you couldn't, could you?'

Lizzie shivered as the two men stared at one another. Their true feelings were clear; neither one had respect for the other and neither was prepared to back down. But it was still two against one, and Vinnie was standing by, watching, the atmosphere tense as no one moved. Lizzie knew that even if she screamed, no one outside would hear. 'Frank, please . . . don't do anything you'll regret,' she begged.

'Shut up,' he shouted, making her jump.

'Your business is with me,' Danny said then, his voice sharp as he moved beside Lizzie. 'Leave her out of this.'

Frank laughed coarsely, throwing back his head in derision. As he did so, Danny whispered to her. 'Run up to the office. Lock yourself in. Draw all the bolts.'

A look of surprise came over Frank's face. He was

frowning, suspicious of them. She wanted to run, but she didn't want to leave Danny.

'Now we'll see what kind of man you are,' Frank muttered grimly, gesturing to Vinnie. 'Let's get on with it.'

Vinnie didn't move. 'We got a witness,' he muttered, nodding at Lizzie.

'She ain't going to tell no one,' Frank shrugged. 'Not if she knows what's good for her.

'Still getting someone else to do your dirty work, Frank?' Danny interrupted quickly. 'That's about the size of it, isn't it? When we were kids and in trouble, I'd look around, but you'd be gone. You were a coward then and you're a coward now.'

Lizzie watched Frank's face fill with hate. He threw himself at Danny. They fell backwards against the lorry and rolled along the length of it, their arms and legs entwined as they fought. When they fell to the floor, Frank's hands were round Danny's throat. Danny's head was forced down on the boards of the pit. Lizzie cried out as Frank seemed to gather strength, banging Danny's head time and again on the wood. But when Frank loosened his grip and Danny was free, it was Danny who rolled on top and gave a blow to Frank's face that make her stomach turn. Frank managed to recover. He looked dazedly at Danny. Coupled once more, their fists and legs scattered the tools spread over the floor. Vinnie stood, watching and waiting. Then Frank grasped an iron bar. Danny got unsteadily to his feet. The two men faced each other, hate and enmity in their eyes. Danny ducked the first blow. The second caught him on the side of the head. She screamed as he staggered backwards.

Frank moved towards him, the iron bar raised again. She started forward, not knowing what she would do, only that she had to help Danny. Before she went far, Vinnie grabbed her. Somehow she made her legs move and pulled away. She reached the staircase and stumbled up it. Below, she could still hear them fighting. Vinnie ascended the stairs after her. She fumbled her way backwards, her eyes locked with his. What was he going to do to her? Slowly he came up each stair. This was not her brother, she realized, but a man whose heart was cold and empty. He did not want a witness to what was happening. Could he kill her, his own sister?

The office was her only escape. She ran into it, thrusting the door closed. But Vinnie was too quick. His hand went round the door, forcing it back. She pressed down on it with all her strength. He let out a surprised howl as she trapped his fingers. The moment they moved she closed it and slid the bolt. Then she slid the top one and the one on the bottom. She stared at the door, listening to the silence behind it. Her heart was beating so fast she thought it was coming out of her chest.

The impact made her scream. She fell back against the wall, her hand over her mouth. She sank down in the corner, watching as another blow came from outside, then another. But Danny was right. The bolts were strong and the door held.

More blows came. Her sobs were deep as her arms went round her knees and she buried her head, trying to block out the sounds. What was happening to Danny? Would they kill him? Would they break down the door and kill her too?

'Oh, God, please make them stop,' she whispered as the tears trickled down her cheeks and on to her wet coat. 'Make them stop . . .'

Bert pulled Benji slowly along as the rain beat hard against them. The old horse could only just move one hoof in front of the other. Bert murmured consolingly, his hand going up to urge him on. They were both drenched. Bert looked helplessly up and down the street, shivering under his jacket. The sky was as dark as night, the rain relentless. He knew Benji wanted to stop. If only they could get to shelter. The warehouse would provide some warmth at least.

When Bert saw the warehouse, he sighed with relief. The rain lashed his face as he led the horse towards it. Beyond the wasteland was a large black car, an unusual sight in this district. Inside the warehouse, Bert found a corner. Tying the rein loosely to a wooden strut and wiping off what wet he could with an old sack, he patted the horse's head. 'At least yer in the dry now, old son. Looks like yer travellin' days are over for a bit.' He took out the nosebag that he had stuffed under his coat and tied it round the horse's head. Benji began to eat. Bert smiled. That was a good sign.

Bert turned away. His mind was on the horse as he walked down to the workshop to find Danny. He tried to accustom his eyes to the gloom. Danny would have to fix himself up with better lights, Bert thought distractedly.

Suddenly he stood still. The blood froze in his veins. Frank was standing by the lorry. What was he doing here? Then Bert saw Vinnie at the bottom of the staircase. Moving slowly towards them, Bert stared at the floor. There was something lying there. It looked like a body. He stopped, his mind confused. What had happened? Was it Lizzie? He moved forward again as a wave of disbelief went through him. It was Danny lying there, motionless.

Then Bert heard a noise, a loud wail, a banshee cry; it was both roar and scream. He was surprised to find the noise pouring from his own mouth. The two figures in front of him were turning, attempting to run, but Bert ran after them; as big and clumsy as he was, he ran fast, the anger inside propelling him.

He lunged at Frank and knew a moment's deep hatred for the man squirming in his grasp. He jerked back his head and smashed it into Frank's face. There was an explosion of blood. Frank fell to his knees, screaming loudly.

Bert stared pitilessly down at his wretch of a brother-in-law. He had witnessed the degradation that Frank had brought to his family, the disregard shown for his own kith and kin. He was an evil man, a coward and a bully. Bert linked his big hands round Frank's neck, increasing the pressure. Frank's fists waved uselessly. Bert was in a kind of trance. At the back of his mind, he knew that he was killing Frank. Nothing could bring back the years that Frank had poisoned, but this felt right, as though there was some justice for animals like him. Not even a piece of wood that crashed against Bert's head, sending his hair flying up in a spurt of red, made him stop. Bert merely turned, untroubled by the pain that only angered him more.

Astonished that his action had no effect, Vinnie ran off.

Bert looked back at Frank, oblivious to Vinnie's departure. Frank's life was draining away, his face turning blue, his lips quivering. Bert tightened his fingers, the ease with which he was snuffing out a life surprising him.

'Bert . . . no . . . don't!' Lizzie stood at the top of the staircase, screaming, her trembling hands covering her mouth.

Bert looked up. For a moment he wondered where he was. Suddenly he realized what he was doing. He dropped Frank like a dead weight. Hurrying to the staircase, Lizzie ran into his arms. He hugged her tightly.

'They . . . they tried to kill him . . . oh, Bert, what have they done?' She swayed.

Bert held her. 'You all right?' he muttered in a thick, shocked voice.

She nodded. 'Yes . . . yes.' They both looked at the door as it swung on its hinges. Frank had run off.

'I nearly did him in,' Bert said as Lizzie gathered herself. 'If you hadn't screamed . . .'

She took a deep breath and nodded. 'I know, I know. But you didn't.' Together they went and kneeled beside

Danny. Blood trickled from his head and ran down his cheek.

'Danny, Danny?' Lizzie whispered, her voice broken by sobs as she bent over him. Bert watched as she gently pushed back the blood-soaked hair. But nothing she did could wake him up.

Chapter Thirty

'Danny . . . Danny . . .?' Even his lashes had blood in them. She tried to wipe it away with her handkerchief. Her voice shook as she cradled his head in her arms.

Suddenly he gave a little moan and came awake slowly. The skin around his eyes was bruised and swollen. Blood was still coming from his head. She wiped it gently away. He struggled to sit up, peering from swollen eyes. 'Lizzie . . . what . . . what happened? Did they hurt you?'

'No. I locked myself in the office.'

'Why . . . why did you come back?'

'Benji went lame. You've got a big wound on your head. It was that iron bar.' Her fingers felt the stickiness.

Bert handed her a rag. ''Ere, gel, mop him up with that.'

She held the rag up and gently dabbed at the wound.

'The 'orse is what done it, mate. We had to come back. I put him up the other end of the warehouse. Then I came down looking for you and I saw Frank and you on the floor—'

'They tried to kill you,' Lizzie interrupted. 'We should tell the police.'

'No,' Danny muttered, '. . . no police.'

'Well, it's the 'ospital, then,' Bert said firmly. 'You've got a blooming great chunk out of yer head.'

Danny looked at Bert. 'No . . . I'm worried about Tom. He'll wonder where I am.'

'But you need to have this seen to.' Lizzie didn't know what to do. He should go to hospital. And what about Frank? If they went to the police would they take action against him? Frank would deny it all.

'The car's outside.' Danny gripped Bert's arm. 'Out the back . . . by the jetty . . . key's in it . . . drive it round the front, Bert. Do like I taught you. Crank it with the starting handle, rev it up and put it into first gear, then second.'

'I dunno, Danny. I ain't never done it without you,' Bert protested, gently restraining him.

'You'll do it. You got to, Bert. Take me to Napier Street . . . my lodgings . . . Tom will have gone home—' Danny was trying to stand up. Bert helped him. Lizzie slipped an arm round his waist.

'There's some bales of hay behind the lorry,' Danny said muzzily. 'I use them to spread over the grease on the floor. Give a couple to the horse on your way out.'

Bert nodded and looked at Lizzie. 'I'll give a toot on the horn, right?'

She nodded. 'Hurry up, Bert, please.'

Whilst Bert was getting the car, Lizzie helped Danny to the small door at the front. He leaned against her, groaning softly, the blood still running down his face.

'I wish you'd go to hospital, Danny.'

He held on to one of the wooden struts of the warehouse. 'I'll be all right. Don't worry.'

'You can't be on your own like this. You and Tom can come back with us.' The cold air whipped across them as she opened the door. Lizzie looked out but there was no sign of Bert. Would he really be able to drive a motor vehicle on his own? Just as she was about to step back in there was a loud backfire. From round the side of the warehouse came a large grey car. Bert was driving it, his large head right up to the windscreen.

'I done it!' Bert yelled through the window as he pulled up with a screech of brakes. The engine shuddered and spluttered. Bert climbed out.

Lizzie opened the back door. Bert lowered Danny on to the seat and pressed the rag against his head. Lizzie slid in beside him. 'Do you know where Napier Road is, Bert?'

'Yeah,' nodded Bert as he jumped into the front once more. 'It ain't far. You'd better 'old tight, though.'

Danny closed his eyes. His head fell back on the seat. It was the worst journey Lizzie had ever experienced. Bert crunched his way through the gears and they went up on to the pavement with a huge bump. Luckily, as it was Sunday, no one was about. It was getting dark and Bert lost his way twice. When they arrived at Napier Road, Lizzie let out a sigh of relief. She looked at Danny. He seemed to have fallen asleep. Was he unconscious, she wondered?

'Go in and get Tom,' she told her brother hurriedly. 'Tell him his dad's had a bit of an accident, so he's coming home with us.'

'Right you are, gel.' Bert pulled on the hand brake and jumped out to knock on the door of the small terraced house. A few moments later, Tom was sitting safely in the front with Bert as he drove them back to Ebondale Street.

His brow furrowed in a deep frown, Dr Tapper wound the bandages tightly around Danny's chest. 'Fractured ribs will heal in time,' he muttered grimly, 'but as for that wound on your head – you were lucky it wasn't any lower, young man. You would have lost the eye.'

Danny sat on the bed in his old room, now occupied by Flo. She had moved her things into the glory hole as soon as Bert and Lizzie had brought Danny in. There was a chest of drawers and a maple wardrobe, but Lizzie had never discovered what Frank had done with all Danny's maps, books and other possessions. Certainly they weren't in the house. Danny hadn't yet asked after them and she was glad.

'I'll mend,' Danny murmured. 'Thanks for the stitching up, Dr Tap.'

'The scar it will leave won't improve your looks, young man.'

'That's the least of me worries.'

Dr Tapper cleared away his things and rolled down his shirtsleeves. 'Remember, no exertion for the next few days. The more you rest the quicker those ribs will heal.'

Lizzie picked up a clean shirt that she had found in one

of Frank's drawers. She had also given one to Bert to change into. Her wet and bloody coat was awaiting a scrub and the soiled rags had been disposed of. Carefully she helped Danny put on the shirt. His movements were slow and painful.

'I don't suppose any of you are going to tell me what happened?' Dr Tapper drew on his black coat. His hair was now pure white, his old shoulders drooping with age. He no longer used a carriage but drove a small black car to visit his patients.

Danny said quietly, 'It's personal, Doc.'

The old man hesitated. 'You know, with injuries such as those, the police should be informed.' He snapped his bag shut. 'I'm an old man, but I'm no fool. My professional advice is to go to the police. Report the incident. But knowing this community as I do, I'm well aware that you'll deal with this amongst yourselves.' His eyes went slowly to each of them. 'As a friend of the family, I would simply say, be careful. You were fortunate today. Next time . . . well . . . you may not be so lucky.' His gaze rested on them a few moments more.

Lizzie glanced at Danny, then followed the doctor to the front room. Flo, Bert and the children were waiting there.

'Is Dad going to get better?' Tom ran across from the table.

'Yes, he's going to be fine.' Dr Tapper patted Tom's fair head. 'But don't pester him. Let him rest.' He looked up. 'And you, Bert, remember I've put several stitches into that cut on the back of your head.'

Bert went red. 'Dunno what done that.'

Dr Tapper had a wry smile on his face. 'No, I don't suppose you do.'

'I'll see you out, Doctor.' Lizzie led the way.

'Call me if you need me.'

Lizzie knew he had his suspicions. She also knew he would keep them to himself. On the island, everyone accepted that rough justice was the only law that counted.

For Tom and Polly's benefit, the story was that Danny had been injured by the engine hoist. Tom had seen his father working with the big chain and hook. If it wasn't secured properly, it could swing perilously in all directions. Polly knew better than to ask too many questions. She was thrilled that Tom and Danny were staying there.

Whilst Danny, Bert, Flo and Lizzie sat in the kitchen, the two children curled up by the fire, drawing.

Flo and Bert lit up their cigarettes. Danny sat stiffly, his face cleaner but the big white patch over the top of his forehead showing the blood beneath. His eyes were still puffy and his knuckles grazed.

'I don't think you should be on yer feet,' Flo said as Lizzie set a pot of tea on the table. 'You must feel rotten.'

Danny smiled crookedly. 'You shouldn't go by appearances.'

Flo laughed. 'You can say that again.'

'How are you, Bert?' Danny asked. 'You got a bit of a wallop too.'

'Didn't feel a thing,' he shrugged.

'Yeah, well, that stands to reason. No sense, no feeling,' joked Flo, nudging Bert in the arm. Everyone laughed again, but the laughter was forced.

'Does Dad know about this?' Danny asked suddenly.

'I went and told him whilst Dr Tapper was stitching you up,' Flo said, looking quickly at Lizzie. 'We thought he'd better know – just in case. He said he'd come down and see you later. I didn't say what happened, only that you'd had a bit of an up and downer with Frank.' Flo turned to Danny. 'I still can't believe yer brother would do this.'

Lizzie sat down at the table. 'What do you think he'll do now?'

'Try again,' said Danny humourlessly.

'He won't stop until he sees you off this island,' Bert sighed. He balanced his thin cigarette on the glass ashtray. His big, drooping eyes blinked several times. 'I'd like to get me hands on Vinnie, too.'

Lizzie shuddered. She hadn't said what had happened at the top of those stairs. She still couldn't believe Vinnie would attack her. There had never been any love lost between them, but doing what he had done today, standing by whilst Frank tried to kill Danny and then coming after her, it was not the act of a man in his right senses. Perhaps Vinnie was sick or mad. She shivered again.

'This time I'll be ready for them,' Danny said. His hand unconsciously went up to the wound.

'What do you mean?' Lizzie stared at him.

'I mean, that's the last time anyone ever threatens me or mine and gets away with it. And that includes everyone under this roof.'

'I'm right with you on that, mate,' said Bert loyally.

'And you can count on Syd,' Flo burst out angrily. 'Frank's a bloody coward, always has been. I just wish Syd and his brothers could meet him in a dark alley one of these nights. Trouble is, Frank wouldn't go up a dark alley, he's too afraid of his own shadow.'

Danny looked at Lizzie. 'I don't want you going anywhere alone for the next few days. Not even up to the market or over to the school. Flo or Bert can go with you.'

'But Frank wouldn't show his face round here, surely?'

'Why not? He came to the workshop.'

'Do you think he'll go looking there again?' Lizzie felt a ripple of fear run through her.

'He might.'

'I wish I'd kept me hands round his neck and squeezed harder,' Bert said with sudden aggression. 'It would've saved us all a lot of trouble.'

'And you'd be on a murder charge,' Danny pointed out. 'Bert, I appreciate what you did for me and I owe you my life, but this is down to me.'

Everyone was surprised when Bert shook his head. 'No it ain't, Danny. I got me own bone to pick with Frank and me brother. And they both know it.'

Lizzie was shocked. She hadn't ever heard Bert speak like this.

'Well, just watch your step,' Danny warned.

Lizzie knew that, despite his injuries, Danny meant what he said, but it came as a surprise when he told them he was returning to the workshop.

Flo choked on her tea. 'What, now? You must be joking. Look at the state of you.'

'What do you wanna go back for?' Bert asked.

'All my tools are there.'

'You think Frank might nick them?' Flo spluttered.

'Anything's possible.'

Bert shuffled his feet. 'To be truthful, I was going to go over t'night without telling anyone. I thought now I can drive I'd borrow yer car and take over food and water to the 'orse.'

'I got an idea,' Flo interrupted. 'Syd'll be over soon. We was going up the pub for a quick one. He can go with you.'

'No,' Danny objected at once, 'I don't want Syd involved.'

'I don't reckon you got much choice,' Bert said with shrug. 'You ain't in no state to go lifting tools, even if you did manage to get over there.'

And what Flo said next settled the argument. 'You gotta sink yer pride, Danny, and let us help. After all, what are family for?'

'Well I think you're all mad,' Lizzie said angrily. 'The horse will survive one night on his own and the tools aren't as important as being safe. You heard what the doctor said. You had concussion and you've two broken ribs—'

She stopped when she saw Danny was smiling at her.

'So you do care?' he grinned, jerking up an eyebrow.

She knew she was going red and that everyone was looking at her. Hiding her blush, she got up and went to put the kettle on.

Whilst the men were away, Lizzie and Flo made up the mattress for Tom beside Danny's bed.

'Don't worry, they'll be all right. They're big enough and ugly enough to look after themselves,' Flo tried to reassure Lizzie.

'You didn't see what happened today,' Lizzie replied shortly. It was all very well Flo saying that. She hadn't been there.

'Well, it's out of your hands now.'

'I still keep seeing it all in my mind,' Lizzie murmured. 'Frank hitting Danny with that iron bar and the look in Vinnie's eye as he came up those stairs.'

'Our Vinnie wants his brains tested.' Flo tucked in the sheet and pulled over the blankets. 'Terrifying his own sister like that.'

'I don't know what he'd have done if he'd got into the office.' Lizzie felt the awful lead weight in her stomach again. She had tried to think of another explanation for his behaviour, but she always came up with the same one: Vinnie had said he didn't want a witness, and, sister or not, she was a witness.

'Come on, it's over. Forget about it,' Flo said, attempting to shake her out of it.

Lizzie knew it wasn't over. It had only just begun. What would they try next and where? Wouldn't it better if Danny went back to Australia? He had Tom to think about. But what would happen if he did leave? She couldn't bear to think of life without him again. At the same time, she could never have him in her life the way she wanted. She was married to his brother.

Later, Bill came down with a bottle of port. By nine o'clock the children were asleep and Lizzie had been over the whole story again, answering all Bill's questions as best she could.

Lizzie knew that Bill was deeply shocked. In silence, he listened to every word that she said. She saw the dismay spread over his face. He was an old man, hoping for a peaceful retirement. He had always known what Frank was, but he had tried to protect Frank from himself. He had hoped that it was not too late for his eldest son to reform. Now Bill was having to face the truth, that Frank would never change.

Conversation exhausted, the three of them sat by the fire. Lizzie wondered, as she had wondered many times before, how their lives would have turned out if she hadn't married Frank. Would Frank have been a better son? Would he now be running the shop? Would Danny have remained in Australia? Would she have married someone else? And Polly . . . what of her?

Polly had brought meaning to her life. She was like her own daughter. Lizzie would have been content to be a loving aunt if things had been different between her and Babs. But they weren't. Babs had shown no love for her own child. How could she have neglected Polly the way she had?

Lizzie thought of Danny, his body bruised and his handsome face disfigured. Her love for him was stronger than ever. She ached for his love, to have his arms round her and to feel his body lying beside her. Fate had not dealt kindly with their love. What was to become of them?

At a few minutes past ten, they heard the sound of Danny's car outside. Lizzie jumped out of her chair. 'They're back,' she cried, waking Bill, who had just drifted off, his cheeks red from the port.

Flo and Lizzie ran to the door. Danny entered looking very tired. The blood had seeped right through the bandage. Syd and Bert were quiet, but they smiled as a strong odour of petrol wafted in with them.

'We're back safe and sound, Mrs F.,' Syd said in a subdued tone.

'Is everything all right?' Lizzie asked breathlessly.

Bert nodded. 'Yeah. There weren't no sign of them.'

'I should hope not.' Lizzie closed the door. 'You don't mean to tell me you really went over there expecting to . . . to—'

'No, no,' said Danny quickly, glancing at the other two. 'All me tools are in the boot, and Benji's got plenty to eat and drink.' He saw his father sitting in the chair. 'Hello, Dad.'

'Hello, son. Well, come and tell me all about it.'

Syd and Flo disappeared into the kitchen. Lizzie left them alone to say goodnight. She watched Danny sit wearily down in the fireside chair opposite his father. She sighed. She didn't know whether she believed him about the reason for their mission over there. But she did know she would have been worried sick if she thought they'd gone to find Frank.

'You remember them old 'urricane lamps we had for the cart,' Bert told Lizzie as he took her arm and steered her to the chairs by the sideboard. They sat down. 'Well, we took them with us. Put all Danny's stuff that was too big for the car in the office and locked it. All the small tools we brought with us. I give Benji a good feed and he was right as ninepence. Tomorrow I'm gonna get him back. Danny said that big lorry he's mending is big enough.'

'What, to put Benji in?'

Bert nodded. 'All we got to do is make a ramp.'

'I hope you know what you're doing.'

Bert grinned. 'No, but Danny does.' He looked bashful for a moment. 'I ain't good enough to drive a lorry yet, but I reckon I can learn.'

Lizzie had to smile. Out of all this, something special had happened to Bert. He'd never been very bright and always felt inferior. Now he could drive a motor vehicle, after a fashion, and the wonder was written all over his face.

Lizzie looked over at Danny, speaking quietly with Bill. He had made an impression on all their lives since he had returned. What would happen if, in the end, he was forced to leave the island?

Chapter Thirty-One

Lil walked into the shop the next morning. She was dressed in a smart brown coat and a new hat. She had her large shopping bag with her, in which she carried her cakes. But before Lil could take them out, Lizzie put her finger to her lips, then led her into the storeroom.

'I won't be a minute, Bert,' Lizzie called.

'Yeah, all right.' Bert continued to serve the customers.

Lizzie closed the storeroom door. 'Danny and Tom are staying here.'

It took a moment to sink in. 'Blimey, what's happened?'

Lizzie sighed. 'It's a long story.'

'Tell me whilst I unwrap these.' Lil began to take the cakes from her bag but stopped when Lizzie told her about Frank and Vinnie's visit to the warehouse.

'Never!' Lil exclaimed, wide eyed.

Five minutes later Lizzie had given Lil the whole story.

'Well, you know what I think,' Lil said angrily. 'I think that Frank needs to be taught a lesson he won't ever forget.' She paused. 'You know, gel, maybe you should've called the coppers even though Danny didn't want to.'

Lizzie shrugged, tying an apron round her navy blue coat. It was freezing in the shop, but as soon as she was on the move she'd warm up. She had curled her hair up in a thick, dark roll round her head, tucking a square of pale blue chiffon into the collar of her coat. 'What could the police do? It would have been our word against Frank and Vinnie's.'

'But it's bloody Frank who's got a grudge against Danny!' Lil spluttered. 'And the way Danny was bashed up, he didn't do that to 'imself, did he? And what about you, then?' Lil added exasperatedly. 'Vinnie wasn't banging on that office door to give you a bunch of roses!'

'There's no proof against Frank. As Danny said, who are they going to believe?

'Well, all I can say is they should be put away,' Lil grumbled. She pulled back her shoulders, pausing for breath. 'How long is Danny gonna stay here for?'

Lizzie shrugged. 'I don't know. Not long, I shouldn't think.'

Lil gave one of her quick laughs. 'Bet the kids are loving it, ain't they?'

Lizzie nodded. She had left Tom and Polly playing happily down in the airey. They seemed to take everything in their stride.

'By the way, Bert didn't come home last night. Doug said he reckoned he kipped here.'

Lizzie nodded. 'He slept on the couch. Just in case.'

'You don't reckon Frank'd try anything here, under everyone's noses?' Lil's pencilled eyebrows shot up.

'I don't know.' Lizzie had asked herself that question so many times she was sick of it. But if he did appear, he would get more than he bargained for. She wasn't going to be ruled by fear. If she was a man, she would probably have gone looking for him, just as Danny, Bert and Syd had. At least it was doing something – though she would never have admitted that last night. In the cool light of day, the beginnings of a deeper anger had taken the place of fear. Why should men like her husband and brother be allowed to ruin other people's lives?

Lil shook her head despondently. 'Can me and Doug help at all?'

'No, I just wanted to put you in the picture.'

Lil sighed. 'Yeah, ta. Well, I better be going, love. You got customers to serve.'

All week they waited, and nothing happened. Lizzie felt close to snapping. She was no longer certain of her own reactions. The anger inside her was like a weapon and she wanted to use it, yet Frank and Vinnie weren't there to use it on. No one had the right to hurt or terrify other people like they had.

She also couldn't help worrying about Danny when he was at the workshop. And she wasn't alone. Sydney kept calling over there to 'have a chat' and Bert, saying he was practising his driving, made constant detours, often disappearing for an hour at a time, as he had now.

On Wednesday, Danny and Bert had brought Benji

back in the lorry. They made a ramp of wooden struts for the old horse to climb up on. The farrier provided new shoes, but couldn't cure lameness. So Bert drove the van and made the deliveries, collecting stock from the market early in the mornings.

A trickle of visitors started calling at the airey. The news had leaked out about Danny. With the scar on his forehead and his bruised face rumours flew everywhere. Boston Brown and Reg Barnes were the first to call, followed by Elfie Goldblum and Dickie. The story was repeated once again. As well intentioned as everyone was, Lizzie was pleased when they had all gone. Flo and Syd came back from the pub with a few drinks. When the children were in bed, they sat round the fire, going over all that had happened once more.

On Sunday, Lizzie and Flo cooked dinner. Bill and Gertie stayed until four. At tea time, Flo and Syd took the children out for a walk. Danny was quiet, not like himself at all. Lizzie was washing up in the kitchen, trying to hide her concern.

'You've been on your feet all day.' Danny came up behind her at the sink. 'Go and sit down. I'll make you a cuppa.'

It was the first time they had been alone. She took off her apron and sat down by the fire, listening to his movements in the kitchen. She sensed the anger in him. He wasn't happy here. Were there too many memories from the past? This was the place he had left, at sixteen, to serve in the war. This is where he and Frank had lived together as they had grown into men.

Danny returned with a cup of tea. He sat in the armchair. The world suddenly seemed to have slowed down around them. The fire crackled, the light of the late afternoon dimming as it filtered through the window. They sat, each with their own thoughts.

The moments ticked by. Finally Danny sat forward, easing himself into a comfortable position. He smiled, a crooked grin, like the old Danny. 'Nothing's changed for me,' he said heavily. 'I want you with me more than ever, Lizzie. But I can't stay here much longer.'

'You're welcome to stay—'

'That's the trouble,' he interrupted her gently. 'I'm getting used to it. I like seeing you at the end of the day, eating with you . . . talking.' His blue eyes held hers. 'And I want more.'

'Danny—'

He held up his hand. 'It's all right. You don't have to say it. I know you won't consider living with me whilst you're married to Frank. But before I leave . . . there's something I want to tell you.'

She felt her heart flutter. What was he going to tell her? Had he decided it was better to go back to Australia? She couldn't blame him. They couldn't live their lives like this. She had that dreadful feeling inside, an ominous dread, and she sat back, closing her eyes for a moment to block out the pain. She didn't want to hear what he said.

'Lizzie, Elsa and I were never married.'

It wasn't what she had expected to hear. Her eyes flew open. She stared at him. 'What? But you said your wife—'

'I never said she was my wife. I told you Tom's mother's name was Elsa, that she was Swedish and she died of pneumonia. And that's all true.'

'But Tom said . . .'

'Tom thinks we were married. I've never told him otherwise.'

'I don't understand,' Lizzie said helplessly.

Danny looked down at his hands, smoothing his thumb distractedly over the cuts and scrapes on his knuckles. 'Tom isn't my son. I'm not his father.'

She held her breath, attempting to understand, to fit the pieces together.

'There were emigrants on the boat going over,' Danny continued. 'Sven and Elsa were from Sweden; just married—'

'You mean Elsa was married to someone else?'

'Yes. Sven was a motor mechanic, hired by the gold-mining company I was going to work for. I met them on the boat going to Australia. Whilst at sea he showed me his books and diagrams. They were all about fuel pumps, carburettors, and other new parts for engines. Sven was going to fit them to the vehicles used for hauling the gravel. The old trucks had gravity feed mechanisms. The gold-mining companies wanted to find out if they could work with the new carburettors. On the journey to Australia I began to learn about my future trade – although at the time I didn't realize it.'

'What happened when you got to Australia?'

'I went to Sydney, attempting to get the postal arrangements sorted out. Then I met Elsa and Sven at the gold-field town of Castlemaine. Sven was working on the big trucks. I had a job underground, in the mine. On my time off I helped Sven in his workshop. He said the motor engine was the gold I was looking for. He suggested I should change jobs. He put in a word in for me with the company.' Danny looked into the fire, his eyes distant. 'One day, I persuaded him to come down the mine, to see my world. I suppose it was a bit of bravado.' Danny swallowed, lowering his head, his hands clenched together. 'That day, the mine flooded. Eight of my mates got drowned. Sven and I were swept into a cavity, an air pocket. He was unconscious, but I managed to hold on to him. It took them two days to get us out. By the time they brought us to the surface it was too late.'

The fire crackled. The room seemed very still. After a while he continued. 'Elsa was pregnant with Tom. I didn't know how to face her. She didn't like Australia or the climate. She was very homesick. And with the shock of Sven . . .' It was another long moment before he looked up. 'Elsa got sick. When the baby came, it was touch and go. For two years I looked after them. Tom became like my own son.' He looked into Lizzie's eyes. 'I got an apprenticeship in the workshop with the company. I never went underground again. Elsa never blamed me. She didn't need to. I blamed myself.'

'No, Danny,' Lizzie protested. 'You couldn't have known the mine would flood.'

'If it hadn't been for me, Sven would be alive today. That's why I've never been able to tell Tom.'

Lizzie said gently, 'You will one day.'

'I don't know. What will he think of me?'

'He'll understand. He'll always love you.' She asked softly, 'Did you write all this, in your letters to me?'

He nodded. 'After Sven's death, I had to stay. But I'd made my promise to you and I hoped you'd understand what was keeping me from returning. Later, when Elsa died, I sent a cable to Dad explaining I intended to come home but it would take me a while to save the money to get our passage back and have enough to set up my own business. I hoped that, even if you couldn't forgive me for not returning, there still might be a chance . . .'

'Bill never received a cable as far as I know. If he had, I'm sure he would have told me.'

Once more they were silent, reflecting on the twists of fate that had kept them apart. Frank's intervention had set the seal on her future. Sven's death had determined the course of Danny's life.

The silence was suddenly broken as a clatter of feet down the airey steps told them the others were back. Flo, Syd and the children burst in through the front door. They were full of the games they had played at the park. As Polly sat on Lizzie's lap, chattering away, Lizzie looked at Tom. Sitting by the fire, his fair hair gleaming, no one would have ever doubted that he was Danny's blood.

There were tears and tantrums the following week. On Tuesday, after school, Tom and Polly sat at the tea table with long faces. Tom and Danny were leaving that day.

'I don't want Tom to go.' Big, wet drops rolled down Polly's cheeks.

Lizzie had grown very fond of Tom. Through him, she had come to know his parents. Tom's blond hair and fair skin were not Danny's, as everyone had assumed, they were from his Scandinavian parents.

'Tom has to go,' Lizzie told Polly.

'When it was my birthday and I made a wish,' wailed Polly, 'it was for someone to play with. And it came true.'

Lizzie sat beside Polly. What could she say to comfort her? 'You can still play at school.'

'It's not the same. Why can't he stay?'

'Because he has to have a home too.'

'He's only got a landlady in Napier Street.'

Lizzie smiled. 'Isn't it much better that Tom only lives a few streets away, rather than in Australia?'

'I s'pose so.'

'When are we going, Auntie Lizzie?' Tom, always hungry, bit into a slice of Lil's sponge. His large blue eyes stared up at her.

'After tea. Your dad took your things to Napier Street this morning. Uncle Bert's driving you over to the workshop.' Danny had packed their few belongings and come up to the shop to say goodbye. She had tried to pretend she was happy for them, that things were returning to normal. But inside she felt as unhappy as Polly.

'I'm not going to wash tonight,' Polly stated rebelliously.

'You'll stink if you don't,' Tom giggled. Suddenly there were smiles again. Tears and laughter mingled as the children finished their tea.

They waved goodbye to Tom as he sat in the van beside Bert. Tom's pale face peered out of the window. Polly ran to the bedroom in tears. Lizzie went after her, pausing at Danny and Tom's bedroom as she passed. She could still smell them there. It hurt.

The days passed and April arrived. Lizzie hadn't seen Danny and she missed him. Polly brought home bits of news from school. According to Tom his dad was very busy at the workshop. He was getting lots of work from the factories. There was no mention of trouble and Lizzie wondered if they had all been wrong about Frank trying again.

It was a bright spring Saturday when a big black car pulled up outside the shop. A man was driving it, a woman sitting beside him. Lizzie's mouth fell open as Babs climbed out. She was dressed in a bright red coat with a black feather boa. Her high heels clattered as she entered the shop. All the customers turned to stare. A waft of cheap perfume floated in.

Bert dropped a sack with a thump on the floor. Babs swaggered past the queue. A lady with a baby in her arms shouted, ''Ere, we was 'ere first. You wait yer turn.'

'Keep yer hair on,' laughed Babs. 'I ain't come here to stand in a bloody queue, missus. 'Ello, then, gel.' Babs sounded as if she'd seen Lizzie only yesterday.

Lizzie's heart pounded under her coat. 'What are you doing here?'

'Charming, I must say.' Babs looked Lizzie up and down.

'Why didn't you let me know you were coming?'

'Why the bloody hell should I?' Babs ran her tongue over her teeth. 'Anyway, I didn't know, did I? I got a friend to drive me over at the last moment.'

The shop was all ears. All heads turned to look at the car.

Lizzie didn't want half of the island hearing. 'You'd better come out the back.'

Panic was welling up in her as she entered the storeroom. What did Babs want after all this time?

'Christ, this gives me the creeps,' Babs muttered as she walked in. 'It's so bloody cold in here. And that stink of veg! Knocks yer blooming socks off!'

'What do you want?' Lizzie demanded again. She looked at Babs with contempt. Why had Babs stolen those letters that Danny sent? Was it because Frank had persuaded her to do so? Babs had only been a girl then, not even sixteen. Still, she had been a worldly wise one. Frank must have bribed her to do it. What did he use? His charm? Money? Promises? Whatever it was, Babs had aided him in his plans to keep Danny away. Lizzie could never forgive her for that. Babs didn't have the right to walk back into their lives whenever she felt like it. But, forcing down the urge to challenge her, Lizzie said nothing, for Polly's sake.

Babs walked around the room. 'I've come to see me daughter.'

That was the worst news Lizzie could have heard. 'You haven't shown any interest in years. You didn't even come to her birthday party.'

'I couldn't. I was ill.'

'Why didn't you send her a present or a card?'

'I was in hospital, that's why. I got a touch of TB.'

Lizzie was shocked. 'Oh, I'm sorry.'

'They put me in one of them places our Flo was in.'

'Quarantine, you mean?'

'Yeah. Don't worry, I'm all right now. You won't catch anything.' Babs shrugged. 'So, you see, I just want to say hello to me girl. Any objections?'

'It depends.' Lizzie didn't trust Babs. She wasn't just going to arrive out of the blue and see Polly, even if she was her mother. Did she know what Frank had done to Danny? Was she just keeping quiet in order to see Polly?

'I don't want Polly upset,' Lizzie said firmly.

Babs glared at her. '*You* don't want her upset. She's *my* bloody kid.'

There was movement at the door and Polly stood there. Lizzie's heart sank. If Polly hadn't appeared there might have been a chance of getting rid of Babs.

'Hello, Mummy.' Polly was dressed warmly in a green jumper and tartan skirt, her long dark hair tied in two neat plaits. She held a pencil in one hand and a book in the other.

Babs plastered on a smile. ''Ello, Pol, love. What you been doing, then?'

'I've been drawing with Auntie Flo. She's gone out with Uncle Syd.'

'Uncle Syd, eh?' Babs cast a smirk at Lizzie before bending down. 'Come and give yer mother a kiss.'

Polly walked slowly towards her. 'Do you like my

picture?' Polly showed her the drawing book. Babs forgot about the kiss when she saw it and jabbed the paper with a red fingernail. 'Who's this supposed to be, then?'

'My cousin, Tom. He's riding a horse like he did in Australia. And there's me sitting in a car. It's my Uncle Danny's car.'

'Your Uncle Danny, eh? I remember him. Went all the way to Australia. Left yer Auntie Lizzie to go and look for gold.' Babs pushed the book back into Polly's small hand. 'You gonna come out with Mummy?'

'Where?' Polly asked curiously. Lizzie's heart sank even further. She wouldn't have the heart to stop Polly if she wanted to go. When Polly asked about Babs, Lizzie's stock reply was 'She'll call one day.' Well, this appeared to be the day.

'Up the park,' Babs replied. 'And maybe we'll go for something to eat after. Make up for me missing yer birthday.'

Polly smiled brightly. 'All right, then.'

'Hurry up, gel. We'll have a nice day all to ourselves. That is, if yer Auntie Lizzie don't put the mockers on it.' She gave Lizzie a black look.

Lizzie didn't want to let Polly go. But how could she prevent it? Babs was Polly's mother. How could she explain to Polly her distrust of Babs? She had always tried to hide what she truly felt for the child's sake.

'What time – exactly – will you bring her back?'

Babs shrugged. 'Dunno.'

'You must have some idea.'

'Oh, flaming heck!' Babs burst out. 'After tea. Does that satisfy you?'

'Polly's bedtime is eight o'clock.'

'Yeah, I know that. It's burned into me brain.'

'Fetch your coat and gloves from downstairs,' Lizzie told Polly. 'If Auntie Flo has gone out, she'll have left the door on the latch.'

Whilst Polly was gone, Babs opened her bag, took out a packet of cigarettes and a lighter. She lit one, inhaling deeply. She had a smile on her face, as though she was keeping a secret.

Polly's eyes were bright with excitement when she came running back in.

'Auntie Flo and Uncle Syd have gone out,' she chattered breathlessly. 'But I've got my things, even my gloves.' All her clothes were bundled in her arms.

Lizzie dressed her and gave her a big hug. 'Be a good girl now.'

Polly nodded and slipped her hand through her mother's. It broke Lizzie's heart to see the little girl walk out so trustingly. She prayed that Polly would remain safe.

By nine o'clock that night, Lizzie was desperate. She was pacing the floor, berating herself for letting Polly go. Her heart was jumping around in her chest. Where were they? Why hadn't they returned?

Lizzie burst into tears when Flo came back from the pub.

'What's the matter, what's happened?' Flo asked.

'She's not back!' Lizzie wailed. 'I should never have agreed to her going out. Who was that man in the car? They could have gone anywhere. Polly could be miles away by now. I might never see her again!'

'Don't panic.' Flo tried to calm her. 'Look, you know what Babs is like. She's got no idea of time.'

'I told her Polly goes to bed at eight.'

'Yeah, well, Babs dunno eight from midnight, does she?'

Lizzie put her hands over her face. 'Something's happened, Flo. I know it. Oh, Polly, why did I ever say yes?' Lizzie sank down on the couch, the tears flowing.

'I'll make you a cup of tea.' Flo turned to Syd, who was standing there with his coat on. ''Ere, Syd, make yerself useful and talk to her, will you.'

The young man sat down. 'She'll be all right Mrs F. It's her mum, after all.'

'That's what I'm worried about,' Lizzie sobbed.

'I'll go and look for them if they're not back soon.'

'But you've only got your bike.'

'Yeah, but I'm fast on it.'

She knew Syd meant well, but he didn't understand. She wished Danny was sitting there instead. He would know what to do.

Polly wasn't back by ten o'clock. By eleven, Lizzie was frantic.

Chapter Thirty-Two

It was the longest night of her life. She was inconsolable. She blamed herself. What had possessed her to let Polly go? Where was she? Why hadn't they brought her back? The minutes dragged by.

Lizzie went to the window. She could only see up the airey steps. She wanted to go out and search the streets, go anywhere and everywhere.

Syd went out on his bike but found no sign of her. He left at one o'clock in the morning. It was four o'clock when Flo came out of the bedroom. She was in her nightdress, her hair was done up in curlers. 'Blimey, gel, ain't you gone to bed, yet?' She screwed her eyes up in the light.

'How can I?' cried Lizzie, pacing the floor. 'What have they done with her? Where have they taken her?'

Flo shook her head tiredly. 'Lizzie, she's with her mother. She's with Babs. Look, if she was out alone on the streets the whole of the island would be looking for her. There ain't nothing you can do.'

'But she hasn't got her nightclothes or her toothbrush—'

'Are you gonna stand there and torture youself all night?'

Lizzie turned her back to Flo. She wrung her hands as the tears spilled over again. She felt utterly powerless.

'Babs'll bring her back in the morning, you wait and see.'

'How do you know?'

'Because she's too much of a selfish cow to want to keep her.'

'She hates me, Flo. I saw it in her eyes.'

Flo moved beside her. 'Whether she does or not, our Babs ain't going to want to sling a bloody great anchor round her neck.'

Lizzie blew her nose. 'It's got something to do with Frank, I know it has.'

'Yeah, well, p'raps you're right. But you can't do anything about it tonight.'

'I'm going to that house in Poplar.'

'What!' Flo grabbed her arms and pulled her round sharply. 'Now you listen to me, you're not going anywhere at this time of night. You don't even know where it is.'

'No, but you do.'

Flo's expression was incredulous. 'I ain't going nowhere except back to bed.'

Lizzie was desperate. She knew that was where Polly was. She had to be there. 'What if Babs takes her away, leaves the island? How will I find her? Where will I start looking?'

'That's daft! Where are they gonna go?'

'I . . . I don't know, but Babs knows that Polly means everything to me.'

'Wait till the morning.' Flo shook her head. 'Come back to bed.'

'No, you go. I'll be all right.' Lizzie twisted the handkerchief in her hands.

'And leave you to hop it out that door? No, I ain't going to bed till you do. And if you go on at this rate, you'll be no good to anyone in the morning.'

Flo pushed her gently down on the couch. Lizzie burst into tears. Flo sat beside her and took her in her arms. 'Here, you silly moo, you're letting your imagination run away with you. This ain't like you. That bloody Babs, she certainly knows how to make your life a misery. But what satisfaction is she gonna get from taking Pol? What about school, feeding and clothing her? Polly couldn't stay at that place.'

Lizzie stared at Flo through red eyes. 'What do you mean?'

'You know what Babs does for a living.'

'I know, all right.'

'Well, exactly. She can't keep Pol.'

'Flo, I don't understand. Why does she lead that kind of life?'

'Search me. To be honest, it was a shock when I went over there as a kid. I saw all the business going on. I got a real eyeful, I can tell you. It was all tits and bums. I thought Vinnie had a really posh job and house till I realized what it was he did. He's a glorified ponce, that's all.'

Lizzie felt her stomach turn over. 'I don't want to know!' she almost shouted.

There was shock on Flo's face. 'Don't go bawling at me. It ain't my fault, all this. You gotta ask youself a few questions here and come up with the right answers. Our Babs might be what she is, but it ain't news to you, is it? You was the one who took Pol on, knowing full well Babs could change her mind any day. Well, I know you was only doing what you thought was right, but no one said it was gonna be easy. It ain't no good having a go at me when things go wrong.'

Flo's words went home. Lizzie swallowed; she was taking out her anger on the wrong person. 'I'm sorry, Flo. I know it ain't your fault.'

They hugged each other close. Flo sniffed loudly. 'Crikey, now you got me at it!'

'If it anyone's fault it's mine. I should have just said no.'

'You didn't, because of Pol and what she would think.'

'She's got to know sooner or later.'

'Well, maybe it's better that it's sooner, eh?'

Lizzie looked at Flo and nodded. She knew that Polly had to learn the truth about her mother, that she couldn't keep it secret for ever. 'You go to bed,' she told Flo again. 'I really am all right.'

'We'll do something in the morning.'

Lizzie nodded. She didn't tell Flo what she was planning. She had made up her mind. If Pol wasn't back on that doorstep first thing in the morning, she was going up to Poplar to find the house. And no one was going to stop her.

*

Lizzie woke with a crick in her neck. She had fallen asleep, fully dressed, on the armchair. She looked at the window. It was daylight. The clock said seven. Easing her head from side to side she sat forward, the events of yesterday coming back slowly.

She jumped up, her heart beginning to race. 'Polly, Polly . . .' she whispered as she ran to the front door. She opened it, but only a cold wind blew down the airey steps. What did she expect to find – Polly standing there?

She ran up the steps and looked both ways. A few people were emerging from their houses, church bells chimed in the distance. Ebondale Street looked the way it always did on a Sunday morning. Deserted.

She ran back into the airey. Her heart was pounding so heavily, she stopped still and made herself take deep breaths. She knew what she had to do. She would go to Poplar and find Polly.

Putting on her navy blue coat and gloves, she looked at Polly's empty bed and her teddy bear. A lump formed in her throat. Where had Polly slept last night? She didn't have any of her things. She never slept without her teddy bear.

Careful not to wake Flo, Lizzie tip-toed to the front door and slipped out quietly. The streets were empty, the docks silent. Idle cranes poked up into the sky, the short ones and the goosenecks alike towering above the roofs. A black and red funnel rose above a terraced line of cottages. She felt small in comparison, but was comforted by the sight. Her hair lifted in the wind and whipped around her face. The air smelled of hemp and tar, fried breakfasts and the beer from the night before. This was her London. She knew it well. She knew everything there was to know about the earth she was walking on. But she didn't know where Polly was.

At eight o'clock, Flo pulled out Sydney's bicycle from beside the stable. Benji lifted his head, made a soft sound of recognition and returned to his leisurely doze. Flo was in a panic. She had woken with a start and discovered the airey empty. She wore no make-up and still had her curlers in, hidden by a scarf.

The handlebars caught on the bracket securing Benji's hayrack. 'Bugger it,' she swore loudly, giving them a yank. A moment or two later she was on the road, pedalling for all she was worth. Her coat flapped against her legs, her throat hurt with the cold air. Thank God Syd had walked home last night and left the bike. Would Danny be at the warehouse? She didn't know what number he lived at in Napier Road.

'Lizzie, you idiot!' she puffed as she cycled. 'Going off like that on your own.' She was crackers to go to Poplar unaccompanied.

Flo pedalled faster. She hadn't ridden a bike in years. Her bum ached, her legs were like lead weights. Why didn't Syd get the bloody chain oiled? He'd been going on about it for weeks. He was always too pissed to ride it when he came back from the pub. Said he preferred to whistle his way home on foot. Saving up for a car, he said.

How did he think they were gonna afford a car and a house when they got married?

Flo sailed round the corners. Her mind darted from one worry to another. Why hadn't Lizzie woken her this morning? It was all Babs' fault. Lizzie was only going to land herself in trouble. What would happen if she found the house and Vinnie or Frank was there? Or both?

'You cow, Babs!' Flo panted as she neared Langley Street. Should she stop at Lil's? No, it would only waste time explaining.

'Please be there, Danny, please.' Her legs went faster and faster. Danny would know what to do. He was the only one who would.

'Ain't seen you on a bike for years!' someone shouted as she flew by.

No, and you're not likely to again, thought Flo. After this, I won't mind if Syd does fork out on a car. At the next crossroads she narrowly missed a baker's van. Shaking and breathless, she skidded to a halt; her heart was doing a tattoo in her chest – she'd bloody nearly gone under those wheels!

She climbed back on again. It was then she noticed that Syd's rusty old bike was a woman's one, and there was a small brass plate welded to the handlebars. 'Queen Mary's Home for Retired Gentlefolk', it said.

It was half past eight by the time Lizzie reached Poplar. In the old days, she pushed Pa up this way, but today only thoughts of Polly filled her mind. She peered along the road at the dirty houses and closed front doors. Everyone was asleep still.

The Shipwright's was down the bottom on the right. She hurried towards it. They wouldn't be open, but she'd knock all the same and make someone hear. The landlord was bound to know where the bookie's house was.

As she had expected, the pub was closed. There were bottles outside in a wooden crate and the smell of stale beer filled the air. Hurrying past the tall glass windows with their frosted glass scrollwork, she arrived in the yard. It was empty, save for a cat sitting on a dustbin. Old sacks, bags, rotting food and boxes were piled up against a wall. The saloon bar door was closed. She banged on it. No one answered.

Someone must be inside. She ran into the road and looked up. They probably thought she was a furious wife, searching for her drunk husband. She ran over to the houses on the other side of the road. The lace curtains twitched, but she knew, even before she knocked, that no one would answer. Who wanted to confront an angry wife on a Sunday morning?

She knocked on another door. A window opened above her head. 'Clear off, you noisy cow!' a man roared, poking out his unshaven face. 'I'm trying to get some kip.'

'I only want to know where—'

'I said clear off unless you want a jerry on yer head.' The window came down with a crash.

'Polly, Polly, where are you?' Lizzie sighed on the verge of tears. The next street was the same as all the others; red-brick houses covered in grime and soot. The only people about were those going to church. She couldn't bring herself to ask the way to a brothel. Coming towards her was a man, his wife and daughter, each carrying a bible in their hand. They crossed the road to avoid her.

Out of desperation she followed them, not looking as she crossed the road. Suddenly there was a screech of brakes. 'What the bloody hell are *you* doing here?' cried a voice from the car that had almost knocked her down.

Lizzie stared, unable to believe it was Babs who was yelling from the open window.

'Auntie Lizzie, Auntie Lizzie!' Polly's voice echoed from inside the car.

Lizzie ran forward, hurling herself at the door. When it came open, Babs sat there, a smile on her painted face. 'Well, look who it ain't!' she laughed, and Lizzie smelled the drink on her breath.

Polly was sitting in the back seat, her eyes full of tears.

'Why didn't you bring her back?' Lizzie heard herself screaming. 'Where has she been?'

'Where d'you think, you dozy cow,' Babs sneered. 'She's been with me, her mo—'

Lizzie fell on Babs, grabbing the red coat and boa, the feathers flying everywhere as Babs fell from the car. The look on her face only made Lizzie more angry. She had to get to Polly, to feel her safely in her arms. Babs was struggling to stand upright as Lizzie fought to open the back door. She had the handle in her grasp when a pain shot through her arm. Someone had grabbed her and was thrusting her back.

'What do you think yer doing?' a voice demanded as she was pushed roughly against the car. She stared into her brother's face. 'Vinnie!' He stood before her, his dark eyes narrowed.

Babs stumbled towards them, pulling on the boa. She poked a finger hard in Lizzie's shoulder. 'Polly's mine. She's staying with me. You got a bloody cheek telling me what to do with my own kid.'

'Auntie Lizzie, Auntie Lizzie!' Polly was screaming in the car.

Lizzie tried to reach her. They couldn't take her away. Babs was laughing as Vinnie got hold of her again, squeezing her arms tightly so that she cried out in pain. 'P . . . please let me have her, Vinnie. P . . . please,' she begged.

His eyes were cold and hard. She knew he had no intention of ever letting Polly go. 'If you want her, you'd better get in.' He pulled open the car door. 'Someone you know would like a word with you.'

Lizzie stared into Vinnie's unsmiling face. She knew if she climbed into the car she might never see home again.

'Well, what are you waiting for?' He gave her a hard push. She fell into the car beside Polly and the door banged. Lizzie clutched the little girl against her. Polly's tears fell on to Lizzie's coat as she hugged her close.

'Auntie Lizzie, I want to go home.' Polly clung to her.

'I know, I know, my love.' Lizzie was shaking, her body numbed, her brain whirling. Was it Frank who wanted to see her? It must be. What would he do? She held Polly tightly, trying to stifle the sobs coming up inside her chest.

The car started up and they began to move off. Suddenly there was a loud noise and the car shook. Vinnie cursed. Lizzie stared at the back of his head and at Babs, who was sitting beside him. She couldn't see their expressions, but Babs started screaming. Vinnie was fighting with the steering wheel. It seemed to go out of control. The car was turning round and round, the houses moving past the windows like a merry-go-round. The car screeched loudly. Babs was still screaming. Lizzie closed her eyes and dragged Polly down on the seat. She knew they were going to crash.

It seemed a long while before Lizzie dared to open her eyes. She had landed with Polly in her arms in the corner of the back seat. As they both sat up, Vinnie was slumped over the wheel. Babs was moaning softly.

Someone opened the back door. Lizzie couldn't see who it was through her tears. She pulled Polly closer. Was it Frank?

'Uncle Danny!' Polly screamed. She leaped into Danny's outstretched arms.

'Danny . . .?' Lizzie mumbled. She slid towards him across the seat. 'What happened. Where . . .?'

He was dressed in his overalls, his big hands reaching out to help them from the car. 'Are you hurt?' he asked anxiously, hugging them to him.

She managed to shake her head. 'No, I don't th . . . think so. I was—'

'Don't talk now. Hold on to Polly.' He pushed them gently on to the pavement. The car had landed up against a wall and the front of a big brown van was up against the driver's door. Vinnie was staring from the window, looking dazed. Danny climbed into the van, reversed it and got out again.

The door of Vinnie's car slowly opened. Vinnie stumbled out.

Polly huddled into Lizzie's arms. 'They wouldn't let me come back, Auntie Lizzie. Mummy said I had to live somewhere else. I told her I wanted to go home. She wouldn't let me.'

Lizzie hugged her closer. 'It's over now, darling. You're safe.'

Vinnie staggered towards Danny, cursing, his fists clenched. Danny ducked the blow, his fists raised as he circled slowly. His punch was swift and sharp and Vinnie's head jerked sharply back. He looked surprised as his hand went up to the large red mark swelling his face. Before he moved again, there was another blow. He went reeling back against the car.

'You bastard!' Babs screamed. 'You bloody bully, what have you done to him?'

'What I should have done twelve years ago,' Danny told her calmly, raising his fists again. Vinnie lunged crookedly at him. Danny moved to one side. The next blow was to Vinnie's stomach and the air poured out from Vinnie's mouth. He fell to the ground at Danny's feet.

'You'll be sorry for this, Danny Flowers,' Babs

shrieked as she scrambled out and went down on her knees beside Vinnie. 'I'll tell Frank, just you wait.'

Danny nodded. 'You do that. And tell him I'll be waiting.' He stepped over Vinnie and on to the pavement. He laid his large hand on Polly's head. 'You're all right now, Pol. You're going home.' He put his arms round them both. 'We're all going home.'

'Call yerself a wife?' Babs screamed after them as they walked away. 'Frank never loved you, never. Even before you were married we was together. He's always loved me. And he don't give a damn about that bloody shop anymore. We're going away, we're gonna leave this sodding island. So it's good riddance to the lot of you, that's all I've got to say.'

Lizzie turned to look at her sister and brother. She was filled with sadness. How had they come to this? Once they were a family.

Then she climbed into the van beside Danny and he drove them away.

Chapter Thirty-Three

Flo and Tom were waiting in the office. Lizzie held Polly's hand tightly as the door opened. Last time she was here, it had been a dark, frightening little room. Now it was bright and furnished, the desk brimming with papers and books. Around the desk there were chairs, a set of files stood in the corner beside a gas ring with a kettle on it.

Flo jumped up from one of the chairs. She ran over and hugged Polly, tears falling down her cheeks. 'Oh, I ain't never been so pleased to see you, young Pol.' She sniffed and put her hands on her hips, looking furiously at Lizzie. 'But I'm bloody mad with you, you dopey cow!'

Lizzie grinned. 'You look it.'

'Fancy running off like that. You gave me the fright of me life.'

Lizzie raised her eyebrows. 'Is there a cup of tea going?'

Danny turned on the gas ring. 'Tom, you get the cups out from the cupboard and push those chairs round.' He glanced at Lizzie with a smile. They had said very little as he drove them home in the big brown van.

'We didn't go to the park like Mummy said we would,' Polly said as she sat beside Flo. 'We just went to a house.'

'What was it like?'

'I didn't like it much.'

'Well,' Flo said cheerfully, 'there ain't no place like home, gel.'

'There was all these ladies. They had only just got up.'

'How do you know that, love?' Flo asked curiously.

'Because they still had their dressing-gowns on. And I saw one lady in her knickers.'

'Well, perhaps they all had a lay-in.' Flo hid her smile.

Polly looked up. 'I ain't half hungry.'

'You can have one of my sweets, if you like.' Tom took out a brown paper bag.

Polly peered into it. 'I like the yellow ones best.'

'I like the liquorice.'

'Your dad punched Uncle Vinnie on the nose,' Polly told Tom, and Flo smothered her laughter again.

Tom looked up at his father. 'Did you, Dad?'

'I'm afraid your Uncle Vinnie and me don't see eye to eye,' Danny said simply.

'I'm glad,' Polly grinned, sucking her sweet. 'I don't like Uncle Vinnie or Uncle Frank.'

'Did you see Uncle Frank?' Flo and Lizzie asked together.

Polly nodded. 'I was supposed to be asleep, but I wasn't.'

'Where did you sleep?' Tom asked.

Polly shrugged, her blue eyes wide. 'Dunno. It was on a chair.'

'Well,' said Lizzie anxiously, 'no wonder you couldn't sleep.'

'Here's a nice cup of tea.' Danny passed out big enamel mugs filled with steaming brown liquid. 'Drink up, Pol, this'll put hairs on your chest.'

Polly giggled. 'I don't want hairs on me chest, Uncle Danny, I'm a girl.'

'I'll have to put some glasses on,' chuckled Danny.

'Why didn't Mummy bring you home last night, Polly?' Lizzie wanted to get the whole story out of Polly.

'Because Uncle Vinnie said we had to sleep in the car after the coppers came.'

'Coppers!' Lizzie shrieked. 'You mean policemen?'

Polly wrinkled her nose. 'I think so.'

'Did you see any coppers – I mean policemen?' Flo asked breathlessly.

Polly shrugged. 'I don't know. There was a lot of noise, but I was sleepy and we had to get in the car.'

'You ain't half had an exciting time, our Pol!' Flo winked at Lizzie. 'You've been on a big adventure, gel, ain't you?'

Polly gulped down her tea. 'Yes, but I didn't have nothing to eat all the time we was in the car. Uncle Vinnie was snoring in the front seat and Mummy was drinking some smelly stuff. I couldn't wake her up and I cried.'

Tom pushed the bag of sweets under Polly's nose. 'There's a yellow one at the bottom.'

Polly helped herself. Looking at Tom, she giggled. 'Uncle Danny saved me and Auntie Lizzie like in cowboys and indians.'

Danny grinned. 'The only thing missing was the horse.'

Everyone laughed. 'What's down them stairs?' Polly jumped to her feet.

'Dad's workshop,' Tom said. 'Do you want to see?'

Polly looked at Lizzie. 'Can I?'

'If Uncle Danny says so.'

Danny nodded. 'Don't go outside, though.'

Lizzie looked at Danny when the children had gone. 'How did you find me this morning?'

He nodded at Flo. 'I was working on the brown van – had to finish it for Monday. Then Flo arrives on Syd's bike.'

'Yeah,' Flo said crossly, 'I was in a right to-do, I can tell you. It was just lucky Danny was here. I didn't know which house he lived at in Napier Street. And I was so bloody furious at you going off . . .

'I didn't think you'd agree with me going,' Lizzie said quietly.

'Too bloody right I wouldn't,' cried Flo, outraged. 'At least not on yer own.

'When Flo told me what happened,' Danny continued, 'I got out the van and drove up to Poplar to find the house. Flo told me roughly where it was. But before I got there I saw Vinnie's car and you and Pol in the back.'

Lizzie looked at Danny. 'I don't know how to thank you.'

He grinned. 'I do.'

They all laughed.

'Going by what Pol said,' Danny commented, 'the police raided the house.'

They sat in silence for a moment until Flo giggled. 'I had to stop meself from laughing when Polly said about that woman in her knickers.'

'It's got its funny side,' Lizzie admitted. Now that they were safe she could agree with Flo, but at the time she had been very frightened.

Flo jerked her head towards the door and the noise coming from downstairs. 'Well, our Pol ain't none the worse for wear. Just listen to them two, having the time of their lives.'

Lizzie looked at Danny. 'What would I have done without you and Flo today?' Above his eye the long, ugly scar reminded her of what he had been through since coming back to the island.

'That reminds me,' Flo said suddenly. 'I got a bone to pick with my Syd, the crafty little sod.'

'What's he done now?' Lizzie asked.

Flo snorted. 'I only rode over here on a stolen vehicle, didn't I? The bugger's gone and nicked that bloody bike. From an old folks' homes an' all. No wonder it wouldn't pedal fast, them poor old codgers hardly have the strength to climb on 'em.'

They all burst out laughing and were still laughing when the children ran up the stairs to see what the joke was. Polly slid on to Lizzie's lap, wrapping her arms round Lizzie's neck. 'I didn't half miss you, Auntie Lizzie.'

'Me too.' Lizzie hugged her tightly. Polly would never know how much.

They were singing the chorus of 'Rule Britannia' as Danny turned the car into Ebondale Street. A large dark motor vehicle was parked close to the shop. Everyone stopped singing.

'Do you recognize it?' Flo leaned forward from the back seat where she sat with Polly and Tom. 'Is it Vinnie's car?'

'No, the van dented his on one side,' Lizzie said quickly.

Danny pulled on the handbrake. 'It's not your brother's, but it might be Frank's.'

'Frank's!' Flo gasped. 'You reckon it is?'

'We'll soon see.' Danny parked at the kerb. 'I'll be back in a minute.'

'Where are you going?' Lizzie grabbed his sleeve. 'It might be a trap.'

Danny bent down and pulled a hammer from under his seat. 'Well, I told Vinnie I wanted to see Frank and I do.'

'But you ain't going to use that?' Lizzie stared at the hammer, her green eyes widening. She felt sick.

'Only if I have to. Now do as I say. Stay where you are, all of you, until I come back.'

'I want to come with you, Dad.' Tom tried to open the door but Danny grabbed his shoulder.

'Not this time, Tom.' There were tears in Tom's eyes, but Danny gave him a wink. 'Good lad.'

Flo put her arm round the boy. 'Yeah, we need you to look after us, mate.'

Danny climbed out, closing the door hard behind him.

They watched him walk towards the airey. Back in the warehouse, with Polly safe in her arms, Lizzie had thought it was all over, at least for today. Frank had receded to the back of her mind. They were all happy again, driving over here, singing and laughing, unaware of what was just round the corner. She closed her eyes. She saw Danny's broken and bruised body and the blood on his face as he lay on the warehouse floor, Frank standing over him.

'I think we should call the police,' she said quickly.

'Yeah, and how long they gonna take to get here?' Flo pointed out. 'And if Danny uses that hammer—'

'Flo, don't! Don't say that.'

'Well he ain't gonna blow his nose with it, is he?'

'Look.' Lizzie nodded at Danny descending the airey steps. They all waited breathlessly. Lizzie had her hand on the door. She didn't know what she expected to see, but she wasn't just going to sit here if Danny didn't come up again.

The minutes ticked past.

They all sighed in relief as Danny came into view again.

'No one's down there,' gulped Flo.

Lizzie sat forward. Danny was moving slowly along the pavement. 'He's going round to the shop. But he won't be able to get in. The front door is locked.'

A few minutes passed. 'Where the flipping heck has he gone to?' cried Flo.

'I think we should—' Lizzie's voice was drowned by a loud, echoing bang. The car shuddered and everyone screamed.

'Christ almighty!' Flo screeched. 'Look at the bloody window! There ain't nothing left of it!'

'Danny!' cried Lizzie. Pushing open the car door, she leaped out. Flo and the children scrambled after her.

'Get back in the car, you two!' Lizzie tried to push them back but Tom broke free. Lizzie grabbed Polly's hand and they all ran after Tom. At the shop, or the remains of it, they stared in. Black smoke was pouring out from the storeroom. Fruit and vegetables were scattered everywhere. An explosion of some sort had broken all the glass. In the middle of the devastation were two figures, struggling with each other.

Frank and Danny rolled on the floor, crunching the glass and squashing the fruit. Lizzie and Flo pulled Polly and Tom close as the two men tumbled towards them.

'Dad! Dad!' Tom cried. They watched helplessly, listening to the grunts, groans and oaths. Glass, newspaper, fruit and veg were strewn everywhere, arms and legs entangled.

The two men rose, grappled and fell towards the door. A few seconds later they were on the street. Lizzie pushed the children back. How could she stop the fight?

'What we gonna do?' screamed Flo. 'They'll kill each other!'

There was a thud and Frank went down. Danny's fist

was still clenched after delivering the blow. He's not holding the hammer, Lizzie thought in relief as she saw blood streaming down Frank's face. It was the punch that had landed him on the ground. He kneeled on the pavement, staring at the blood over his hands, his nose streaming. Lizzie watched as he seemed to sway, then topple over.

Danny moved forward.

'Don't, Danny, no!' Lizzie screamed. She was terrified he would kill Frank.

Just then a car swept into the kerb, a large black shiny one. It was the biggest Lizzie had ever seen. All four doors opened at once. Slowly, but impressively, a short, thin man climbed out. He looked around at the mess. His hair hung down on the collar of his expensive looking camel overcoat. He was smoking a cigar. Other men followed, their faces shielded under the brims of their hats. Lizzie recognized him as the bookie, and this was his gang. He stared down at Frank, who was holding his face in his hands and groaning.

'What do you want?' Danny muttered, pulling the hammer from the waistband of his trousers.

'You won't need that,' growled Ferreter. 'Put it away.'

'Why should I?' Danny held the hammer in both hands. 'The odds ain't in my favour. They weren't last time either.'

'I heard,' Mik Ferreter nodded. 'Nasty business, that.'

'You heard all right,' Danny snarled nodding at his brother. 'First hand.'

'Now that's where you're wrong. I was a bit put out meself when I got a whisper of what happened.'

'It's your turf,' Danny challenged. 'Or so I'm led to believe.'

The bookie stared coldly into Danny's angry gaze before replying. 'Your not wrong there, son. And anyone disputing that has to answer to me. There ain't a dog that pisses on this island without me knowing.' He looked slowly down at Frank. 'Is there, Frank, me lad?'

Frank moaned, trying to stem the blood that poured from his broken nose.

Ferreter laughed nastily. 'Yer making a mess on the pavement, cocker. As a matter of fact, I'm having a little spring clean of me own. Don't do any harm every now and then. Pick him, lads, before he shits in his pants as well.' He nodded to his burly escorts; two men blocked Danny's path as the others bent down, pulled Frank from the ground and dragged him into the car.

'Your old man has pushed his luck once too often,' the bookie told Lizzie as his eyes went curiously down to her hand. He raised his black eyebrows. 'That's a nice bit of jewellery you've got there, love.'

Lizzie looked down at her ring. 'What do you mean?'

'I mean, yer gonna have the rozzers round here soon about yer window. Before they come I'd get rid of it if I were you. That is, if you value yer freedom.'

'But it's my wedding ring.'

Mik Ferreter laughed. 'Yeah, course it is. And you know who give it to you.'

Lizzie stared in disbelief at Frank's guilt-ridden face in

the back of the car. Again, the years melted away and she recalled the day he had given it to her. She had told him it was a Dearest ring and he had replied, in surprise, that she knew more than he did. Why hadn't she realized then that such a valuable item was not Frank's to give?

She looked at Mik Ferreter, his dark eyes coolly studying her finger. 'It was stolen,' she breathed, not asking a question but telling herself. As she looked questioningly at Frank he turned away, unable to meet her gaze.

The ring was the only thing of value that Frank had ever given her; the symbol of their marriage and commitment to one another. The value had been in that, not in how much it was worth. She would never have betrayed Frank, even though she had not loved him. As long as the ring was on her finger, she was his wife.

Lizzie slid the ring slowly over her knuckle. She stepped forward and held it out towards the bookie. Ferreter stared at her, a flicker of curiosity in his dark eyes. She looked at Frank, then opened her fingers.

The ring fell, catching the light as it tumbled. The little splash from the drain was all that she heard. Like her marriage to Frank, the ring was gone for ever.

Chapter Thirty-Four

'What's Bill going to do?' Ethel asked as she swept the last shards of glass into the pan.

Lizzie secured the sack she was holding, tying a firm knot. 'Dunno. I think he'll retire now. Gertie wants him to go and live with her.' She placed the sack beside the others, ready for disposal.

'What? You mean, they'll tie the knot after all these years?'

Lizzie nodded. 'They just never got round to it with Bill working so hard.' She smiled. 'You wait till Pol knows. It'll be all round the school that her grandma and grandpa are getting married.'

Sitting back on her heels, Ethel laughed. 'Just shows it's not too late even in your dotage.'

Lizzie sat down on a wooden crate with a sigh. 'I don't know how Bill's going to take it if Danny identifies the body.'

Ethel laid the brush and pan down. Both women had turbans on and wore trousers, their shirtsleeves rolled up over their forearms. The empty shop was filled with dust and the door was open to let it out.

'Do you really think it's Frank?'

'From the description, yes.' Wisps of dark hair curled out from Lizzie's turban. Distractedly, she pushed one of them back under the cloth, recalling the shock last night when a policeman had brought the news. A week after the explosion a body had been recovered from the river. A formal identification was necessary. It was Danny who had gone to Limehouse to fulfil the duty.

'Would the bookie really have – you know?' Ethel began uncertainly.

Lizzie shrugged but felt certain Mik Ferreter would have no qualms about meting out his own form of justice to anyone who betrayed him. 'He said Frank had pushed his luck once too often – so unless Frank talked his way out of it . . .' Her voice tailed off.

'Did you tell the police that?'

'We had to. I mean, with the shop in the state it was, they wanted to know all the ins and outs. With all the unrest in the country lately they seemed to think that Frank was involved in some kind of political uprising.'

Ethel burst out laughing. 'Sorry, but that's daft, knowing Frank as I do.'

Lizzie agreed with Ethel. Anyone who knew Frank realized his sympathies were directed entirely towards himself. But, had his plan succeeded to set fire to the building, everyone in the place could have been killed. Had Frank hated them all so much?

'Thank Gawd it was a bodge job,' Ethel sighed, 'and just made a mess. Think what would have happened if Danny hadn't arrived in the time to stop him.'

They had managed to clear the debris but all the windows were still boarded. Only the open door let in the daylight. 'The police said it was a crude incendiary device that backfired,' Lizzie explained. 'And they came to the conclusion Frank was in with the political agitators.'

'What about the business of the ring?' Ethel asked curiously. 'Did you tell the police about it?'

'No, I left that bit out.'

'No wonder, if it was stolen.'

'I was lucky no one noticed before. It was a lovely ring.'

Lizzie felt for the vacant space on her left hand. Her heart gave a little flutter as she thought of what she had done. But throwing the ring away had been an outward sign of her inner determination to start again.

'I'm really sorry,' Ethel said quietly. 'You loved that ring.'

'I love me life more, Ethel. And I intend to get on with it.'

'You sound different, you know.'

Lizzie knew what Ethel meant. She felt different inside, more sure of herself and less uncertain of her future, which was odd in a way. She didn't know what she was going to do about the shop – her livelihood. Bill was going to retire, although he had told her he wanted her to start again, that he would even let her have money to put new windows in and buy stock. But she wasn't rushing into it. She wanted to make the right decision for her and Polly. 'Well, I've done a lot of thinking in the last week,' she said quietly. 'With Babs disappearing it's down to me to decide what's best for Polly.'

'Do you know where Babs is?'

'No. Someone told me they thought they saw her at the train station but couldn't say for definite.'

'Poor old Pol,' Ethel sighed. 'How is she?'

'I think she understands a lot more than she lets on.' Lizzie's overriding worry was that if Frank really was Polly's father and if it was him lying dead on that mortuary slab, how would they all feel then?

'What about Danny?' Ethel asked with a curious frown.

'What about him?'

'You know what I mean,' grinned Ethel.

Lizzie smiled. 'You sound like your mum.'

The two girls burst into laughter. Ethel's eyes opened wide. 'Tell you what, you and Pol and Danny and Tom could all move back to Langley Street. Number eighty-two is empty now. After all the police raids on the knocking houses, old Symons would be only too pleased for you to take it over again.'

Lizzie sighed. 'I don't even know if I'm a widow yet.'

'You've been one for five years,' Ethel answered drily, 'the amount you saw of Frank.'

Lizzie's green eyes were far away. 'I couldn't go back to Langley Street.'

'Why not? Mum and Dad would love it. It'd be just like old times.'

'But it's not old times, is it? It's the here and now.'

'Crikey, you have changed.'

Lizzie nodded slowly. 'I don't want to live with ghosts, Ethel.'

'You're not afraid of ghosts are you?' Ethel chuckled. ''Cos I can tell you right here and now, ghosts won't last long round Langley Street, not with old Vi on the loose. It's supposed to be ghosts that do the haunting not the neighbours.'

They laughed again until Lizzie stood up, stretched her back and glanced round the shop. 'I think we've just about finished in here. Ethel, I really appreciate you coming over to help on your day off.'

Ethel smirked. 'I've enjoyed meself, really. All this excitement.' She clapped her hand over her mouth, her hazel eyes wide. 'Fancy saying that when Danny is out looking at a dead body.' She went pink. 'What time d'you think he'll be back? Wonder what happened?'

Lizzie nodded to the small green Singer car that was pulling into the pavement outside the front door. A tall figure in a grey suit climbed out. 'Here he is now. We'll soon find out.'

Half an hour later, after a cup of tea in the kitchen, Lizzie stood at the door of the airey, hugging her friend goodbye. A soft April breeze swirled down the concrete steps. 'Thanks for everything, Ethel. You sure you won't have a lift?'

'No thanks. I'm off up the market while I've got the chance.' She added in a soft voice, 'I really am sorry, Lizzie. I know what a bugger Frank was, but it must have been a shock all the same.'

Lizzie nodded. 'It was, even though I was expecting it.' She cleared her throat. It hadn't sunk in yet that it really was Frank's body they'd found.

'I expect it'll be in the papers,' Ethel sighed.

'Yes. I'll cross that bridge when I come to it. Gossip only lasts till the next bit.'

'See you over at Mum's soon then, like old times.'

Lizzie watched her friend climb the airey steps. She didn't know if it was possible to return to old times. She certainly wouldn't move back to Langley Street. She wasn't sure she wanted to stay here either. She had saved a little money and put it by for a rainy day. Had the rainy day arrived, she wondered?

She closed the door. There was half an hour before collecting Polly from school. Enough time to talk to Danny on their own for a while. He stood by the fire, his elbow resting on the mantelpiece. For all Frank had done, neither of them wanted him dead.

Without a word, he took her in his arms.

She leaned her head on his chest. 'Do they know how he died?'

'He drowned, the police said. And there's no evidence to suggest foul play, but . . .' Danny held her gently away from him. 'You'd better sit down. I've got something else to tell you.'

'What?' Lizzie clutched his arms. 'What's wrong?'

Danny pushed her gently into the armchair. 'The police were going to arrest Frank. He had set up a house at Whitechapel.'

'You mean a brothel?'

Danny nodded. 'And it was with Babs.'

She stared at him. Her voice shook as she asked, 'How do you know?'

'The police inspector said they had a tip-off. Because of all the unrest in the city, they're having a crackdown.'

'So that's why they wanted to know if we'd seen Babs?'

Danny nodded. 'She faces arrest too if she's found.'

With difficulty, Lizzie composed herself. If she was honest it was no longer the fact that Babs had no love for her as a sister that hurt, but it was hard to accept that Babs and Frank had formed a relationship that seemed to have endured. She looked up at Danny. 'And Vinnie?'

'He's at Bow Street. Nothing to do with the brothels, but for receiving stolen goods. Some of the charges, including a West End burglary, go back years. Like Frank, Vinnie must have upset a few people in his time.'

Lizzie felt tears of anger spring to her eyes. 'What's so unjust is that the bookie won't answer for his crimes,' she said bitterly. 'If it wasn't for him—'

'That's where you're wrong,' Danny interrupted. 'The police have found new evidence against him and closed down his businesses. He was the last person to see Frank alive, but the police have no proof of murder. It's my feeling they're going to make another charge stick.' He looked back into the fire. For a moment he stood there deep in thought. He had loved his brother, if Frank had never loved him. That was the tragedy, Lizzie thought sadly. It could have been so different.

Lizzie stood up. She laid her hand on his shoulder. As

he turned round she saw the grief in his eyes. He drew her into his arms. A warmth flowed slowly back into her body, a love that was immeasurable.

'I love you,' he whispered. 'Marry me—'

She put her hand up to his lips. 'Don't ask me yet.'

He gazed into her eyes, sighing heavily. 'I've waited twelve years to say that, I suppose I can wait a bit longer.' His arms folded tightly round her. 'Just don't forget that as each day goes by, it won't come again. I want to wake up with you beside me each morning. I want to look after you and the kids. I want us to be a family.'

A family . . . yes, it was her dearest wish. But it was too soon . . .the memories too fresh in her mind.

He undid the turban round her head. Her black hair tumbled over her shoulders and her green eyes shimmered as she stared up at him. 'That's better,' he told her. 'This is the girl I remember.'

She looked up into his dear face. She knew he loved her and that she loved him and they were now free to let that love grow. Love was a blessing she would treasure and never take for granted. And whatever the future held, life would be rich with the fruits of that love.

POCKET
BOOKS

A Dorset Girl

Janet Woods

When her mother and stepfather perish in a fire, Siana Lewis finds herself destitute, with a younger brother and sister to support. Although her prospects seem bleak, Siana's beauty and intelligence will attract the attention of three men.

Daniel, her first love – the man who will betray her.

Francis Matheson, the village doctor, who admires Siana's determination and thirst for knowledge.

And Edward Forbes, the local squire. A sensual and devious man, Edward is used to getting what he wants. He desires the beautiful peasant girl from the moment he sets eyes on her – and he's determined to have her. Whatever it takes.

'A thoroughly enjoyable saga with a delightful heroine and vivid characters' Anna Jacobs

ISBN 0 7434 6799 X

PRICE £6.99

POCKET
BOOKS

Beyond the Plough

Janet Woods

Now a wealthy young widow, former peasant girl Siana Forbes has overcome her humble beginnings to become mistress of Cheverton Manor, the handsome estate which her infant son, Ashley, will one day inherit. When the man she has always loved, country doctor Francis Matheson, asks for her hand in marriage, it seems her happiness is complete.

But trouble lies ahead. An unexpected tragedy means Francis must leave for Australia – a land where danger and hardship await. Left behind to raise a growing family, Siana too has problems when a sinister figure from her past emerges, determined to cause havoc. And a terrible ordeal suffered by her stepdaughter on the night of the harvest supper leaves Siana with a heartbreaking choice. Will she be able to overcome the odds stacked against her and keep her family together? And will she ever re reunited with her beloved Francis?

ISBN 0 7434 6800 7

PRICE £6.99

POCKET
BOOKS

A Handful of Ashes

Janet Woods

After an unhappy period apart, Francis and Siana Matheson have settled into a loving marital relationship in their comfortable Dorset home. Siana's only sorrow is that so far she has been unable to bear her husband another child. Francis however is content to be a father to his grown-up daughters and his young son, Bryn, born while he was overseas.

But Siana is hiding a secret. Although she hates keeping something from her husband, the need to protect all concerned has left her with no choice. She must keep quiet and live with the guilt of her deceit.

No one can keep the truth hidden forever – and when Siana's shocking secret bursts into the open, there will be tragic and far-reaching consequences for the close-knit Matheson family.

ISBN 0 7434 8401 0

PRICE £6.99

POCKET
BOOKS

A Sovereign For a Song

Annie Wilkinson

WINNER OF THE ROMANTIC NOVELISTS' ASSOCIATION'S NEW WRITER AWARD

An impoverished miner's daughter growing up in the small village of Annsdale, near Durham, young Ginny Wilde yearns for adventure. But she gets more than she bargained for when her dark good looks, fiery spirit and beautiful singing voice capture the attention of Charlie Parkinson, her employer's unscrupulous brother.

Fleeing the wrath of her irate father, Ginny heads for London where she embarks on a successful career as a music hall artiste. But, unable to escape Charlie's influence, Ginny finds herself increasingly unhappy as she is sucked into his louche, womanizing lifestyle. Can she ever find the courage to leave Charlie and return to her beloved north-east? And will she ever be able to recapture the heart of her one true love, miner Martin Jude?

ISBN 0 7434 6882 1

PRICE £6.99

POCKET
BOOKS

The Soldier's Wife

Rachel Moore

World War II is over – and the troops are coming home.

Bound together by their weekly knitting circle, Carrie, Velma, Gwen and Shirley supported one another through the bleak wartime years. Through good times and bad, they kept each other's spirits up, taking comfort in their unique bond of friendship, longing for the day their men would return.

Now at last their husband have come home. But it's not easy adjusting to married life again – and two of the women have painful secrets to hide. Shirley doesn't know if she can live with the guilt of her deceit. Gwen is terrified of being found out. Having tasted independence, Velma plans to ask for a divorce. And, married just two weeks before her husband joined up, Carrie must get to know her beloved Archie all over again.

In a gossip-fuelled village like Penhallow accusations abound and rumours fly. Their marriages under increasing strain, the four women will need each other as never before.

ISBN 0 7434 6800 7

PRICE £6.99

POCKET
BOOKS

These books and other **Simon & Schuster/Pocket** titles are available from your book shop or can be ordered direct from the publisher.

☐ 0 7434 6799 X	A Dorset Girl	£6.99
☐ 0 7434 6800 7	Beyond the Plough	£6.99
☐ 0 7434 8401 0	A Handful of Ashes	£6.99
☐ 0 7434 6882 1	A Sovereign for a Song	£6.99
☐ 0 7434 8373 1	The Soldier's Wife	£6.99

Please send cheque or postal order for the value of the book, free postage and packing within the UK; OVERSEAS including Republic of Ireland £2 per book.

OR: Please debit this amount from my:

VISA/ACCESS/MASTERCARD ....

CARD NO ....

EXPIRY DATE ....

AMOUNT £ ....

NAME ....

ADDRESS ....

....

SIGNATURE ....

Send orders to: SIMON & SCHUSTER CASH SALES
PO Box 29, Douglas, Isle of Man, IM99 1BQ
Tel: 01624 677237, Fax 01624 670923
bookshop@enterprise.net
Please allow 14 days for delivery.
Prices and availability subject to change without notice.